CHRISTOPHER MURPHY

UNFOLDING GRACE

novum ◢ pro

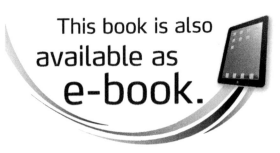

www.novum-publishing.co.uk

© 2022 novum publishing

ISBN 978-3-99131-653-4
Author: Christopher Murphy
Secondary Editing:
Roderick Pritchard-Smith
Cover photos: Elena Shitikova,
Minnystock, Vadym Lavra,
Oriontrail | Dreamstime.com
Cover design, layout & typesetting:
novum publishing

www.novum-publishing.co.uk

Climate neutral
Print product
ClimatePartner.com/16547-2201-1002

CONTENTS

The ensuing story is just what it is, not simply a fable to entertain, it is a tale that simultaneously asks questions and explores the possibilities of another way of living. Could there be a different narrative of what creation (meaning human temporal life as we here on Earth comprehend it, the question of the 'afterlife', and what may lie beyond) is and how it actually works? It explores what may be discovered if we delve a little deeper inside ourselves, to see, realize and experience the prospect of being more than simply human, living in a way that is more connected and aligned to the All that constitutes the Universe, way beyond the level at which most of us are presently doing. We have an immeasurable untapped capacity for soulful living that offers an expansive, more-than-human evolution and a return to what may be our true state of being.

"The Kingdom of God is within."

Yeshua

This quote is simply saying that everything (Universal Wisdom) is there, available for everyone, all the time, passing through and alive within every particle of our (all of us) being. Each and every one of our particles contains the 'Kingdom of God', if we are present and connected to and with ourselves does this then give us access to the All that is? This book contemplates what such an opportunity might look and feel like, that is, the journey from where we are now back to being in alignment with the All that Universal Wisdom is.

Chapter 1

New Year's Day 2000

As he stumbled and mumbled through the deep recently fallen powdery snow, Roar again attempted to recall the events from the previous evening at the much-hyped New Year's Eve party marking the beginning of this promising new century. He felt that he knew exactly why he found it difficult to remember the details from last night's festivities, any of the conversations he had taken part in or with whom and now, why he was here alone, his head throbbing, trudging through the thirty-centimetre deep snow on Skiphelle Beach at 6.30 am on the first day of the first month, of the much-vaunted new year, 2000.

What had happened at the grand centenary celebration? All he could feel was a sense of dread and that sinking feeling that came upon him every time he had, once again, overdone it with the booze. Where was his beautiful partner, Elisabeth? He knew deep down that she loved him and would never normally leave him to wander alone in his current state. That was the unspoken part of the arrangement within their pseudo-relationship – he would drink too much at social events and she would usher him away before he could do too much damage, often driving him home and cajoling him into bed before his antics went too far.

It was still several hours before the coming of the rising sun would end this long winter night. As the small crescent moon shone along with the star-filled sky reflecting on the blanket of pristine white snow. It was minus fourteen degrees, Roar Moerk was comparatively lightly dressed so he was now starting to feel the impact the cold and his own self-disregard was having on his body. He stopped in his tracks knowing it was time to do something about it, somewhere from within his befuddlement he decided he would call a taxi, go home and speak with Elisabeth.

It was quite dangerous to be outside in these low temperatures in a state of inebriation without the protection of proper multi-layered winter clothing. He felt quite numb but had no thoughts for his own safety. He looked quizzically down at his gloved hands and noticed again the hole in the thumb of his right-hand glove, a two-by-one-centimetre burn hole and his thumb within was reddened and felt quite tender to the touch. Pulling off the glove to take a closer look, Roar suddenly felt light-headed, the ground began to spin, there was no longer any pain as his body pitched lifelessly forward, headfirst into the soft deep powdery snow.

Roar Moerk was Norwegian born in Droebak, a small-picturesque town that many would consider only to be a village, situated approximately forty kilometres south of the capitol, Oslo, on the eastern coast of the Oslo fjord. At the age of thirty-nine, one hundred and eighty-eight centimetres tall, relatively attractive with sandy brown hair and deep blue eyes, he had never married and had no children, that he was aware of, and didn't really want to have any. Roar had never been a driven career minded man, more a lackadaisical opportunist that fell into his undertakings but seemed to have a talent for choosing mostly successful ventures when he did so. Quirkily charming in his own way, he always had a twinkle in his eyes, his broad smile was never far away and almost always knowing how to take the edge off a situation with his perfectly timed disarming comments. Outwardly charming but inwardly deceptive, there wasn't anything he did, even if it seemed to be helping someone out, that wasn't for himself, for his own personal gain. As far as Roar was concerned, he was number one and deservedly so, if a task didn't ultimately bring him more recognition, sexual favours or wealth then it was not a task he would consider doing.

He and Elisabeth owned a luxurious three-bedroom apartment in an expensive modern complex just north to the centre of town. Parked outside was a brand-new Audi A6 2.8 Quattro for him and a small Peugeot 205 that Elisabeth had bought back in 1995. Roar also owned a spacious ten-bed ski lodge in the mountains at Hemsedal, purchased from the proceeds attained from the sale of his shares of an investment in an Information Technology company just before the announcement of a profit warning occurred, dramatically crashing the share price.

Roar was the only child of Harald and Solveig Moerk. Solveig loved him dearly and had spent many years of her life providing for his every whim. She would literally do anything for him, give him anything he asked for, spoiling him completely.

A devoted housewife and mother, Solveig met Harald at college and it was the first real relationship for both of them, they both knew immediately that this was the partner they were looking for. Harald was tall, determined and strong willed, he knew exactly what he wanted, he was in control and he needed a relationship where he was the boss. Solveig had always been quite timid and unsure of herself, she had shied away from any attention, she found it hard to be decisive and allowed her parents to control her life. When Harald came along, dominant, so similar to her father, she just knew she needn't look any further. She could escape the confines of her family home and set up her own nest with Harald who would always provide for her. He was so sure and dependable, that's what she loved most about him.

Harald had spent his whole working career at the same local bank from the day he left college to the day he retired, early, as the manager of the branch. He was completely dedicated to the bank; it was his first and only true love. His other loves came in the following order, checking in with his broker regarding his share investments, steak and red wine for dinner, golf at least three times per week and now after retirement every day possible, cigars and cognac, gardening around the retirement villa in Spain, evening strolls along the beach with Solveig, oh, and a bi-monthly catch-up with Roar if he was available.

They would also spend six weeks at their summer cabin in Stavern, situated in southeastern Norway. It was, in reality a complete change from their villa in Spain having very few, basic facilities which included an external, primitive composting toilet where you throw a few handfuls of sawdust down the hole after completing your deposit. On the other hand, it was situated on a large plot of land in much sought-after, idyllic and secluded spot close to the water's edge with its own private beach and small jetty. Being at the cabin meant indulging in the simple life for six weeks of the year in an area of Norway that often has beautiful summer weather, although it can be pretty dreary if the rain sets in for a few days or even weeks. Harald would spend hours fishing off their small wooden jetty or bobbing around in the little family dingy whilst Solveig busied herself with cleaning, washing and preparing the meals in-between hours of sunbathing with her stack of magazines and romantic books close by.

Harald and Solveig rarely spent much time together in conversation, it was just the way it always had been, they got on with their own interests and responsibilities, it was an unwritten agreement. Even when they were together at mealtimes and in the evenings, they rarely spoke to each other more than a few words about the weather or other practical issues, Solveig immersed herself in chores around the house whilst Harald read the newspapers, puffed on his cigar and watched the evening news on TV. Outwardly it seemed idyllic, very settled, a well-to-do couple with everything they needed – great pension, early retirement, beautiful villa in Spain, even now they had only just turned sixty-five, what more could anyone wish for?

They each had their own bedroom and rarely shared the same bed, making love had never been very exciting, more clumsy, uncomfortable and often embarrassing for both of them. Rather than discuss how they could make it better, both had kept their thoughts internalized and inwardly decided it best to retreat into their own worlds, their own private closed-off bubbles of safety and security. The idyllic life is not always what it seems to be.

As a child Roar was often left to his own devices, even when he was quite young, as his mother busied herself around the house making everything just perfect, spotless and dust free with not a single item out of place, except for Roar's room where everything was chaotic, just the way he liked it. When it became too messy, he would feign a headache or a tummy upset and convince his mother to make it all better again, including putting every one of the strewn items back into place. This continued until the day he left for university in the city of Bergen on the west coast of Norway. Being a very bright, observant child, he soon learned that his devoted mother could be easily manipulated, Roar abused this knowledge, ruthlessly bamboozling her at any opportunity. He became accomplished and persuasive in the ways of deceit and manipulation. In the end, he could convince almost anyone that black was white and was able to sell a story or product almost at will.

Roar was pampered and soon became very entitled, expecting everything he wished for even before he asked to have it. Self-serving, self-indulgent, narcissistic, over-privileged and arrogant he expected to be the centre of attention. He soon learned from the way he treated his mother how to treat all women, they were for his convenience or pleasure, to be used and discarded at will, he conveyed an almost complete lack of respect. As the years went by, he learned how to disguise his disrespect behind his charm, but it would always shine through in the end. For two decades Roar had played the field to become a specialist in one-night-stands and short-lived romantic relationships. He left many sad and disappointed young ladies in the wake of his almost unfailing charisma. Eventually, the word of his deceitfulness spread and his infamy often entered the room before he did.

He didn't see his father very much at all and never really developed any sort of close relationship with him. There was always a cool, almost emotionless distance between them. For Roar it never occurred to him to miss his absent father, he invariably had his mother diligently standing by, thus he and his father became completely ambivalent to each other.

Roar's latest venture that started five years earlier along with his childhood friend Anders, was a rapidly expanding Information Technology company based in the centre of Oslo which was proving to be very profitable as the IT market seemed to be in exponential growth. It was a project that consumed much of his time. Due to the excellent market conditions the company had already grown rapidly, currently employing twenty-five people and expecting to double in size during the next two years. They were focussed on the field of Rapid Application Development Solutions at a time when many large companies and organisations were in the process of converting their legacy system to modern technological platforms.

Roar was a busy man, doing all the things he wanted to do, living the life he wanted to live. In between unavoidable breaks caused by his small physical niggles and injuries, he was addicted to working out at the gym, running in the forest during the warmer months and participating in winter sports when the snow was on the ground, alpine skiing and ice-skating being his preferred activities. The winter season in the Norwegian mountains could start in early November and last until the end of April, which meant many weekend trips, including early Friday finishes to beat the weekend traffic exodus, with often late Monday morning or even afternoon starts.

Working late, he and his colleagues often ordered take-away food and drink. On other occasions they would attend late afternoon and evening meetings in the bars and restaurants close to the office in and around the centre of Oslo. His office was also equipped with a very large and comfortable sofa that he sometimes used after a late night at the office and particularly when they had had a few drinks at one of the local bars.

Recently there had been more late nights, more drinks with colleagues, more overnight stays on the office sofa or at one of the local hotels as often happens during Christmas party season in the city, which stretches from November to January. It all started on Friday, December 8th 1999, after they closed the office early at 4pm, with all twenty-five members of staff, having drinks and finger food as a precursor to the evening's traditional Christmas dinner at Det Gamle Raadhus (The Old Town Hall) restaurant just around the corner from the office.

As the drink flowed and the sound of conversation escalated, Roar popped back into his office to finish off the last few emails before closing down his computer. Anneli, one of his lead developers, knocked and entered without waiting for a reply. It was 6.30pm and they would be leaving for the restaurant in fifteen minutes. They had both felt the attraction to each other but so far had never acted on it as they knew from experience the amount of damage an affair could cause, the fact that they both were in committed long-term relationships and had been for several years, not that it would normally stop Roar from trying his hand at any opportune moment.

Anneli, now a little more uninhibited due to the four glasses of red wine and two shots of aquavit, advanced provocatively towards Roar and stood just a few centimetres from him, held both his cheeks and gently urged him up from his chair until they stood face to face. With her high stiletto heels on she was exactly the same height as Roar. "I'm going to have you tonight," she whispered brushing her lips over his ear, turned and slowly swaggered out of his office again.

Roar sat back into his office chair for a while contemplating their interaction and feeling the disturbance and the excitement within himself. He had imagined many times what it would be like with Anneli, she was tall and athletic with olive skin, jet black hair and intense dark brown eyes. She had a feline, slinky, sexy way of moving and a stunning smile, she was also twelve years his younger. There had often been furtive glances between them during the past eighteen months that she had been part of the team, but he had always suppressed the urge to make advances or flirt with her, this time he knew there was nothing that would stop him availing himself of such a wicked opportunity.

In his mind he was already calculating and constructing his excuses for not returning home after the Christmas party – excuses that he knew Elisabeth would never believe but would accept as she always did. He could see her face in front of him now, those penetrating blue eyes that knew him better than he knew himself, that simply asked him for the truth. He knew somewhere deep inside himself that Elisabeth wanted only the best for him, that she actually knew his every move and through that brought an innate knowing to him, but he stubbornly refused to accept it. He thought to himself, 'How can it be that I know so well the obvious sensible choice and yet at the same time want the exact opposite that may cause hurt and confusion both for myself and for my partner?' He knew that this evening he would once again betray Elisabeth and by doing so betray himself, the excitement outweighed the honesty and the truth. He quickly replied to the last email of the week, switched off his computer and walked out of his office and into the party.

He texted Elisabeth to say that something urgent had come up, wrote something about a large contract in Trondheim. He would have to return to the office after the party was over as he needed to complete the work which would take him well into the night.

Elisabeth knew what was in the message even before she opened the text, she could feel the energy of it as she knew Roar's selfish ways only too well. She had reached a point where she no longer had any real expectations, knowing that he would just continue his egocentric lifestyle with no true regard for her or anyone else. She needed to look after herself now and make the changes that would bring joy and harmony to her own life, with or without Roar.

She knew somewhere deep inside him there was a beautiful tender man screaming to be heard, but he was so consumed with self-interest, recognition and personal and material wealth that she doubted she would ever see the true Roar. She deleted the message without answering, switched off her phone, returned to her book and mug of hot chocolate and decided she would have a lovely hot bubble bath and turn in early for the night.

The party ended as it was always going to. Instead of returning to the office, Roar and Anneli booked into the Plaza Hotel for the night. After each making separate exits from the party, they met up in the hotel foyer. Roar didn't look once at his phone to check if Elisabeth had replied to his message. Both intoxicated, they fumbled through a quite forgettable twenty minutes of attempted sexual activity before quickly falling into a zombie-like alcohol induced sleep. Awaking at 9.30 the next morning, both with pounding headaches, they ordered breakfast via room service with a side-order of paracetamol. After consuming the food and tablets they began to feel more alive again which led to a much more successful sexual encounter that started in the bedroom, by way of the shower and back into the bed. By the time they came up for air midday was already behind them and they knew it was time to leave, returning to their individual partners and whatever versions of guilt, if any, they chose to carry with them.

Since the day of the office Christmas party, they had tried to meet in stealth as often as possible which unsurprisingly, yet tantalizingly, had been a lot of fun and excitement for both. Lies seemed to come easily for both Anneli and Roar, they invented a project that they worked on together, needing to work extra-long hours to get it completed. This required staying in Oslo at least two nights per week, perhaps three, and sometimes even working on Saturdays. They were regulars at the Plaza, eating dinner at the restaurant and spending hours in sexual exploration in the hotel bedroom. Even when they didn't stay the whole night, they would book the room for four hours then make their way home late in the evenings. Of course, they kidded themselves they were doing this undetected but in reality, they knew that their partners and indeed their co-workers would and consequently did 'smell a rat'.

NEW YEAR'S EVE

Elisabeth had always been very observant. Knowing Roar as she did, she knew full well he was seeing someone else, it was impossible not to know, there were literally dozens of signs. His every movement gave him away, his every expression and every word that came out of his mouth spouted untruths. She continued to consider her options for a new single life, the whole relationship with him had prepared her for this process and she was astonished to feel how calm she was and how simple it would be. She could even pinpoint when his most recent bout of indiscretion had all started – the text on the night of his company Christmas party; she felt it then and she could feel it now. But tonight was not the moment, they were after all about to attend the New Year's Eve party. All their friends and everyone in the town had been waiting for this special evening – parties everywhere, along with the most colossal fireworks display that had ever been seen in Droebak.

Roar was very chirpy as they prepared themselves for the party, getting showered and ready for the event. Elisabeth had not had a drink for the last two months; she had never been very keen on either the taste or the effect of alcoholic beverages and no longer seeing any reason to continue had decided to stop drinking completely. She had spent many hours at the local yoga studio during the past two years and in December had practiced every day for at least two hours. Her body felt great, very trim and slender although she had always looked after herself, and now at thirty-four she looked better than ever, the few tiny wrinkles in the corners of her eyes only enhancing the beauty that shone from within. Lately she had been feeling that there must be more to this life than the way she was currently living, that although Roar had treated her well previously, she now felt that his level of disregard for her was beyond uncomfortable, even abusive and could no longer tolerate it, as to do so was to accept the abuse. She needed to love and respect herself which she could not do inside this out-of-balance disrespectful arrangement that their relationship had become.

Roar, on the other hand had already opened a bottle of his favourite full-bodied Amarone red wine and with over half the bottle already consumed he was well on his way to another forgettable evening. Or was he? As he sipped on his wine, he recalled his meeting and the heated, passionate sex with Anneli the previous night. She really was athletic and resourceful in so many ways, and he was intoxicated with excitement just at the thought of her. He wished he could be with her this evening, and he knew she felt the same way. The more time they spent together the more they seemed to melt together in their love-making. It felt perfect, open, physical, non-verbal, exciting and frantic, they couldn't get enough of each other, just the thought of her ignited his desire and lust.

As Elisabeth stood in the shower shampooing her hair, she heard the bathroom door open, and Roar came in. During the last month he had shown no interest in her, nor attempted to have any physical contact. They had rarely seen each other let alone been naked together. All these were tell-tale signs of his current encounter with infidelity.

Roar took off his clothes and entered the shower behind her and without saying a word took both her breasts in his hands, squeezed far too hard and pressed himself forcibly against her from behind. She froze as feelings of disgust washed over her whole body; feeling quite startled she had a knee-jerk reaction, lifted up her foot and stamped her heel down on his toes. Roar was shocked, more from her reaction rather than the pain in his right foot.

"Please do not touch me," she said regaining her calm. "Get out of the shower and use the other bathroom now, please go!"

He hobbled quickly out of the shower, out of the bathroom with his proverbial tail between his legs. He knew she knew what he was doing and had known about the other times too, but usually accepted or pretended to accept his thoughtlessness and disregard, but she would always succumb to his arrogant expectations. This time was very different, there seemed to be a new strength about her demeanor, a steel in her voice. It was different for Roar too, as he couldn't get enough of the physicality with Anneli.

Beyond the feeling of hurt and disgust and that she had actually been violent towards him for the first time ever, Elisabeth was pleasantly surprised at the power and steadfastness of her own conviction, the certainty of a better, more truthful way of living was pulsing through her body, a feeling that she could shed the shackles of her past self-demeaning ways and live what ought to be a more forthright, self-loving way, not just in the future, but right here and right now. She felt the attachment to being in relationship with Roar candidly melting away, she felt her own self-respect growing stronger and an inner glow of love for herself spreading out from the centre of her heart. This, she knew, was the starting point for her to begin living her life in full, not in subservience or controlled by the whims of anyone else.

Both now ready for the party of the century, as it was being billed in the auspices of their little town, they stood in the hallway putting on their winter layers and winter boots. It had snowed all day and now that the skies had cleared, the outside temperature was dropping rapidly. Minus ten, at the moment and probably much colder later, it was going to be bitterly cold at midnight when they would be standing outside watching the grand fireworks display. Roar, wearing a black suit, white shirt and dashing blue paisley tie pulled on his navy-blue cashmere overcoat which would generally keep him warm moving from one house to another but not for standing outside in the freezing cold for thirty minutes or more drinking champagne and watching a fireworks display. He had packed a backpack, which was commonplace when attending parties in the Norwegian wintertime; his essential contents were; two bottles of Amarone red wine, one bottle of Bollinger rose champagne, one- half bottle of Rémy Martin XO cognac, a pack of ten Cuban Montecristo cigars, one pack of cedar cigar matches and one lighter, one pair of black brogues and the most essential New Year's Eve accompaniment, a large pack of extra fireworks for their own private display. Boys, and men, do love to play with their fireworks.

Elisabeth, looking absolutely stunning, impeccably made-up and in her figure hugging, thigh length, deep blue woolen winter dress with black stockings and black leather boots, her thick, blond, chin-length, bobbed hair under her Russian style fur hat and a long faux fur coat, had also packed a bag with several extra layers for the outside activities later in the evening: the usual set of accessories, makeup, lip gloss, hair brush, perfume, shiny blue patent leather stiletto heeled shoes, adorned with sparkling diamond-like sequins and two bottles of her favourite San Pellegrino sparkling water, also making sure to pack her own set of keys and not to depend on Roar in any way.

They waited for the taxi to pick them up at the pre-arranged time of 8pm. Roar, who had been watching Elisabeth intently, still a little uncomfortable with the previous exchange in the shower, chanced a flattering comment in a vain attempt to get into her good books, "You look so beautiful tonight, Elisabeth."

"Thank you Roar," she replied confidently, curtly saying, "I know, I am stunning, am I not?"

Slightly taken aback and for once completely lost for words by the power and confidence she radiated as she claimed her own beauty, Roar then stood in silence for the next five minutes until the taxi arrived.

The party was being held at a local community hall and over one hundred fifty people would be attending. It was to be a friends and friends of friends' party, so most of their local friends and acquaintances would be attending. The ticket price of eight hundred Norwegian krone per person included a three-course meal with limited wine, beer and water during the meal. If you wanted any other drinks they would have to be brought in as the hall did not have a bar. Included in the price of the ticket was the music played by the local disc jockey.

There would also be a magnificent firework display at midnight down in the town centre, at the local harbour which would be launched from specially prepared barges outside the harbour walls. The display which would be free of charge, had been privately funded through donations, and would also be visible from outside the community hall, although anyone who wished for a closer view could make the short journey down to the harbour.

Elisabeth Lysne had now been in a relationship with Roar for almost six years. She had grown up in Droebak and had known who Roar was for many years before they became lovers. She knew him to be a well-known charmer, player, ladies' man, wannabe playboy, his reputation was known to the whole town. When he had first approached her, she rejected him immediately, but he was relentless. She had never known anyone so persistent, he never gave up, no matter how many times she said no. In the end, after nine months of his unrelenting offensive, he had worn down her resistance to the point that she gave in to his charm, even though she knew his reputation full well. He convinced her that he would change for her, that she was the one he had been waiting for. And it was, in the beginning. He was so attentive, loving and considerate and would do anything for her and wanted to spend as much time as he possibly could with her. She fell in love with him and believed that he had changed.

After two years of dating, travelling to exotic destinations, experiencing different cultures, they agreed to commit to each other and live together. They bought an apartment, moved in together and she realized it was at this point that his attention for her gradually changed. He slowly became more easily distracted and throughout the next four years they had many discussions, debates and arguments as to what was expected in their relationship. In the end it was as if they were from two different planets, two entirely different perspectives on what a relationship should be. It seemed that after he had 'captured' her heart with his charms it was as if he now felt that he could deposit her in the apartment and then go off and do exactly as he wanted with no regard for how she felt about it.

They had such different interests: Elisabeth liked to communicate, meditate, exercise with gentle yoga classes, read and walk in the countryside, along the coast or in the mountains. Roar liked fast moving winter sports, football, running and lifting weights at the gym. He had shown some interest in Elisabeth's pastimes and hobbies early on in the relationship but that quickly waned, and he was focused more and more on all the activities he wanted to do as well as his business and socializing with his friends and colleagues.

They had tried for a while to find enjoyment in each other's interests. Elisabeth would travel up to the cabin in Hemsedal with Roar along with some of his friends and their partners. Though not keen on alpine sports she would join them on the slopes to ski but would quickly be left behind and discarded as they exercised their well-honed skills with no regard for her novice level of skiing competence. In the end it became boring and lonely to be with them skiing and partying in the mountains. They would all join the raucous after-ski partying and get drunk almost every evening, having nonsensical conversations about nothing in particular. Eventually, Roar would go skiing most weekends during the winter and Elisabeth would stay at home or attend yoga classes or travel to the odd weekend yoga or meditation retreat. He worked during the week, sometimes staying over at the office and most weekends they would do their own thing in their own places. They saw each other less and less, hardly ever communicating anything of consequence, until they arrived at this current place in time, in what looked very much like the end of the line.

Winding the clock onward four years until the present moment and this is where they have come to. They no longer even discuss their relationship and the way forward, there didn't seem to be much point anymore. Roar knows how to treat a woman in order to get what he wants but when he has that his attention span quickly diminishes, and he is off on the quest for the next interesting event or whatever he can get excited about. His next thrill, the next party or skiing trip, a chance to get away for the weekend, anything that would quell the unrest that seemed to continually drive him forward – or was it driving him backwards towards his own imminent self-destruction?

Sometimes the greatest revelations in life appear during the darkest moments, giving us an unexpected opportunity to expand and evolve as human beings, or conversely, we can contract and fall into the energy of desolation,

victimisation and self-pity, thus reducing ourselves to even less than we previously were.

For Elisabeth it had never been more crystal clear. She had woken up, shaken into greater awareness, given a full and thorough view of, 'what is not living life in full'. She had been shown everything that life, for her, is not about thus she was given what living life is meant to be. She could no longer be in this abusive arrangement that was such a poor excuse for a relationship. This degrading compromise she was in, was at best, 'you scratch my back and I'll scratch yours', to at worst, for her, manipulation, mental and psychological abuse. She could no longer live with such levels of self-disrespect.

To be in a relationship, she realized, is to be in an ever-developing awareness and soulful evolution, first with herself and to what she held as the greatest universal deity or power that, she thought, some may call God. Personally, she would like to call it Universal Light, the energy that we are all part of, that holds everything in its divine power. Subsequently, to bring that true inner connection to all other relationships great and small, fleeting or permanent, to bring everything you truly are to all that you do and with everyone you meet. She was tired of living so constricted and contracted, it was time to live her full self in everything she did, and this meant that any relationship that was not true would have to change completely or become a thing of the past. And in doing so, realized how she would like to live her life, free from deceit, free from holding back, free from allowing herself to be manipulated, so as to live her life in a more truthful way.

She had become conscious of the fact that she could not blame Roar for her predicament, she had known who he was from the start, made all her own choices and allowed herself to get caught up in the excitement of the game, for that is what it was and, in fact, still is. There was never anything real, just the thrill of the hunt and being hunted, the then hunter now had other prey in his sights and would pursue it until the bitter end, whatever that turned out to be, and for her there was definitely nothing to be gained, no truth waiting around to witness that and be positioned as the victim, she thought to herself. She also had to let go of the images she had carried through it all, images of a devoted and kind husband and two beautiful children in a happy and comfortable home.

There was a contented feeling of settlement and total acceptance within her, a perception of knowing where she was really going for the first time in her life and this is what she would reflect, purely that impression of her full self, in every single encounter and communication with others. She felt years of disappointment and agitation beginning to slip away, her body starting to feel lighter, the residual gloom lifting from her mind and a sense of freedom permeating through her whole being.

They arrived at the party at 8.15pm after the short taxi journey in silence. They stepped out into the night and breathed in the cold, crisp and somewhat refreshing evening air. It was certainly going to be a chilly one. Elisabeth had agreed with the taxi driver that he would pick them up again at 1.30am, Roar saying nothing, immediately thinking to himself that it would be far too early for the New Year's Eve party of the century to end.

As they stepped inside the foyer, the heat from within the venue was like a blast of hot summer wind in their faces as they quickly found the cloakroom and deposited their winter attire and changed shoes before making their way into the main hall. It was decked out with Christmas lights and year 2000 banners, bouquets of flowers and frosted glass tealights on all the tables that were covered with deep midnight-blue tablecloths and sprinkled with masses of small year 2000 golden glitter, with golden coloured charger plates and a combination of light and dark blue serviettes. Underneath the charger plates they would find several sheets of multi-coloured paper stapled together to form the evenings song book.

There were three long-tables, made up of several smaller tables, arranged in rows with seats for fifty people at each one. Most of the seats were taken but as they already knew they would be seated in the middle row on the side facing towards the vestibule they had just entered through; they made their way in that direction. As they moved through the hall they were greeted by several different people and engaged in polite conversation with each one until they finally arrived at their seats, which were situated close to the stage end not far from the DJ and near to where a microphone had been set up. The microphone was for the evening's speeches and for anyone who cared to entertain or indeed, had anything else to say.

It is somewhat traditional in Norway not to take these kinds of events too seriously even though they are often quite rigidly structured with a master of ceremonies that introduces all the speakers and who guides the formal part of the evening until the dinner is completed, then music and dance takes over. There is also a lady's speech performed by a man, a man's speech performed by a lady, a speech in thanks of the food and many other smaller speeches and toasts that the master of ceremonies keeps control of. There is also a tradition of making up songs that fit the event. A well-known melody is used but the words of the original song are changed, usually in a jovial manner to fit the occasion. There are also lots of well-known drinking songs and chants that may spontaneously erupt as the alcohol begins to flow in full.

As they sat down in their seats Roar clumsily placed his collection of booze on the table in front of him banging it down as if to attract as much attention as possible, he left the champagne in his backpack as he would put it outside to chill for a little later. Elisabeth took out her bottles of San Pellegrino placing them gently on the table. On the opposite side of the table were a couple they had never seen before and who they would discover to be Mikal and Annelise, the placement had been planned this way to encourage new acquaintances and connections. To the right of Elisabeth was a man called Eric who she had met before at one of her yoga sessions at the local yoga studio. To the left of Roar was a young lady named Veronica who worked at the local supermarket, so almost everyone knew her as she was so visible in this small community and because of her refreshing bright, bubbly and outgoing personality. Roar immediately turned on his charm with Veronica, much to the dismay of her boyfriend Bjorn, sitting in the next seat further along the table. Softly shaking her head, Elisabeth, not wanting to react to Roar's blatant flirting struck up a conversation with Mikal and Annelise. She whispered, more to herself than those around her, "It seems some things will never change." Then quickly changing the topic, asked Annelise and Mikal, "How long have you been living in Droebak?"

She soon discovered that they had moved to Droebak from Oslo during the previous summer. Selling their three-bedroom apartment in the Ullevaal area, had given them the equity to buy a four-bedroom house with a good plot of land here in Droebak and as their twin boys were now almost six years old and about to start school, they wanted them to grow up in what they thought was a safer place. Mikal was a police-lawyer specializing in tax fraud and tax evasion and Annelise was about to open her own arts and crafts shop, including ceramics and picture framing, down in the centre of Droebak. She also intended to create her own ceramics workshop by converting their garage, selling her works along with the artistic creations of other selected artists, in her shop.

They were both fascinated to hear about Elisabeth's lifestyle and her interest in meditation and yoga, saying that they would love to try yoga as they often felt stressed by their own lifestyle, so much to do and far too little time in which to do it.

Elisabeth was a teacher at one of the local secondary schools, she told them. She had known very early on in life that she would work in education. She had finished her bachelor teaching degree at twenty-two and had since specialized in languages. She spoke Norwegian, English and Spanish fluently and was also a competent German speaker. Elisabeth's mother was originally from Manchester in the United Kingdom and had always spoken English with her as well as her two older sisters and younger brother. The family had holidayed in Spain, often travelling there between two or three times every year. She had also taken a six-month sabbatical there after completing her degree.

The call to order had arrived and the meal was about to begin, people were milling around greeting each other, a few still looking to locate their seats for the evening.

The three-course meal they were expecting had been pre-ordered, so everyone knew exactly what they would be receiving. There were two options for each course plus a vegan/vegetarian menu. As the first course starters were being served around the room, Elisabeth felt a soft tap on her shoulder; her sister Annette, three years her elder smiled broadly at her. They stood together by the table and gave each other a long loving hug and chatted for a while.

Elisabeth spoke quietly in her sister's ear, "I have come to the point in my relationship with Roar where I can't accept the way he is anymore. I know he is up to something, working late most nights and supposedly staying over at the office. I feel I have given away my own self-respect in this pathetic liaison and it's now time for me to claim back my own self-worth, I truly deserve better than this"

Annette nodded in agreement, she had been at school at the same time as Roar although he was a year above her, she knew him well or rather, knew about many of his escapades. Several of her girlfriends had succumbed at one time or another to the advances of Roar and she had always felt that Elisabeth had made a huge mistake becoming involved with him, that she could do much better. Not wanting to rub salt into her sisters wounds, Annette replied, "If you want to get away from him for a while you know you are more than welcome to come and stay with us for as long as you want to."

Elisabeth replied, "I may take you up on the offer very soon."

The sisters loved each other dearly and could be open and truthful with each other but they had gone through the same discussion regarding Roar many times to the point that there was no point anymore. Roar was so engrossed in his conversation with Veronica that he hadn't even noticed the arrival of Annette and as she moved away, back to her partner, she purposely bumped his chair on the way, but still no reaction he was too focused on the disarmament of this young lady beside him at the table.

The starters were now on the table and the waitresses and waiters came around with the wine, both still and sparkling water, as well as canned beer. Elisabeth had chosen a fennel and orange salad, preferring that to the offer of rakfisk, which is a traditional Norwegian dish of fermented freshwater trout or char, and its accompaniment of flatbread with butter, sour cream, finely sliced onion and leek. Roar was already devouring his rakfisk, washing it down with gulps of wine, as though he hadn't eaten for the previous week.

He had surfaced from his conversation with Veronica to scoff his starter and was now focusing on Mikal and Annelise, well mostly Annelise, as was his norm. He was very loquacious and droll, particularly after a bottle of wine or two, who's counting, with lots of self-irony as well as a spattering of sarcasm as he soon had both Annelise and Mikal enthralled as he told stories of his exploits, investments and skiing adventures.

"We were skiing off-piste in Verbier on a quite remote run quite late in the day. We knew the terrain quite well as we had been here several times before. We were almost through the forested area that would lead back onto one of the main ski-runs, when I spotted a flash of bright orange colour in my peripheral vision. I stopped, as did my friend Joachim skiing behind me and we went to investigate. The orange colour turned out to be the arm of a lady that had become lodged head down in a ditch under a fir-tree, skis stuck in the snow and unable to maneuver herself to release the skis or get out of the ditch. She had been there for over an hour and was completely exhausted and resigned to freezing to death. We pulled her out, she was uninjured but really shaky so we escorted her all the way to her hotel." With his full-on charm, he entertained them until the next course arrived, they hardly got a word in and he learned absolutely nothing about them apart from their first names.

Meanwhile Elisabeth and Eric had been deep in conversation and realized that they had many similar interests. He was also a teacher, although he worked at a nursery school in the neighbouring village of Son which was about twenty-five minutes' drive from Droebak. Eric was forty-five, divorced and had a daughter, Emma, who was fourteen years old and they lived in a flat on the outskirts of town in an area known as Heer.

Eric's preferred pastimes ranged from yoga and meditation to walking and cross-country skiing in the mountains and also included food-foraging, especially for wild mushrooms which he had learned from his father who had been a man of nature always out in the wild and often taking Eric along with him out into the forest, all year round, no matter the weather, rain or shine, snow or ice. They had camped out spring, summer, autumn or winter, sometimes even building their own snow holes to spend the night in.

There were constant stoppages in proceedings with toasts, songs and speeches that were fun for most of the attendees except Elisabeth in her sobriety, who now purely observed, without judgement as the people around her became less inhibited and the noise levels grew louder until it was difficult to hear herself speak or think. She found herself pondering upon why people needed to drink so much alcohol to have, what they called, 'a good time'. Living with Roar these past years had given her ample opportunity to reflect on how much he would change in the space of only a couple of hours, from being a calm reasonable man to becoming an aggressive womanizer without inhibitions. It was as if he was possessed by a demon, she guessed that this was why alcohol is often referred to as 'the demon drink'. It was interesting to see such a large group of people drinking and how the atmosphere had changed from the joyful gentle encounters of meeting one-another to what now was a more raucous, edgy, aggressive vibration. It was only 9.30pm, so what would it be like at 1am, she wondered?

The wait staff had cleared away the dishes from the first course and were now arriving with the main, for the vegan/vegetarian they produced a beautiful honey-roasted hot root vegetable salad. For the meat-eaters they delivered the current traditional

New Year's Eve food, roast turkey dinner, and for the old-style traditionalists, 'Pinnekjoett' which is cured and dried smoked lamb ribs served with boiled potatoes and a swede-mash which for many is the main meal consumed on Christmas Eve too.

In the far corner of the hall Elisabeth spotted her old friend Siv with her husband Christian. Even though her food had arrived she wanted to go over and have a chat with them, so leaving her salad on the table, off she went. Roar sat and watched her walk away and even through the fog of alcohol he could still register that there were changes afoot, he could sense a new air of authority about the way she moved, no arrogance but a fullness and openness. His thoughts were disturbed when Mikal said, "Roar, your wife is very beautiful, you certainly are a lucky man."

"Yes," he said curtly yet contemplatively, "undoubtably very lucky."

Elisabeth and Siv were very close, they had literally grown up together, through nursery school and all the way through to college, they had a very open dialogue and kept nothing from each other, told each other everything. Siv looked at Elisabeth and immediately said, "You look amazing Liz, what's going on?"

"My life is about to change forever, I don't quite know how but I can feel it through my whole body, I feel it so clearly, I am changing, evolving in a way, to something grander than I have been before," she replied.

They continued to discuss how Elisabeth felt and she told her that there would be big changes in her relationship with Roar and that she would probably leave him quite soon. Siv thought silently that that would not be a minute too soon. Christian listened and nodded, he had been a classmate with Roar and had felt the wrong end of his spiked humour too many times and thought that it was about time he got what he really deserved. For Elisabeth it was great to feel the love and acceptance from both of them and she told them how greatly she appreciated their concern and friendship. She realized that everyone she had met this evening and every interaction was further indication of how communication and connection in relationships should be and that anything less than full openness and transparency was abusive. It also indicated for her how, for many years, she had accepted so much less than she deserved and that there was no longer room for any more abuse. She promised them that she would come back over to them when the dinner was completed, left them and then made her way back to her seat. Feeling as she walked back that her own acceptance of a relationship that was less than loving was in a way choosing self-abuse, she was responsible for everything relating to her own situation.

As she sat down in her seat the next speech began, it was to be the lady's speech which is given by a man in honour of all women. Henrik Bjerke, the local jeweler, delivered a speech that was humble, witty and completely loving and honouring of women. Elisabeth received every word and knew that this was an ideal that not many men, if any, lived up to but in truth why should any woman accept less. It made so much sense to her and yet in general we avoid living the way this man had presented. Why is that? What stops us living this way, she contemplated a while upon her own question to herself. And she expanded, why should we not treat men exactly the same way, there is no difference between us. Why do we constantly try to mess each other up? We dishonour, we compete, we ridicule, we belittle, we banter, we disenfranchise, we do everything that is not loving or respectful, which harms us, whilst the opposite would be to do everything that is loving, that heals, that we ought to make our every action a healing, loving movement or interaction.

The first thought that came to her was, that it is the 'self', the I, the me, that is the greatest problem we all have, that is what stops us from being completely true with each other, that is what stops true love. The conditions we put upon each other taints everything we do. She had never had so much clarity before, it seemed that she was being given an unending stream of revelations, she could actually feel her own clarity and awareness increasing. This was truly a turning point in her life, a moment of expansion, another step along the way to become or, in fact, return to the All that is within her and indeed everyone else.

She finished her salad and poured another glass of sparkling water, turning to her left she observed the empty seat where Roar had been. He's around somewhere, she thought, chatting up someone else no doubt. He doesn't seem to have any control over his urges when he is drinking, he becomes possessed and not in a good way. She caught herself having these thoughts about him and wondered, was she judging him, what right did she have to judge others, he knew many people here at the party, maybe he was just having a chat with one of his friends. She did a quick scan of the room; he was nowhere to be seen. She let go of wanting to know his whereabouts and accepted that she had chosen to put herself into this situation so it was entirely her responsibility to do something about it. Roar had his own responsibility, and she would no longer judge whether he acted upon that or not.

Roar was out in the cloakroom, putting on his overcoat, boots, hat, scarf and gloves. His mobile phone had been constantly buzzing in his pocket for the last half hour. He lit up a cigar, buttoned up his coat and went outside into the freezing night, he knew instinctively that it was Anneli and that something untoward must have happened. They had agreed not to meet until they were both back in the office on Tuesday January 2nd. They had planned to stay over at the Plaza after work and he had not expected to speak to her before then.

He walked outside feeling a little groggy from the wine, the cold air shocked his only area of bare skin, his face, but that was enough to give him an immediate sobering effect and a thought flashed through his mind that maybe he should consider a little moderation in his consumption of alcohol. The thought disappeared as quickly as it came. He trudged off through the snow, into the starlit, clear and freezing night.

Anneli had been confronted by her partner Sven about her absence from their relationship during the last few weeks, demanding to know what had been going on. Sven had acted totally out of character, become threatening and aggressive, she was frightened that he might even harm her physically. She had fled their apartment in Oslo and was now at her sister's house in Nesoddtangen, which was a short ferry ride from the centre of Oslo, also about a thirty-minute drive from Droebak.

Sven was a very successful business-to-business sales consultant at a large Norwegian international telecom company based in Oslo. He travelled extensively, mostly throughout Scandinavia, although there were quite regular trips to India to negotiate multimillion dollar contracts with their outsourcing business partners located there. He loved Anneli deeply, they had always been open and intimate with each other. In March they had planned to take a four-week Hawaiian adventure holiday with a stop-over in San Francisco. It had been great fun planning all the hotels, beaches, flights, stops and escapades they would experience along the way.

He felt that recently she had become distant and aloof and continually avoided spending time together. He had questioned himself for thinking dark thoughts but in the end, he had realized that she was definitely avoiding him. It felt to him as though everything they had was slowly slipping away, he also felt devastated and betrayed.

December had been a quiet month, it seemed that many companies had gone through their preparation for the turn of the century and were bracing themselves for the moment the clock ticked to 2000, hoping their computer systems would not crash. He spent this time catching up on paperwork, much of which he could do from his home-office. This also highlighted how much time Anneli spent at work. As the days and weeks passed by, he saw less and less of her, she became distant and his every attempt at intimacy was bluntly rejected. He became more and more suspicious; he just knew that something had changed and not in a good way.

He was gravely saddened, almost grief stricken, didn't know which way to turn or who he could speak to but this quickly gave way to anger and frustration. He wanted to know why, who, when, and yet he knew the answers to his questions would crush him.

She had denied that there was anything going on and insisted that it was all work, an important project that needed to be delivered by the end of January. That it was all very tiring but had to be completed and could mean a promotion for her. He had persisted, angrily pushing her on to their sofa demanding to know why she had continually rejected his sexual advances, saying that being tired had never stood in the way before. He knew instinctively, it wasn't hard to read, that she was seeing someone else, he needed to hear the truth, now. He felt that he could explode, he could lose control of his senses completely if he didn't get answers.

Anneli had always been a very physical and demanding lover, at times it had been too much for Sven, he had been the one refusing her advances. Sometimes they would make love for hours and still she wanted more when all he wanted was to sleep. Some Sundays they would stay in bed for most of the day, making love, napping and eating, it had been gloriously exacting. From this to complete rejection, for Sven there could be no other explanation, tiredness simply did not compute.

"I haven't told him anything, but he knows and he won't let go of it until he gets answers," she told Roar as he trudged through the snow, "What are we going to do?"
Roar tried to think, well, in the excitement of it all, he hadn't really given it any thought whatsoever. He did know that he was not ready to leave Elisabeth and be with Anneli – they were just having fun. He needed time to think. He didn't know how to answer her question, he just mumbled, "I don't know."

They talked for a few minutes as she told him she had taken a couple of bags and moved to her sister's place and would stay there for now but she would have to talk it through with Sven at some point during the next few days. They agreed that she could book into the local hotel at Skiphelle, just south of Droebak and that he would come to her as soon as he could get away from the party, which may not be until well after midnight, probably more like 2am.

She felt a little calmer now, as in all honesty she had not considered the consequences of what they had been doing. She realized that she had been consumed by the buzz, by the collusion and intrigue of the deceit in which they had partaken. For her, excitement was the antidote to a mundane life. As soon as she felt constricted by her lifestyle, something new had to happen and it didn't matter if she hurt herself or others, there was always collateral damage around Anneli.

Elisabeth was chatting to Eric about an upcoming yoga retreat he would be attending on the island of Crete, some of the most sought-after yoga teachers from around the world would be there. He would be attending a two-week Ashtanga retreat at the end of April during the Easter break. Elisabeth felt that this type of yoga was far too physical for her and much preferred a gentler, more meditative form of yoga. She had practiced Ashtanga yoga many times finding that it was not suited to her body, it was physically challenging and didn't feel caring or gentle enough for her.

Roar returned to the party and was now slumped down in his chair; Elisabeth turned to look at him. He took up his half-full glass of wine and gulped it down, quickly pouring a new one. With a troubled look on his face, deep in thought he stared at his own wine glass sitting on the table.

"Are you okay Roar?" she said, "You seem a little distracted."

At that very moment he had what could best be described as a blind impulse, a bolt from the blue, or was it a fed thought from a darker place, it was though, a way to get away from the party a little earlier. "Yes, I'm fine, I was just thinking, I would love to go down to the harbour to see the fireworks display close up. Let's do it," he said, knowing that Elisabeth would not be interested.

He knew she wouldn't want to leave the party for the fireworks display and that she had already booked the taxi for one-thirty. He saw this as a perfect way for him to leave the party and meet Anneli at the hotel.

"You know that I am not interested in standing outside in the freezing cold to watch fireworks but if you want to go, then go. I will make my own way home when the taxi arrives," she answered curtly.

The dessert arrived, almost everyone had chosen cloudberry cream which is a simple mixture of whipped cream, sugar and wild cloudberries giving a smooth texture with a sweet yet tart flavour and was a great Christmas-time favourite for many Norwegians. Various bottles of spirits and liqueurs appeared on the tables, Cognac, Irish Cream and Amaretto, amongst many others.

Elisabeth had chosen the fruit salad due to her intolerance of dairy products. At the same time the wait staff were also serving coffee and tea, for what is a good liqueur without a cup of hot coffee? Roar poured himself a substantial cognac, offered it around to the others nearby, then topped up his coffee with a little more cognac. He then recounted a tale of building up his last business to those around who chose to listen, how he sold it just before the shares crashed, making a killing, almost incriminating himself for insider trading at the same time.

The music was playing, many people were dancing. As the clock started to creep towards midnight, Roar made a show of asking politely if anyone would like to join him to walk down to the harbour to watch the firework display. Not expecting anyone to say yes, he was quite surprised when the young couple next to him, Veronica and Bjorn accepted saying that they would be meeting up with some friends down there and he was very welcome to join their group. He reluctantly accepted, at the same time thinking that he would easily lose them in the crowds and make his way to the hotel which was only a ten-minute taxi ride from the harbour.

At 11.30pm, Roar, Veronica, Bjorn and about twenty other people that had decided to make their way down to the harbour started to leave the party. Roar had packed his backpack, taking the rest of his cognac, the champagne and his own fireworks, wrapping himself up in his hat, coat, scarf and gloves and with the others, went on his way. Eric left at the same time to make his way to his brother's house.

Elisabeth took this opportunity to wander around the hall and connect with friends and acquaintances that she knew well and others that she had recognized but never really had a conversation with. This far into the event, it often became difficult to converse with people that had spent the evening drinking whilst she had not. On several occasions she had exchanged no more than a few words with someone and knew immediately that there was no point to the conversation, there was no-one home. She just excused herself and moved on to the next. The hall was gradually emptying as everyone made their way outside to watch the firework display from afar. At 11.50pm she went into the cloakroom, put on her extra layers, her hat, boots and coat and made her way outside.

As she stood outside with Siv and Christian, before they asked the question, she knew they would ask, she had a flash of insight – a sort of knowing about Roar – pass through her body. She felt and knew deep down, that this night was the end of the way that it had been and that from now on everything would change. This would prove to be true in many ways in a very short space of time. "Where is Roar?" asked Siv.

"Going his own way," she replied gently, "as he always does and probably will do until the bitter end."

They all fell silent; it was 11.58 and they awaited the new year count down. They could hear some far-off explosions as prematurely ignited pyrotechnics shot up into the sky.

Hundreds of people were packed tightly in the bitter cold night, thronging the street around the tiny harbour, waiting for the countdown and the following barrage of sights and sounds. Roar, bottle of cognac in hand, weaved his way through the crowd looking for a good vantage point, bumping and stepping on toes he managed to push his way through to the front, irritating many along the way.

Five – four – three – two – one – 'Happy New Year', the huge cheer went up, the champagne corks popped and the sky erupted into a kaleidoscope of multi-coloured lights and thunderbolt explosions. The bombardment of the senses continued for the next fifteen minutes as the crowd oohed and gasped at the magnitude of the fiery display. Never in Droebak's history had so much money gone up in smoke in such a short period of time, and the crowd loved it. As the display reached its pyrotechnical crescendo and the last bombs exploded, lit up the sky and boomed out over the mostly inebriated audience, Roar remembered that he too had some fireworks.

As the crowd dispersed, he took out his fireworks and lit up one of his cigars. Placing the fireworks way to close together he began to light the fuses with his cigar. Before he had managed to light half of them the first one erupted into life shooting a sparkling fountain several metres up into the air, then the next one came to life, then the next and this lit the remainder of the fireworks placed on the ground. People close by ran for cover and Roar, a little slow in his current state of inebriation was covered in a shower of burning sparks. He frantically ran and attempted to brush them from his coat and hat, comically he dove headlong into a pile of snow that had been cleared from the road around the harbour by the local council snow ploughs. He extinguished himself but then felt a sharp pain on his right thumb and quickly pulled off his glove and shook away the last of the glowing ember that was stuck there.

Cold and somewhat embarrassed he began to make his way back through the remains of the crowd on his way to search for a taxi to take him to the hotel. He worked his way up to the main street, Storgata, the prime thoroughfare through the centre of little old Droebak. He moved along to the one and only taxi rank beyond the town square, shocked when he observed the length of the queue waiting for taxis, he decided he would walk to the hotel. It shouldn't take him more than twenty-five to thirty minutes to get there, he thought.

The name Droebak originally meant, 'steep hills' which described the whole area the town was built on. You couldn't really walk anywhere in Droebak without going up and down the hills. At the south end of the main street, a steep hill with a narrow winding road, with no footpath and normally too narrow for cars to pass each other had now become even narrower due to the heavy snowfall. Beneath the lightly packed snow lay a coating of compacted black ice which made walking uphill almost impossible, treacherously slow and quite dangerous in his intoxicated condition. By walking at the very edge of the road, almost in the ditch, he was able to avoid the ice but had to pass through the deeper snow which made for frustratingly slow progress. The only saving grace was that it was such strenuous work getting up the hill that his body heated up and he didn't really feel the cold too much. As he crested the top of the hill the road flattened, and he knew that he was past the worst point and the rest of the walk would be mostly flat until it took him back down, almost to sea level where the hotel lay.

Through these physical efforts and the cold night air Roar's mind had begun to clear and the fog of alcohol started to lift. He suddenly stopped in his tracks: A huge elk stepped out of a wooded area and stood at the roadside, no more than ten metres in front of him. Nature often gives us signs in the form of symbolism, there are no coincidences and everything that happens means something. Was this confrontation with the elk a great stop moment for Roar or would he simply choose to continue on his somewhat wayward path in life?

Elisabeth arrived home at 1.45am, took off her winter layers and went into the bathroom to get ready for bed. She took a long, close look at her face in the bathroom mirror and smiled, looking into her eyes she observed a deep sparkle she had never really noticed before. She felt very spacious as if the whole of the universe was within her. She smiled again as she felt the freedom that this gave her, the sense that her life was opening up before her. She had changed and could no longer look back, for the real truth lay in the present and the future which also included the past as that is where she was ultimately returning to. She could feel the enormity of what was taking place in her life, great revelations and realisations were unfolding within her. She had always felt that there was way more to life than the physical temporal outplays we humans busy ourselves with. She had felt several times previously that she had lived many lives before this one and that there was a cycle to complete, to live life in a way that was more consummate, more evolved. That we are not here on Earth to play around, to fight, squabble, to greedily amass wealth for ourselves. We are here to expand to a level of humanness that is to live in a way that is in service for all of us. She was aware that it was not simply a question of the physical, human past but the past as in where she was before all her human incarnations, the past and the future as one, at one with and returning to her soul. Her whole body was ignited with a new awareness, there was a tingle in her every particle, she could feel and sense so much more than could be seen with the naked eye.

Eventually she made her way into the bedroom and got into bed. As she lay there, she could feel Roar, she could actually feel the turmoil he had within him and through all his undoubted narcissism and showmanship she could see that he, deep inside himself, was vulnerable and hurt. That he was actually living his life acting out a roleplay in order to avoid dealing with what it was that was harming him. Instantaneously she inherently knew that absolutely everyone had that same beauty, the same glorious essence deep inside and she could see all the layers of untruth that Roar and people in general, wrapped around themselves to avoid being that true essence. Elisabeth could feel her own layers of protection, deceit and falsity, below these layers she felt the hurts and the pain of lifetimes of living the opposite of what she truly was, living this grand illusion or rather the ignoble delusion that human life had become.

During the stillness of the night as she slept, there was a majestic settlement within her body, a deep confirmation from within, that this was the new foundation for life and from this platform she would grow further, she would no longer dither in the spuriousness of the fraudulent construction of deceitful interactions of human life, rather petition truth with every movement of her being.

They stood at the roadside, ten metres apart, looking at each other, each waiting for the other to make the first move. Could this be a sign, some sort of message for Roar, and what did it mean?

Now this was a full-grown bull elk around three hundred and fifty kilos and standing well over two metres tall. Fortunately the elk had already dropped its antlers but none-the-less was still a formidable obstacle standing before him. Once again Roar, choosing to ignore the sign before him, stepped forward. The elk immediately turned and trotted back through the snow into the woods.

Thirty minutes later, after falling three times on the icy descent down the steep part of the road to the hotel he arrived bruised, burnt and bedraggled at Room 106, Anneli let him in. He didn't look or smell particularly well in his fireworks-singed clothes and with a strong smell of stale alcohol, she stepped back a little in shock. "What happened to you!" she exclaimed.

He shrugged, threw his coat, hat and gloves on the chair in the corner of the room, then kicking off his shoes he sat down on the bed. A wave of relief and exhaustion swept over him simultaneously as he made himself comfortable, propped up against the headboard. He felt dizzy and he had a headache, so he closed his eyes for a while to regain control, then replied, "I can tell you all about it later, now, how's it going with you?"

It was now just past 2am. Anneli had already been in the room since 12.45am. During that time she had ignored the frequent ringing of her phone as Sven had tried to get in touch with her. As they talked it was more and more difficult for Roar to focus, Anneli repeatedly asking him if he was listening to her and saying that they had to discuss what they would do next. The pain in his head increased, he tried in vain to follow the conversation. In the end he slumped over on the bed, seemingly unconscious, Anneli unsuccessfully tried to rouse him. He was breathing steadily and she assumed he had been overcome by the alcohol and tiredness, so disappointedly she let him be. She remained in the room for a while contemplating her next move and reasoned that there was little point in staying there and decided to call a taxi and return to her friend's house.

The taxi arrived almost an hour later, she took one last look at Roar who seemed to be sleeping deeply, turned and left the room.

Roar awoke in a very confused state a few hours later not really understanding where he was. He closed his eyes again, trying to think it through, but his mind was a complete blank. Eventually, he remembered getting ready for the party and what he thought was a frosty atmosphere between himself and Elisabeth. A flash of her beautiful smiling face came into his mind then suddenly morphed into mocking laughter disappearing as quickly as it came. He sat up on the bed, all his clothes on and as he moved, he felt the throbbing inside his brain more intense than ever before.

"Why do I do this to myself?" he mused. "I have no idea what has happened, what I have done or how I got here in this room. Why would I come here alone? Or has someone else been here?"

He re-opened his eyes, focusing on the contents of the room and quickly realized he was in a hotel, but where? He drew the blinds and looked out, it was still dark, there were lights in the distance and what seemed like an open expanse of water in front of him, it was probably the fjord. He walked over to the desk and picked up the hotel literature, now relieved it was the Skiphelle Hotel, at least he was not too far from home. As he thought of home he was again reminded of Elisabeth, she was so sensible, and would no doubt be home, all tucked up in bed right now.

For years now he had had post drinking episodes when, after a certain point he couldn't remember anything at all of the prior evening's events. Gradually, during the following day some images of the often-unfortunate events would return and he could then, to a certain extent, piece together the turn of events of the night before. It could be quite embarrassing when sometimes weeks or months later he might meet someone and they would open a conversation with him, he would strain to remember but often concede that he didn't recognize them. They would then narrate a story telling him of their antics together or of his drunken escapades. More than once, he had been given a sudden slap across the face by an unfamiliar and irate young lady for something he didn't know or recall he had said or done.

The gaps in the memories seemed to be getting bigger, he thought that he somehow should stop drinking so much, or even that he should stop drinking completely. He had said this to himself so many times before but as soon as the opportunity to drink reappeared, he welcomed it with open arms, and to be honest, with great relief. With relief from what? Why do I need to drink so much and why can't I stop drinking after one or two beers? He knew instinctively that he was asking himself what could be the most important questions in his life so far. He couldn't think about that anymore just now, it made his head throb even more. He opened the minibar and took out a bottle of Farris sparkling water, a row of miniature spirit bottles stood neatly to attention beckoning for him to indulge; he refused.

It's New Year's Day, he thought, I can change this, I can stop drinking, he thought, as he closed the door on the row of decadent little soldiers. He drank the Farris sparkling water, decided to go for a walk to get some fresh air, put on his outdoor clothing, found the room key and made his way to the exit.

It was a gorgeously vivid dream, harmonious, peaceful and still as Elisabeth sat against the palm tree on the white sandy beach gazing out over the tranquil azure ocean. The dream slowly faded as she roused from her refreshing sleep. It was still early in the morning, around 8am as she opened her eyes and stretched out her body. She felt truly amazing. She had not slept so soundly in many years, her new-found purpose was pumping through her veins, confirming once again that her life was changing, permanently.

She put on her dressing gown and wandered out to the kitchen to put on the kettle, made herself mint tea and took a look at the latest New Year's Day news on TV. The headlines were a mixture of local news about the great firework displays around the country and on the other hand there were several incidents in which people had lost their lives due to house fires caused either by unattended candles, carelessly discarded cigarettes or irresponsible handling of fireworks. There was also international coverage of all the fabulous firework displays from all the capital cities around the world.

Her thoughts returned to Roar as she started to wonder where he was, she couldn't let go of the eerie feeling that something had happened to him. She did love him, but in some way that love had changed. There was a greater understanding for who he was, including both his wild disregarding side that not only harmed himself and potentially everyone around him and for the hidden side he seldom showed to anyone, the hurt, vulnerable and sensitive man that he allowed no-one to see. She contemplated the fact that he may never allow that real Roar, the true man he was underneath all the outward charm, carelessness and macho bravado, to stand forth in this life, and the fact that they would now presumably break up and go their own separate ways, without him ever revealing his full and true self.

He had done so much to destroy their relationship that it was difficult to see that there could be any way to heal it. He didn't seem to have the will or indeed any interest at all in preserving or resurrecting what they had had together, let alone developing and expanding it to a new level.

Relationships cannot survive, thrive and evolve if they are not nourished, enhanced and continually enriched. Anything that is not enrichment is debasement or abuse. In the end it is a simple equation, there is no room for tolerance, for this is a sure sign of abuse, reciprocated with a dose of judgement. The equation is imbalanced, therefore not truly loving and must be attended to in some way.

Alexander and Mona were standing on their balcony overlooking Skiphelle Beach, breathing in the cold early morning air. The last of their guests had left and they had tidied up the house after their party, taking a short breather before retiring to the bedroom. They looked down to the beach noticing a lone figure in a dark overcoat and hat plodding through the deep snow. A combination of the starlight and house lights on the opposite shore reflecting off the still fjord lit the figure up in silhouette. It was an unusual sight to see as the figure stopped and started, making very slow progress along the shore, close to the water's edge. Fascinated they followed its progress; the figure had almost reached the far end of the beach when it stopped twenty metres short, didn't move for a short while, then suddenly fell forward, face down in the snow. They stared in disbelief for a short while as the figure lay there unmoving, eventually they turned to look at each other simultaneously realizing that this was a very serious situation and they sprang into action.

Mona called the emergency services as Alexander put on his coat, gloves and boots, grabbed a torch, several blankets from the cupboard in the hallway and quickly made his way down to the beach.

The emergency services took all the details they required; an air ambulance helicopter would be dispatched as soon as possible. They estimated that it would take approximately fifteen minutes to arrive. As Alexander approached the prone figure, he instinctively felt that this was a desperate situation, it was bitterly cold and quite isolated in regard to getting emergency assistance.

Droebak is a very small town and if someone behaved eccentrically, or in any way that made them stand out from the crowd, it was noticed and it was discussed by many of the inhabitants. In the case of Roar, everyone knew him, or at least knew of his alcohol and women-related antics. He was often the topic of the town gossip and frequently not seen in a positive or very respectful light.

Alexander struggled to move the inert body, he cleared away snow from the right-hand side, laying out three blankets on top of each other and eventually rolled the man onto his back laying on the blankets. He checked for vital signs of life and detected a faint breath and a weak pulse; he knew it was imperative to keep him as warm as possible. He tried vainly to revive him or get some kind of response, but to no avail. This was a life-and-death situation. He maneuvered him carefully into the recovery position. He checked the man's pockets for identification, finding Roar's wallet. Alexander packed Roar tightly into the remaining blankets, making sure to wrap one gently around his head, then examined the contents of the wallet, finding a driving license, recognizing the name although he hadn't recognized the face. He took another look at the drawn face before him, this time seeing Roar and recognizing him, took out his telephone, called Mona asking her to pass on the details to the emergency services. Alexander knelt close to Roar, constantly checking his breathing, which remained stable, slow, but very shallow.

From the moment Mona called for help until Alexander spotted the approaching helicopter and waved his torch so that they could pinpoint where to land, was only seventeen minutes and then another three until the helicopter was on the beach and the medics were attending to Roar. They checked him swiftly, put him on oxygen, wrapped him in space blankets and whisked him away. Within twelve minutes of leaving the snowy beach in Droebak, Roar was on a hospital stretcher being wheeled into Ullevaal University Hospital in Oslo.

It was now 10.25am and the low winter sunshine lit the snow atop the trees of the forest covered hills on the opposite side of the fjord. It was still very cold outside as Elisabeth, who was just finishing her breakfast smoothie contemplated where she might go for a walk. There was still no sign of Roar, and she had no expectation that he would show up any time soon. She went to the bathroom to prepare herself for the day. As she stood in front of the mirror cleaning her teeth, she heard the house telephone ringing in the distance. She finished off, walked through to the living room to where the phone continued its incessant bleating. "Hell," she didn't even complete her greeting.

"Is that Elisabeth Lysene?" the voice on the line asked.

"Yes, speaking, how can I help you?"

"My name is nurse Helene Kristiansen, I'm calling from Ullevaal Hospital regarding your partner, Roar Moerk," she replied.

Elisabeth felt a pang of anxiousness in her stomach as she asked, "What's happened?"

She explained that Roar had been flown to the hospital earlier this morning in an unconscious state with no visible injuries other than a small burn on his thumb. He was still unconscious and they had determined that at some point during the night he had suffered a brain hemorrhage. He was in a coma at the moment although his vital signs were stable.

Elisabeth asked about coming into the hospital; the nurse replied that Roar was in the Neuro Intensive Care Unit and would be having vital procedures and medications during the next few hours so she may not be able to see him, but she was welcome to be there whenever she wanted to come.

After the phone call ended, she thought to call Roar's parents in Spain but decided to wait until after she had been to the hospital and had more information to give them. A walk would help clear out the cobwebs from her mind, she thought and, putting on her warmest full-length padded coat, fur-lined boots and gloves, thick woolen hat and scarf, she stepped outside.

Chapter 2

NEW YEAR'S DAY 1900

Roar, still sleeping, felt the mist clearing from his mind, could feel the light in the room even before he opened his eyes. There was something different, he felt peculiar. As he opened his eyes, he knew that he was no longer Roar and yet somewhere in the distance he was. He was she; her name was Grace Lightfoot. Had she been in a strange dream in some far-off land, somewhere in the future or somewhere in the past? She only knew that this vivid, profound experience changed everything – she felt that she was two people in one, both male and female, that she lived both in the past and the future, and that now, the present was a pivotal point in her evolution as a human being and more. The present was both the past, the future and the current moment all rolled into one. She could still feel the presence of Roar with her and yet she was herself, in full.

It was New Year's Day 1900, the first day of the twentieth century. In London it was cloudy, damp and chilly at around five degrees this early morning. Grace was alone in her attic room, at the top of the house in Kensington, where, from her one small window she could look over to the leafless trees in Hyde Park, no-one stirred so early on this January morning.

At the age of twenty-seven she had already been the house-keeper in the House of Darcaster for the last three years, one of several homes belonging to the renowned industrial family. George Harald Darcaster, normally based at the head office in Manchester, was the current head of Darcaster Industries and this home was his base whenever business called him to London. His wife, Alexandria, seldom accompanied him when commerce called him to the South of England.

Darcaster Industries were very profitable, though originally solely based on cotton import and mill production. Towards the end of the 1880's they had diversified, expanding rapidly by investing in many of the leading technologies of the time. By 1894, when the Manchester Ship Canal opened along with Salford docks, the area was in its heyday, the third largest port in Britain. George Darcaster was also involved in the opening of the world's first purpose-built industrial estate at Trafford Park, Manchester. Through the remaining years of the nineteenth century, Trafford Park attracted many new companies within the heavy industry sector.

The Darcaster wealth increased exponentially, George became an exceedingly rich man and by 1898 he had purchased a huge country estate in the hills to the east of Manchester, renaming it Alexandria Hall, in honour of his wife. The walled estate covered three-thousand-four-hundred-fifty-acres, including two small farms, four gate-houses, forests, streams and a river, lakes and moors with fishing and hunting rights. There were thirty-five outside servants including those allocated to the farms and gatehouses, in addition to the seventy inside servants tending to the forty-five-room house and the separate servants' quarters. Having moved away to the countryside to protect himself and his family from the polluted air in central Manchester, Darcaster now had interests and business ventures in many areas of the country, including London.

Grace had been born in Manchester; her parents worked as servants for many years in the House of Darcaster, from the time they had lived in their great mansion in central Manchester, to when in the summer of 1898 they had moved along with the rest of the household to Alexandria Hall, through to the present. She had grown up in the Darcaster household, but rarely saw any of the Darcaster family, as she had been strictly schooled in avoiding contact with them by her parents and the other servants. Both mother and father rose through the servant ranks until her father now worked as the butler and her mother as the housekeeper. Grace had attended a local board school from the age of seven until she was ten, although both her mother and father were literate and had taught her to read and write well before she started school.

Grace, aged eleven, started work in the Darcaster household as a laundry maid and progressed during the next twelve years to become the head housemaid directly responsible to her own mother for whom she had deputized on several occasions in times of her mother's illness. She had also spent time assisting in the kitchen, particularly during festive seasons, birthday parties and other events. Mrs. Darcaster had noticed her dedication, effectiveness, attention to detail and her all-round understanding of the workings of the house on many occasions and had duly discussed this with her husband. When they opened the London house, they felt it natural to ask Grace to take the post as she was more than qualified to run the much smaller house in Kensington and to organize appropriately whenever necessary.

For the last three years during her tenure at the Kensington house, whenever the house was otherwise empty, she had spent much of her free time either browsing in Darcaster's own well-stocked library or on clement days she would walk along past the Royal Albert Hall and up through Hyde Park, all the way to Euston Station to visit the W. H. Smith & Son Railway bookstall, where she could always count on an invigorating read for a reasonable price. Grace loved to read and could spend hours deciding which book to choose. During this process she had become very familiar with the manager of the stall, Mr. Richard Billings, an elderly gentleman who possessed, what she realized was an unfathomable wisdom and knowledge of writings both ancient and modern.

Grace had been alone in the house for almost four weeks since Mr. Darcaster had last been in London on a ten-day business trip, but he would be returning the day after tomorrow. As always with her constant attentiveness she had maintained the house in perfect condition, and everything was prepared for his arrival. Everything, that is, except for herself; she shivered with fear at the very thought of his arrival. She dreaded the return of this large, repugnant, arrogant man and everything he stood for: She feared for her own safety, for her own life.

She walked down the stairs to the spacious new bathroom that had recently been installed on the first floor. It actually had a large new-fangled bathtub with hot running water that poured out through a faucet. She would bathe every day when she was alone in the house. If Mr. Darcaster or any member of the family were home, she would wash in her room. She opened up the faucet and allowed the water to slowly fill the bathtub. As the bath ran, she went back upstairs to choose her outfit for the day. She did not have a uniform as such but was expected to dress neatly, clean and tidy at all times. As the fashion for ladieswear was gradually becoming less complicated, less bulky and ladies in general were becoming more active, the clothing became lighter and less restrictive, much to her relief. The clothes for the day chosen, she laid them out upon the bed, picked up her toiletries and a towel and made her way down to the bathroom.

As she lay there in the soothing hot water she looked down at her thighs, where once there had been large deep purple bruising, there was now small, faded blue and yellow patches. Her upper arms were the same, it seemed there were marks wherever he laid his hands upon her. She shivered in disgust and felt her neck and throat where he had choked her until she had almost lost consciousness. She observed her own body, noticing that her breasts had become a little larger and were tender to her touch, scrutinizing her normally flat stomach, she could see a definite bulge; she knew that she was with child. She shuddered with apprehension at the thought of what was to happen next. She was hopelessly trapped and had nowhere to run to, no way out of this abhorrent situation. The only option was to be open with him and hope that he would care for her in a decent and proper manner. She knew instinctively, based upon his previous loathsome behaviour that he would be more likely to treat her in a severe and heartless manner. But what could she possibly do?

It was at least three months since her last bleed, she could not afford to delay broaching the situation with him any longer.

In two days, when he arrived, the outcome of his reactions to her disclosure would probably shape the path for the rest of her life and she had a terrifying sense of foreboding, that something beastly might transpire at the hands of Mr. George Darcaster.

George Harald Darcaster had inherited the Darcaster Industries when his father, who had been sixty-one years old, suddenly died of a massive heart failure, without any prior warning. George, at the time of his father's death, was twenty-nine, had worked with his father every spare minute he could, learned the business inside out and was more than prepared to take on the company. Not only that, but he also had great ambitions to further embellish what his father and grandfather had built. He had a ruthless streak, was prepared to take considerable risk in achieving maximum profit and was not regarded highly by the workers he employed, quite the opposite as many cowered at the mere mention of his name.

George was completely ambivalent towards his workers; on the one hand he knew that he needed them to do his bidding and provide him with his much-treasured profits and on the other he had a very unhealthy disdain towards them, detesting every one of them. For him they were necessary vermin, valuable to him only in terms of how much profit he could achieve from each one.

Since the early 1870s when the unions had emerged, his hate had been doubly ignited. He detested the unions with an unrefined vehemency, he saw them as criminal pillagers here to mulct him personally of his hard-earned dividends. He fought them tooth and nail at every twist and turn and had recently recorded a huge victory against them. After a prolonged period of lockouts, they were forced to accept the implementation of new machinery which meant a reduction in the number of employees he needed, and increased efficiency under terms of payment governed by him. After years of fighting, and with the recent recession, the powers of the unions were now considerably weaker which meant that he and many other company owners could more dictate the terms of employment for the workers, allowing for the implementation of the most recent time-saving technologies and the slashing of the workforce, again giving them more profitable financial results.

He had no thought for those forced out of work, they were mere numbers for him, his focus was upon growth, expansion and profit. He looked upon life as a challenge, to be the greatest he possibly could be, which for him could only be quantified materialistically by how much of the market share he controlled, how many companies he could acquire, grow and merge into his empire and how many people he was able to command. He was a true workaholic, living and breathing business, feeling it was his true lifeblood.

In his own mind, George felt superior to all others, that he was the premier, most intelligent businessman, that he was a natural born leader and that one day he should also lead this country, to become the prime minister. His father had always encouraged and cajoled him to work unflinchingly to become top of the class, be the most intelligent pupil, the best sportsman, and in business together he had recognized that George had a drive and perspicacity way beyond his own. George knew that the world was there for him to exploit and to take whatever he desired, that opportunities were limitless for a man with such a boundless Machiavellian astuteness. His every move, thought, word and intention came from his aspiration and dedication to self-gain, to self-fulfill and to self-satisfy. A very dangerous man, as he had no real boundaries or true sense of good and bad, right and wrong, truth or untruth. A law unto himself and to his own chosen deities, who were the gods of self-gratification, recognition, status, wealth and profit.

It was 10.30am and George sat in the Birmingham office preparing for a busy day of meetings that would take him well into the late evening. He would then dine and stay the night at the Birmingham Grand Hotel before making tomorrow's train journey to London Euston, eventually arriving at his London house at approximately 6pm. This morning he had indulged in a full

English breakfast at the Grand, including eggs, bacon, sausages, tomatoes, mushrooms, black pudding and fried bread, in addition he also devoured delicious buttery kippers and kedgeree which was a dish from India that had become very popular. It consisted of spiced rice with smoked fish and boiled eggs. The sheer volume of food he had consumed now reminded him he needed to consult his physician as he endured a severe bout of scorching heartburn shooting up into his chest and throat.

As with his obsession for work, everything he did, was done wholeheartedly with every ounce of his fiber. It could be the way he ate voraciously and voluminously or when he hunted, he had to be the one at the forefront to perform the kill, and any relationship was for him to dominate, he must be the one in perpetual ascendancy. Being second best or kowtowing to anyone else in any way was not an option and never would be.

At forty-nine and a leading industrialist, a man who had worked hard and played in the same way, he was starting to feel his own mortality, feel how all these years of non-stop activity had compounded in his body. He ran his fingers through his now thin, grey, receding hair and reflected how, only ten years ago it was so thick, dark and lustrous. He thought about how his joints ached in the mornings, how difficult it was to bend his knees, the stiffness in his back and how his once lean, muscular body was now covered with layers of fat, and in particular the large ever-expanding paunch where once there had been a flat hard stomach. He contemplated how simply walking upstairs caused him to be short of breath.

Dry gin, madeira port and brandy were his preferred tipples of which he indulged in on more evenings than not. What previously had been a weekend activity had now become more-or-less daily. He found drinking often to be medicinal, a drink or two – or three, helped him come down and relax in the evenings. He even used alcohol as an aid to sleep, which was often disturbed by the acid-reflux he constantly suffered when he lay down to sleep. On the occasions he would drink in excess he would often wake disturbed and unrested, with often a black hole in his memory, whole periods of time would be blank. Some memories of the cruel and heartless acts he perpetrated upon Grace would slowly come back to him. He would simply shrug them off; she was his servant, and he was after all, entitled to do as he wished. That others would be hurt as a consequence of his actions did not concern him, at least, not on the surface.

Richard Billings stood behind the W.H. Smiths bookstall at Euston Station, in the late morning of January 2nd, 1900. It was a cold, bright, sunny day and the bustle had returned to London's streets after the Yuletide festivities. Richard had a real passion for his work, he treasured his books, loved people to have beautiful books and adored being with and conversing with his customers. This morning he had brought along something from his own private collection, one of his many treasured reads, and stowed it away underneath his old hand-made wooden cash box, the box he had meticulously designed, constructed and carved himself, twenty-four years ago. The chosen book written by Radda Bai, a collection of Russian writings translated to English, entitled, 'From the Caves and Jungles of Hindustan'. It was a descriptive and fascinating spiritual journey, also containing somewhat critical observations and brutally honest views of the British rule in India.

Richard, after studying Classics at the University of London had served almost forty years in the civil service and had been stationed in Bombay for fifteen of them. He had seen the brutality and the ruthlessness of the British war machine that had driven most Indian natives into absolute poverty. The colonizing British occupancy of India oversaw the syphoning off of the enormous temporal riches of this majestic land directly into the coffers of a select few entrepreneurs and their unscrupulous well-positioned collaborators in this country. He had seen it with his own eyes, the total injustice and ensanguined atrocities perpetrated in the name of Great Britain and Queen Victoria. It was something Richard could never forget, never purge the grotesque memories from his mind.

Certain members of the British establishment undoubtably had the deaths of millions of innocent Indian people on their hands and they would, at some point, sooner or later, stand before the court of Karma, as they were beyond the reaches of any true temporal justice in their current positions of power. True justice was an unconceivable concept for the prevailing system based on the entitlement and dictated by the war-mongering conquerors that put the acquisition of riches far ahead of the value of human life, and in particular the value of the lives of those that were considered to be of lesser-nationalities.

He was the third son of Henry Billings, a landowner in northeast England who had provided Richard with a not insubstantial lifelong and greatly appreciated benefaction that he supplemented with his meagre remuneration from the bookstall. His father had passed away twenty years ago, and his older brother Barnaby now ruled the roost and would not interfere with his father's wishes in regard to Richard's yearly reimbursement from the family estate. From his long years of toil in the civil service he had saved a sizable sum which was safely deposited in the London & County Bank, Islington High Street branch. A frugal existence meant that his nest egg never diminished. He had never married and expected he would eventually bequeath his monies to the hospital at which his nephew Samuel was a prominent doctor. The work at the bookstall was not a necessity, it was simply a joy to be out amongst his fellow Londoners, to connect and converse with his many regular customers. This was much more satisfying than to sit alone in his small but adequate three-bedroom house, although he did love to tend to his pretty and well-cared-for garden in Barnsbury.

He spotted her, carrying an armful of books, as soon as she entered the station. The young lady normally shone as bright as sunshine, but he could see immediately that her movements were troubled. Today she was definitely not herself. The usual graceful glide across the station hall floor was laboured and staccato. She tried vainly to smile as she approached her favourite bibliosoph, but the tendrils of worry and despair sat far too deep. Richard had always been very reserved in his approach to those of the opposite sex which meant he had never married. His shy awkwardness and red-faced blushing had always left him too embarrassed and lost for words in their presence, although with age and not inconsiderable wisdom his bashfulness had, to a great extent, diminished. At this instant though, his clumsy shyness disappeared completely, replaced by genuine concern and care for he knew instinctively the seriousness of this situation.

"My dear friend, what ails you so much that it takes away the light from your beautiful smile?" he asked in surprise at his own candor.

A flicker of light sparkled in her eyes and a smile creased her lips before gently subsiding again as she said, "Ahh Mr. Billings, it is a personal matter that I may not utter a word lest it be tainted with impropriety."

His concern grew deeper, but he decided not to press any further in fear of insulting or even frightening her away. He did so enjoy the company of this delightful young lady. She would speak only the words that were given to her to utter, if and when they were there for speech. She had a natural openness and honesty that emanated through her every word.

"And how may I be of assistance to you today?" he smiled.

She was there to thank him, returning all the books he had kindly loaned to her from his private collection and carefully handed them over, informing him how wonderfully enlightening they were and that she hoped one day to read them again. Amongst the books were some he had obtained through his membership of the Theosophical Society and were written by the mildly controversial Madame Blavatsky, describing the ancient wisdom brought to humanity through world teachers of the past. He reached down, from underneath his old cash box and brought forth the book he had selected for her from his own library, 'From the Caves and Jungles of Hindustan'. Offering it to her he said, "This is for you, you need not return it. I have another copy at home. Keep it as long as you like and pass it on to someone else when you have finished with it."

She started to shake her head, but he insisted that she take it. Her curiosity overcame her depressed mood. Taking the book, she thanked him profusely. Her spirits lifted, as in between his sporadic customers, they had their usual long deep conversation encompassing diverse religions, their purpose in life and modern-day society and any other tangents their discussion diverged upon.

Two hours later, she was on her way home; tomorrow evening Mr. Darcaster would arrive, she thought as a chill ran down her spine. She knew she couldn't afford to wait any longer, she dreaded his reactions, what would he say, what would he do?

It was getting late, George sat feeling quite exhausted and extremely full after polishing off his sponge pudding and custard desert, washed down with port. It had been a momentous evening with huge new shipbuilding contracts for his newly acquired shipyards at Canning Town in East London that would transform Darcaster Industries. Government contracts were always hard fought, and it paid to lubricate the palms of certain members of Parliament to edge out the competition. As he celebrated with a cigar and large brandy, he contemplated the next day's journey down from Birmingham to London. Suddenly, he felt a flare of burning pain shoot up through his chest. He pushed away the brandy glass and swore he would soon see his physician to prescribe him some medication to alleviate these awful pains and discomfort. He knew already that he had a poor night of sleep ahead of him, so he further delayed his evening quietude and pulled out a copy of the Birmingham Daily Gazette which he read from cover to cover before retiring to his room.

To help ease the effects of his burning acid reflux, he had already requested the hotel staff to provide him with several extra pillows he could use to prop himself up with during the night. He now prepared the pillows so that he could spend the night half-sitting in the bed, hopefully this would give him the rest he needed so he could deal with the enormous amount of paperwork he needed to attend to on the train journey to London.

Grace awoke early in the morning, well before sunrise on January 3rd, thinking of the books she had returned to Mr. Billings at the bookstall. She had written a letter to him in a sealed envelope and slipped it inside the cover of one of the books. On the envelope she had written, 'If you do not see me at your bookstall during the next seven days, please deliver this letter to the police. Signed, Grace Lightfoot.'

The letter inside read as follows:

> *To whom it may concern,*
> *My name is Grace Lightfoot, I work for Mr. George Harald Darcaster, employed as his housekeeper at his London abode in Kensington. During the past two years Mr. Darcaster, who is a married man, has forced me to take part in lewd sexual acts against my will on many occasions, most often when he is under the influence of alcoholic beverages. He often becomes enraged when I refuse his advances, beats me and forces himself upon me, he will not take no for an answer.*
> *I now fear for my life as I am with his child and have no option other than to inform Mr. Darcaster of this situation which I will do so when he arrives back in London on January 3rd, 1900.*
> *I pray to God for a fair and just outcome,*
> *Yours sincerely*
> *Grace Lightfoot*

Grace had much to do to prepare everything for his arrival this evening. He would want a three-course dinner with all the usual trimmings as well as his favourite beverages and cigars, which were well stocked in the cellar. She would make sure his bedding was freshly aired and that every surface was spick and span with not a grain of dust in sight. He was a perfectionist and wouldn't accept anything less or anything out of place. To not prepare thoroughly was to unnecessarily garner his ire. She would also need to spend several hours in the kitchen preparing his dinner, with freshly purchased ingredients to be collected in the early afternoon. She went about her day trying to concentrate on her activities and thus avoiding thoughts of what may be to come later this evening.

It was early Wednesday afternoon, on the first part of his journey, he sat in the first-class carriage on the Midland Rail service from Birmingham to London; the journey would take between four and five hours, so he had booked a seat in the dining car for a late lunch. Whilst on the train George waded through copious amounts of paperwork and prepared himself for the four meetings he was to have during the following day. He would then leave for Liverpool on Friday morning. He had to attend to vitally important business in Liverpool on Saturday 6th, the urgent shipping of military equipment and ordnance to Cape Town, which were supplies for the British Army in the ongoing war against the South African Boers. His stay in London would be very short before he was back on the train heading north to Liverpool.

Surprisingly he had slept quite well the previous night and was in a good mood. He had cleared and prepared the necessary paperwork in record time and was now seated in the dining car. Including the coffee and brandy he sipped, it had been an extremely tasty five course lunch. Feeling content with himself, he settled back and puffed on his cigar and let his mind wander. His thoughts drifted to his London home and what awaited him there, he closed his eyes and saw Grace lying naked on the bed in front of him, her firm young body...

"Excuse me sir," the voice shook him from his reverie. "Aren't you George Darcaster?"

The man standing in front of him was Sir John Simmonds. They had briefly met at a formal dinner in London the previous summer.

"Yes, Sir John, it is I. Please join me."

The two men spent the rest of the journey in deep conversation revolving around the Boer War, the armaments industry and the prospects for business in this new century.

Richard had left the books returned by Miss Lightfoot in a pile on the edge of the desk in his study-come-library. There were books everywhere and it looked quite untidy although he knew the exact place of every one of them. This morning he would put everything in its rightful place before he left for the book-stall. He busied himself around the study. accidentally knock-ing over the small pile of books onto the floor, and as he turned, he noticed a white envelope flutter out from the books landing on the rug. He stooped down to pick up the envelope reading the words on the front and stopped in his tracks. He read them again, 'If you do not see me at your bookstall in the next seven days, please deliver this letter to the police'. With that a fearful shudder passed through his body.

As the afternoon preparation wore on, she found it more and more difficult to stay present within herself. She became distracted to the point that her hands were shaking as she prepared food for the evening. When she heard the clattering in the hallway, she froze almost dropping the knife in her hand. He had arrived and in-stantly there was a feeling of cold icy fear at the pit of her stomach. She had thought it through, he must be told at the most opportune moment, it could not wait until after dinner when he would be too drunk and too aggressive, it was too soon to speak to him as he walked through the door, he needed time to settle in. It was now 6.30 and dinner would be at 8pm. She gauged that after he had seated himself at the dinner table would be, if there actually was one, the most opportune moment to tell him of her predicament.

Later on, she was moving around the dining room, making sure everything was in place for the dinner and putting the fi-nal touches on the table decorations, when a noise from behind startled her. She braced herself for what was to transpire as she turned around to face him.

"Good evening, Sir," she chirped with as much vigour as she could muster, avoiding his direct gaze. "How was your journey?"

He grunted an acknowledgement and moved to his seat at the head of the table, sat down and asked what she had cooked for him this evening. She took the time to describe all five courses detailing the components of each and how they had been prepared. He smiled, seemingly satisfied, fleetingly showing a glimpse of what was perchance, a kinder side of his personality.

'That sounds exactly as it should be, bring me the first course then.'

Grace took a deep breath, her knees were shaking, she almost turned away but something inside her made her stay. She knew that this was the opportunity she needed, she had to face him now, tell him what he had done.

'Please sir, before I bring the food there is something of grave importance, I need to broach with you.'

'Can't it wait until after dinner?' he snapped.

Her resolve shaken but still intact, she gently, yet firmly replied, 'No Sir, it cannot.'

He looked at her in surprise, 'Come on then, out with it, girl.'

Another deep breath, and the words that had been bottled up inside her for so long poured forth in a stream of emotion and a flood of tears until she fell into silence feeling completely exhausted. Enervated, she looked directly into his face, into those dark, brown eyes for any sign of emotion or compassion; there was nothing. His face reddened, deep furrows etched their way across his brow and his eyes grew colder and more intense. She feared he would explode, he said nothing for quite some time, then simply asked her without emotion, to bring him his food.

The meal proceeded in silence, the only words uttered were, 'port', 'gin' and 'brandy' when he required them to be put on the table within easy reach. He grew more and more sullen as the meal progressed, gulping in his food and washing it down with plenteous quantities of his chosen beverages. Grace became more timorous as each course was delivered, until, at last, he sat back with his coffee, brandy and began to puff contentedly on his cigar with a smile-come-smirk on his face, as though he had come to a conclusion, or a satisfactory decision regarding her unwanted pregnancy.

'Wait here,' he said as he stood up and walked away from the table into his study.

She stood by the table and waited for what seemed an eternity. She heard him opening and closing draws, grunting with malcontent as he remonstrated around his room.

'Get your hat and coat quickly,' he barked as he returned five minutes later and began to give her instructions.

He handed her money and a letter.

'This is for Doctor Smythe, he is an old friend of mine and he will be able help you, go to the end of the street and take a Hansom cab. Doctor Smythe's address is on the envelope. When you arrive, give the letter to him, he knows exactly what to do. Here is some money for the fare both to get you there and for your return journey. I will await your return here. Go now, straight away, do not dally.' With that he ushered her out of the door, coat and hat in hand.

George knew that Smythe was not a real doctor and not a real friend:, He was an inconvenient necessity. He was a man of exceedingly dubious character that he knew would do what was required, if the price was right. He was somewhat expensive but very discreet, that is why he had been so successful in his despicable trade for the last twenty years. George had used Smythe's services in the past without expediency, he was certain of both his illegality and of his criminal integrity to his paying customers.

He did not give the fate of Grace a second thought once he had decided on his course of action, this was just like any of his business decisions, the most effective route, maximum profit and minimum disturbance for him. His problem was now quickly and effectively resolved.

Grace stood outside the front door shivering with both fear and cold, feeling shellshocked at the icy and heartless manner she had been treated. Even though she had tried to prepare herself for it, there had still been a faint hope of some form of empathy from Mr. Darcaster. She slowly regained her composure, putting on her hat and coat she walked with heavy steps, unsteadily down to the end of the street to the line of Hansom carriages. The cab drivers were huddled around an open brazier on the street corner desperately trying to keep warm whilst waiting for a fare. As she approached, a young man stepped forward out of the huddle and jauntily asked if he could be of assistance.

She gave the cabby the destination address, then climbed wearily into the cab not entirely sure of her own fate but knowing that it would be life-changing or even worse. She had heard stories of girls being subjected to horrible treatments, being permanently damaged or even dying at the hands of some of these back street charlatans. It was cold inside the carriage. She shivered and pulled her coat more tightly around her, took hold of the blanket on the seat and wrapped it around her lower body and legs. The journey was torturous, she tried to keep herself orientated as to their whereabouts in London but soon lost all sense of direction although she knew they were heading east. The roads grew narrower, and she became more worried and confused, until eventually the carriage stopped outside a row of modern three-story townhouses. The cabby pointed to a red door, she thanked him, paid and stepped out of the carriage.

Once inside, Grace gave the letter to Doctor Smythe. He opened it and gingerly looked inside, took out a letter and read carefully to himself:

> *Dear Barnaby,*
> *This young lady, Grace Lightfoot is in need of your expert services. Unfortunately, she is with child and out of wedlock, please perform the necessary procedures to terminate this gravidity. I trust you will find the enclosed reimbursement to your satisfaction.*
> *Yours sincerely,*
> *George H. Darcaster*

Barnaby Smythe, now aged fifty-nine, had once been a student of medicine but had inherited his father's pawnbroker business in Villiers Street much earlier than expected, and therefore did not complete his studies. He did however follow very closely the medical developments as they transpired, training himself in the very lucrative field of abortion as a discreet sideline. He became very adept and through his pawn business was able to acquire all the equipment and anesthetics he needed. Through twenty years he had never lost a single patient, that he knew of.

His wife, Andrea, was both his lifelong companion, his able-bodied nurse, anaesthetist and his very first patient. After two very difficult births they had not intended to have any more children, when Andrea fell pregnant for a third time, they decided it was much less risky to perform an abortion than to go through with the pregnancy. The success of this operation had fueled his medical pride and led him to initiate a sagacious back street practice for middle- and upper-class ladies. Both were fully aware of the illegality of their enterprise and yet they knew they were protected by the necessary discretion of their clientele.

'Come this way and tell me all about your predicament, young lady,' said Andrea gently.

As Grace told her about the situation, she was met with sympathetic replies. She began to feel a little more composed, less ill-at-ease. She was led down a flight of stairs into a warm, clean, brightly lit basement that was decorated with everything one would associate with a doctor's surgery: charts and anatomy posters, skeletons and medical equipment. There was a screen in the corner behind which she could remove all unnecessary clothing, once prepared she lay on the treatment bed, covered with a sheet.

Andrea spoke to her softly and told her she would apply a chloroform mask to anaesthetize her so she would sleep and wouldn't feel a thing. She woke up approximately one hour later, feeling very groggy and nauseous. It took her several minutes to regain some form of clarity as to where she was and what had happened. Andrea spoke to her again, advising her to be calm and not to move too quickly, that the chloroform would soon wear off. Grace was told she may feel some pain in her abdomen and that there may be some small amounts of blood over the next few days until everything settled down. She was also informed that the operation was successful and there should be nothing more to worry about. Grace looked under the sheet and saw that a large dressing had been bandaged around her. She was to change the dressing regularly during the next few days.

As Grace sat in the Hansom carriage on her way back to Kensington, she felt utterly exhausted, filthy and abused, she felt a hate for George Darcaster well up inside her. She did not want to return to the Darcaster house to see that man, that abomination within, yet knew there was no other choice. She stepped gingerly out of the carriage, paid the cabby and climbed slowly up the steps to the foreboding front door and let herself in.

George heard her enter the hallway, got up from his desk in the study and walked out into the hallway.

'Is it done?' he asked.

'It is,' she wearily replied.

'I understand you will need to rest for a few days, I won't be needing your assistance until I return three weeks hence. I will leave further instructions on my desk before I leave in the morning, and I will stay at the Grosvenor tomorrow evening and leave for Liverpool from there.' He coldly turned his back and walked away into his study without the slightest enquiry into her wellbeing.

She knew now, more than ever that she had to find a way out of this situation, out of his clutches and start a new life somehow, somewhere. She felt like a mouse locked in a cage, the cat held the key. She painstakingly climbed all the stairs up to the top of the house and the solace of her attic refuge. Closing the door behind her, she got ready for bed. Exhaustion soon flooded over her as she quickly fell into a deep coma-like sleep that would last for fourteen hours.

Without consideration or even the slightest thought of his young housekeeper, the next morning George busied himself, ate and was gone by 10am. Hailing a cab that would take him to Canning Town for his first meeting of the day, he contemplated far too important affairs to allow himself to be distracted by domestic issues. He was driven by providence, 'the King of King's, Wealth and Prosperity', 'the Demon Greed' and the 'Attainment of Recognition'. Nothing could throw him off the scent of gold and glory that was his destiny.

Grace awoke in the early afternoon, still feeling exhausted, with a dull throbbing pain in her lower abdomen and a pressing urge to relieve herself. With no option other than to go down to the bathroom where she could cleanse herself properly, she took the parcel with extra dressings Andrea had given her and made her way carefully downstairs to the first-floor bathroom. The old dressing was completely soaked with blood, she quickly removed it, cleaned herself up and replaced it with a fresh one, remembering that there could be bleeding for a few days, then made her way down to the kitchen to prepare some food for herself even though she didn't feel very hungry.

She cut herself a slice of bread coated it with jam and made a pot of tea, sat in the kitchen, again contemplating her lamentable situation. She did have a small amount of savings but that wouldn't last more than a few months if she wasn't able to find employment very quickly. Slowly she managed to force herself to consume the food with the tea, she then sat for some time to find the energy to climb the stairs once again. Eventually she made it all the way to her room, got back in bed and was almost instantly asleep.

The next few days went by in a blur, it was light outside, she felt dizzy and confused, not sure of what day or time it was, the memories of Doctor Smythe and Andrea came back into her mind. She realized that she was in danger, felt the sodden dressing underneath the covers and decided that she must get to a hospital, otherwise she may perish here in this bed, in this God forsaken house. It took a huge amount of effort and willpower simply to get off the bed. She changed the dressing as best she could, put on her clothes and made her way down the stairs. She put on her winter coat, hat and gloves and went to leave. As she opened up the door, everything around her became blurred, the walls began to quiver, she lost consciousness and fell to the hallway floor.

It was Monday morning at home in Barnsbury. Richard, who had just cleared up after breakfast, was in his study preparing to make his way to the bookstall at Euston, when his eye fell upon the letter from Miss Lightfoot. In a sudden impulse, ignoring the words she had written upon the envelope, he picked up his letter opener and slit open the top of the letter with a deft flourish and pulled out the note within. He read it several times.

> *To whom it may concern,*
> *My name is Grace Lightfoot, I work for Mr. George Harald Darcaster, employed as his housekeeper at his London abode in Kensington. During the past two years Mr. Darcaster has forced me to take part in take part in lewd sexual acts against my will on many occasions, most often when he is under the influence of alcoholic beverages. He often becomes enraged when I refuse his advances, beats me and forces himself upon me, he will not take no for an answer.*
> *I now fear for my life as I am with his child and have no option other than to inform Mr. Darcaster of this situation which I will do so when he arrives back in London on January 3rd, 1900.*
> *I pray to God for a fair and just outcome,*
> *Yours sincerely*
> *Grace Lightfoot*

Richard was both sad and outraged, he felt the hate of this upper-class supremacist attitude and the self-entitled chicanery that ran through George Darcaster, disgusted that a man in such an eminent position could abuse such a lovely delicate young lady. He knew immediately what severe danger she was in and that the police would not protect her. They were controlled by the rich and powerful elite and contacting them would only dig a deeper grave for Grace. Servants that became a problem often had a habit of disappearing without a trace. They were necessary to the running of the households but were in fact resources that could easily be replaced.

By opening the letter, he had now chosen a path of no return, he had to do something. He must try to save her from this precarious situation. He would take the bull by the horns, visit the Darcaster house and demand to see Grace. The intransigent unrest in his body told him that if he waited for seven days it would be too late, immediacy was imperative, he must act now. He prepared himself for the unusual day ahead as best he could, left the house, walked down to Kings Cross and boarded a Hansom cab, gave the cabby the address and sat back whilst the wily cabby picked his way through the busy London traffic.

He steeled himself for a difficult confrontation as they approached the Darcaster residence, knowing that physically he would not be able to contend with George Darcaster who was known for both his wealth and his erstwhile athletic achievements in his younger years. There was also a not inconsiderable age disadvantage. The cabby pulled up the carriage. Richard asked him to wait, expecting that he would not be at this residence for very long. He climbed down and walked up to the front door. As he reached the door, he noticed it slightly ajar, turned the doorbell and heard it ring clearly in the hallway beyond. He waited, nothing stirred, no noise at all came from within. He tried again and waited once more, nothing at all. He decided to open the door and as he carefully pushed forward the door, opening it just enough for him to enter before it stopped, blocked by something on the other side. He looked down at the lady's booted foot before him lying in the hallway. He immediately squeezed in through the opening and saw as he had feared the prone body of Miss Lightfoot.

Richard knew enough first aid to check both for her pulse and to check she was breathing, yes, but both were very weak. He tried to revive her, there was no response and there was a large swelling on her forehead. He got up and walked briskly down to the cab to ask the cabby for assistance. He duly obliged. Richard picked up the set of keys and Miss Lightfoot's bag and locked the door after the young cabby who was a stout lad and was able to lift-up the petite Miss Lightfoot and place her gently in the carriage, half sitting-half lying. Richard asked him to take them to Charing Cross Hospital where his nephew Dr. Samuel Billings would be able to help them.

Again, the cabby darted his vehicle nimbly through the heavy London morning traffic and made hasty progress to the hospital and upon arrival the cabby once more carried the unconscious young lady, this time out of the carriage and into the hospital. It was very busy, people everywhere, Richard raised his voice.

'Emergency, this young lady is seriously injured.'

A young man in a white doctor's coat approached them. Immediately Richard enquired about his nephew with such authority that the young doctor scurried away and reappeared within just a couple of minutes.

'Please come with me,' he intoned.

They were led up one flight of stairs and along a corridor, shown a door on the left. Dr. Samuel Billings and a nurse greeted them cordially and indicated that they put the young lady on the examination bed. Richard gave Samuel Grace's note and informed him of the circumstances from his perspective, so he knew exactly what the situation entailed. Dr. Billings asked them to wait outside as he and the nurse took over the situation. Outside the door, a little further along the corridor was a small seating area, Richard thanked and paid the cabby handsomely as he left, then promptly took a seat awaiting the outcome.

Samuel knew instinctively that his Uncle Richard would never call upon him if it were not a life and death matter. After swiftly reading the note, he gave his nurse instructions and they went to work together on what was not such an unfamiliar case. Personally, he thought it much better to legalize the termination of unwanted pregnancies during the first weeks of pregnancy rather than have women risking their lives at the hands of careless back-street abortionists with little interest in the survival of their clients.

Miss Lightfoot had lost a considerable amount of blood and had also become extremely dehydrated; it was imperative to staunch the bleeding and rehydrate her as quickly as possible.

Chapter 3

ROAR'S AWAKENING

Elisabeth had walked for two hours through the deserted streets, along the coastal path and through the park, not meeting a single soul along the way. Everything looked white and pure, the blanket of fresh snow hiding all the cracks and imperfections that lay below. If only it could always be this way, but the snow will at some point melt, and everything hidden will once again be revealed she thought, just like life, the cracks, the indoctrinated ideals and beliefs, and the undealt with issues that are often hidden somewhere inside, will always resurface in some way, at some point. Would it not be best to actively seek them out and not unnecessarily conceal anything, then we wouldn't need the snow of false gestures and idiosyncrasies as facades to hide the pain, sorrow, anger and frustration we carry around inside us?

Completing the walk, she returned home and decided to get herself ready to drive to the hospital in Oslo. It was 2.30 in the afternoon and the sun was already waning. Leaving now would get her to the hospital just before darkness fell, although with so much snow and clear skies there would be much light to be reflected. She had packed a small overnight bag as she expected to stay there at least for tonight.

She arrived at the hospital; Roar was on a ward comprised of private single rooms available for those with the correct level of individual health insurance. She stepped in to see him lying there connected to a diverse selection of medical equipment continually monitoring his condition. She had been informed that he had undergone a successful minor brain surgery, that he had every chance of making a full recovery although there may be some memory loss and other slight short-term aftereffects. Standing at the side of his hospital bed looking down at his sallow, drawn face, with his head wrapped in bandages, she wondered how it ever came to this, why she allowed herself to become a part of this charade, part of his life. She shook herself out of her own self-pitying reverie by physically moving her body into a different position, shaking her head and moving around to the other side of the bed.

'I've come too far to let his sorry state drag me back into the prison I have released myself from. I will not have any sympathy for him, his condition is all of his own doing, emotional reactions will neither help him nor me,' she said out loud as she moved around. 'In fact, emotions will only hinder recovery and compound his, to be honest, self-induced state of ill-health and his habitual ill-behaviour that he has indulged in the whole of his life to this point. The only way to really help him is to be completely transparent, withhold nothing and to speak only the truth, no matter what.'

She could feel her own authority growing within her body as she articulated her words. Amazingly she felt her love for him expand. There was no pity, no attachment, no expectations of any form of outcome, she felt more settled inside than ever before.

Elisabeth sat down in the comfy armchair placed next to the bed, her thoughts immediately sprang to Roar's parents, that she would have to call them soon. She got up again, looked at Roar for a few moments, turned and left the room. She asked the nurse where she could find a public payphone, and with these directions she left the ward and made her way to the phone booth in the main hospital lobby. As she walked, she thought of Harald and Solveig, how they might take the news, calming herself in preparation for their expected reactions or non-reactions, as the case may be. She knew how attached Solveig was to Roar, her only child, her doting obsession, the eternal mother of her aging baby boy. She realized how harmful such a symbiotic, almost parasitic relationship must be. Neither could truly gain anything real from it. Each interaction between them only ever compounded the toxicity within the relationship.

She imagined Harald's reaction to be nothing less than a cold acceptance and yet she knew deep down there was a love that he held back, love that he saw as emotional weakness. Again, this was a harmful relationship with lifetimes of wounds, behaviour patterns never dealt with, poisoning them both from the inside.

She lifted the receiver and dialed the number. They were sitting on the terrace in the evening sunshine when the phone rang and Solveig went to answer. Elisabeth knew that there was no way to pack it in gently enough for Solveig not to become hysterical. After greeting her warmly, Elisabeth carefully and gently said:

'Let me first say that Roar is doing well considering the situation. He is in hospital recovering from a small brain hemorrhage.' She went on to tell Solveig exactly the information the doctor had given her earlier.

Solveig had burst into tears, crying hysterically for her baby son until Harald had taken the phone from her and listened solemnly until he had all the information, asking questions to fill in any gaps there might be and to make plans for their immediate return to Norway. Elisabeth promised to let them know if there was any change in Roar's condition as soon as she could. Putting the phone down Harald turned to console his overwrought wife, to make sure she had all the information and persuade her that the situation was not as bad as it could be. He held her in his arms until her sobbing abated and told her he would organize the first possible flight back to Oslo.

After the call, Elisabeth returned to sit with Roar and settled into the armchair with a pillow and blanket. She took out her book, The Consciousness of the Atom by Alice A. Baily and began to read. Enthralled by the book she hardly seemed to notice the hospital staff coming and going, until a few hours later a nurse asked her if she wanted to stay the night and if so, she would bring in a foldable bed with appropriate bedding. The hospital room also had a private bathroom which she could use as required. Elisabeth was prepared to stay the night, so began to get ready for sleep as she now had begun to feel the late night from New Year's Eve.

After consoling Solveig, Harald had immediately called the SAS flight desk at Alicante airport, who had willingly obliged with first-class tickets on the 9.15 morning flight to Oslo. They packed large suitcases as they had no idea how long they would be in Norway and prepared suitable clothing for when they stepped off the plane into the freezing Norwegian winter, the winter they had, for many years, always tried to avoid. It was currently fourteen degrees Celsius in Alicante and in Oslo a shivering minus twelve.

They ate a light dinner and prepared themselves for an early-night to bed and an early-morning rise and departure to the airport. Harald had ordered a taxi for 6am as the trip to the airport was approximately fifty to fifty-five minutes and as always, they would be at the airport at least two hours before departure time. Tomorrow, Sunday January 2nd, the traffic at 6am would definitely be very light so no fears of delays in transit. Harald and Solveig got ready for bed and both drank a large cognac to relieve the stress of the situation and to help them sleep, allaying their fears of what might happen to their only son.

It was 5.35 in the morning. Elisabeth, lying on the fold-out bed in the alcove at the side of the room, was disturbed by close-by movements and by the lights which had become brighter in the room. She sat up and rubbed her eyes, observing the activity by the bed, both a nurse and a doctor stood talking with Roar who was now slightly propped up on pillows. She silently slipped on her dressing-gown and slippers and made her way over to the bed.

Roar was awake, his bloodshot eyes stared blankly up at the doctor who was attempting to gauge the severity of his condition. Roar didn't seem to understand where he was or what had happened. When he saw Elisabeth, he gave her a weak smile of recognition that soon melted back into concern, worry and confusion. He tried to speak but couldn't seem to control his mouth, all that came out was slurred gibberish. The doctor looked at Roar and said, 'Don't try to speak for now, just answer with a nod or a shake of the head when I ask you questions. Do you understand me?' Roar nodded.

Dr. Karlsen then proceeded to ask several questions to determine the extent of his patient's injuries. Roar could hear, and understood the instructions he was given, he could feel his whole body, move his arms as normal but although he could feel his legs, he had difficulty moving them. They felt extremely weak. Dr. Karlsen explained that he had suffered a minor subarachnoid hemorrhage, which is a type of stroke caused by a ruptured brain aneurism resulting in bleeding in the brain.

'Luckily someone saw you collapse and alerted the Air Ambulance, getting you here to hospital very quickly. We performed a procedure called clipping which requires a small incision into the brain. We successfully repaired the aneurism, but it may take some time before you are fully recovered. There can also be some permanent complications, but you are most likely to make a full recovery and what we have observed so far is giving us every indication of that. Your speech should improve quickly during the next few days, although there may be a permanent defect, only time will give us the answer to that. In the meantime, if you have any questions, you may write them down and we will answer as best we can.'

The nurse left the room and returned two minutes later with a small hand-held whiteboard and a packet of marker pens.

They determined that the last thing Roar remembered was waiting for the taxi to go to the party on New Year's Eve but couldn't really discern whether the memory loss was because of the brain hemorrhage, the amount of alcohol he drank until about 11.30pm, as witnessed by Elisabeth, or most likely, a mixture of both. He was advised that from now onwards, any further consumption of alcohol would seriously endanger his life. They warned him that during the next weeks and months he needed to be extremely careful, not only in regard to alcohol, but the fact that his body would be very weak and that he would probably need much more sleep than normal. Work would have to be kept to a minimum, preferably not at all for at least thirty days. The condition of his body would probably not allow it anyway.

Roar felt overwhelmed, he closed his eyes, as if to say, that's enough for now, and it was, he needed to rest. They left him alone with Elisabeth. She allowed him to rest, showered and made her way to the hospital canteen to get some breakfast. She realized that Roar's parents may already be on their way back to Oslo. She knew how efficient Harald was. There was no point calling them in Spain now, they would probably be here during the next few hours. She took her time giving him the space he needed to rest. When she returned to the room, she could hear the light snoring she recognized so well. She put on her hat, coat and other outside apparel, made her way down to the main entrance and went for a morning walk.

He heard Elisabeth leave the room but continued lying still with his eyes closed as he contemplated his new-found situation. Roar couldn't remember anything from New Year's Eve but he did recall the vivid dreams he had experienced, the dreams that seemed so real and tangible. Could this have been a real 'past life experience'? It felt like he had been living in Grace's body, could he really have been this woman one hundred years ago? He felt as if he was the person experiencing horrific abuse from a cruel and heartless man, from a man with thoughts only for himself, focused only upon what he could get out of life, caring not for anyone else, abusing a young woman so fiendishly.

He then thought of his own selfish way of living, his continual betrayal of Elisabeth and yet, here she is again, caring and looking after his welfare even though she knew of his treachery. He thought of all the women he had used, all the business colleagues he had manipulated; he was so conscious now of what he had done, that it had all been for none other than himself. He realized that he needed to change, that this dream, this lesson from the past had given him a chance, a wake-up call, but at the same time he felt a deep hurt inside, the hurt that Grace had suffered, a hurt he carried within and ultimately only he could heal.

Roar felt a huge appreciation for Elisabeth, how she had stuck by him through everything, all the deceit, the deceit that did not fool her, she knew how he had been and what he had done. He thought more deeply about her, how she had looked at him on many occasions, a knowing wisdom way beyond his own, how he thought he had fooled and outsmarted her. He realized now that he had only bamboozled himself, thinking he was better, superior to her and to so many others. How pathetic that all seemed now, lying there in a hospital bed, fortunate to be alive. He could also perceive so much more at this moment, including the truth of his own behaviour. He felt he had been, in a way, repeating the behaviour that he himself, as Grace, had been the victim of one hundred years before.

How could he want to treat others in such an inhumane way after experiencing it himself? He also realized that Elisabeth had changed in her attitude towards him. He felt her love and yet also he sensed her steadfast detachment, that there was no longer any need for anything from him on her part, that she would tolerate no more of his abusive ways. Weariness and regret overtook him and again he fell into a deep sleep.

Elisabeth returned to the room nearly two hours later, saw that Roar was asleep, sat down and started to read. She hadn't read more than a few pages when the door opened. In came Roar's mother, Solveig, in a fluster, closely followed by Harald dragging along two huge suitcases. The silence shattered; Roar awoke with a groan; Solveig, who was about to speak to Elisabeth immediately ran to the bed exclaiming, 'Roar, my poor baby!' The tears flowed down her cheeks as she sobbed, 'You poor thing, mummy's here now.' She buried her head in his chest.

Roar groaned again and blinking the sleep from his eyes he tried to speak but everything came out in gobbledygook. He looked up at his father and pointed to the whiteboard, which Harald passed to him. Elisabeth stood up and let them know she would give them some time together; she left the room. Eventually Solveig lifted her head and she and Harald questioned Roar for the next thirty minutes or so until they seemed satisfied with all the answers he wrote on the whiteboard. He let them know what had happened and for a change he honestly admitted that he suspected that his drinking habits were probably the cause of the brain hemorrhage and that he needed to do a little soul-searching into how he had been living his life. This was undoubtably a consummate wake-up call that was impossible for him to ignore. He felt he had no other choice now; change was of the essence.

Elisabeth returned a little while later as Solveig and Harald were about to leave and she noticed that they seemed more at ease, Roar was asleep again. They said they would take a taxi and check in at the Saga Hotel which was only a few minutes-drive away from the hospital. They would get some dinner and come back later in the evening and stay with him during the night so that Elisabeth could get a good night's sleep and attend to anything she needed to. Off they went wheeling their suitcases behind them.

Elisabeth had to admit to herself, she was glad to see them, and she no longer felt irritable in their presence as she had often previously done. She pondered on why this was, why had they often made her so exasperated? She then realized that it had not been them at all, it was her, she made herself irritable. She had, in a way, been judging them for the way they chose to live their lives, judged their choices, their habits and behaviours. What right do I have to do that, she thought? Everyone, including me, has the right to choose to a certain point, as long as it is not directly harmful to others. It has been the same with Roar, he has made so many choices that I have reacted to, that I have judged, some of them may be sad, and harmful to himself but I can't condemn him for them. If he chooses to have affairs with other women, it is up to me to then choose what I believe is true for me, not fly into anger, blame or any form of recrimination. Although some choices may bring much sadness, they can be taken without too much emotional reaction or in fact, without any emotional attachment at all. It may be that I could step back and breathe deeply for a while to allow for a sensible and truthful response rather than retort immediately with an emotion-dripped castigation or to wallow in my own self-pity.

She walked over to the bed: He was still sleeping, she picked up the whiteboard and read the words written there, 'I have no other option now, change is of the essence.' She raised her eyebrows in surprise, it brought a smile to her face as she remembered how, many times, he had said quite similar words with a huge hangover after a heavy night on the booze. This though, she instinctively knew, was different and above all it was the truth. If he continued to live what he thought was his normal way of living he would not survive much longer. So many have made this hard-living, partying lifestyle their normal that most look upon anyone that does not live this way as being abnormal, weird or as boring party poopers. This massive form of self-abuse, she thought, has now become the new normal, whilst self-care and self-love have become the new weird. What a truly crazy upside-down, topsy-turvy world we live in. In truth, it has been this way for such a long time but now it seems to be accelerating in a downward spiral of human self-destruction.

She sat down again, suddenly realizing that no-one had informed Anders, Roar's partner about recent events. Anders Abrahamsen was an unassuming, gentle man who had known Roar most of his life. They were as alike as chalk and cheese. He was quietly confident and had an inner strength that, to a certain extent, held Roar's exuberant impulsivity in check, most of the time. Elisabeth thought the world of Anders. She immediately went down to the phone booth, called him and let him know what was happening and that it was unlikely Roar would be back at work before February, even March, depending on how quickly he recovered. Anders faithfully promised to stop by on Wednesday evening to see how Roar was by then.

True to their word, Solveig and Harald returned to take over the observance, and much sooner than she had expected. Roar had not been awake so she had little more to tell. After a brief conversation they said their goodbyes, she would return after breakfast tomorrow. It was a little warmer outside, but the snow had started to fall again, lightly at first but soon became a blizzard that made it very difficult to drive. She was relieved to be driving Roar's four-wheel-drive Audi, which was built for bad weather and great for wintery roads. By the time she arrived home there was already eight to ten centimetres of new snow on the ground. Fortunately, they had parking spaces in the subterranean garage under their apartment block so needn't worry about parking in the snow. There was also a lift up from the garage to their apartment on the third floor, so once inside the garage she was protected from the weather.

Entering the apartment, she felt the stillness brought on by the heavy snow outside, no movements. People mostly stayed home in this kind of weather, either waiting for the new ski tracks to be prepared after the snowfall or not daring to go out in case they fell and broke an arm or something worse. Young children were the great exception, they just loved to play in the snow, seemed not to notice the cold, they created their own play, their own world of adventure, with snow castles, tunnels, ski jumps and mountains. She felt the return of the broodiness that often reappeared, her own desire to have children that had so far gone unfulfilled, that, she ruminated, may never be actualized.

As she was preparing dinner, her thoughts returned to Roar, looking so vulnerable, lying there in the hospital bed unable to speak. What was to become of him? A wave of pity passed through her, coming and going without residue, just not sticking to her in any way. That's no longer the way I will live my life, she thought, sympathy is like a poison, it's an energy coming through someone else, an energy looking for a way into my body to suck away my life-force, my own power, like a parasite drawing away my blood, leaving me depleted and subsequently more susceptible to further invasion, ergo even greater depletion.

This energy of pity or sympathy is around me all the time and I simply need to choose not to conform to what it brings, the poison that this energy contains within it or brings through, is constantly searching for a point of entry into my body, relentlessly. It's like a switch, it's either on or off, it is not allowed to enter. If it's switched off the other, true choice, true energy will be switched on. She pondered. How do I keep the true Light energy switched on permanently?

Roar had been dramatically affected by this episode, something deep inside him has shifted, she could feel it and was certain that over the next few days her perception would be confirmed. That didn't mean she would continue in this relationship, if what they had together could actually be called a 'relationship', for in truth, she had known for a long time that it was not what anyone could call a genuine intimate relationship, it never was and never had been.

To begin with, he had laid on the charm and was super attentive but even then, she could have seen through his beguilement if she had wanted to or simply chosen to do so. She instead elected to settle for less than she knew was acceptable, discarding her own self-worth. For does not every woman deserve to be adored, cherished and honoured by their man, and indeed, on the other hand, does not every man deserve the same from his partner?

She contemplated further. It appeared to that in almost every relationship, everywhere, women and men settled for less than what would be true for a loving, wholesome relationship, thus in settling for less, in whatever form that may take, they settled for their own acceptable yet unacceptable level of abuse and self-abuse. For was not unconditional respect and love, being honoured, adored and cherished, the absolute minimum that should be acceptable from and for anyone in any true relationship?

For, do we not, in these arrangements that we call our relationships often settle for much less than the minimum we ought to? Do we not deserve to be loved unconditionally, enjoy complete respect, to be unreservedly honoured, adored and cherished? What is it that happens when we live from the dark energy of what is not true love and consummate respect? Could it be that we attempt to control one-another in a multitude of different ways? Maybe it is in the form of put-downs, threats of violence, obsessions, charm and persuasion, maybe in a form of unarmed combat such as being in competition

with one-another. All this can be quite blatant and plain for the eye to see, it can be quite openly disguised as a form of banter, or it can be in a more hidden and devious way in the form of insidious psychological terror.

I have allowed Roar to control me, to manipulate and to blatantly lie to me, so why did I choose to go along with all of this, she thought. The whole town probably knows what Roar has been doing and yet I pretend to be oblivious to it all, for what, what do I get out of it? Doubtless they see me as a victim of a philanderer, a poor foolish woman being duped by this garish scoundrel of a man. I see myself as a victim, as they do but why am I choosing this victimhood consciousness, when I am so aware of what is going on? Is it easier to be in it rather than to step out and confront it, or indeed to confront what is the root cause of my lack of self-worth? There are so many questions coming to me now, so much to be answered and in fact I know that every single answer is within me, no-one else can do it for me, no-one else can be blamed, there is only me and my own choices.

As she prepared her fish chowder, she realized that all this contemplation was part of her way forward in life, that with each step, each question answered, each level of resistance removed, she became more detached from what most would describe as normal life, but what she now saw was anything but normal for her. In many ways the life she had been living was a farce, a ridiculous satire completely bereft of truth, completely lacking in any form of purpose. How many people had real purpose in their lives? She thought about purpose for a while, thought about her colleagues at work and wondered about their purpose.

She could recall the conversations, the day-to-day chit-chat, the complaining about the pupils, the complete lack of enthusiasm, with just enough energy to get through the day so that they could get home in the evening and open a bottle of wine, or even two, to relieve the stress and anxiousness. By Wednesday they couldn't wait for the weekend. They fantasized about Friday afternoon, about their free-time plans. They planned and dreamed about their next holiday, their next skiing trip, which TV shows they would watch or the latest movies they might see. Any distraction would do to avoid being present with themselves – to avoid being present with the children they were meant to be here to serve.

For many it seemed that the only reason to work was to make enough money to enable them to enjoy their time off. Every enjoyment seemed to be intertwined with drinking wine, beer, cocktails or cognac and spirits, no real questioning of what life was about or why we are here on this planet Earth. Their purpose in life was to enjoy free-time, which could basically be interpreted as 'the purpose of being more and more self-indulgent and self-satisfied', not really caring what was going on anywhere else as long as they could enjoy the sunshine, the skiing, all their chosen forms of distraction and entertainment like TV, films, theatre, music concerts, good food, junk food and of course the different beverages, the essential accompaniment for any and all occasions.

What had become of the real commitment to the children, to truly connect and communicate with them in a way that allowed them to learn genuine care and respect for themselves, the teachers and each other? Where was the absolute obedience to be in service for the children, rather than see them as obstacles to overcome each week until they could get a well-earned rest at the weekend? Where was the duty, the unequivocal devotion to offer truth, raising the children up above the deceit and degradation of society? The next generation may bring the changes that are, for now, beyond us. The current generation though, seemed lost in the corrupted illusion of what human-life is touted to be. We seem to be fed and to accept, this dark deception that comes at us from every angle at every opportunity and across every form of media and paradigm.

There was a sliding scale within the school, of how her colleagues worked. Some had completely and utterly given up and wanted only to survive each day, each class they taught, get through the weeks and months, the school terms and the years. To such an extent in fact, that it was to get through their whole teaching career until the day they could retire and do only what they wanted to do. Whilst others were more inconsistent, some days they would be quite joyful and bring that to their work, whilst on other occasions they would bring to school exactly what they were experiencing in their home lives, trying to put on a brave face but not managing to prevent the dis-ease they were experiencing from seeping through into their attitudes and treatment of both their pupils and colleagues.

She stopped herself, she had to feel where she was in all these thoughts: Were they just ideals to pursue or was she, herself, actually realizing all or any of it, was it her own living way? She knew that she was devoted to all her children and was there for them. She knew that she connected to all of them, she had no favourites, she would not allow any to be excluded no matter what the circumstance. She also realized that there was no perfection in what she was bringing but more importantly her every intention was for the true good of each and every child. They were all the same to her, all equal. She didn't work for her own self-satisfaction, but she knew that she did a great job for all the children. Others had noticed the difference in the way she was at work, the joy that shone from within her, the love that the children had for her and the academic results her classes achieved. If the children were respected, connected and well communicated to, this would allow the joy within life to unfold and there would be no limits to what they may become. For, if we continued in the current vane all we achieve is to teach our children how to be stuck in the same rancid mud along with ourselves. If we climbed out of the mess and reflected on what life can be, they would be offered the opportunity to reject what has been and to live life in a different way.

Already during the evening Roar had become less dependent on the whiteboard and could make himself understood, although for some reason his thoughts came much quicker than the words seemed to exit his mouth which often caused his speech to become a little incongruous. There was an observable disconnection, his thoughts moved forward as the words belonging to the previous expression were still trying to exit his body. Although he did feel more present and alive after his evening nap. Through the adversity of the whole situation, he felt fuller in a strange way, something that he had never felt before. He had woken up happy to find his parents in the room but a little disappointed not to see Elisabeth there. His parents told him to expect her after breakfast tomorrow.

The medical staff appeared at regular intervals and were very surprised and delighted with the progress he was already making, letting him know he should be careful and not to rush into too much activity. Roar wondered how long he must stay in hospital; they had replied that it would be at least a few more days as they needed to monitor and observe his condition as this was a very vulnerable time, shortly after the initial hemorrhage. Roar did not argue or complain, although he did feel much better, he knew how quickly he became exhausted and the need for sleep came like a wave washing over him.

It was Monday morning on January 3rd, 2000, the first day back at work for most of the population of the country after the often-extended Christmas break. Anders Abrahamsen addressed the staff that were gathered in the large meeting room. He told them about Roar's whole episode, the emergency helicopter ambulance, the subsequent diagnosis and current condition on his road to recovery. Anneli sat completely still, afraid she might give away her duplicity. She said nothing but wondered what would have happened if she had stayed, what a mess that would have been. Another member of staff asked why he was at Skiphelle in the early morning all alone? Anders had no answer, Anneli remained tight-lipped, wishing everyone would stop asking questions. They all returned to their duties and projects, back in their own offices to get on with the year 2000.

Anneli sat in her office feeling the anxiousness rising, wondering how many others would be asking questions about why Roar was there, what he was doing and with whom he was doing it. There was a knock on the door, Anders entered the room. Anders was a an astute, observant and forthright man, he also knew Roar better than Roar knew himself. He had seen the signs and was already certain that Anneli and Roar were having an affair. He sat down opposite Anneli, looked her resolutely in the eyes and said, 'Now, tell me what really happened at Skiphelle.'

She felt her anxiousness rising up through her body, her normally eloquent and composed self-confidence was shaken as she stuttered in a higher pitch than normal. 'What do you mean?' was all that she could eek utter.

'You know exactly what I mean, you were with Roar at Skiphelle,' he replied.

She could not hold it in any longer, the pressure from every angle had diminished her defences. She had avoided speaking to Sven who was trying to call her constantly, her parents had called to ask what was going on, Sven had called them too, her friend wanted to know how long she planned to stay. Now, Roar was in hospital and Anders was here demanding to know what was going on. She covered her face with both hands and started to sob uncontrollably, Anders got up, closed her office door and waited for the sobbing to subside. Anneli raised her head from her hands and through the tears retold her story to Anders.

She told him about the Christmas party and all the clandestine meetings up until the New Year incident, that she separated from Sven and was temporarily living with a girlfriend and how she and Roar had spoken on New Year's Eve arranging to meet at the hotel by the beach. He had arrived late, looking bedraggled and what she thought was drunk, they had talked for a short while but he had fallen asleep. She tried to wake him up but he didn't respond. He stank of alcohol so she had assumed that he was just very drunk. She made the decision to let him sleep it off and rode back to Nesoddtangen in a taxi. As far as she knew he was okay until that point. She had left before 3am and knew nothing of why he was on the beach a few hours later.

Anders thanked her for opening up, saying that it would not be wise to try and visit him in the hospital as both his partner and his parents were there most of the time. Anneli remained seated, thinking to herself, what a mess she had gotten herself into. Someone always seems to get hurt when I get myself into these crazy situations, I can't keep doing this, she thought. She slumped back in her seat, shaking her head slowly from side to side. I can't do this anymore, why do I need this excitement when it always destroys what I already have. Maybe I need to talk to someone professionally about this, get some support, some help with it.

At the hospital, Roar had been taken to do some further tests, Solveig and Harald had left to get some breakfast. Elisabeth arrived to an empty room, one of the nurses had informed her of the situation and that her husband was making a great recovery so far. She had informed the nurse, a little too sharply, that they were not married and instantly felt the acid within the tone of her voice. It actually hurt to feel it, how must that have felt for the unsuspecting nurse? It just goes to show how every little thing matters, every word, thought and intention is a form of energy we send out to those around us.

A few minutes later Roar trundled into the room in a wheelchair pushed by a young attractive nurse laughing at something Roar had said. Elisabeth instantly felt a pang of irritation. The thought immediately entered her mind, there he goes, flirting again, when in truth she had no idea what had been said between them or in what context. She batted the thoughts away, realizing that it was a judgement of him based on his past behaviours. Now he had to make all his own decisions and live with the consequences of those choices. She could not and had no intention of changing his way of being, that he had to do for himself. The thoughts dissipated and she became fully present in the next moment. He looked up to her and smiled, 'Hello Elisabeth, great to see you.'

'Hi Roar, lovely to see you too, up and about, it looks like you are recovering nicely. How are you feeling today?'

'Well yes, much improved, it seems my body is recovering quite quickly and I am being very well cared for.' As he glanced to the nurse who smiled at his remark.

His speech had already improved vastly although there was a certain amount of slurring, mumbling, gaps and words that came out almost on top of one another, though she could now understand everything he was saying. He got up from the wheelchair unaided and walked slowly to the bed and climbed in. His legs were still felt very weak and he became quite exhausted after just a few movements. The nurse left the room: They were alone together whilst he was fully awake in her presence for the first time since the party on New Year's Eve. She sat close to the bed and asked him if he was well enough to talk about what had happened and what had been going on before that.

He sat in silence for a while, he was feeling both his old way of being and what could be the new, more open and honest way for him to be. It was as if he could feel all the indiscretions, all the lies and deceit he had perpetrated over the years, all at the same time. He also felt how badly he had treated Elisabeth during their time together as a couple and that this could no longer continue, but at the same time, he recognized this old pattern inside himself, a dishonesty, a need to protect himself from hurt, shame, guilt and so many other hidden layers of ingrained behaviour. He became conscious of the pause, the long pregnant pause, and that he was on the verge of a decision that could potentially change so many elements of his life, a decision to commit to change, to be truthful, honest and transparent. He chose to say yes to change, yes to absolute honesty, or at least honesty to the best of his current abilities. He could feel how much of his life had been lived in deceit, with lying to and manipulation of others, he could feel how much pain and sadness there was inside him, that he needed courage to stand up and feel all that needed to be felt.

He took a deep breath and said yes. He spoke slowly, controlled and carefully trying to avoid causing Elisabeth any distress or pain. She stopped him and told him what she already knew about his most recent affair, when it had happened, who it was, which evenings and nights they had been together. She explained that over the years she had learned to read him to an extent that she knew the moment any untruth was uttered by him, which was, in fact, most of the time.

'You think you have been clever and manipulative but the only person you have fooled for the last two years is yourself. Having said that though, I have allowed you to fool me but that was not your fault, it was my choice,' she told him. 'Don't try to spare me any pain, I have already felt it all and yes it does hurt but I have mostly let go of it, I just need to hear it all from you, honestly and completely. This will help you just as much as it will help me, so do not hold anything back.'

Even so, after expressing all this, she felt herself bracing for what may come, because even though she had dealt with much of his philandering she also knew that it would probably be much worse than she had ever imagined. He spoke slowly and as clearly as he could manage for the next thirty minutes as she listened solemnly to all his sordid details, all his deception and dishonesty. When he stopped, he had emptied as much as he could. She asked simply, how he felt about what he had done and the fact that he had now been open and honest about it.

Again, there was a long pause as he tried to get a grip on the turmoil spinning around inside his body, at the sheer scale of his own duplicity. He felt the shame and self-disgust almost overwhelming him as he spoke. 'I feel afraid, naked, exposed and defenceless.' The tears rolled down his cheeks as he tried to get to grips with these so unfamiliar feelings. 'Like an unprotected, undisciplined child with no-one to look after me, no mother, no father, no-one to help me decide what I should do now, completely helpless.' The emotion in his voice seemed to increase the difficulty in getting the actual words out of his mouth. He stuttered falteringly; his words seemed to run into one-another as he fumblingly expressed his feelings. For Roar this was for an unaccustomed and sensitive experience. He continued,

'My insides are a pandemonium, I'm nervous and confused, yet there is an enormous feeling of relief and, in a way, respite, a reprieve from the anxiousness, stress and excitement of my deceitful escapades. It feels like I have hit the reset button and everything can change from now on.' He fell silent and looked at Elisabeth.

Elisabeth said nothing, sat back trying to take it all in, and she knew it all or at least had suspected much of it but it had been even more than she had imagined. She was desperately trying to keep her cool, to not react to all this abuse, that he had almost certainly been with another woman during the day and had sex with her that same evening on many occasions. She didn't really want to ask that question but forced herself to do it, for she knew and he knew, and he confirmed that had been the case on some occasions.

Slowly, finding in extremely difficult to keep the anger and disgust out of her voice, Elisabeth replied, 'Do you realize how abusive that is to me, how everything you have done, is abusing me, it's so difficult for me to sit here just now and yet I feel I have to take this to its conclusion, whatever that may be. I have played my part in all of this. I knew you before I agreed to go into a relationship with you. In choosing to say yes to you somewhere inside I knew I was saying yes to abuse. I also need to get to the root cause of why I did this to myself. We are in a way, partners in this crime, together. I am more disgusted with myself than I am with you, it's incredible that I allowed myself to be violated in this way."

They looked at each other, not speaking for a few minutes until once again Elisabeth spoke, "Am I not worth more than you have given me, worth more than I have settled for? What has happened to my own self-respect? I don't think you have respected me because I have had such a low level of respect for myself, what more could I expect of you? I chose to be with you, a man that has so little self-respect that he almost kills himself through his own lifestyle choices, then what does that say about where I am with my own self-esteem? I have settled for so much less than I deserve, less than anyone deserves. You can continue on the path you have been on, that will only lead you to self-destruction and early death, but I will no longer accompany you along that way. I have stepped off this roller-coaster to oblivion.

My self-respect is growing, my self-awareness is expanding, I will move away from this abusive relationship, I can no longer accept the abuse that seems to be all that you have to offer.'

'You probably will not believe this, but I will change, I have begun to change already,' Roar said in little more than a muttering murmur. 'I know telling you all the sordid details of what I have done is corroborating and cementing the vast betrayal I have engineered but in doing so it is freeing me from the lies I have lived and need not live anymore.'

'For my own sake, I need to explore every nook and cranny, leave no stone unturned in getting to the root cause of my own acceptance of your maltreatment. So, I am willing to hear everything you have to say but remember where your past words have come from and be sure to hold yourself to truth,' Elisabeth replied. 'I will not walk away yet, I need to unravel everything I can, but at some point, leaving the relationship may become the only real option.'

After a few more minutes of silence, Roar then told her of the vivid images, that felt more like recollections from the past, that he had experienced whilst in his unconscious state. The time spent in the body of Grace Lightfoot was much more than dreams or memories. He could remember every movement, every feeling and every word. He could also describe the scenes from the streets of London in 1900 that would have been impossible for him to do before he collapsed. It felt like he was Grace, and she was him, they were the same being, the same essence. He told Elisabeth of the abuse he had suffered, the loneliness and the entrapment, the rapes, the beatings, the pregnancy and the illegal abortion. He didn't know if he/she had died that day in the hallway.

Roar talked for a long time and in truth it did seem that he had actually lived and experienced all the words he expressed; how could this not be the truth. She had never heard him speak this way before with so much presence, empathy and insight. She knew Roar, this was not the flippant, conceited scallywag she had persevered with for last few years. This was something, someone else. There was a definite change in him, but how long would it last and when he gets back on his feet will he simply return to his old life?

Roar began to tire, he had difficulty keeping his eyes open, he needed to rest again. Elisabeth told him to take a nap and they could speak more later. She decided to take a short ten-minute drive to Vigeland's Park, where she could take a walk and clear her head from all the thoughts that had started to swirl around inside her mind. She knew these repetitive thoughts were generated by the emotional reactions to what Roar had told her, reactions that came from the un-dealt-with hurts both from her current and previous relationships, and from certain events in her childhood. Maybe she also had pain and hurt, and in a way a momentum from lives she had previously lived, similar to the way in which Roar had described his experiences to her. If he has lived other lives previously, then presumably he is not the only one. Could it be that we all live many times over? Then is it also true that we carry the Karma of those previous lives so that this, in combination with the experiences of the current life, brings us to the present point, and what we are at this moment living?

It may seem like reactions are caused by the actions of someone or something else but that may, in fact, not be the whole truth of the situation. Could there be some external dark force that instigates and ignites the thoughts, that has us believe that we are individuals, separate from all others? If we become free of individuality and the wants and needs of the 'self', is there then nothing within or outside us that can provoke deleterious emotional reactions? Is it not so then that every futile outplay from the dark external forces that seem to be constantly upon us are in fact nothing more than opportunities for growth and expansion further into the Light of our true origins, rather than feeble attempts to draw us back into the dark realms of reactionary human life constructed by the deceitful forces of spiritual creation?

The sky was clear and the sun was already way passed its zenith and the short winter's day would once again turn to a long cold night. Elisabeth parked the car and walked into the green parkland and immediately started to feel more composed, more present within herself. As she moved, she sensed her whole body, the way her feet trod upon the ground, how the fibres and joints of her body gently shifted, feeling her whole self at one in space and her surroundings.

As she walked upon the well-trodden, compacted snow her questioning about Reincarnation returned to her awareness. She let herself feel the inquiry within her whole body. Yes, there was a knowing within her, an ancient feeling of spaciousness, wisdom and Light. She could feel that it was true, that we do live within the science of Karma with an obligation of living responsible lives. Everything we do does affect our future lives and all other beings living their lives, everything is inextricably interconnected. She felt it was not simply about her living a truly good life for herself, her next life and lives thereafter. She also realized it was about her living responsibly, in service for everyone else too and that no-one should be left out, everyone and everything was affected and everything mattered. The reflection to all, of her responsible living way, was paramount.

She wondered where she was whilst Roar was incarnated in London in 1900. Was it possible to be anywhere on the planet? How many lives had she lived, what had she experienced, where had she been, what had brought us here what is our true purpose in being here? There were so many questions and yet she did not feel disenchanted. She instinctively knew that she had all the necessary answers inside her. What she needed to know would be revealed whenever it was called for. The answers were there and the deeper her connection with her inner-most essence the more the answers would be revealed. What is this inner-most part of our being, is it not the pure observing love, the steady unmovable serenity found deep within us all, could we simply describe this as the Light within or the essence of what we truly are?

She pondered further: What is it that stops us from being at-one with our essence, this soulful Light? What is it that gets in the way of such beauty that resides within all of us? For, if we all could live from that inner sacred place, there would be no abuse anywhere on the planet, harmony would be the norm. There is, though, a darker energy available, a force we all can choose to allow through us. Instead of our Light, we align to the dark force of spiritual creation. It almost feels schizophrenic, we have the soulful Light that has only truly loving intentions, but we also have the other part, this wayward rascal, the careless conspirator, the despot, the selfish scoundrel, the one that is run by spiritual creation instead of the Light. This irresponsible aspect of our being is the part known as the spirit and may often be referred to as the ego. This spirit may well be a delinquent reduction departed from the soul; a part of the whole we are from that has chosen separation and the way of spiritual creation instead of the Light from which it has departed.

The outplay of the spirit comes in a myriad of forms that differs for each one of us, it may be the despotic dictator, the executor of genocide, the seems-to-be do-gooder philanthropist trying to repair his tarnished public prestige, the greedy businessman's charity donation to reduce his own tax bill, the fanatical preacher, the nice friend giving the words of sympathy instead of the truth of what needs to be expressed. Indeed, any emotional expression is its connivance. The deviousness of the wily spirit knows no bounds, it will not only abuse others it will readily abuse the very body in which it resides; it cares not. It seeks only excitement, drama or any other encounter or ordeal on the scale of temporal experiences. It will do anything to distract the human part of the being from the Light. It will cause delay in any way, preventing it from a return to the way of the soulful Light that burns within every being.

The gross and immeasurable amount of disturbance this recalcitrant spirit has created within each of us has

caused, and continues to cause, deep unrest, dis-ease and chaos in every corner of the globe. Name any war, injustice, hypocrisy, disorder, crime, deceit or any other violation and behind this, the fractious spirit is there to be found.

If the way we now live is controlled by the guiles of the spirit, then how do we return to the living way of the soul, for that is where we need to go, that is where true truth is to be found. It is quite hilarious and, at the same time calamitous to use the phrase 'true truth' for it exposes the truths we are given. The truths that we are fed and educated to believe, are in fact based on lies and illusion produced by what could be described as a grand union of collaborating spirits in the form of consciousnesses that are designed to capture each and every one of us in disparate ways. Until that is, we can realize our way free from these self-chosen forms of individual enshacklement. Truths we are taught are nothing more than ingrained falsehoods. Tragically this is what our whole society is built upon, a complete and utter illusion that we are all convinced is the truth of human life.

She had come full circle, entering the car park she arrived back where she had started, feeling with awe and amazement the power of the wisdom that had come through her during the walk. She felt very confirmed in and committed to her chosen path; that she would allow Roar the space he needed to embrace or reject what was on offer to him, that was actually on offer to everyone. She now knew he was also feeling the inner conflict as everyone else does in some way, although he may be very confused about it considering his near-death experience.

Maybe for most people to see the lies, see the corruption and at times, the complete insanity of how we live our lives, a traumatic experience is the only thing that can wake them up from this self-induced ignorance we choose to call a normal life. In fact, this universal wisdom is on offer to everyone, it flows through all of us, all of the time and it is simply a choice of which source

of energy one chooses to align to. We either stay in the prevailing energy to continue obsequiously on the current path into our own inadvertence, or we choose what we could describe as, true service, the universal Light, divine intelligence or God's wisdom, the 'What Is', that is everything the current way is not.

She got in the car, felt the deep stillness and settlement within her body then drove back to the hospital.

Roar was awake when she arrived back at the hospital and the room was full of hospital staff. She had to wait outside until they had completed all the investigations they were undertaking. This was a teaching hospital and it looked like they were having a lesson in post-brain-hemorrhage care in Roar's room. Fifteen minutes later she entered the room to see a rather bemused Roar sitting up in bed with a wry smile on his face. He told her that the specialist had said he was recovering well, his leg-strength was improving rapidly, his speech was also coming along nicely, and he seemed emotionally stable, at least at the present moment. He had asked if he could go home and after a short discussion, they had agreed that he could have a physical and psychological assessment the next morning to discern if he was ready to leave. They would also prepare the required medication to take at home if he were to be discharged.

Two days later, just before midday Elisabeth collected Roar from the hospital and drove him home, out to the apartment in Droebak. His parents would stay in Oslo one more night, then they too would drive out to Droebak and stay with their old friends who lived in a large house just a short walk from Roar and Elisabeth's apartment, before returning to Spain the following week if all was well with Roar's recovery.

'Roar, how are you feeling about being home, what will be your next steps, how do you want to live your life going forward?' Elisabeth asked after they had settled in for the afternoon.

She continued, 'Three big questions in one, I know, but it's so important for us to have an open and honest communication and that we are totally transparent with each other. There can be no more deceit. I can't live my life with someone unwilling to show me everything they are. I don't even know yet if I can be with you even if you are willing to change your ways. I don't even know if I can be all that I ask myself to be, I only know that it is my intention to evolve as a human and soulful being and this is what I will strive to do and be, with or without you.'

After a short silence, he replied, 'When you ask me these questions my first thought, my first inclination is to go into the kitchen and pour a glass of wine to ease the anxiousness that the questions cause. Or maybe no, I'm not sure that the discomfort isn't already in me before you ask. It seems like the questions are asking me to feel what is already there.

'I know that my drinking so much, well, and all the rest of my wild behaviour, is to avoid something that asks me to look deeper into the hurts I have not dealt with, and through that to be more, to live more in truth than I currently am doing. These changes will require not drinking and not filling my time with anything and everything I possibly can. I have to be committed to what I need to look at that will enable me to face what is required to change my deleterious patterns and offset the momentum that has been my wayward living.

"I feel utterly vulnerable and exposed, completely naked with nowhere to hide, like I'm being smacked in the face whilst tied to a chair. There is no real option other than to meet head-on what needs to be faced and yet I can feel resistance as though it is being pumped around my body in my blood. There seems to be an intransigence in my every cell. Part of me feels like something disconnected from me, almost a separate vibration through my whole body that is screaming 'No', and yet within the no there is a resignation that there has to be, at some point, an inevitable yes. There is a turmoil, a fear of what is unknown and yet it is known, it is a familiar pull towards what I know is the truth and yet there is such great obstinacy. So, in answer to your question about how I feel now, I feel terribly anxious.

"The first steps for me to take are the steps of learning a better way of looking after myself, not the way I previously regarded number one, only me. Which was not looking after myself, it was more like abusing myself, I did what I pleased, had the excitement I wanted, thought it was fun. Pumping iron, getting drunk with the guys, skiing, taking risks, driving dangerously, flirting, chasing other women and being the real alpha male. It was all abusive to myself and everyone else around me. My body has certainly sounded the fire-alarm, given me a huge warning signal. The doctors have confirmed that I can no longer live this way. If I do not take heed, I may not live much longer, I know I need to fundamentally change the way I live my life. If I did continue to live like that and the doctors were wrong, I still do not want to finish my life at the bottom of an empty bottle.

'To stop drinking alcohol has to be my first priority. It has almost certainly been the greatest contributing factor to my near death. I know it is an addiction, I have to have a drink. I mean I will use any excuse to have a drink but the thing is, I don't know any other way. It's been this way for so long. I know how pernicious drinking would be for me and I can feel a sort of self-preservation kicking in just at this moment but I'm afraid there is something else within me so strong that will try to override my current sensibility and pull me back into my usual habits and antics. I guess you could call it an urge to indifference, carelessness and self-neglect. I realize that I need a whole new level of looking after myself but at the same time there is this feeling of apprehension, of not being enough or capable to manage to make the changes needed. The pull to drink is so powerful, it is the first thought that comes into my head whenever there is a moment of sadness or being alone with my own thoughts. I know I need to take a deeper look at why I drink in the first place, try to get to the root cause which I feel is hidden more deeply inside me and yet it's here within me, so it can't really be so far away.'

Elisabeth spoke quietly. 'There are many people in similar situations to you Roar, some that will recover fully or close to it, then return to their old ways, eventually resulting in a new traumatic episode or even, sooner or later, their untimely premature death. Others do change their lifestyle, give up their unhealthy habits and addictions but instead of taking a holistic view, they focus on the physicality, choosing other habits to keep them fit without going any deeper into what caused the problem in the first place, without looking at the origin of the matter. Then becoming addicted to something else instead of the alcohol which may help the physical body, but it does not deal with the underlying causes that are then left to further fester, until they may eventually manifest into some form of illness, dis-ease or even an injury through accident. I say accident because even this is due to how we live or it is to show us something that needs our attention. In the end it's not simply a question of healing the body, the whole being needs to heal, body, mind, spirit and soul. Actually, not the soul, it does not in fact need to heal as it is everything it needs to be right now, it simply offers the Light and the path back to the truth of what we are.'

She continued, 'I feel we people in general are constantly being torn between two opposite poles, the one we all know so well that wants to party, have what they seem to believe is a great time, drink, do drugs, smoke, eat junk food, actually be in total disregard of our own bodies, wake up ill the next day and do it over and over again, rewind and repeat. Whilst at the opposite pole, we have a harmonic, aware, alert, caring part that is open, lovingly communicates, has unfettered self-respect and complete regard for every particle of the body it inhabits and holds the same consideration for every other being. We are in a way the third part, the position in the middle being torn between the two extremes. If we align to one, we are no longer aligned to the other, there is no neutral gear to idle in. So, we are either in league with this wayward, couldn't-care-less part that we could call the spirit, or we are aligned to the opposite, which is the essence of what we truly are, the soul and the Universe beyond. Each one could be described as an energy. One is a nourishing, loving, caring, true energy, whilst the other is a selfish, disregarding, wanton and deceitful energy. When we drink, live for and from emotional highs and lows, distract ourselves from the present, get lost in addictions, obsessions and hobbies, we are in truth aligning to the harmful, destructive spiritual energy. Consequently, we cannot align to our true natural way of being, the way of being that most of humanity has disconnected from, the healing soulful way. We can only align to one energy, or the other, at any given time.

'When we do anything else that aligns us to this harmful spiritual energy, we do it to cause a distraction from living as our true self, the being we truly are. Our natural tendency is to return to the truth of who we are, although there are several layers of defence mechanisms obstructing the way, as well as our much-practised patterns of wayward and destructive behaviour. It can begin in childhood, when we are hurt or traumatized in some way, abused, physically or emotionally neglected, ignored or any other event that somehow negatively affects us. A small child is more in its natural state, very open and vulnerable and as hurts build up over the years the child may develop methods of coping and defensive behavior in order to not feel these hurts. These protective mechanisms become ingrained, they become our behaviours and our reactions, all to avoid the ill-feelings that have been encrusted around our very being.'

Roar thought for a moment. 'I see how my parents are together, there is no real intimacy between them, they don't really communicate very much at all. It's all really quite cold between them. They just did their own things and that was the accepted way. I remember being on my own so much, seeing my friends out with their parents, going skiing or to football matches, swimming in the fjord, on the beach together. When I was old enough, I would tag along with other families, often with Anders, his parents and his sister, and if not them, anyone who would take me with them. I was quite impertinent and sometimes the parents of my friends would refuse my persistent overtures. My reaction to that was to become more and more persuasive and manipulative. As I grew older, I would feign rejection to play on their sympathy so that they would almost always allow me to tag along.

'I never thought much about my parents just doing their own thing, Mum's main duty or way of passing the time was to do anything for me, as long as it was in the home setting or at our summer cabin. By the time I was fifteen, as I looked much older than my actual age, increasingly, I did my own thing, came and went as I pleased. I would tell my mum I was staying over at Anders' house and would be going to all-night parties with older kids. There was always alcohol or dope and it soon became a regular thing, partying every weekend, which also led to a lot of casual sexual relationships. I didn't really care who I slept with as long as it was someone, a girl, it didn't matter who, I wanted the company, and the excitement. I would be very disappointed and irritable if I didn't have a sexual encounter, even for one night during weekends. As the years passed, the weekends were extended into the weekdays and partying; drinking and sex, in a way, became my main purpose in life. Even in the work environment I would take any and every opportunity to get my fix in order to lubricate my addictions.

'This grew into my way of living, the main focus in life. When I got together with my male friends, I would often become the focal point because of my seeming success with girls. The guys would talk about which girls would and wouldn't, we rated them, judged them, their bodies, their performances in bed, we wouldn't let a girl pass by without all of us looking her up and down. It's just what guys did and still do, I still look at all women and something inside me automatically calls judgement on them, rates them into categories. It feels like a right men have, that I have, because we men are the dominant gender. It was the same for all the guys, we all felt it, that we were above women and could pass our judgement upon them. Although when I think about it, about the discussions we had, there were some that didn't really have much to say and they probably do have more respect for women.

'Wow, I realize how bad this is, it's complete disrespect for every woman on the planet. I guess most men everywhere think, at some level in this way. It is more pronounced in some, and I'm ashamed to say it happens all the time with me. It is an addiction to me, it's so deep-rooted that it seems to happen naturally but now I can feel how arrogant, abusive and disdainful it actually is.

'This is so exposing, I have never considered that the way I act, the way men in general act towards women is everything other than normal. I don't mean in extreme cases such as rapists, pedophiles or people that beat their partners or anything that is physically or mentally abusing. It was just men having a bit of banter about the opposite sex, I always saw as being harmless fun.'

"Yes, Roar, but at what point does your harmless fun become abusive? Have you ever considered how the women feel about your critical appraisement, those objects of your fun know what you are doing, and most would rather not be ogled in that way? There are, of course, women that crave such attention, but, again, have you ever thought why they want it, why they flaunt themselves for men, why they sleep around? Could it be that they have been brought up in a way that has left them with issues about their own worthiness, that they are not good enough and that any attention from men in their eyes is construed as good attention. I know that if I had had more self-esteem, I would never have allowed you or any man like you, into my life. Could it be that what women need from men is respect and decency, men that are not simply look-ing to get them into bed, use them and move on to the next con-quest? For, in truth no women want to be treated badly. So many have been manipulated, brainwashed, cajoled, forced and encour-aged to live and behave in a way that is harmful to themselves. This is not to say that it is only women that have been on the re-ceiving end and that yes, men have also been deceived, indoctri-nated, abused and maltreated in many similar and disparate ways.

'I know, I have let you abuse me for so long, I now know that there is a way out of it, a way to break free of old harmful pat-terns and re-imprint the way I live. I didn't have a clear enough sense of self-respect and self-love to avoid falling into this trap with you but now things have changed for me, and I am quite sure they can change for anyone else, including you if you can let go of whatever holds you in it.'

'Something has already changed within me Elisabeth,' he said. "I almost had to die to even consider stopping the way I've been living, and I know it is just a tiny step but it is a step away from the way it has been until now. I know I have to change everything; it is a daunting task but I have no other option.'

She could see that Roar was starting to get tired so they agreed to have an early night; Elisabeth had already prepared a bed for Roar in the guest room as it would be quite some time, if ever before she would want to share a bed with him. They got ready for bed, said good night and went to their separate rooms.

As she lay in bed, she thought about everything Roar had said, all the different women he had been with, even during the first months of their relationship. She thought about how difficult it would be to forgive him for all his infidelity and betrayal. This allowed her to realize her own part in it all, her own acceptance of placing herself in this situation and her own self-deception, acting for so long as though nothing untoward was going on, knowing full well, who he was and what he was doing. At some point she knew what was happening, by donning her convenient cloak of victimhood, she was choosing to live in that abuse too, until now that is.

He was never going to change his spots, not until something this serious happened, and it could be that not even this will be enough, in this life, this time around. If she had been a willing participant, which she was within this relationship, hmmm on second thought not really much of a relationship, more like a duplicitous arrangement to avoid taking full responsibility for herself, then how could she be the one to forgive? It was obvious for her now that if she had an equal part to play in this deception, nay self-deception, then there is no reason to forgive anything. There is no blame to apportion. She could, though, embrace the learning and accept in full the lessons now on offer. It is sad that all this has happened, but it had to transpire in order for her to see more clearly and learn to be aware of how much abuse she had been accepting. She now had the opportunity to never accept this kind of abuse again.

If, in situations where there is a perpetrator and a victim that willingly enter into harmful arrangements, is there ever a call for forgiveness? What is forgiveness? Is it one person pardoning another for something unacceptable or atrocious they have, in a way, willingly had done to them within a so-called relationship? Onlookers from the outside often see these relationships with all their seemingly one-sided malignancy without knowing the wretched details of the arrangements between the two involved parties but the participants within live their ingrained patterns and behaviours as though it were normal deportment. It could then be easy to fall into judgement without knowing the full truth of the situation. Those within the relationship often judge each other, their spouse or accomplice whenever they forgive them for any misfortunate occurrence that takes place. Thus, forgiveness becomes nothing more than judgement and acceptance of the evil ways that simply ingrain and re-enforce the existing ill-patterns of the arrangement, making it ever more difficult to gain release from it.

This brought her back to her own view and opinion of herself and what she had been saying to herself; that this is what she deserved to get from life, that she could not expect more than this. Those tired old words she had spoken to herself so many times before reverberated in her mind.

'Appreciate everything you have and get on with it, no-one has the perfect life, the perfect relationship and there are many people out there much worse off than you,' she had told herself.

She knew now that she would no longer allow these words to control her way of being, she had now stepped beyond them. She realized, yes, that she should appreciate what is true, but this was a false form of gratitude, it was settling for what she was not and in doing so it would be continuing to live in acceptance of the abuse she had tolerated.

Everything she had in life at this moment was a reflection of how she had lived until now. Surely if she changed the way she lived, then life would also reflect back what these changes emanate outward. As the days went by, she felt more resolve, more truth in the choices she made and that gave her a true strength, a knowing certainty of where she was now headed. It also allowed her to feel how she had always adopted an attitude of being less than the men she had been involved with in her life and that this felt like an age-old consciousness that she had lived with, not just in this life, but for many lifetimes before. It felt almost as if she had been born with it and that it clung to every particle within her body. Worse than that, it seemed to pollute everything, it was in the air around us all and ran through the body of every woman and every man until the moment they could see it for what it was and choose to renounce it, let it go from their bodies and set themselves free from it.

She could see it, feel it; it no longer controlled her. It is pure evil and she chose to reject it. It was within her purpose now to reflect in a way that is untainted by it.

Sleep washed over her.

In the other room Roar fell asleep almost before his head touched the pillow. All the discussion with Elisabeth had left him quite exhausted and yet he felt exuberant and much lighter within. It was as if all the lies he had lived had been cleansed from his body, all the deceit was no longer necessary, and a great weight had been lifted from him. He fell into a deep unmoving slumber and his breath became so still and shallow that it was almost imperceptible, almost as though he had taken leave of his body.

Chapter 4

GRACE'S TRUTH

The medical staff worked on Miss Lightfoot for the next two hours. Through surgical dexterity, years of medical experience in treating what must have been thousands of similar cases and of course their innate wisdom, they stabilized and subsequently revived her to consciousness.

As she was coming back, she had a sense of a man she may become or in some way be a part of, in a time far hence from here. She knew that the choices she now made would impact not only who she would become in this life but for many lives henceforth. These choices would not impact her lives alone but all the lives of all those around her, now and onwards into the future. This would be the greatest of responsibility that she and all others may take. She could also feel that nothing would change from the way it is now if each human being did not choose for themselves a way of responsibility. She opened her eyes, in more ways than one, and in a particular way, she hoped they would never close again, at least not in this life.

'Where am I?' she croaked, 'What happened?'

'Hello Grace, you are at Charing Cross Hospital and everything is going to be fine, we are here for you now,' replied nurse Brightwell. 'This is Dr. Billings.'

Samuel Billings then explained the whole situation to her, that the book seller from Euston Station was his uncle Richard who had read her note and found her unconscious in the doorway of the Darcaster house in Kensington. He immediately, with the aid of a cabby, had rushed her here to Charing Cross Hospital. They arrived not a moment too soon. They had managed to stop the bleeding, re-hydrated her body and, in truth, saved her from imminent death. She now needed to be extremely careful and to take much rest for the next two weeks.

The tears rolled down Grace's face, they were both tears of relief to be alive and yet tears of dread for what was to come. She simply couldn't go back to work for George Darcaster, to be abused again, she couldn't go to the police as it would be his word against hers and they would never believe the servant ahead of the rich industrialist. Her only option would be to find menial employ somewhere else and without any references, as she had only ever worked for the Darcaster family, she was convinced she would finish up homeless on the streets like so many others in the lower echelons of this unjust society.

A little later a nurse came in to ask how she felt and if she would be able to receive a visitor, as Mr. Richard Billings was waiting outside. She nodded and the nurse left the room. Two minutes later there was a gentle knock on the door and Grace gave permission to enter. He walked slowly, almost sheepishly into the room looking quite grave as he moved towards Grace in the bed.

"How are you, Miss Lightfoot?" he inquired.

She was at a loss for words, confounded by a mixture of extreme gratitude, almost overwhelming dread for her own future and abject embarrassment of the situation and circumstances she now found herself in. And once again the tears began to roll down her cheeks.

"Thank you, Mr. Billings," she stammered in between her light sobbing. "I am truly thankful for what you have done, but in truth I am both happy and sad to be alive."

She then went on to explain her predicament and the complete horrendousness of her imminent plight. Richard fully understood the severity of her dilemma and had already given the situation much contemplation. For him, in the end it was quite simple to transpose her unfortunate precarious situation into one of benefit and positivity for them both.

'Miss Lightfoot, I have a proposition for you to consider, you may think this inappropriate but it is the best I can offer you at this moment in time.' He paused as she looked at him with curiosity.

'I live in Barnsbury, not far north of Kings Cross Station. I have a small property with three bedrooms, in which I live alone. I live a very quiet and simple life between the bookstall at Euston Station, my own private book collection and tending to my much-cherished garden. At my advanced age I have begun to find it quite tedious to attend to all the household chores as well as caring for the garden and my own little athenaeum of books. What I am trying to say to you Miss Lightfoot, is …'

Again, he paused for a short while, as though the words were stuck inside him.

'When you are well enough to travel, I can offer you a position of employ in my humble household as my housekeeper. It may not be such a grand post such as the House of Darcaster, but it would be a safe haven for you to recuperate and re-establish yourself in fast employment. I cannot offer you the wages you might be accustomed to, but it is a live-in position with all food and necessities included and thirty pounds per annum for you travail. You do not need to answer immediately, take all the time you need to consider this.'

He had hardly finished speaking his words before Grace blurted out, 'Yes!' She paused for a couple of seconds, 'Yes, yes, yes.'

She had no doubt whatsoever, after all their conversations over the past few years, that this was the most honourable man she had ever met and this proposition from Richard Billings was the answer from God to all her prayers.

"Thank you so much Mr. Billings, you are truly an angel sent from God, I would be delighted to work in your employ for as long as you want me to do so. This is the second time you are to save my life in such a short space of time, thank you with all of my heart.'

Both, much relieved, joyfully continued to discuss the more practical aspects of what this co-habitation would entail. There would be much to prepare before the house would be ready to receive this young lady. Amongst it all, a bedroom must be put in order, cleaned and cleared, as there is currently an abundance of books deposited in there, yet to be classified and placed in their correct locations. They would all need to be sorted and shifted as soon as possible.

They eventually arrived at the subject of her clothing and other belongings, as at some point, she would have to return to the Darcaster house to collect them. She realized that she had less than three weeks before having to face George Darcaster upon his return. She would have to stay in hospital for at least three more days to ensure she didn't start bleeding again, so consequently that would still leave her plenty of time to go there and retrieve the few belongings she owned. She could recoup her accoutrements preferably under the cover of darkness, as she hoped to leave without notice of the watchful eyes of anyone in the neighbourhood. She didn't have much more than could fit in her one battered old trunk, so it would take less than an hour to be done with it. Neither did she want to incriminate anyone else, her intention was to simply disappear without a trace. They agreed that as soon as she was fit enough to travel, they would retrieve all her belongings.

Grace grew tired and Mr. Billings realized it was time to leave, he had much to prepare, it was best to get started as soon as possible. She was asleep before he left the room.

Five days later, they pulled up outside the Darcaster residence in the Hansom carriage. They had deliberately located the same cabby, Joseph, that had carried Grace into the hospital as she had expressed her wish to thank him for his part in saving her life. It was a little after midnight and the houses along the street were shrouded in darkness as all three of them entered the house using as little light as necessary. Grace quickly gathered her belongings, packing them into her trunk; forty-five minutes later she was completely satisfied she had everything that belonged to her. Joseph carried the trunk out to the cab; Grace placed a pre-written letter on the small table in the hallway and she carefully locked the door behind her. She gently slipped her set of keys through the letter box and turned away with the intention of never returning. Joseph drove them sedately home to Barnsbury, dropped them off and made his own way home for the night.

Although it had been a late night, she woke up early the next morning, prior to the stroke of 7am upon the clock, feeling more freedom than she had ever done before. Her body was healing well, and she had suffered no further setbacks after her traumatic experiences. It was still dark and cold outside and quite chilly inside the house. There were fireplaces in every room, but it was impossible for them to burn all night. Every morning the downstairs fires and the coal-fired cooking-range in the kitchen would be cleaned out and re-lit, gradually warming up the house,

Grace had now been living at Mr. Billings's house for two nights and this was her third day. She loved it more in every moment that passed. He had created a budget for the weekly food and household expenses, today was also the first time she would be going out to buy fresh food for their dinner. They had been for gentle walks around the area pointing out the shops where he generally would buy his provisions. They had discussed all the practicalities of the household including a schedule for bathing and other more private activities. The bedroom had been cleared for Grace and she would take the time during the following weeks to adorn it in a more feminine manor.

As she entered the library, which was probably the largest room in the house, though the cluttered state created an illusion of a much smaller size, she took in the scene, every spare inch of every wall except for the area above and around the large open fireplace and the one large window, was bedecked in shelving crammed with books. There were also stacks of books on the floor and covering the large desk and desk chair in the centre of the room. In the far corner beyond the fireplace, in what was probably the warmest corner of the room, stood two well-worn, walnut-framed dark blue velvet armchairs with a small dark stained oak wine table in-between. There was a small stack of books on the table including one that was open. She thought inquisitively that these must be the books Mr. Billings was currently reading. She picked up the thin emaciated open book and looked, expecting to read what was on the pages but it was all in a strange symbol-like script she had never seen before. She would later discover it to be Sanskrit.

They sat together at the small dining table in the compact ante-room which was in reality part of the kitchen area. There was a lull in the conversation whilst they finished the last few morsels of their meal, when quite unexpectedly Mr. Billings asked, 'How do you feel within yourself now and what are your feelings in regard to George Darcaster and what he has done to you?'

Grace finished chewing, swallowed and carefully laid down her cutlery whilst pondering upon the question. Eventually she responded. 'This has been a thoroughly ghastly experience for me. He has subjected me repeatedly to so much pain, humiliation, perversion, degradation and if not for you, my certain annihilation. I feel such antipathy and repugnance. I feel nauseated at the very mention of his name and I feel the fear of what may happen if ever we were to meet again,' she said with what could only be described as resentful bitterness. 'He absolutely disgusts me!'

Richard was quite taken aback by the venom in her voice, he had never felt or heard such contempt in her words. He could feel without doubt a burning, harmful hate emanating from and through her, so powerful that as she uttered these words it seemed to change her from the beautiful soul that she is, into a revengeful fiend hellbent on retribution. He knew that if she allowed these feelings to remain within, without true healing, then they would fester and consume her very being, and in doing so, complete her destruction that was started by the actions of George Darcaster. A thought flashed through his mind, that he must save her again, but no, this time it would be her own responsibility to save herself from her-self. He then quickly realized that he could only guide her to a certain extent, the rest was up to her. Only Grace had the power to make her own choices. It was up to her to seek the resources she needed and call for the guidance required to help her see all of her seeming misfortune as an opportunity to grow and expand beyond the mere physical and mental reactions to the situation.

He knew he had to tread carefully, it could be quite easy for her to misconstrue his advocacy as non-supporting or even uncompassionate, but he needed to express the truth, to withhold nothing.

'I understand how hurt you must feel by all that has been in-flicted upon you by George Darcaster. These hurts will sit deep within your body and need to be healed completely, nothing should be allowed to remain inside, it all needs to be brought up and out for true healing to commence and be rendered in full. This will understandably take time and of course a willingness on your part to evolve over and above the abuse and all of what has been before. It is of the utmost that this be understood and that you comprehend in full the importance here.

'As long as you allow the thoughts of what has been done to you to spin around in your mind, you allow his deeds to remain entrenched within your body. His power over you will remain strong and will further injure you, never giving you reprieve from the pain and the scars he has wrought upon you. Do you understand this, Miss Lightfoot?"

She nodded. 'I understand and please call me Grace, Mr. Billings.'

'I will, as long as you call me Richard,' he replied.

'Richard, I do understand, yet it feels so far away, that I may have peace of mind and no longer re-live all those horrendous episodes in that house. How can this ever be removed from my body, from my mind?' she wondered.

Richard began, 'There are many considerations and aspects that may need to be addressed; for full and true healing it is im-perative to leave no stone unturned. It is important for you to be completely at ease within your healing environment as well as with the people you involve in your healing process, for no-one can heal alone. You will need to express absolutely everything to and with someone you are one-hundred percent confident in, someone you can trust completely. You can do this with me but if you would prefer to talk with another woman, I can ar-range that for you.'

Grace quickly replied, 'I have full confidence in you Richard, I can tell you everything that has happened and how I feel about it. There is no need to involve anyone else in these matters. Although first, can you please explain how this might work, how the pains within can be removed from my body? How can I stop the constant thoughts of the brutal savagery I have undergone from churning over and over in my mind?'

Richard paused, he didn't want to confuse her and yet he didn't want to hold anything away from her. He said, 'Grace, could it be that there are two types of light in this world, or to make it simpler, let's say that everything is either from the true soulful Light or on the other hand, from dark spiritual creation. All that is evil is produced when men and women choose to live from spiritual creation and all that is true and virtuous is produced when we choose to live within the Light of the Soul. Everything, both Light and dark exists within the universe around us or in other words they/ we all reside within, what I would describe as the body of God. The realms of spiritual creation which may be only found here on this planet, are but a speck on this tiny plane of life, all of which resides within the beauty and Light of the universe which may all be contained within the body of God. As this miniscule aberrant malfunction here on Earth is originally from Light, thus, someday in the future this constructed misconception that is spiritual creation will also return to the Light so that everyone and everything will be reunited in oneness with the All that is the One Light.

'We humans have for many centuries been both the puppets and the purveyors of the spiritual creation that corrupts the Light of the universe. Only here on Earth it is we that must return to the Light from whence we originally came. We are the wayward spirits incarnated as humans, that have separated from the soul to which we all must one day return. We play out our wanton games and imprint our deviant ways in this world of creation in our vain attempts to delay that return to our inevitable, unequivocal future. In order to facilitate this return, we must understand to what extent we have left our true selves behind, accept the responsibility of what we are and what we have done, then step back onto the path of restoration, towards the oneness of the All.'

Grace sat nonplussed for a few moments as she absorbed Richards words – she didn't comprehend everything he was saying but somehow recognized it as truth simply due to the timbre of his voice, the resonance of which vibrated throughout her whole body. Her mind could not assimilate all he expressed but the particles of her body seemed naturally to align to the reverberation of his voice.

'My head cannot seem to fathom all the words you are saying but somehow my body knows that you present the truth, please continue,' she whispered.

Richard went on. 'Could it be that we have all lived many lives, walked hundreds, maybe thousands of times in the fog of this grand illusion that temporal life here on Earth is, and yet we fail to discern what is real and what is not. We actually choose not to determine the truth because we have been so committed to the lies that we have created for ourselves in the falsity and righteousness of expressing what we think is our own free will. Now we have no choice but to continue on this unending wheel of death and re-birth until we all can walk free of this illusion of our own creation. Each life we experience, every interaction we engage in, every breath we breathe, are all either remarkable opportunities to take steps away from our ill-ways, or quite the opposite, we move in the knowing that we further entrench ourselves in this stinking swamp of evil self-deception.'

He paused for a few moments to give her the space to digest the words he had expressed. Richard looked directly towards Grace and she nodded for him to carry on.

He continued, 'Absolutely everything that happens at any given instance, in any of the lives we live brings the possibility of both Light and dark, for they are opposites. The offer of Light of the Universe is instantaneous, always there, always first, we refute the Light to choose the dark which is the deceit and evil of spiritual creation. In choosing one, you reject the other. No single human being is capable of walking a middle path for that simply does not exist. The difference between Light and dark may not always seem so clear, as the dark often closely imitates the Light to mask its own deceit with further intricate deception. As we walk farther along the path of return to the Light, we learn to feel and read the prevailing forces, thus becoming aware and capable of greater discernment of the truth, or in truth perceive the lies that are the dominant and current way we live here on Earth.

'If you now think about your own life and everything that has happened to you, the occasions that have caused you pain or joy or any other feeling or emotion, then contemplate upon the lessons learned or not learned during that encounter. You may then see the potential in everything that happens, but it requires discernment. Do you respond or react to situations that arise? If a dark force assails, do you have some kind of reaction, are you then aligned to dark spiritual creation, do you accordingly contribute to and expand this evil force and contribute to the extension of the variation of its expedient existence?'

As she sat there transfixed, with a puzzled look on her face Richard continued. 'I can answer that for you,' he said.

'To begin with, you, I, we, all react, with an outplay that is either internal, external or both. That is, until we align ourselves to the Light and learn how not to allow the dark forces of spiritual creation into our bodies whenever, through our lack of awareness, we unwittingly choose to do so. We could say that due to the ways we have lived for so many centuries, humanity now lives and is almost in its entirety moved by this dark energy. Spiritual creation cannot function without its energy supply, which comprises of the sum of the energy contained within the emotional reactions of the all but-a-few, the few that walk in clarity and live solely and soulfully in the Light. Spiritual creation is unwittingly fueled in this way by the vast majority of humanity who choose not to know what they inherently know, oblivious or not, to the dark forces.

'Most of us, unintentionally at best, are aligned to spiritual creation. We accept this evil energy, this tainted power, into our bodies and through this give away control of our minds, our intentions, our words and our actions. We become its puppets. Thus, everything we express comes from this alignment. It becomes everything we believe we are. You see Grace, we are like empty vessels, only our alignment gives us the intelligence and wisdom from which comes our expression. We can only

116

express from the energy that comes through us, be it Light or be it dark. We can either express from the majesty and wisdom of the Universe or we can express from the reduction that is the perversion named evil spiritual creation which only exists here on this tiny planet of ours.'

Grace smiled. 'So, you are actually telling me that we have only two choices and if we do not choose we are actually choosing anyway, by default choosing the opposite. Does that also mean to say that my thoughts are not really my own, that because of my alignment my thoughts will be given to me or generated by the energy that lies behind it. So, you are saying that I don't think my own thoughts. That does sound quite absurd to me.'

'Exactly!' exclaimed Richard. 'You can probably imagine how difficult that might be for some people to accept. Some of our learned thinkers might simply write these teachings off as complete tomfoolery, but once experienced it is impossible to ignore or deny. If you think about egotistical people, women or men, that care only for their own gain and their own pleasure, that can toss aside anyone who gets in their way, can use and abuse others without remorse, they are not evil but they do allow evil to run them. They are aligned to the forces of spiritual creation. Their thoughts are purely self-serving, but in truth their every movement fuels the cause of these malevolent dark forces. Others around them, that associate with them, that have been maltreated by them, react to their words and actions and thus allow these forces to enter them as well, taking on the energy they emanate and so too contribute to the ill-cause of the dark evil.'

Grace stirred uncomfortably in her chair at the thought that because she hated and despised Mr. George Darcaster and what he had done to her, she too was contributing to the evil at hand.

'Paradoxically, those that bring through the energy of the Light are vastly more potent, for the Light is the wisdom, intelligence and communication of the Universe or it could also be described as God's Light. Just as the dark forces, the Light is also in and through us all the time. Aligning to this true Light is making the choice to return to the true essence of what we are.

Choosing and living from the Light is the choice of simplicity. It is much easier to live in the Light than to live in the complication and deceit of spiritual creation. Because it is simple, beautiful and above all the absolute truth, it has been and always will be, attacked by those wayward spirits dedicated to supporting the confederation of dark evil. Once again it is not the individuals themselves that attack those that live from the Light, but the energy and the dark consciousness that they allow to move them. Once aligned to the evil spiritual creation they are controlled by it and will do it's every bidding until they can be freed from it, until each individual realizes that they are not part of it and so embrace the path of Light, the return to soul.

Grace sat back in her chair as the power of his words helped her to settle more deeply within herself.

'By choosing, in full, to live in and from the Light, we may become beacons that step out of the illusion created by the dark forces, relinquishing self-motivated actions, realizing that we are here to shine for everyone, all of our lost brothers and sisters, our luminescence reaches far and wide, touching all. Many who are ready, may be pulled towards the Light as moths to a flame. There is no preaching, no convincing, no persuasion. We live in and by the Light, others then respond or react to what comes through. The power of the Light is not selective, it pervades all, the insight it brings is not for us alone, it is given to us to be in service for all.

'The power of Light is like the flying seeds of the dandelion flower blowing in the breeze, spreading where the prevailing winds will disseminate, knowing not where they will fall. The dandelion is the most prolific of plants. Its plan for reproduction, though not perfect, is simple and successful. It has the power to land and germinate almost anywhere, bringing its beauty and Light to the most desolate of terrains. Maybe one, maybe many will germinate to full fruition, they too may be wafted on the breeze to spread seeds of their own and shine as beautiful yellow suns for all to see, lighting the way for many more. Thus, only living in full, in the Light of the universe, rejecting the evil ways of spiritual creation, can bring about the changes humankind needs, to evolve beyond what it has sadly become.'

'It does sound very beautiful to live in this way but how do we change from being ensconced in what you call spiritual creation, to being able to live within this Light of the Universe?' asked Grace, again feeling the acceptance of everything Richard had said resounding deep within her body.

'It is all here, both Light and dark, within us all of the time, everything we have the possibility to be, flowing in and around us in every moment of every day. The Light is here first and is the body of the universe; spiritual creation is but a minute aberration here on this tiny insignificant planet within the enormity of all that space is,' he continued.

'The problem can be that we have lived this life, and perhaps many lifetimes before, developing different strategies and patterns of avoidance based within spiritual creation. We use these to circumvent everything that is there on offer to us to facilitate our inevitable return to the Light. Is it not natural that we would want to look more deeply into this, actually become students of ourselves and the two energies that abound, in order to uncover what the truth of life really is? Due to the nature of this dark and corrupt illusion, we have wandered, deluded, often aimlessly through the abomination it is, through all our many lifetimes up until the present, increasing the tension of our separation and an accumulation of internal hurts. We have built up ways and patterns of continually avoiding feeling these hurts by constructing artificial layers of protection, or what some might call defence mechanisms, around them which become both forms of ill-behaviours and sets of nefarious ideals and beliefs, that run on loop through both our conscious and unconscious hours of existence.

'It could be said that, in reality we have complicated everything there is about human life to avoid the simplicity of the truth of what we are and what we all will eventually return to. We have all lived before. During our many lives we have been both bathed fully in the Light and far away from it scurrying through the dark shadows, but one thing is certain, this is that you, I and many others have known this truth before. It could be said that we are closer to the truth in this life, that is why we are now so readily pulled to return to the Light. We may possibly make a swift return to the level of knowing, a level of connection to the Light that we have lived in previous lives, or it may take many lifetimes if we struggle to recover and heal from the hurts that we carry within us. It is also a question of dedication and obedience to the Light, for if we are not in obedience to the Light, then the only other option is to be in obedience to the opposite thereof. It is either black or white, Light energy or dark energy.'

'How do you know all of this? Where does it all come from? Is this information readily available and widespread and are there any teachers of it nearby?' She had asked four questions at once, totally engrossed in what Richard was offering.

He had a wry knowing smile on his face as he took the time to answer her questions, he instinctively knew that she had encountered the true work of the Light at some point in her previous incarnations and thought to himself joyfully, that she already knew that too.

'Grace, there have been many students and presenters of the teachings of Light, which to some also may be known as the teachings of the Ageless Wisdom. This almost certainly dates back as far as a teacher known as Hermes Trismegistus that could be as much as ten to twelve thousand years ago. Since then, there have been several well-known and as such to us, unknown teachers. Many of the known presenters of truth have been described as philosophers or prophets, such as Zarathustra, Patanjali, Pythagoras, Siddhartha Gautama, known as the Buddha, Yeshua, known as Jesus, Mohammed and many other lesser renowned servants of the Light. All of these brought through the teachings of Light, the Ageless Wisdom, in different ways, in their own expression thereof.

'Since their passing and the passing of subsequent years many of these teachings have been transformed and corrupted into religions that have given rise to much untold suffering through judgement, persecution, pain and bloodshed, taking the teachings so far from their original intent. Spiritual creation will always try to possess mankind in order to debase everything that is of or from truth. It will always attempt to create division and destruction. So too, has it contaminated the teachings of every Ageless Wisdom teacher of the past, often represented in the form of the modern-day religions now known to the world. Could it be possible that every religion we know today, is the result of the dark subversion of mankind? It is still possible to see the true good or the truth that was at the inception of the teachings, but you can also see that spiritual creation-controlled man has taken this truth to form it into his own handywork, for his own benefit. Where there is not true equality for all, both women, men and all persuasions, all people from all countries and all walks of life then maybe the truth has been left behind.

'As far as I know there are no living teachers located locally to us at this present time but there are several students such as myself that are knowledgeable in the Ageless Wisdom. There are always teachers here incarnated upon the Earth though not always accessible within all lands.

'Everything tempered by the force of spiritual creation will be corrupted. Our purpose is to live free from this corruption and as the beacon of Light, shine for everyone so that they too can feel the truth. To do this work, the work of Heaven on Earth is never for oneself alone, but for every being equally. When we align to the energy of true Light, we can then emanate the Truth based upon that energetic choice of Light over dark. There is only the one energetic truth and that comes from the Light. Doing good deeds from an alignment to spiritual creation is thus not in the energy of truth, it is still spiritual creation even if it seems to be of materialistic, physical or psychological benefit to some that are deemed to be deserving.'

Richard paused for a few moments realizing that all this could be too much for Grace to comprehend. He looked into her eyes, he could see her understanding, that she followed his discourse without too much confusion. He sensed that she was aligned to the vibration in his voice rather than trying to digest every word he spoke.

He continued, 'I know all of this because it has been given to me as I have aligned to the Light, becoming a student of it and myself, and because I have been aligned to it in many previous lives. This enables me to return to it when again called to do so. As you know I spent many years in India during which time I had the great fortune to meet a Swami who recognized me from a previous incarnation. He re-introduced me to the teachings of the Ageless Wisdom, allowing me to re-ignite the spark and re-kindle again the eternal flame within.

'This Swami was said to be ancient, at least one-hundred and twenty years old and yet when I met him, he appeared quite youthful, tall and strong, no more than fifty years old, without a grey hair in his long sleek, jet-black mane. This man of indecipherable age maintained his great health and vitality through his constant presence and almost flawless way of living. He considered everything in every moment, his full and unwavering attention was serenely focused upon the return of all beings to one truth and the one brotherhood we are all equally part of. It was he and the enormous wisdom that poured forth from him that assisted me in freeing myself from the constraints of the dark energies that controlled not only me but most other men on this planet.

'He also taught that many that do return to the study and living of the Ageless Wisdom teachings may suffer then from debilitating illness and disease and may even pass quickly from this life due to the sheer volume of amassed karma through lifetimes in the wilderness, that the body clears from the returning wanderer that is the spirit within. The clearing of karmic imprints occurs when the etheric reprobate embraces the light in full, thus inducing a swift return to its magnificent origins. This swift return and passing over from the present life can often be a preparation for incarnations to come.

'During my time in India and in particular my study with the Swami, I learned how to decipher the ancient Sanskrit language. I acquired a Sanskrit copy of the yoga sutras of Patanjali. Learning these living lessons in the original language has served me well and does so still today as each sutra offers new depths of wisdom each time it is read and then lived. You could say it presents to us an opportunity to choose and follow a true ever-deepening living way.'

Grace sighed, trying to think about what Richard had said, now becoming slightly distracted and a little confused, asking, 'Of what benefit has this work of Light been to you personally? How has it improved your life?'

Richard understandingly, chuckled gently. 'Grace, it is not for me, although initially and in part for many years, it may have been so, until I realized a fuller truth of what I had endeavoured upon. There was though an immediate knowing deep inside me that what was being revealed was ancient and true. Every particle in my body ignited, my whole being seemed to come alive to it. Whilst upon this return to the Light, the way of returning to the soulful being that I am, I realized that until I let go of the image of me being a self and all the emotions, beliefs and thoughts related and belonging to that self, the path would be shrouded by spiritual creation. The 'self' that we think we are, I found to be one of the greatest obstacles impeding our way back to the truth of who we genuinely are. The self is the great complicated illusion that is fooling the whole of mankind, for it is a fabricated reality that is but a temporary anomaly only existing as long as we all contribute to allow the lies to persist. Layer upon layer of convoluted deception concocted to confuse and reduce our innate magnificence to be but a morsel of what it truly is. Self is then the disabler of truth, harmony, love and radiating the brilliance of the universal beings that we all are. The temporal rewards and anguish of mankind that seem so real are the result of the deceit of the self. Rewards, or suffering, are not as they seem, but are rather a paltry guise, a thin veneer upon the tensions and hurts of separation from what we truly are.

'Contrary to the complication of the prevaricated self, it is quite simple. In truth there is no self, consequently there are no benefits for you nor I in being the I, the me, the self.

'As I gradually relinquish my own identification with the self-illusion, so has the life I am currently living improved, not as a goal but as a byproduct of this abnegation. Though I am fully active out in this world at my grand old age, I have become more and more detached and unaffected by both the atrocities and the everyday goings-on around me and yet I am more loving and caring of each and every person I see. I have no great desire or need for luxuries or fanciful possessions, though I do have this adequate home and more than enough savings to restfully live out whatever remains of this life. All in all, my life has improved because I am no longer captured by the stress and anxiety of the harsh world around me, for I know it is naught but an illusion being fed to us all by the forces of the dark.'

Once again, as Grace registered his voice deep within, something inside her felt decidedly uncomfortable, a part of her was squirming around, not wanting to hear all this talk of there being no self. A facet of herself protesting, how could there not be self, as this is all that I am? She forced herself to re-focus, to continue to hear the depth, vibration and beauty of Richard's words.

'Now, though it has not always been this way, I work not just to sell books. My purpose is to stand forth and allow the Light of truth to radiate through me to all others. My personal benefit from living in this way is that I have been released from the chains of spiritual creation, freeing me from the grand illusion, though I still must live within it, with and for all others.

'From the first moment I saw you, I felt the Light within emanating from you, Grace. I see it burn brighter each day. You and I have had many discussions prior to your hospitalization. I can feel that you have been called back to the Light and that you seek the truth in your own way, as do many others. You may reject all that I have to say to you, claim that it may not be for you, though I seriously doubt that. There need not be any persuasion, the truth will be sought out by each one of us whenever we are ready to assimilate it into our lives, for this is more than acquiring knowledge, it is a living form of wisdom that lays bare the deceit of time.

'I know I have presented you with a great deal to ponder upon, you need not try to digest it all immediately though all the answers are already within you and from one answer many others may grow. Do you have any more questions, and how do you feel about all that I have said?'

She shook her head and yawned, it was getting late and she was suddenly feeling tired. 'It is all so overwhelming. You are actually telling me that everything I have done, the way I live, everything that is around me, it's all untrue, all false, it seems absolutely preposterous and yet it feels palpable, as though I could almost touch it with my hands, with my whole body. I think I need to sleep on it and see how it all feels in the morning. It is time for me to clear up the kitchen and get ready to sleep. Thank you so much for all this Richard.'

George Darcaster arrived late in the evening in the pouring rain, at his house in Kensington as was planned three weeks prior. He fully expected his evening meal to be ready and to have his young housekeeper ready to serve him, fit and well after her recent procedure. As he alighted from the Hansom carriage, paid the cabby and turned to look at his house shrouded in darkness he knew immediately that something was amiss. He scurried through the cold winter rain up to the house, fumbling in his overcoat pocket for the keys, getting thoroughly drenched. He let himself into the darkened hallway, dropped his trunk noisily on the tiled floor and shouted angrily for his housekeeper. He furiously searched the drawers in the hallway for a packet of those Swedish safety matches and eventually, through a whole torrent of swearing and vehement grumbling, he lit several gaslights around the house, promising to strangle the housekeeper if he ever laid his eyes upon her.

George climbed the stairs up to the top floor where Grace's room was situated. The door was wide open, he went in and lit the wall lamp. The covers on the bed were turned down and the white sheet was covered in a huge dark stain, his face physically dropped in shock at the extent of what was surely dried blood. His mind went immediately to how he must discard all the evidence of what happened here, who did he need to contact to clean up this mess and not have anyone investigate further?

Is she alive, he thought, do the Metropolitan police know anything about this? He checked every room in the house, finding no trace of her. He then realized he had not looked through her belongings and returned to her room to find everything she owned had been taken. He felt a little relief and then his anger intensified and he went back to the hallway to pick up his trunk. As he picked it up, he noticed the trunk was sitting over another stain across the tiled floor, lifting the trunk he also saw her set of keys lying on the floor nearby. More proof that she was alive and had fled. As he turned to walk to his study, he noticed the envelope on the table addressed to himself in her handwriting. Once again, he dropped the trunk with a dull thud and proceeded to pick up and open the envelope. It read:

Mr. George Darcaster,
You will notice that I have left your employ and any monies owed to me, you may keep. After you left the house the last morning you were here, during the proceeding days I became progressively worse and the bleeding did not stop. As I was leaving the house to try to get some help, I collapsed in the hallway but fortunately I had opened the door and was discovered by a kind passer-by and consequently rushed to the hospital. Due to expert help I survived, I had very little blood left in my body and was very close to death, but they pulled me back from the brink.
All this is registered with the doctor at the hospital and consequently deposited in the hands of a lawyer, included in this deposit is a full list of every episode that you have brutally abused me for your own evil pleasure, every threat and every sexual misdeed, every beating and exploitation. This will never see the light of day as long as you do not try to find me or come in contact with me in any way. I hope never to see your person again.
Yours sincerely
Grace Lightfoot

George was absolutely fuming, he read the letter again. He knew he could be put in a very difficult position as his wife had already substantial grounds to divorce him based upon his previous malefactions, and that would surely cost him a pretty penny. He felt somewhat helpless, not knowing where she was, not knowing what she might do in the future. He needed to get the upper hand somehow. He considered that her parents were vital members of the household in Manchester and that he could use them in some way, but he knew how important they were to his wife and that she would never go along with harming them in any way, let alone terminating their employ.

She was not threatening him now and if he just let her go then he would probably not have any problem with her. He should get everything cleaned up and organize a new housekeeper as quickly as possible before the next visit of his wife. He would somehow have to explain to her that Miss Lightfoot had left his employ without any notice and simply disappeared. There was also the considerable possibility though that his wife already knew the housekeeper had left. If Miss Lightfoot's parents have been informed, they may inform his wife so he must tell her at the first possible opportunity.

He would pay some of his men from the factory handsomely to come over with a cart and dispose of the bed and anything else that could be incriminating. This could be quickly arranged in the morning from Canning Town.

He realized that he had no food and nothing was prepared for him to stay. He would have to find an alternative abode until everything was returned to normal. He gathered all the necessary items and locking up the house again, he walked with his trunk down to the end of the street and took a cab. He barked indignantly at the cabby, 'Take me to the Grosvenor Hotel, and do it quickly.'

Not coincidently, the following day a letter arrived addressed to Mr. and Mrs. Arthur Lightfoot. It was from Grace who had, with the help of Richard sent this letter to inform her parents that she no longer worked for George Darcaster and had taken similar employ at a smaller establishment in another area of London. She did not give them an address to reply to and they immediately became worried even though the letter asked them not to be so. She told them that she was in very good health and her employer was a kind elderly gentleman, she could not have asked for a better place to be. She also promised to write to them regularly and would come to visit sometime in the near future.

Later that day the housekeeper, Evelyn Lightfoot, Grace's mother was conversing, as she often did, with Alexandria Darcaster, Mr. George Darcaster's wife and lady of the manor. They spoke about local events and happenings, neighbours and children and inevitably Grace became the topic of the conversation. Evelyn told Mrs. Darcaster about the letter she had received, that Grace had left the Darcaster house in London and was now with employ elsewhere. This had been quite disturbing news for Alexandria for she knew her husband well and immediately suspected that he was somehow to blame. Her mother told Mrs. Darcaster that Grace was in good health and thought well of her new employer.

Alexandria felt very uneasy and would certainly question her scoundrel of a husband when he next arrived home. She thanked Evelyn and abruptly ended their conversation saying that she had something important to attend to.

Three weeks later, Grace had physically fully recovered from her ordeal and could now do all the household chores without a problem. Through the regular conversations with Richard, she did feel somewhat lighter in her disposition but there was still a cloud of unresolved pain that cast a shadow across her demeanour. It was very difficult for her to let go of all the rape, abuse, violence and the trauma of the illegal abortion that had almost cost her life. There was a burning, unforgiving resentment and hatred that twisted in her belly, a relentless abhorrence gnawing at her being and the reoccurring revulsion at the images of her ordeals that she couldn't seem to release from her mind. She had said to Richard that she could tell him everything that had happened but to express the details of this nightmare she had lived through had, so far, eluded her.

She knew instinctively that if she did not elucidate clearly, the pain and devastation that she still held within could hold her in its wicked grasp to deteriorate and possibly destroy the quality of the rest of her life. She decided that the next time she and Richard spoke she would divulge the full and complete magnitude of her personal desecration.

As often was the case, after dinner they sat in his study-cum-library in the old threadbare armchairs and chatted about all things, both daily practical tasks and duties and deeper more existential subjects. This evening Grace, as she had promised herself, had opened the conversation about how she was feeling, the reoccurring nightmares and the ill-feelings that wracked her body.

Richard, in his wisdom had simply stated that the hurts that we carry have to be felt because if they become buried beneath layers of avoidance, they become harder to deal with. His gentle advice was to feel them but don't let them consume you. Then there is the process of describing them, expressing everything that has happened and all that we feel about it. It is in a way a method of taking control, gaining ownership of them and in doing so it enables us to release them, cleanse them from our body, then throw them onto the bonfire where they belong, never to return.

They sat late into the evening: Grace described everything that had happened to her, from the first time he had forced himself upon her to how she had resisted and had been beaten for her efforts. She described how aggressive and roughly he had treated her, choked her until she had fainted. Each time he would come, he had beaten her into submission. She told him how she had in the end given up and not resisted, not wanted to be beaten any more. She told him how her skin crawled, how disgusted she was with herself, the feelings of ending her life, throwing herself in the river or under the path of an omnibus, anything to stop the pain.

She had adapted, accepting the abuse, as his visits were quite infrequent, and she had much time for herself in between. This would be her lot in life, and she excused it by saying to herself that it was much better than many others, much better than living on the streets. She had come to think that she, as a servant girl, didn't really deserve better than this coming from such a lowly background. The pregnancy and the forced abortion had been a stark reality check, bringing her back to her sense of propriety, breaking the hold of what had become her ingrained submissive thoughts and passive acceptance.

Everything came out, she expressed how she felt about all that had happened. There were floods of tears and sobbing as her pain was released. At the end of the evening there were sparks of relief and yawns of tiredness and exhaustion from the discharge of the poisonous energy from her body. She was completely drained and yet she felt new life running through her veins. This was a huge clearing of much of the ill-feelings, the pain and emotions she had been holding on to.

She literally fell into bed that evening and slept a deep dreamless sleep for ten hours with no reoccurring nightmares, no tossing and turning, just complete stillness and tranquility.

Never had she slept this well in her adult life. She awoke the following morning in a new light. She realized that this was potentially the greatest release from the captivity of her past she had ever experienced. Suddenly though, she felt the clouds of old hurtful memories beginning to form. Sitting up in bed she simply brushed them away, thinking, I'm not letting you take control of me today; this is my body and this is my life. She got out of bed and joyfully engaged with the day.

When she arrived in the kitchen looking a little sheepish, Richard was sitting at the table eating the breakfast he had prepared for both of them.

'Breakfast is served,' he remarked merrily, 'I trust you are well slept?'

She smiled openly at his joviality. 'Yes Sir, very well, thank you so much for your kind regard,' she replied, joining in the merriment.

'How are you this fine morning?' he continued in the same vein.

'I feel wonderful, our conversation yesterday evening has certainly helped me clear out some of the hurtful debris I have carried around with me, especially in regard to my time in London. I slept so well and awoke this morning feeling somehow resurrected and fuller in myself than before, my joy for life rekindled and revitalized. You are truly a master of human cognizance and perception, again you saved me from a dreadful fate,' Grace replied gleefully.

Richard grinned. 'It is not I that saved you, I am but a willing catalyst, it can only be you that chooses to save yourself, or a more fitting description would be, it is you that chooses to walk once more the path of truth upon this earth. As for being a master, yes, I am, as are all others who choose to live from and with the Light, which as you know is equally on offer for everyone. We all have the same vast unrealized potential to bring through the wisdom of the Universe, it is always simply a breath or a movement away.

'It is a beautiful thing to express in full all that you have inside and all that flows through you, holding nothing back. For in holding back, the energy of the 'unsaid' remains within the body, becoming malignant and ultimately could be the cause of a multitude of illness or disease, both of mind and body. I can already sense the change in you Grace, the change brought about by simply expressing all the pain you held inside. This has cleared much of the ill that was retained within your body. You may well discover that there is yet more to clear from your body, there may always be new layers of undisclosed and guarded secrets of the past to uncover. We have experienced so much during so many lifetimes and we still walk with the patterns and momentums of the past until every stone is turned and every hurt is vanquished.

'This true way can be walked with your newly uncovered joy; it cannot be walked with trepidation and reticence. The process can, at times, be painful but the expansion on offer can be truly divine, the pain is only the result of how you choose to perceive it, welcome it for what it can bring. The clearing and healing, that comes not just for you but for everyone you know, the whole of mankind, for it is a fact that all and everyone are interconnected and duly affected by everything in some way.

'So, Grace let us make an agreement here and now, that there never remain words unsaid, no matter how hard or painful they may be to utter, let them always be spoken in full. There may be times when you or I walk in the wilderness of dark spiritual creation and do not feel to speak, we may lock ourselves away to avoid contact with each other or others. When this occurs and is perceived, it is truly the moment to seek reconnection as this can be the next offering, the next step in our return to the full embodiment of the universal Light. For without doubt, in the time to come there will be moments such as these, please remember it is not perfection we seek, for hidden within perfectness are the devious tendrils of spiritual creation. There is no true perfection whilst we dwell here on Earth, though it can be said that we may well reach an enigmatic state of perfect imperfection.'

Grace became serious. 'I will always strive to express fully in everything that I have to say, always. It does seem so unjust that society does not allow this, that we are separated and segregated, only those with opulent wealth that control the general public are allowed to speak what is for them the truth and yet for most others, most common folk, this is but convenient prevarication. Must we only speak truth in one-another's company lest we be denounced and ridiculed, even arrested and incarcerated. How do we give this to others that don't know what we are talking about, this must be for everyone, it is surely wisdom all should have access to?'

Richard spoke again. 'It is not so simple and the powers of spiritual creation fight the Light of truth at every step. They will do anything to prevent the awakening of the masses that have willingly succumbed to its control. There can be no preaching, persuading or converting of others. This becomes a need for others to understand and to change and in that wanting lies once again the deceptive control of the dark forces. As it is with you and me, Grace, there is some kind of universal plan, a magnetic pull to meet and communicate with those that are constellated to be together in one way or another, to be with those that are ready to awaken and step upon the way of soulful return. When connection to the Light is chosen, the power of the Universe can impulse through us and actualize the events and incidents that are called for. Sometimes it may be extreme and life-threatening as you experienced or it could be a simple sentence, a look from a passerby or even sharing a carriage on a train journey. Nothing is coincidental, everything means something, nothing can be nothing and everything has to be something of great meaning. Within the Light there is nothing of insignificance, everything is equally glorious and majestic.

Grace smiled as she felt the absolute gloriousness of what Richard was saying and felt how his words warmed the particles of her body and she felt at-one with him.

'It is often, not the words that are spoken rather the reflective movement and the heavenly vibration, conveying the offering of Light, to be at one with all, that may or may not be seen, though at some level will always be felt. It is within every facet of our lives, every breath and every gesture, thought and intention, absolutely all that we do is the whole that we reflect to every man, woman and child. No matter how we align, to this energy or that, to the Light or to the dark, all that we take in is all that we bring through to everyone both incarnate and disincarnate.'

She nodded agreeing completely with the whole of her being as Richard continued.

'As far as the way of society is concerned, yes, it is unjust, cruel and often heartless. It is almost devoid of the true truth; deceit, greed and corruption abound, yet there is Light, there are those that exude veracity and transparent candor. We mostly look upon our lives in the context of this one life we currently live, at least most people I know view it this way. They see life often from the point of view of how it is for themselves first, their own family and close friends second and don't really care too much about what happens to the rest of humanity. Many wealthy industrialists and nobles attend their churches at the weekends to appease their selected deities, whilst during the week they perpetrate despicable acts upon thousands, in the name of their preferred God's – control, greed, debauchery, comfort, fame, luxury and affluence.

'They do not consider the effects of Karma. As I said earlier, they view life in terms only of this single life. They live at this current time, convincing themselves so, when deep down they all know that they are much more than just humans in physical bodies, a not inconsiderable fact they choose to ignore. Life then becomes exclusively about them and theirs, about what they can achieve in this life or at the other end of the scale of wealth, about how they can best survive or where to get the next meal from, how to feed themselves and their children. Everything they do, no matter what station in life becomes insular, more inward focused, more and more separated from each other.

'Karma is the great leveler, even a despicable despot has to die at some point. When this happens there will be a certain recompence and then when this person re-incarnates, they may well be born again as a victim of despotism, or may come again as a sick and outcast leper, for in the end it will be to reap as is sown. Be a purveyor of evil in one or more lives, Karma will bring its timely riposte with its own form of counterpoise, thusly no crime committed is without reciprocation and forfeit.

'Every time we align to spiritual creation, we build up our negative karmic abundance. This will subsequently determine our location in and for our next life or lives to come, where we will again be given opportunities to align to either the Light of the Soul or spiritual creation. Aligning to and moving in the Light enables the purging of ill karmic footprints and re-imprinting of the ill-imprints of spiritual creation with truth, bringing about the possibility of the accumulation of a positive karmic balance.

'There is also, one unmistakable truth that cannot be refuted; we are not from here, we cannot stay here, we all must return from whence we came; our future is written in the past and the past therefore is our future. There is no other option, there are only levels of delay. No matter how much we try to avoid our future, how much we prolong this illusion of life on Earth, we all will one day return to what we truly are.'

Grace enquired: 'How is this return to where we came from supposed to happen, if we all must align and live from the Light to get there? Just look at all the crime, all the injustice, the nauseating inequality, is there anyone living in this way now? None that I can see. Look what has happened to me, this takes place all the time and others are not so lucky as I have been to have someone like you come along, that really cares. How long will it take for people to change?'

Richard paused to ponder a little upon her words. 'Yes, there is great resistance from humanity to re-align to the intelligence and communication of the Universe, the Light of God. It is difficult to explain the All that is. Suffice to say that the All is accessible to everyone and within that access lie the answers to everything. The more we surrender to the truthful Light, the greater levels of access to the Ageless Wisdom can be attained. This is a process both of personal healing and a renouncement of every construct we have believed to be truth, that isn't.

'From birth, in this current life as in previous lives, we have been schooled within the prevailing ill-conceived systems in a way to keep us in check, to know our place and not step out of line. All the way from a young baby girl to now as a woman, you have been taught through the restrictive and destructive guidelines of this corrupt society that you must serve men, that you do as you are told, that you are not as important as the boys or men, you are not good enough and many other divisive indoctrinations. This is complete and utter nonsense as everyone is the same, everyone is equal, the same in their essence, anything that implies difference or some being better than others is an obvious sign of the dark forces being at play. This more often than not results in girls and women having issues with their own dignity and worth, from taking on unobtrusive reticence to being completely submissive and introverted.

'In other words, society is set up for men in general, and in particular, rich men, that see themselves as superior and entitled. It is they that make society's rules and regulations, it is they that control what women can and cannot do, they decide that women are second class citizens, at best. They set up women to be crushed by this male tendentious culture that they are convinced by the ill-forces of spiritual creation to think they own and control. The real truth is that they are the ones that are owned by the consciousness that they are affiliated with, the consciousness within spiritual creation, that we can call 'supremacy'. They are mere puppets dangling from the strings of the dark forces, thinking in their self-sanctified, conceited arrogance that they are supreme, completely deluded and deceived by this evil force from within spiritual creation.'

Thoughts had begun to spin around in Grace's head, drawing her away from the attention she had on Richard's words. She realized that she had slouched down in her chair and immediately sat up straight again, re-aligning her to presence and allowing her to re-connect with the wisdom of Richard's words.

'It is not the evil men of this world that we should hate for they are just the same as we are, the only difference is how deeply within spiritual creation they have been submerged, how much of themselves they have conceded. Yes, they have chosen this alluring fate though it is not for us to judge, that is the lot of powers beyond our control, for what is enacted in the name of spiritual creation shall surely one day return to the Light via the re-imprinting of their karmic misdeeds. When in our lives we encounter such wayward beings, for in essence they are the same as we all are, it is not a moment for avoidance or fear, it is a moment for love, acceptance and a grand opportunity for learning, taking further steps on the path of return. For each person, such an actuality is constellated by the universe to afford us a learning which gives the possibility to evolve further back to our future, and the future of all our fellow beings either incarnated now with us or still residing on the spiritual planes of life.

'Everything we encounter in life is a potential lesson that could aid us upon our way back to becoming the soulful beings that we truly are.

'And about this journey back, it is as you may imagine, different for every one of us, different for each individual person. There may be similarities, but everyone has come to the point in life they currently occupy by way of their own separate route and in doing so, have their own set of experiences and their own sets of hurts and pains they have suffered and may have concealed within themselves; they have also built up their own portfolio of ideals and beliefs. Therefore, Grace your own set of hurts, ideals and beliefs are your own self-chosen obstacles preventing you from accessing the Truth. It is your own responsibility to explore, accept and release them from your body. Deal with everything, let nothing remain undiscovered. Lay everything out, feel it and let it go.

'This may seem an insurmountably daunting task to begin with, but that is simply the poisoned voices of the dark forces whispering to us that it is so. Its never-ending goal is to delay as long as possible from the inevitable, undeniable return to Truth. For the true truth, which is pure Light, lovingly encapsulates yet obliterates the insignificant flaw which is spiritual creation. Once you understand how the dark forces work it is much simpler to disarm them. If you can look at it from this point of view, that our default state, our natural way of being is Light and that the dark continually tries to cloud over to stop us feeling the power of the sun. The clouds of spiritual creation have become ingrained in the way we live our lives. They control the patterns and behaviours, our thoughts and beliefs and yet we know the sun is always there and it will in the end shine through the darkest of clouds.

'If our basic nature, our very essence, is luminosity and the brilliance of pure Light, the power is here within us to burn away all the conniving threads of spiritual creation, all of these congenital and implanted ways of

'being' hold little sway as we move in sequence and in collaboration with the All. It is understanding the magnitude of the power the energy of the true Light can bring through. At the same time, it is a new and yet familiar positioning with an instinctive comprehension of exquisiteness without any need for perfectness. No expectation of getting it right or being wrong but a humility of knowing that through this alignment all that is given to you is not for you alone, it is for everyone. It is not something to take home and keep in secret for the benefit of oneself, it simply does not work in that way. It is something that comes through the body simply to reflect and shine out again for all others. The Ageless Wisdom can never be owned or held in place, it can only ever pass through a vessel or being, giving them the choice to live from it or to reject it.'

Grace interjected. 'It all seems so elusive, so far away from where I am in my life at this moment in time. It feels too much for me to comprehend when I try to think about what needs to be done.'

Richard continued: 'All this said, it is understandable that this may seem overwhelming at first and there are some basic steps that can be taken, although everyone has their own levels of understanding so it will vary greatly. One simply beautiful yet grossly underestimated practice is that of a loving self-regard. This may sound a little narcissistic to begin with, yet ultimately it is almost exactly the opposite of narcissism. You could say that narcissism is the dark perversion of loving self-regard which appears as superiority. Through true self-love, in the end, you do not love yourself for your self, you love you for everyone, including your self. There can be many components, facets and angles that make up the whole of what loving oneself may be.

'There is also the reconnection with our innermost selves which is truly loving and caring and can be done quite simply in just a few minutes.

'We can try a little experiment if you don't mind, a short meditation.'

She nodded willingly.

'Find a comfortable sitting position that will allow you to sit still and undisturbed for the next few minutes.

'Bring your attention to your body, consider your whole being for a few moments. Try to feel all the different elements of what makes you the complete, perfectly imperfect living person that you are.

'Just close your eyes and feel the whole of you from top to toe, feel your every particle, stay in and with your body.

'If your mind begins to wander just bring it back to your body, be with you, within the whole that you are.

'Feel everything that you are, feel each divine particle.

'Experience the flow of each in and out breath.

'Feel the sacred connection to the All through your heart.

'Feel the everything that you are both within and beyond the physical delineation of your body.

'Can you get a sense that you are much, much more than just a human body with a human ego?

'You are a part of the universe. You are made up of universal particles that maintain your universal connection.

'Maintain the awareness of your breath and the delicate quality of its movement.

'Do you see, hear and feel the wayward spirit within that wants to drive your thoughts away from the magnificence that you are?

'Can you feel the pull to return to this sacred place that is your soul and the majesty of the All that is?

'Open your eyes and stay with your body and the connection to all that is.

'In just a few minutes we can access or reconnect to the divine communication that is from Heaven. It is with us all of the time, we ourselves choose to not be connected or we actually choose to be connected to the dark forces instead.'

Grace opened her eyes; she could feel the unfathomable stillness of her innermost being. She smiled gently and nodded in her agreement and oneness with Richard.

He continued: 'Loving self-regard is deeply caring for all that you are within, including the delinquent spirit that seeks to constantly disrupt, disturb and delay the return to this wondrous unanimity that we are all from. On a more practical level it also means connecting to your body and listening to the messages your own physical body sends to you. Not allowing abuse or abusing your own body in any way by overriding these messages and this applies all the time and in everything you do. As everything that happens affects, in some way, how you move and hold the body, the way you think about your body and your whole self, anything you put into the body and every intention thereof. Everything starts with how you regard yourself, and if that regard is not loving then how can it be possible to hold others in any true form of loving regard?'

Grace listened intently to Richard's words and wondered about her own way of being. In particular, she considered the way she thought about herself. She realized how much self-judgement she had lived in and correspondingly how she had judged other people, not necessarily in the words that she spoke but certainly some of the thoughts she had. She had innumerable times berated herself for her own lack of worthiness, particularly during the last few years in London.

Richard continued. 'Practising this loving way leads to deeper awareness, a greater attention to every detail of life and thus a deeper form of caring for oneself. It encourages the development of nurturing daily routines and rituals like meditation, that support the ever-unfolding connection to the divine universe, emphasizing the power of presence within each movement we make and every word we speak. Self-nurturing and self-care are integral parts of developing a true loving way, but to others this may be seen as self-indulgence or even egocentric. It may also feel a little this way at first, until it is fully appreciated that it is being done to enhance our service to the All, for the All. It may also lead to a deepening within oneself which opens up opportunities for profound levels of healing and the letting go of unresolved hurts we often carry with us throughout life. This true form of self-love can be an enormous step along the way back to our true natural state, which is, in simplicity an observing, all-beholding stillness, a state of being love.

'By focusing on this nurturing way, we may also discern what love truly is. Love has nothing to do with emotions. It is actually a re-attainable and completely natural state of being, a beholding, caring observation that exercises no form of comparison, competition, jealousy or judgement. Of all the emotion-based depictions of love, none hold its true meaning. All are emotional, reaction based, none contain true harmony, stillness and joy, and none evoke the real truth in any way.

'Strange as it may sound, it allows everything that is needed, to happen in order for each individual to unfold along their own individual paths back to the same universal One Soul that we all come from. If a person has to learn through falling victim to a robbery or another through an accident or illness, then this may well come to pass. These are opportunities we are continuously given as offerings of soulful expansion. If we deny what is on offer, at a certain point in time, a more obvious message or event may come along giving once again an opportunity to evolve. It could be that everything that happens to us at any time may be an offering to be discerned. We could use emotional reactions in order to avoid what is there to be understood and embodied or we may learn to observe free from emotion and respond in truth to the offering of evolution we are being given.

'And it is plain for all those who want to actually see it as it is. Humanity is mercilessly out of control, the majority clearly living firmly entrenched in the realms of spiritual creation, living life almost entirely from their emotional reactions. They often behave like depraved animals as you know only too well, and you have felt that brutal force of that depravity many times during your sojourn at the Darcaster house. This is all part of what we could call the dark plan, using emotion, to divide and conquer, to instill hate, fear, revulsion, passion, desire, lust and a multitude of other destabilizing emotional ways, in its vain attempts to prolong this constructed illusion of human life and postpone the inevitable return of all beings back to the One Soul. We are en-masse bamboozled and ensnared, as we constantly choose to not be what we truly are, not because we don't know better, we choose not to know or understand what is going on due to our on-going momentum through lifetimes past and of course our serpentine attraction to the attachment of being an individual.'

With that, Richard smiled and stood up to leave for the book-stall. Grace sat awhile after he had gone, pondering upon everything he had expressed, feeling the effects of his words within her body. She wondered about her own choices that kept her entrenched within spiritual creation and for how long she had avoided living from the Light. Had she needed to be abused so horrendously to enable her to break away from the clutches of the dark plan? How many lifetimes had she wandered aimlessly in the wilderness of spiritual creation?

Chapter 5

ROAR'S REVELATIONS

He awoke twelve hours later knowing fully that he was here in his own body but at the same time he had the feeling of some of the lived experiences from what he truly felt was his previous life as Grace, much of what she had experienced and the words she had heard now vibrated within him. The wisdom of what he once emanated seemed to infect the particles of his body, the potential of what he could reflect to others almost brimming over.

It quickly faded into a fog of concern as thoughts of his present quandary crept into his conscious rumination. He was swept into a pulse-raising samba of speculation, pulling him in all directions until his body began to react. Coldly sweating he felt his own blood pressure rising as his heart began to pound. He could feel all his senses on edge as his fight or flight response kicked in. Panic was set to stampede, when from somewhere deep inside he felt a message, 'Breathe Roar, breathe gently, follow your breath, come back to yourself, just breathe.' He did just that, he lay there breathing, focusing on his in-breath and his out-breath, following its passage in and out of his body, reconnecting with himself, breathing his own breath, calm washed over him again as he returned to the present and no longer allowed the distracting and disrupting barrage of thoughts to assail his being.

He came back to more of the stillness he had first awakened with and feeling more removed from the minor panic attack that he had just a few moments ago suffered, considered objectively this episode he had experienced. He gave himself space to contemplate. This was quite unusual for him as he was generally somewhere else, rather than being present in his own body, his mind would be thinking about what should happen next, next and next.

He sighed to himself as the truth came to him, that at some point in time (he could not remember when, it felt like it had been going on forever) he had started to use fabrication and beguilement as effective weapons of getting from life exactly what he wanted. He could see how, for him, this had become a deeply-rooted pattern of behaviour, so much so that it was impossible to conceive of the magnitude of his own deceit and self-inveracity. Living his life, based on untruths, had necessitated him always trying to stay one step ahead of everyone else he was in relationship with, family, friends, work colleagues. It was all the same, it was the way he was.

The original lie, or lies whenever they were, and all this sickening congestion within actually feels very ancient and stymied. Maybe it was a way of being that was so deeply rooted within him that it may have been something he had indulged in during other life-times, a pattern from within that was easy to repeat? Although, his dreams of Grace, and her inherent honesty seemed to contradict this, at least for this one other life.

Still the problem with a life based on lies is that it always requires new lies to cover the lies of the past, it becomes an unending chain that is almost impossible to break when it becomes so ineradicable. In addition, he was realizing that the way mankind lived was a monumental lie which meant that he was lying from within a plethora of lies. So, this is how it has been until now, until I almost died and still the behaviour does not want to relinquish its hold. The only way forward is to repudiate all of it, to completely abandon everything that was his normal, but in truth a normal yet utterly abusive way of life. He shivered at the thought that nothing could be the same. He was after all a bon vivant, a connoisseur of life and all its comfort, luxury and licentiousness. He felt the gloom descend as he thought about how difficult it would be for him now, donning the energy of a victim of life, he started to sink deeper into the doldrums. Suddenly he realized that he could not wander onto the path of hopelessness and pulled himself out of whatever energy had grabbed him, he sat bolt upright and returned to himself in the present.

Positively, he gently and playfully admonished himself. He thought the first step is to realize what has been going on without putting expectations on any speed of change, or even change at all. There was so much here to be relinquished and yet everything that he needed was readily available, at any time, within his own body. It's incredible to feel how far removed the life he had been living was from what his body, his dreams and his past life were telling him at this moment. How easy though, it was to slip from one state of being into the other, how old thoughts could almost instantaneously and surreptitiously take over the clarity without him even noticing. How dedicated he had been to his injurious lifestyle, how much effort it required to maintain all the lies and deceit, how complicated it all had been. He had thrown himself into it wholeheartedly, completely obedient and overly enthusiastic, he had made it his living way. What if it was possible to have the same obedience to living from the Light, from absolute honesty, how would that be?

He realized that living from the Light and honesty would be much simpler, it would actually be free from complication, there would be no deceit, nothing to hide, complete transparency. Just the thought of this made him feel lighter and more joyful, then immediately darker and solemn as thoughts of all the decadent pleasures he would have to renounce began to spin around in his head. Images of a beautiful, naked Anneli lying prone in front of him, her firm, sensuous, athletic body anticipating ... he broke off the chain of thought. Surely there was a more temperate path to be taken, knowing the true answer even before he had asked himself the question. There was only dedication, either to the dark or to the Light, although to move from one to the other was not without its pitfalls. A lifetime of wallowing in spiritual creation with all the ingrained patterns of behaviour would not be easy to relinquish, decades of willingly submitting himself and his thoughts to dark control, accepting the rewards of his obedience to them.

He felt a wave of guilt sweep over him as he realized that even in his daydreams, he could betray Elisabeth. He stopped and thought about the feeling of guilt that had been so strong a few moments ago, where did that come from, what is guilt really, is it a true feeling or is it an emotional reaction? He felt it was judgement of the fact that he had fantasized about Anneli, that this was a wrongdoing, but is that truthful? Right and wrong predicate the guilt via judgement based on one's individual ideals and beliefs, but are these individual ideals and beliefs true? Everyone builds up their own set of ideals and beliefs and none are exactly the same, so who or what decides what truth is?

How can there be truth if everyone has a different truth, it doesn't make sense. How can laws be made if no two truths are the same? Laws are made by Governments. Governments are supposed to govern for the people, but this is no longer true. They are influenced by lobbyists from large corporations and mega-rich financiers to create favourable laws for chosen companies and people, to enable them to make more profit, avoid paying tax and to ignore rules and regulations that protect the individual members of society, society as a whole and the environment. Basically, this is a description of corruption, the whole system is fraudulent from top to bottom. This also means that almost every living person is tainted by it, to a certain level due to ideals and beliefs and their own personal view on what the truth actually is.

By this time his head was spinning, and he felt that he was starting to become a little confused as he asked himself multiple questions at the same time. He stopped, breathed again slowly to regain his composure allowing the questions to come out. What is it like to not be corrupt then? Does that mean that anyone not free from ideals and beliefs must be contaminated by it, in that case what is the true truth, if that even exists?

Another thought suddenly appeared: what then is going on with all the mainstream religions around the world, are they also infected by this debasement, are they also peddling lies and deceit? Is there anything, any institution, any living being that is free from this? Has there ever been anyone in history untarnished by this dark force of nepotism?

He knew the answers to all his own questions as he also knew instinctively that everyone else knows the reply to all intrinsic questions and yet, like him choose to deny themselves access to these answers, in fact they mostly refuse to even ask the questions in the first place. Yes, there is a true truth, it comes from a place of surrender and spaciousness with acceptance of the All, without judgement, competition or comparison. It is a space within us all. This space has been shrouded and buried deep within, covered by layer upon layer of concocted and defiled illusion-based ideals and defence mechanisms, created by and in reaction to the evil forces of spiritual creation that seek to control all men and in doing so, all earth-bound sentient beings.

He realized that there may well be groups or organizations somewhere upon the planet that do live in a way that affords them a true connection to Ageless Universal Wisdom, although he had not, until recently witnessed any evidence of this. He felt that it was a matter of opening up and enabling connection to this true source of wisdom and intelligence. There were in fact simple choices that were also connected to detaching from the multitude of emotions that seemed to enshroud, confuse and complicate everything. Consequently, it followed that ideals and beliefs are connected to and controlled by our emotional choices that become entrenched within our bodies. He knew that everything he could remember, everything he had experienced so far in this life had been for him and him alone. Within that realization it was possible for him to deduce that these had been emotional choices simply for the pleasure and excitement, seemingly oblivious to what was the deep disregard for himself, his own body and to the lives of so many others, which was also a form of ingrained self-abuse and vulgar arrogance. This was choosing not to live from the true source of wisdom and intelligence, this was the exact opposite. It was black and white, dark and Light and his way had been living from the dark domain of spiritual creation. He had not been connected to the Light from whence the true truth emanates.

He continued to answer the questions himself. There may have been teachers and prophets in the past, there may even be teachers and presenters of the truth somewhere on the Earth right now, probably on the opposite side of the planet, in Australia, perhaps? It seems though that there is very little Light shining through the darkness at this moment in time. Although he could now feel that there was Light shining on him, otherwise he would not have been given this wake-up call and all the messages both from the past and in the present. He had lived under the auspices of spiritual creation for so long and what he had seen and done in his lifetime was lightyears away from the truth. He confirmed for himself that he knew everything that was corruption and in doing so he automatically knew the opposite, that both of these options were a question of obedience to one way or the other, the energy of separative spiritual creation or the energy of the Light of the Soul.

He also realized that this Light shining upon him, was shining upon everyone, it's just that in general we live our lives and choose to be oblivious to the Light that shines brightly, all the time, for everyone. He contemplated the wake-up call he had been given, that it had almost ended his life. Could it be that he had received calls to attention, messages from the Light many times prior to this one, that he had ignored them until it was so severe that he could no longer ignore it. Is this what is happening to everyone, is this why lifestyle sickness and disease is now completely out of control? What then will it take to shake humanity out of this deceitful spiritual creation-fueled stupor they are caught up in?

Furthermore, there seems to be some truth and there may be some truthful and honest people within all religions he thought, although looking at some of the actions and atrocities carried out in the name of certain religions it is easy to see that they have been corrupted by the dark mendacity of spiritual creation. Divisive politicians bear false witness, gaslight, and defraud the public in the name of their chosen religion and the deity they call God. They mercilessly, often unilaterally, surreptitiously at the behest of the armaments industry, go to war upon nations that otherwise refuse their overt attempts to control them. Priests, self-proclaimed men of God, sexually abuse young children, clergymen of many denominations indoctrinate, incite and recruit in the cause of holy war, encouraging others to perform evil deeds. Is it not so, that even the most minor of these evil deeds is of pure corruption and therefore infects the whole that it is part of?

It could be said that most religions come from the same source, from world teachers, often called prophets, whose words convey the truth that comes from the Light, which could be seen as the one true religion. That it may be the wisdom and intelligence of the Universe presented through these teachers and prophets of the past and present. Thus, the truth of what and who we are is presented for all and how easy it seems to be for derision, defamation and delusion to hail its poison upon anyone presenting it.

Sadly, humankind, corrupt and deluded, controlled by the dark ills of spiritual creation, takes these words to form them into a vehicle for their own self-serving, individualistic and nefarious purpose. Thus, leaving behind all Truth and moving it into debasement and depravity.

Every time the truth is bestowed upon humanity, every time a true presenter emerges laying forth the wisdom of the ages, the forces of spiritual creation will recoil. Then they will, through the masses of controlled men, aggress, disparage, defame and stigmatize in an attempt to diminish the Light that is shone. They will assiduously assault the Light with every weapon within their vindictive poisonous arsenal, they will stop at nothing for they know they are originally from the Light and vainly fight against their own inevitable return from whence they came.

Roar stopped, where had all this reverie come from, he pondered, what was all this Light and dark energy, all the foresight and wisdom? He felt clearly that he had been fed this wisdom from a place beyond himself, that there was no way he could have just thought these thoughts, he realized that he was some form of conduit for something much greater than himself. He was beginning to understand, in more ways than he could fathom at this time, that his life had changed, nothing would ever be the same again, He was still Roar Moerk in name and in body, but every other aspect of his being was opening up to the magnificence of the universe within.

Later that afternoon Elisabeth and Roar were sitting in the living room, in the corner where there was a small round oak table between two leather arm-chair recliners. Behind this small constellation was a large set of oak bookshelves that were full of Elisabeth's books. There were two modern floor-standing reading lamps whose heads peaked over the outer side of each chair, ready to peer down upon whichever books might be read. Roar was not one for reading books. Elisabeth's chair by the window was well used and always had a couple of blankets available to keep her cozy whilst reading. Roar had never really used his armchair until today, he never gave himself space to recline and read, it had always been too sedate, he was always a man of motion, on-the-go. The whole corner configuration was set upon a soft, deep, white sheepskin rug, protecting the gorgeous nut-brown stained, under-floor heated, oak-hardwood flooring.

Roar had told Elisabeth all about his experiences from the past with Grace and about the revelations that had come through after he had woken. Elisabeth had smiled knowingly. She recognized the nature of the revelations Roar had been having and knew immediately that he was at a point of no return, no return to the old Roar, the old self-centred, self-destructive way of being. She felt a glowing warmth within her chest, it was a melting away of a layer of self-protection, a defence she had put in place over the years, a distancing away from him in order not to feel the hurts that lay beneath, not just from her life with Roar, but long before, some of it was truly ancient and probably from many lifetimes' past. She allowed her heart to open more, not just to Roar but to everything and everyone. She felt the spaciousness and the healing within as age-old hurts began to slip away.

She smiled openly and asked him: 'In truth Roar, what do you feel about me, about women in general, how you have looked upon us and about the way you have behaved towards all the women in your life? What has caused you to act in this way? It doesn't matter what you say, your words can no longer hurt, so do not hold anything back or try to be nice to safeguard my feelings. What you can say now may be a great healing first of all for yourself and ultimately for everyone. Whatever we do or say has a ripple effect that reverberates around the planet, every thought, movement, word or intention, everything matters. If we deliver anything from the energy of spiritual creation that is hurtful towards one woman, we are hurtful towards all women and as all women are connected to all men, we are hurtful towards everyone. Nothing can be stand-alone, everything is interconnected.'

He sat back in the recliner and closed his eyes as he felt the truth of Elisabeth's words. He breathed slowly, simply following his breath in and out of his body, several thoughts came to him simultaneously, like a package of realizations delivered from above.

'There has always been something special about you Elisabeth, something that makes you stand out from all the other women I have known. From the first moment I saw you I wanted to be with you. You may laugh and think that this is the way I am with all women, which is partly true, but there is more and there is a difference, it's as though we were destined to be together. There is something about you that is calling me to be much more than I have thus far become, asking me to stand up, not just for myself but for everyone. It may seem a little crazy to say this; it feels like our connection to each other is on a much deeper plane than our normal everyday human interactions. Yes, I have for years now fought both an internal and an external fight against this connection, to the point of my own imminent death.

'I have been in denial of this from very early on in our relationship, fighting it more and more as our bond become stronger. As we grew closer at the start of our relationship, it came to a point when I started to back away, choosing to indulge in anything that would give me respite from the pull towards you because it threatened all my well-practised and deep-rooted patterns of behaviour. I could sense what this feeling within, asking me to be more, would mean. It was asking me to change everything I knew, all my behaviours, hobbies and activities, that nothing would be the same. I was torn between this enormous pull to be with you and the fear of giving up everything and walking into, what I told myself was, the unknown. The safety and security of my tried and trusted patterns of behaviour are all I have, and it feels like I'm stepping off the edge of a cliff into an abyss of uncertainty.

Elisabeth shifted her position in the chair to look more directly at Roar, seeing the new-found honesty in his posture, sensing a more surrendered vibration in the words he expressed. A gentle smile moving her lips and creasing the corners of her eyes.

'Another question popping up into my thoughts now is, if I could feel this pull and at the same time feel my own internal resistance to the responsibility that a relationship with you was calling for, then why throw myself so wholeheartedly into it, at least in the beginning? I guess it's a question of which force is the strongest or could it be something else, could it have something to do with my past lives and the fact that I have previously lived in a completely different way? My blatantly abusive resistance to you is so harmful to both of us and anyone we know, which makes the choice of the true way to go so obvious. Whatever it is that comes through you to pull me away from my harmful lifestyle is undoubtably truthful. It came to a point where there were so many conflicting thoughts within me that it felt like I was under constant tension and always anxious.

'The easiest way to avoid the tension was to do all the things I've always done but now do them even more intensely, knowing deep down that the answer is quite the opposite. I know now that it is far simpler to live in truth than in the extreme complication of what I contrived my life to be. The old way is the way that brought constant stress and restlessness whilst the true way, brings more settlement, stillness and harmony. The easiest way for me to avoid the truth was to avoid you, Elisabeth, by committing myself more fervently to doing everything I'd always done before with even more effort and dedication. Maintaining the lie that my life was, became far more convoluted than the simplicity of the truth.

'I made sure I was busy at work, I would chase other women, I had to exercise more, drink more, smoke, never stay in one spot long enough for me to think about what was causing all the tension. In the end, my body had to give me one huge warning, almost killing me before I would listen, before I could arrest my abnormal, but for me normal self-abusive lifestyle. This was in fact slowly killing me, I was slowly killing myself, you could call it a slow form of suicide, all in order not to feel the truth of what was going on inside me.'

As he spoke, Elisabeth had realized that she was no longer looking at Roar, that her body had stiffened with tension and that she could feel her teeth tightly clenched together. She had to physically massage the muscles around her jaws to unclench them, to stand up for a few moments to release the agitation within her body. This was a process for both of them to go through and there was much to be felt, released and cleared from their bodies. She sat down again in the chair and signaled Roar to continue with a little nod of her head.

'I have never really cared about any of the women in my life, either before or after I met you. This attitude started very early on in my life when I spent much of my time with my mother and quickly learned how to manipulate her to get anything I wanted. I also saw how subservient she was to my father, she waited on him, thanklessly, hand and foot, she also did the same for me. I always had the right words at the right moment to persuade her to do my bidding. These manipulative talents were soon turned to the girls at school and from there it became my way of being, you could call it an addiction, I had to get my own way with any girl that I turned my attention to, and they were often a year or two older than me.

'All the guys at school used to look to me for advice about how to get the girls and we used to discuss in detail how each girl was, what we could get from them, how willing they were, rate how they looked and if they performed sexually or not, how good or bad that might have been. We were merciless, hyper-critical and we lied constantly to each other about what we had done with the girls. We would spread rumours about any of the girls that didn't give us what we wanted. If they refused to have sex then we would tar and feather them with vicious rumours about how easy they were. Girls, sport, football, skiing, and drinking are all we really talked about.'

Roar stopped for a moment, picked up his glass of water from the table and took a sip, although he seemed to be somewhere else, deep in thought, there was something he had just realized. He sat still for a further few seconds with the glass still pressed to his lips but without drinking. He then replaced the glass and continued with whatever he had presently received.

'There is a strange power that seems to have control over adolescent boys and then men in general, that makes them always view, no, look up and down in a very lascivious way, almost every woman they see. It can sometimes be done in a split second so the woman hardly notices, whilst others blatantly stare unashamedly, not caring what others may think, their lustful thoughts open wide for all to see. It feels like we are all part of a huge and powerful consciousness that captures men, no matter the culture, religion or country. In fact, in some places and/or communities, it is so overwhelming that women are at risk every time they walk alone outside. It feels like I, and most men I know, look upon women as inferior to us men. Sorry, let me rephrase that, I and almost all the men I know see women as inferior to us men, that women are objects of lust and desire that are here for our pleasure. We actually have our own way of instantly judging every woman we know or meet, see on TV or any other media or even simply walking down the street. No woman is exempt from this.'

Elisabeth knew Roar was speaking honestly as she recognized the situation, he was describing to her. She had felt it so many times in the past, felt the stares, the glares, the salacious comments and gestures, how it made her skin crawl.

'We were a gang of teenage boys that were interested in sport, partying, smoking marijuana and having sexual encounters with girls. There was no talk about the existential questions of life, it was all about what we could get and from whom we could get it. We talked about every girl we dated, kissed, groped, had sex with, we talked about every girl we knew, every girl and every woman we saw. We had to look at every one of them and give them a rating or a value as we saw it, our right to judge all. Eventually it became a competition, feelings didn't matter, all that we cared about was how far we could get and another number to count, another notch on the belt.

'There was an awful way of rating each girl by the hour of the evening or by the number of beers that had been consumed. It was all so degrading and ignominious, but it seemed that it had always been that way and we just continued to exercise our arrogant rights of male dominance. The funny thing is that it was all bravado, not knowing who we were, not knowing how to be ourselves, simply falling into this ready-made trap, a way of being because everyone else was doing the same. We made fun of each other, of every situation, it passed as a playful banter but in truth it was hurtful and we used irony and sarcasm in an attempt to jovially laugh it off. Each jab of ridicule, each sting we gave or received engraved the hurts and behaviours deeper into our bodies until this was the only way of being. This was always the way we behaved with everyone. It was about one-upmanship and ridicule, it was about judgement and arrogance, emotion and reaction, never letting our true feelings surface, complete falsity and internal poverty.'

Roar had never spoken so honestly before but, even so, his words caused Elisabeth to cringe, she wanted to hear the truth but at the same time the truth was brutal. She had to tell herself that this is the energy we have all conformed to and even cringing and complaining about it is a reaction to it that further feeds its continued circulation. At that moment she was able to, once again, smile as Roar continued his narration.

'Furthermore, this type of male dominance, male supremacy consciousness takes hold and can suck men into even deeper levels of depravity. Now this is not prevalent in all men but it can be seen that some men take this baseness much further, they seem to have no limitations, no sense of propriety or morality. No young person is spared, they even do the same with young girls and boys, age holds no boundary nor restraint for their salaciousness.'

Elisabeth nodded her agreement as Roar continued.

'From as early as I can remember, I observed that boys and men had the upper hand. Society, in some way, categorized men as superior and women as inferior to men. It's like an unwritten code. From early on there has always been talk of equality for women and that Norway was at the forefront of the fight but these are basically empty words. We had one of the first female prime ministers in Europe, Gro Harlem Brundtland in 1981, but this did not change the way men objectify women. It didn't change the overall attitude of men. In fact, it has steadily deteriorated, becoming more ingrained and unchecked than ever before.

'We are now at a point where women are even more aligned to that same male consciousness, increasingly they collude with this objectification, they seek attention and play into this ugliness. What is it that drags women down to the level of debased men? It is they, the women that hold the potential to change this ill way of being. It is they that hold the beauty and sacredness within. Is it not women that have the potential to lead men out of the duplicity of the spiritual creation they have entrenched themselves in? You and all other women hold the key Elisabeth; I now feel you pulling me out of the gloomy morass that I have been so deeply rooted in for so many years. You are the only woman I know that emanates that divine sacredness, the stillness and poise that is a super-powerful reflection to me and all other men, that asks men to be who they are, to step away from abusiveness and to live life truly.'

'Roar, you hit the nail on the head,' Elisabeth spoke with calm authority. 'It is true, that I and all women are here to reflect this true beauty to all men, without exception, but that does not mean that men are to sit and wait for women to realize themselves first. Men must also reclaim themselves from the illusion that they are different from women, that they are superior to women, they must accept that they also are tender loving beings and not the macho superior and arrogant creatures many of them think they have become.

'Women should present their femaleness and fullness of who they are first before they adopt any label or role depicting what a woman should be doing. These labels have been given to women by men who wish to control them, labels such as wife, mother, daughter and many others. A woman is always a woman first before she does any of these activities. A woman is a woman in the activity of being a mother, which means she is a sacred being that may be feeding a child, the feeding of the child is not what defines who she is, it is simply an activity performed as the full beautiful divine being, she is.'

Roar felt he had to move, he stood and walked over to the kitchen, picked up a bowl of fruit and placing the fruit on the table between them, returned to his seat. As he moved, he felt Elisabeth's words reverberate within him, that what she was saying was exactly the same for men. A man is a man first, what he does, is done in the energy of the man he chooses to be.

Elisabeth continued: 'Women can be more successful in business, and they are often successful. This part is mostly accepted although even here a great many men do have problems having a woman as their boss, often deliberately sabotaging and causing disruption wherever possible. The problems arise when the woman, as a business leader, engages with men and other women, not from her femaleness and sacredness but in reaction to the male energy, when she undertakes to out-compete the men to attain her success. This form of success is then not true success. It engages the dark energies of competition, comparison and judgement to crush others and become their superior. When a woman spends her life in this male energy, which is in fact alien to the female form, what kind of impact can this have on the physical body and what will be the long-term psychological effects of this sustained self-abusive way?'

Roar was in complete agreement; he had seen women in his line of business and how they had competed with the men, the savagery and cold-heartedness of the cut-throat ambition knew no boundaries. Women, like men, would do anything to achieve their aspirations, no holds barred.

Elisabeth could see that Roar was attentively listening to her as a new stage of the relationship was developing. 'Everything is interlinked, years of competition rather than cooperation, comparison rather than congruence and judgement rather than acceptance, likely will cause great disharmony within the body as this is overriding the natural equanimity of femaleness.

'If the woman were to reflect her true femaleness and divinity to the men around her, instead of competing with them, she could inspire through reflection for them to be more like their true selves, without comparison and judgement. Not playing into or engaging with the male supremacy consciousness in any way, what kind of impact do you think that might have in a business setting, or any other setting for that matter?'

As he listened intently to what Elisabeth had to say, he nodded slowly as he contemplated the divisive ways he had manipulated and contrived to achieve his own wants and needs. Also, how some of the women he had encountered in his business dealings had used him to get what they wanted. Ah, but he had also used them to get what he wanted, although false and treacherous, it had been a mutual agreement, both getting something in return.

Sensing Roar was too deep in contemplation to answer her question, she continued, 'If a woman were to be in complete self-honouring, loving and adoring every particle of herself, not expecting or wanting men to confirm her, free from self-loathing and without any issues about her own self-worth, how would that reflect on society as a whole? How would society in general react to such a truly independent woman with the attributes I have just spoken about? I think we know. As the old proverb says, "the nail that sticks up its head, will be hammered down".

Society, as it is in this current time, would not take lightly to women being themselves in full and not conforming to the "rules of the game". The dark forces will do their upmost to crush any woman who shines too brightly, or in fact, any man that deigns to present truth in this manner.'

Elisabeth paused to glance at Roar, he returned her look as they held each-other's gaze for a few seconds. Roar thought that Elisabeth, as she had spoken, was describing herself in so many ways. He saw the bright light burning deeply within her eyes, felt it pulling him towards her.

She added: 'It is the same every time a person or a group of people live and reflect a different, more truthful and responsible way of being. They are immediately "put to the sword". The haters will crawl out of the woodwork and use every means possible to try to discredit, defame and destroy if they can, any who purvey the reality of our corrupt worldly truths, mercilessly they are ready and eager to stamp out anything that challenges their ill-ingrained narratives. This overarching dark supremacy consciousness fights desperately to disavow the Light from shining through, although at some point in the future spiritual creation will be overwhelmed by the unstoppable reflection of the Light as humanity realizes the depth of the illusion it has suffered through, for millennia. The Light will never cease as spiritual creation is but a tiny blemish within the magnificence of all that the Universe is.'

Roar struggled with the magnitude of what Elisabeth was presenting here, he understood the depth of the lie he had been living but at the same time there were forces within him that did not want to let go of everything he had ever been and done in this life. If he were to change, to become a beacon of light, to live in a way contradictory to everyone he knew, that he would be attacked and defamed, how would that be? On the other hand, how could he return to what had almost killed him. He thought about a middle way but knew that this did not really exist as an option for him.

Elisabeth was reading Roar, had he had enough? She felt she could go on. 'Maybe it is all linked to the general deterioration of society. The more we women accept this consciousness, whether we join it, complain about it or fight it, we are then feeding it, helping it maintain itself and even grow stronger. Any reaction does not impair or stop the initiating energy, it increases and intensifies it, literally dousing the flames of evil with high-octane fuel. To have any lasting effect, it may take many women to return to their divine sacredness and the beauty of their inner selves. Yet it starts with just one to realize and reflect to others that may start a chain reaction. Society is spiraling out of control, and yet there are those in control that continue to manipulate this downward vortex. This evil of spiritual creation is Machiavellian, calculating, sinister and above all else, uncompromisingly relentless.

'There is only one way to impact this scheming consciousness, by not trying to have any impact, by not engaging with it in any way. It is possible to hate it in a way that is emotion free from a place of complete detachment from it, and with an all-encompassing beholding love for all our fellow, lost beings entrapped within it. It is a consciousness that thrives and expands due to our engagements with it. Give it no more fuel and it will slowly be extinguished. There is a long road ahead with many twists and turns before we all can relinquish this consciousness, yet each person that manages to disentangle themselves from this labyrinth of lies contributes immensely to its eventual deconstruction and dissipation.'

Elisabeth stopped, she felt the impact of her own words upon both Roar and herself. She looked towards him again and smiled broadly, receiving his own beaming grin in return. She knew he understood everything she had said but was he willing to take it all onboard and live his life in a different way?

⸍

Chapter 6

NO END, ONLY RETURN

They stood amongst the huge crowd of mourners that had gathered in Hyde Park along the route of the funeral procession. London's streets were often full of people swarming and milling around upon their daily travails but never had either of them seen so many people in one place at the same time. It was the morning of February 2nd 1901: Queen Victoria had died on January 22nd and her body was to be transported through Hyde Park on its way to Paddington Station then onwards by train to Windsor where she was to be placed in the mausoleum she had originally built for her departed husband Prince Albert who had died forty years earlier in 1861.

Grace and Richard gradually worked their way towards the exit of the park, through the thronging crowd as they headed northwards towards their home in Barnsbury. It had been a very solemn occasion guarded by an immense military presence. The passing of a monarch seems to evoke a mixed bag of reactions and of course a massive crowd of mourners and even greater numbers of curious onlookers, which in turn brought out the devious teams of pickpockets determined to turn a profit from such a huge gathering.

They walked for some time in silence feeling the strange atmosphere in the air, as if everything had changed and yet all was still exactly the same. The passing of a monarch meant nothing more than the fact that a new artificial figurehead would be put in place in her stead to act as the leader but was in truth a planted puppet of the elusive supremacists that lay behind this pompous facade.

They had previously discussed the prospects of life, death, and the cycle of Reincarnation, past lives and what if anything might come next, whether there was a heaven or hell and what other lives they may have lived previous to this one. They both had feelings of having lived earlier lives but were not able to say exactly who they formerly were.

'What kind of life do you think Queen Victoria will live if she reincarnates and why do you think she was born to be Queen and become the ruler of the Empire? Do you think she might become a princess once again or what else do you think Karma has in store for her?' Grace asked Richard.

Richard had been walking along pondering upon the same theme.

He spoke: 'I would imagine that being Queen for so many years and ruling over so many people not only in Britain but all around the British Empire would carry a lot of Karma, although the monarchy has very little real power to create political or humanitarian changes. They are, in truth, essentially powerless marionettes; their strings being pulled by the political and financial elite that conspire in the shadows. She has though been the figurehead of the expansion of the British Empire and under her flag, millions of people have been either slaughtered, enslaved, worked or starved to death. This British Empire has been and still is to a certain extent one of the most savage and brutal regimes ever to exist in the whole of history as we know it. I don't really know how to measure the amount of negative Karma that Queen Victoria could have accumulated and how she might recompense for the inhumane, heartless treatment of millions of fellow and equal human beings that she has so resolutely represented. It does seem that certain people of power have no issue with allowing the dark forces through them, that drive the annihilation of great swathes of peoples in order to increase their own personal position, power and profit.'

Grace had read many books covering the exploits of the British expeditions to foreign lands and most of them had painted glorious all-conquering images of how our valiant and brave pioneers had tamed the savages of far-off worlds. Richard, on the other hand, had personally witnessed other darker aspects of British colonization.

Richard continued with no trace of sadness or judgement in his voice, 'It's difficult to say what her fate might be when she returns in her next incarnation, Karma can seem to work in strange ways at times, but in the end, everyone must in some way atone or recompence for all accumulated Karma. She may well return once again as a princess or even a prince, to be given the opportunity to live her life in a different way, atoning for her lives past. Living a life of such entitlement is very difficult because there is an extremely powerful consciousness that holds all within it, making it almost impossible to break free from. Being captured and controlled by this supremacist consciousness of monarchical entitlement, may ultimately lead to many lives of suffering similar fates as those most hurt and brutalized by it. Every life though presents an opportunity for learning and to break free from the ingrained patterns of the past.'

Grace listened intently as they strolled northbound. 'How does it all work then, this process of living here as human beings? Can we also reincarnate as animals or insects?' she asked.

Richard spoke: 'I'm not really sure about this but I would say that most animals do not have a soul, although a few may do, there are some animals that do have distinctly human-like behaviour. Insects probably do not.'

'Consider that it may all be tied to living responsibly, with that I mean living a life that is focused on the true betterment of all, the enrichment of humanity and not only on the advancement of ourselves, as individuals. We all come from souls originally and we are part of the same One Soul. We all shall return from whence we came but as long as we play this game of separation and individuality, of abuse, hate, war, inequality and division, we will not be capable of this. We must then continue upon this cycle of birth, living, dying and rebirth to do it all over again and again until we all can live our lives in harmonious togetherness with everyone else, only then can we all leave here permanently, on to our next level of unfoldment. As long as we, humanity, continue in the illusion that we live this one life and so, either depart from here to heaven or hell, or any other version of this in any other religion, we will continue to live without aware-ness of the fact that we are much more than human, that we are truly multi-dimensional beings entrapped within this self-cre-ated miasma called life on earth.

'It is also important to become aware enough to discern the difference between the Truth and what is not true, yet named as truth, because without this acuity it is easy to be led astray with the deception of good and bad. Being labelled good or bad does not mean that either of them is truthful. Doing good can be the greatest beguilement that can throw us completely off course and condemn us to many lifetimes in the wilderness, for there is good and there is true good or in other words, the Truth. Ask yourself the question, is it possible to serve others without the expectation of any form of self-gratification, that there is no focus on prof-it for you when doing good deeds for others. And beyond this, is it possible that self-sacrifice in order to help or please others, can also be connected to a want or need of the self to be recog-nized, in some way, for these benevolent actions? Is this not also being untruthful?'

They had exited Hyde Park at Lancaster Gate, passed the newly built Underground Railway station of the same name and made their way along Sussex Gardens headed in the direction of Regents Park. The dispersing crowd became ever thinner as they moved away from the park.

Sensing Grace's full presence in their conversation, Richard continued: 'If we think back to Queen Victoria and all the dev-astation and depravation she has overseen from the lofty perch of her mighty throne, ensconced within her most opulent sur-roundings, might it be possible that her next life could be as a beggar on the very streets of London. Would it then be true for us to sacrifice our own health or wealth to aid this person or would she or he need to experience some of the measure of the destitution and pain she had previously ruled over? Of course, as long as it is of no detriment to ourselves or indeed not for our own personal gain or self-satisfaction, then it may be a splendid reflection to be of assistance to those who are in dire straits, no matter the Karma they may carry. Unfortunate as it may seem, everyone is exactly where they need to be right now to be given the opportunities they need to evolve out of their current level of delusion within this global illusion.'

As Richard spoke, Grace could sense the truth in his words. She could feel how she had lived her life oblivious to the grander scheme of things, had unquestioningly accepted her given station in life and the class differences of this discordant biased society. But now she was starting to see how everything was an illusion, a huge game of creation and distraction, she could either be a pawn being moved within the chessboard or she could observe detached, to help deconstruct the evil deceit playing out.

Richard continued: 'Look at your own situation, you have experienced some horrific abuse at the hands of George Darcaster. You were close to death and yet it was the letter you wrote that I felt the impulse to open, and thus come to your aid, resulting in your survival. I somehow knew that you had much more to expound and communicate in your current life and so I was drawn to do what was needed to ensure that would happen at this juncture. Mr. Darcaster was the evil hand controlled by spiritual creation, engaged to stop you from your true call in this life. We must continually be aware as there is always another Darcaster, another conduit of the dark force to attack the Light that we bring through. It is the dark energy, not the person it is expressing through that is the evil force, although that person has, in one way or another, chosen which force they have aligned to. Anyone allowing through such evil cannot be excused from their choices and should be held accountable for any ignominy resultant thereof. Yet through reactions such as judgement and blame we do not diminish this poisonous energy. Quite the opposite, we amplify it to bring even greater devastation and suffering. Within all this there is always an opportunity to access greater wisdom and thus further unfoldment along the way of evolution.

'An example of this increased pain and suffering could be, in your situation, the acquiescence to what happened, thus becoming a life-long victim of the, comparatively short period of time that you were in these, no doubt extremely painful and traumatic situations. If the trauma and pain is allowed to fester inside without being healed, it increases its potency to the extent that it can destroy your whole life. It can eventually manifest into both physical and mental sicknesses or even drive you to take your own life.'

They wandered through Regents Park, onwards towards Camden Town and further to Barnsbury.

'Realize the true culprit, which in your case is the dark supremacy consciousness, the evil forces of spiritual creation that control George Darcaster's every movement. Learn to hate this without emotion and learn of its machinations in order to overcome it. Do not hate the man it has controlled in order to harm, and thus control you. For in truth, he is also a victim of its evil connivance just as much as you are, if not more for he must assimilate and deal with the resultant Karma in his lives to come.

'You may also ask yourself, why has this happened to you, how was it that you came to be in this situation. If everything happens for a reason and all is based on the Karma of this and your previous existences, what have you experienced and what have you allowed yourself to undertake or be part of in your past lives?'

Grace stopped walking, she felt irritation, anger and disbelief. She felt like screaming but simultaneously she knew that Richard would not say anything that would in any way harm her. He was the most honest, truthful and gentle man she had ever known. Richard waited impassively, looking directly at her, allowing her all the space she needed to digest his words and to find her response.

After a couple of minutes, she replied. 'It is difficult to believe that I may have done such despicable things in my past lives and that I would now be subject to this pain and suffering that I have had to endure. It was not only the episodes with George Darcaster, but it was also all the time in between his visits, all the dread, all the self-disgust, and the feelings of letting down my family. Are you actually saying that I have been a person such as Darcaster, that I have perpetrated the same despicable acts as

I have now experienced?' She knew the answer, as soon as she asked the question.

Richard replied: 'Explaining the nature of the wayward spirit that totally controls the human body until we realize the situation we are in, is not so simple because it is in a way designed to thrive on complication and will continue on this capricious trajectory until it is called or pulled to re-align to the Truth. It thrives on illusion, diversion, derision, duplicity, opposition, emotion, hypocrisy and cunning. The spirit will stop at nothing to avoid true integrity and responsibility, yet it may well give a close impression of doing so or even choose to do quite the opposite. It is genderless and yet in each new life it must present as either man or woman, although the human and its body, man or woman, is only allowed to access a tiny portion of the spirit's intelligence so the person rarely understands the extent to which it is being manipulated by forces that seem normally to be way beyond its control.

'In its many-faceted existence, it complicates and distracts itself to avoid the hurt it feels which has been caused from its original separation from the soul. This is the greatest hurt, the original pain felt by all, not only by this recalcitrant aspect of the being. This is often why we seek to relieve our pain through all forms of distractions that take us away from our presence within the body and that is why the spirit continually seeks out experiences, whether these are highs or lows are of no matter. The only goal is not to feel the separation it has inflicted upon itself.

'The spirit knows of its own immortality, that it has and will live many more lives, until it eventually, inevitably returns to oneness with the soul. Thus, the spirit will connivingly convince its human personality that it is a mortal and that it must journey on one of the many offered options of what we know as afterlife. It is predictable but nonetheless unpredictable. For this fractious character, human life is a playground, an arena of entertainment. It matters not what kind of life it shall live for all life is an experience, a thrill in one way or another. Human pain and suffering are simply part of its grand adventure into its own world of creation. Every episode, event, ordeal and encounter are simply other ways of avoiding feeling that original hurt and delaying its inevitable return to the soul it separated from.'

Grace wondered how all this could be, a spirit, the human itself and the soul, all part of the Universe and yet playing out what seem to be insignificant little lives down here on this tiny planet held in and surrounded by the power and enormity of Space.

Richard spoke: 'There is an ever-present reminder of where it separated from within every human body. Everything is built from and of the divine particles of the Universe and thus within every particle of the human body lies the wisdom and intelligence of the Universe which constantly and magnetically, pulls the misguided one back to its origin, back to soul. Not only that, at the depth of each human being, at its innermost heart, there lies the connection to the eternal glowing spark of the soul with its ever-knowing, ever-loving observation that one day will re-ignite every disconnected being, inspiring their return to soulfulness.

'It is not to say that you have performed the same evil deeds as Mr. Darcaster. Although the fact that this has all happened to you tells us that there is a reason and that there is something for you to learn and evolve from. Of course, it could be that you have abused someone, or several people in one way or another in a previous life, thus causing you to suffer abuse in this life. We have lived so many times before so that it is quite possible, we have all been similar to Darcaster or even worse, and it is also possible that he has been the victim of the very abuse he now perpetrates upon others.

'Most important, is to receive what is on offer, accept what has happened and feel the opportunity it now brings for you to walk clear of that contamination. Do you wallow in the dark energy of the poor victim, the unfortunate woman defiled by this uncouth villainous man, or do you choose the Light, to see these acts of depravity for what they really are? Do you continue to live in the realm of human being only or do you choose to live from the whole of the divine being that you are, in connection to All that is?

168

'In the end, it comes to a point, as we learn to live our lives in awareness and presence within the purpose of what we know we are here to do, that the clouds will lift from our countenance, allowing us to see and feel more clearly the loving imprints from our past. It may not be the detail of the lives but the energy and alignment of the community or movement of which we have been part of that can be felt and brought through as a living radiation into the present. If we allow ourselves to feel the loving footprints of the past and accept the times we have slipped into waywardness, for certainly all have done so, the now and the future may become the crystal-clear Truth of oneness with All.'

Grace felt Richard's words and realized how true they were. She felt how destructive the malignant energy of accepting the role of the victim was and how it could crush the life force from her if she maintained her status as the willing participant. She knew instantly that she would linger no longer in the domain of persecution and victimhood, for only the path of internment, decay and self-destruction lay there.

She asked: 'I sometimes have quite vivid dreams that seems to be in a time far from now, could this be dreams of the past or dreams of the future? I feel that it is not me and yet it is me in another body in a different space, in a place, a country unfamiliar, at the same time it feels well known to me. It feels very real when I first awaken, almost that I am two or more people in one, but still the same. It then gently fades away and I am simply Grace again but there is a residue knowing that I am more than just me in this one life. Does anything like this happen to you, do you feel any other lives that you may have lived? Am I experiencing this because I lay so close to death such a short time ago?'

He smiled again as she asked her multiple questions. 'Ah yes, dreams, that can be a very convoluted and perplexing subject to contemplate although it may be quite simple. We could look at it from several angles, although if we are distracted, disconnected and emotional in the way we live our daily lives then we may find that our sleep will be tainted by exactly the same components and constructions, often resulting in a poor quality of sleep and dreams to match, dreams that are not of a heavenly phenomenon, rather the opposite. They are interspersed with the dissonance of our own ill-living ways. This may not always be the case and in the end, it is always a question of discernment.

'Sleep, as you know, is a vital aspect of living in a human body and as everything else in life it is important to do this in a true fashion. You may feel that sleep is sleep and that's something the body just does but there is more to it than that. As I have said many times previously, everything matters, everything is equally important, and it is important to do anything and everything in a loving way. I'm not just talking about sleep but also the way we move, whatever we think or do and our every intention behind all that we do. Everything has a natural cycle including the human being and the whole being that we are. These cycles should not be disregarded as they are crucial to our soulful evolution. Is it then possible that the human being has a natural cycle of work and rest, motion and repose, that can be felt when the being is truly honouring of its own body? The body actually knows when it needs to move from the phase of motion over to repose.

'It could also be that there is, during the rest period, an optimum window for the being to sleep and be rejuvenated so that it maximizes its opportunity for growth and expansion. When we sleep irregular hours, the body often becomes tired, the demeanor less vital, more contracted and the Light diminishes, we become more distracted and less present in the moment, so we know that this has a great effect. Is it not natural that this disturbance is then carried over into our dreams and thus the dreams often will be from the energy in which we are currently living, therefore the dreams are most likely from the darker side?

'On the other hand, if we live our days in a loving rhythm of work and rest, in connection to our body, respecting the signals the body actually sends to us, sleeping when the body calls for the sleep, could we then bring that rhythm into our sleep? Then would the dreams we have be more likely an extension and an expansion of the loving way we live during the day? Would we then have meaningful dreams or could this result in less dreaming and more time spent in the inner stillness that we all are, deep within? Could the dreams and impressions we have in this reposeful state be from the energy of the wisdom and intelligence of the Universe? Could they be from the past lives we have lived in oneness with the Light?

'There have been many times during the last twenty years that I have awoken from slumber, knowing that I have received an impress of ancient wisdom and yet it is only there as a simple feeling, an insightful glow within my body. As I have slept, I have opened myself to the All that the Universe is. In doing so, I received healing and clarity, thus enabling the next level of access to the intelligence and wisdom that is constantly flowing in and through us all. It seems that as I establish greater connection to the living purpose of this life; open and obedient to the true energy of Light, what is received becomes grander and more powerful for the cause of the battle for truth between the Light and the dark. Through our day, every moment brings with it a choice to be on one side or the other. Do we live for and with the Light of the Soul, or do we support and walk hand in hand with the evils of spiritual creation?'

Grace sighed, asking: 'How can it be so cut and dried, it all seems so harsh, there is no room to relax, no time to simply read a novel or take a walk in the park without this war between the Light and the dark taking precedence? It seems unfair to expect one to leave behind everything one has known, everything one has believed, to examine every thought and inclination they experience. This would disturb the mind and the health of every individual willing to commence this incogitable undertaking. How can it be so, it all seems so overwhelming?'

Richard replied, 'How can it not be so black and white? If we simply consider that we are from the magnificence of the Universe, from the divine fiery Light that encompasses the All that is and can be. Anything that is not from this will be a disturbance, a dark blemish within the Light, a malignant throbbing sore within the purity. Is there a difference between relax and repose? When in the state of repose, we stay connected to deepen within the Light and yet we may or may not be moving or doing, something or nothing in particular. It is simply giving your whole being the opportunity to sink deeper into the arms of God, to receive the next installment of his universal wisdom.

'Then there is a question of reading a novel. Of course, we can read books and novels but as I have said, there is nothing that isn't something, so reading a novel is also something. If it were a novel pertaining to the truths of the universe and exposing the dark evils that keep us shrouded from our true Light, then, by all means, read it. If it is purely for entertainment value, this is another matter, are we then present within our body or lost in the images of the written words within the book. Everything we do either heals or harms. There is no neutral ground, even though it may seem so. Neutral ground is yet another weapon in the great arsenal of dark deception, it seems harmless enough but lies in the area of distraction, comfort and security which as we can imagine, diminish our awareness and presence. Neutral ground or staying neutral is not making a choice of our energetic alignment, so no choice means we are not choosing the Light and therefore choosing the fed, neutral alignment which is yet another deception of the dark forces.'

She stopped walking, Grace could see and understand Richard's point of view but there was something inside her that didn't want to accept all that he had to say. She still wanted to have the choice of enjoying a good story to take her away to distant shores and experience other lands through the words of great authors. She stopped at the thought of the great author, who was writing the book that gave her the beautiful images: Why had it been written and what energy had the author chosen to write the book in? If we read books that are written by authors with the intention to purely entertain and distract the reader and of course make profit for themselves, what energy or force do we allow into our bodies? This must be the same for everything we do, the way we speak to each other, the way we prepare and eat food, the music we listen to, absolutely everything contains either the energy of Light or that of spiritual creation.

Richard waited until she was ready to walk again. 'Is there something you would like to say?'

Grace replied: 'Yes, what you said caused me to consider more deeply some of the things we take for granted in life. That absolutely everything must be considered. By blindly doing something that has always been done a certain way without thinking, is then not choosing which energy we align to. When we are not consciously choosing, we inadvertently or preferentially select the jurisdiction of spiritual creation. It is a huge deception, everything is a trap, it is so staggering, how is it possible to escape it all?'

He replied: 'We must first discover and understand the enormity of what is at play here and also realize the true magnificence of what we are. Consider that everything we have believed or idealized in the past or the facts that we have been taught as so-called truths by our parents, teachers, clerics or parliamentarians, are all part of the grand deception. It is sad but true that it is a tiny minority of humanity that have not been taken in by this grand illusion. Absolutely everything we hold as truth, hold as an ideal or a belief needs to be re-assessed, picked apart and resurrected within the fiery Light of the soul. Nothing is so small as to not be considered. Know that every thought that has been thought, has been given to us from the energy attracted by these ingrained deceptions. It is difficult to see the scale and the extent of the subterfuge when we are comfortably wallowing within it.

'We are born into it, although we do also carry momentum from lives past. Each time we reincarnate we have the potential to walk towards the Light and yet our previous patterns and momentum can quickly lead us astray. The forces of spiritual creation have put in place the complete system of living designed to catch each new-born child and immediately begin their evil work upon them. They are relentless, they will use any agency in their unending determination to prevent every human being from realizing the full magnificence of what they truly are.

'The parents we are born to have most often unknowingly, yet knowingly, conformed to the dark system, believing it to be the true way, although at some level they still know the truth. They teach, train and indoctrinate each child in ways that gradually cause them to lose connection with the Light they are from, as they too conform into the system of illusion. All other aspects of this misbegotten society then pull the children further away from their true origins and deeper into the depths of dark spiritual creation until the point that the grand deception they are indoctrinated into is the only truth they can see and comprehend. This is the same for everyone in different ways and it continues relentlessly throughout all our lives until we are so far removed from the truth, so embedded in our ideals and beliefs that when truth is presented to us, we fervently deny it, denounce it as humbug, fantasy and lies. For some of us though when we receive a message or some other form of re-awakening, we see the truth before us, realize there is more to being human and embark upon our way of return, back to soul, back to the Truth.'

Grace interjected: 'I love my parents so much, they were really good to me, looked after me as best they could. How could they be living from within the realms of spiritual creation? They only ever speak well of others and are generous, law-abiding citizens. It is difficult to believe that they do not live from the Light. But now I can see how they, like me, have settled into their place as servants within this society, accepting that they are less worthy than those above them. They have conformed, as we all do, to the system that is in place. They have chosen to be good rather than bad, chosen to be secure within the enforced structure, not to rock the boat in any way. If everyone chooses this way, we will remain incarcerated forever.'

Richard went on: 'Grace, your parents are just as lost as we all have been. I am sure you can see and feel that your own re-awakening came from our meeting but even prior to that, by heavenly design. There are no coincidences in life, subsequently through our conversations, and some of the books you bought or borrowed, you were pulled towards the Light. Although it was your traumatic experiences at the hands of Mr. Darcaster and your near-death encounter that was needed for you to truly want to seek the deeper truth and your purpose in this life. The Universal Light works in ways that may be for now beyond our comprehension although in time I am sure all that needs to be revealed will be made manifest.

'The way of the Light of truth appears difficult because we are viewing it from within the complication and dominance of this spiritual creation-instilled fabrication of what we see as earth-life. It is from within this realm of spiritual creation that confusion and mischief abound, giving the impression that anything outside of it is where the complication and difficulty is found. Stepping out of the dark and living from the Light unravels the dark entanglement and brings in a way, unfathomable simplicity, a simplicity beyond simple. It simply is.

'When we live in this complication, we allow ourselves to be taken over by the impulses of the dark forces. We allow our thoughts to be controlled by evil energies or consciousnesses. We allow these thoughts to spin wildly around in our minds, repeating and repeating, engraving them into our ideals and beliefs, controlling our reactions, taking us further away from our true selves. We think of what is 'good for me'. The self comes first, and we often go no further. Others seem not so important. Living from within this dark energy delivers to us all the world we now live in, a world that is cruel and hateful. It creates everything that is harmful, all that destroys and kills in whatever guise it dons. It matters not, if it harms anyone in any way. Then this, surely, is from spiritual creation. Living from within the system of dark spiritual creation, we have without doubt, lost our way.'

Richard slowed his pace as he knew they had not far left to walk, noticing the rays of sunshine peeking through the dispersing, reddening, early-evening clouds just above the horizon.

He continued: 'If we look to the British Empire as it stands now, it is glorified as being great and positive, bringing untold riches to our shores for the benefit of all that are under its rule. If we look at it from within the energy of simplicity, we immediately know that there is absolutely nothing of truth in the way the British forces and businesses exploit every country they have invaded. It is not about bringing a better way of life to foreign shores. It is purely the unleashing of supremacist privilege and arrogance at the cost of millions of lives. In India alone, millions have starved to death whilst our British Empire ravages and strips bare the resources from under the noses of these famished peoples. Our armed forces have decimated all forms of resistance and even now they are waging wars upon the peoples of Southern Africa. Our young men are conscripted into the military and sailed off to these foreign lands, expected to fight, kill and die in the name of Queen Victoria and Great Britain. Many thousands will never return. They are simply cannon fodder, a resource to be used in the quest of greed and untold riches for just a handful of rapacious, predatory self-centered men and women that have sold themselves to be the instruments of the evils of spiritual creation. Britannia may rule the waves and much of the known world, but the malicious force of spiritual creation undoubtably rules Britannia.

'For some it is easy to register when events and occurrences are blatantly evil, but for those lost within its consciousness, they may be blind to it all, or choose to be so. When life becomes solely about oneself, engrossed in only what riches and power can be forgathered, interested in what is beneficial only to the self, then there are only the colours and flavours of spiritual creation to be seen. The Light is firmly withheld beyond the compacted layers of spiritual creation and only evil is on show for all. Though it is not always so; the deviousness of the dark forces has many ways to bamboozle the human being.'

They stopped to pause for a moment, both knowing that they were a mere stone's throw away from home, wanting to stay in the flow and to complete what was there to be said and listened to before they arrived.

He continued: 'Look to the London Workhouses, these were initially created to help the poor and less fortunate by giving them food and shelter and, of course, work. These have now become just like prisons for men, women and children alike. The conditions they have to live in are horrific and those who own and run them force even the children into unpaid labour from which the masters make their fortunes. The people, children included, are ill-fed, castigated and abused, often becoming sick and even dying from malnutrition. Those on the lowliest rungs of society are now imprisoned, punished and exploited, once again for the financial advance of greedy profiteers, undoubtably controlled by the energy of spiritual creation. How did these establishments, originally designed to help the unfortunate then become the tools of avaricious exploiters, what makes men take advantage of their fellow beings? Even small children are not spared their gluttonous unscrupulous attention. Were these heinous do-good creations ever meant to care for the true welfare of the poor and less fortunate, or is "doing good" also part of the evil dark plan? The plan set forth by the grand disunion of ethereal soul-separated miscreations is to perpetuate their forlorn attempts to remain disconnected from the Oneness of the All.

'In the world we now live in with so much that is obviously reprehensible and often totally abhorrent it is easy to determine all that is evidently bad, such as sexual perversion, slavery, war and murder. And thus, we are often oblivious to the inherent corruption and deceit that lies behind most of what is the "good" – our unscrupulous, discordantly constructed systems of governing and living offer to all. "Good" is then so deceptive, it could be postulated that it is much worse than the more obviously injurious, "bad". "Good" is designed as part of the evil spiritual plan to keep us away from the true truth of what we are and why we are here, to ensure we continue in our disconnected slumber instead of awakening to the true reality of our origins and walking upon our path of return to the One Soul.

'Look to the schools run by priests, monks and nuns who swear to serve their God, to love and cherish all equally, and yet even they admonish, beat and abuse the children within their care. Are they connected to the true Light of Heaven, God and the Universe or are they sold to the forces of spiritual creation? Are they not masquerading in their holy garb and supposedly

177

doing good and righteous work of God, whilst bathing in the forces of evil?

'Within the Light there is no abuse, there is no exploitation of others, there is no self-gratification at the expense of any other beings. Should we aspire to be in true service for all sentient beings, we would recognize that there are no inequalities and no exceptions, no-one is to be left out. Whilst we are human in our human bodies, we will err, but could our intentions be truly loving?

'Is it our intention to live from simplicity, aligned to the Light, present and aware within our own bodies? We will have thoughts, but can these be mostly of true good and true benevolence, expressed through us from the Light? Can we care for ourselves as we care equally for all others and will we live in service for the All, not for the I or the me? Again, there is no perfection within the Light, as spiritual creation cannot be simply swept aside. It has for years, and lifetimes, weaved its wicked tendrils deep within all aspects of society and thus into every being on the planet. By shedding the complication, living from the stillness and simplicity of the soul it may be possible to cut the tendrils and dispel the evil imprints that hold us shackled to spiritual creation.

'As you can imagine, we all have been indoctrinated layer by layer into this illusion of what life is until the true essence of our being is buried beneath blanketing layers of untruths that we think are our truths. Our being becomes what is above and within all the layers, no longer in connection with its loving essence, shrouded by all the dark blankets. Each layer contributing to the one above it, compounding 'what is not', until we no longer recognize the contents of those lower constricted layers that are providing us with our current view on reality. These are all the strata of complication, designated to keep us confused and disconnected from the Truth. Not until we begin to remove each blanket, layer by layer can we reveal first the previous untruths that have led us to the current untruths that we think are truths, then those beyond them, until we begin to become once again, aware of the Light within.'

They had begun to walk slowly along the street, as if they knew their conversation was about to reach its conclusion. Side by side they stepped forward towards whatever lay ahead.

Richard spoke again: 'Could it be that there is no Truth until the Light inside is revealed, and here it is within us all, wherein lies the simplicity of knowing who and what we truly are? Here we find the joy, stillness and harmony. Here we know, observe and feel the love of God and the immensity and majesty of the Universe.

'It may be that we must accept our current level of complexity and complication; acknowledge all the layers we are engulfed by, resolve to uncover and return to the Light that we truly come from. Each layer we unravel will reveal a new one, it is an epic journey, not towards a long-distanced goal in the future, but a return from whence we came. With each revelation of the evil that we have been dedicated to, every illusion we have happily played our part in, every abuse we have felt and everyone we have abused, we feel the pain of where we have been. Let this not deter us from our return. Each hurt that is healed and each revelation made manifest, allows for the expansion of the Ageless Wisdom of the Universe within us. Let each step be not of regret and recrimination, let each step be of joy and love for all that is rediscovered. Each hidden hurt divulged and relinquished and every painful experience renounced will rekindle the Light of joy within.

'As each layer is uncovered, each revelation exposes the "what is not". We resurrect ourselves and move deeper into our path of return, the return to what actually is, the grandness of the Heavens and beyond.'

They arrived home in Barnsbury.

179

Chapter 7

SUMMER RELAPSE

It was Friday, July 21st, 2000, and Roar seemed to be fully recovered from his New Year's Day ordeal. He had returned to work on Monday, February 7th as a man deep in the process of change. He had communicated with Anneli many times, both by email and telephone during those weeks of recuperation and they had both quickly seen the writing on the wall as regards any future relationship between them. Anneli had subsequently given in her three-month notice at work, but had been allowed to leave with full pay almost immediately after handing over her remaining projects to other members of the team. Roar had not heard from nor seen Anneli since and had no idea what had become of her.

At this time of the year most businesses were either closed for the summer vacation or at best, running a skeleton crew. It is almost impossible to do any form of business in Norway in the month of July, but an ideal time to get through any administrative and planning work that needed to be done. Roar and Anders had been alone in the office all day and had agreed to have dinner at the Mr. India restaurant in the next street, close to the office. Anders would be flying out to Crete the following day to spend some time with his family at their summer house close to Chania.

It was just after 6pm, they were the only guests in the restaurant and had been given their favourite table, as they often frequented this eatery and were well-liked for their regular patronage. Since his brain hemorrhage Roar had been living carefully, had steadfastly refused all offers of festivities and other drinking opportunities at both work and in private, by the sheer force of willpower and a little knowing wisdom from the recent experiences ingrained in his body.

It had been a scorcher of a day, topping thirty degrees Celsius in the shade and as they ordered their drinks both Roar and Anders decided they would like a chilled Kingfisher beer along with the poppadom's and their starters. The Kingfishers arrived and Anders looked quizzically at Roar as he lifted the beer to his mouth as if to say, are you sure you should be drinking that?

Roar immediately smiled and said: 'It's okay Anders, a couple of beers and that's all, I have it all under control.'

'Listen Roar, I know what you have been through and I don't want you, me or the company to have to go through all that again,' Anders replied. 'I know you haven't been drinking so far this year and you have been amazing, like a new man at work. Not getting distracted by your party friends or by any of the ladies that you often flirt with, which has helped the company make steady progress even through the tough market conditions we seem to be going into.'

'I love it when you nag me Anders,' Roar said flippantly, taking a deep swig from the beer.

The meal continued and by the time they had paid the bill they had both polished off four 330ml bottles of beer which wasn't a great amount compared to Roar's previous heavy volume of consumption. As they stood up, Roar felt a little dizzy and stumbled slightly as he moved away from the table. He definitely felt a little strange and lightheaded as they left the restaurant and knew he needed to get home as quickly as possible. He said goodbye to Anders, hailed a cab and was on his way to Droebak, and it was still only 8.30pm.

Elisabeth was not home when he arrived; she often met with a group of girlfriends for a few hours on Friday evenings. The friends would take turns meeting at the different homes of the group members for dinner and serious, or at times not so serious conversation. Everyone lived locally so it was usually within walking distance, although Elisabeth sometimes drove as she was the only member of the group that didn't drink alcohol. When she did drive, she would usually drop off one or two of the others along the way if they were ready to leave with her. Tonight, she had walked to her friend Anne-Catherine's house, as it was only a twenty-five-minute stroll, the weather was so beautiful and would still be light when she walked home about 10.30pm. The summer evenings in Droebak could be spectacular, the sun setting behind the hills on the other side of the fjord at around 11pm and it never really becoming completely dark.

Roar took a cool shower before getting to bed in the spare room, as had been the norm since he had returned from the hospital. Although they had had many deep conversations together, they still slept in separate rooms. They had become more open and communicative with each other during the past six months, but they still were not physically intimate. Within the transparency and space that they gave each other, there was no inclination as yet towards sexual intimacy. He did, at times feel the hunger for sex and excitement that was his old way of being but would quickly realize that the force behind his thoughts did not come from a loving place and his urges would soon subside. This evening there were no thoughts of women and sexual encounters and just two minutes after he had climbed into bed, he was fast asleep, in a deep coma-like slumber.

Elisabeth arrived home just before 11pm. She noticed Roar's keys left on the telephone table in the hallway, his shoes haphazardly scattered on the hallway floor and his jacket lying over the arm of the chair. This was unlike Roar to leave such a mess in the hallway, although it had been his normal way before he had stopped drinking. She could smell from his jacket that he had been in a smoky environment but that was probably from the restaurant he was going to with Anders. She had an uneasy feeling that all was not as it should be – she hoped that he had not done anything stupid. She went upstairs and prepared for bed and when ready she silently glided into the spare room to check up on Roar. He was fast asleep, breathing very softly, almost baby-like and as she bent forwards, she caught the faint smell of beer on his breath. She wrinkled her nose and cringed slightly as several thoughts attempted to enter her head at the same time. She slipped out of the room and went to her own bed and climbed in.

As she lay there in the dark, she was again assaulted by thoughts, reactions, like probing tendrils seeking an entry point, trying to take over both her body and being. She stayed calm and focused on her own breathing, taking several minutes simply thinking about and being with her own breath until she was completely present within herself.

Her immediate reactive thoughts had been to take hold of him, shake him awake and demand to know why he had been drinking, but she had not allowed this to take control of her and had rebuffed it almost immediately. She had thought how stupid and irresponsible of him to drink alcohol after all that had happened to him. Again, she had not allowed this judgement of Roar to take over, it had remained on the cusp of her awareness, like a vulture watching over a death scene, but she was not going to allow it to take precedence.

Through her calm deliverance she felt and instantly knew how to respond to what had happened, perceiving the truth thus avoiding spiraling down into the gaping rabbit hole of cascading reactions onwards into a labyrinth of accusations, judgements and recriminations. Yes, she would speak to him about his evening, but he was not her responsibility, she was not here to save him anymore. She would simply reflect the truth from her place of calm stillness, nothing more, nothing less. If he is to climb out of the hole that he has dug for himself without falling back in again, he needed to have the gumption to climb out himself. Even if he falls back in again, in the end only he can choose to climb out and stay out. There is no perfection as she knew herself. Roar could not be perfect, and she needed to allow him the space to be imperfect without any expectations about getting anywhere at some future point.

It was now approaching midnight, which was well past her normal time for sleep. She would usually be in bed around 9pm and no later than 10. Elisabeth felt truly settled as she nestled down into her light summer duvet. It was time for sleep and the morning would bring what it needed to bring. She drifted off into a deep dreamless sleep, totally surrendered to the flow of the universe through and around her.

It had been a late evening for Elisabeth, and she slept soundly for over eight hours. She awoke to the sounds of the seagull's morning chorus as they glided, stooped and dived above the fjord. She was immediately wide awake and ready for the day ahead as she prepared herself for her ritual morning walk. Without much ado, she clambered into her sweats and made her way out and down to the local harbour, which often was part of her morning coastal walk.

The sun was already quite high in the sky, having risen at 4.30 am. It was already close to twenty degrees Celsius and another scorcher of a day was on the cards. It was Saturday morning and even in this small town there were already signs of life stirring, people walking dogs, gulls squawking and birds singing. Summer in Norway could be quite short, but the days were long and the people seemed to adapt, to sleep less in the summer and then catch up by sleeping more during the long dark winter nights.

She made her way along the coastline, past the harbour and headed along the coastal road towards the centre of town. How glorious it felt to walk in stillness and connection with herself, at the same time fully aware of all the sights, smells and sounds that pervaded her close environment, it was truly joyful to be Elisabeth Lysene.

She took the wooden steps down to Parr Beach and as soon as she stood upon the sand, she removed her shoes and socks, folded up her leggings, walked down to the water's edge and stepped into the sea, allowing the clear, tepid water to gently lap over her feet and ankles. During warm summers, the Oslo fjord would heat up quite considerably and the water temperature in the sea could rise to as much as twenty-three degrees. She stepped further out until the water reached her knees and walked gently along to the other end of the beach marveling at the sunlight glistening on the almost still waters and appreciating just how gorgeous the simple things in life are.

This moment of clarity was so perfect, it led her to think of how complicated life could become if she became engrossed in activities, actions or thoughts that took her out of the present and into her head, thinking of what might have been, what could be in the future or the 'what if I had done things differently, where would that have led me?' Complication, she felt, is totally unnecessary. It simply means that I have become entangled in a reactive state, a state of being that is not even me. If I walk around in thoughts about, or concerns for, what happens to myself or indeed others, what energy am I then moving in? There are only two options, am I here, with me, connected to myself and the All that is, or am I lost in distractive or destructive thoughts as I move my body around, as I walk here along the beach? As I am walking, are my movements and footsteps impressing the energy of the Light, or am I moving within the confines of spiritual creation and further entrenching that?

She sat down on the sea wall at the end of the beach and took in the glorious diorama out across the sparkling blue fjord over to the green, undulating forest-clad hills on the opposite shore. She could feel the beauty around her and yet could sense the falsity of the world and society in general. She could receive these beautiful images through her eyes but realized how blind she actually had been for so many years. She could feel the residue of her own self-deceptive arrogance and that of humanity in general. The belief that, on this planet, within our solar system, the galaxy and the Universe, or even the many Universes, that our eyes could determine all that was there to be seen and base all our systems of living on that, now seemed so foolish! She had believed that if it was not seen by the naked eye then it didn't exist, if we couldn't picture it then it was not there. We even have firmly established sayings such as 'seeing is believing' that enforce and entrench our own arrogance. If we do not see it then it does not exist. Society was built only upon what the first five senses can determine. Sight, just as with all our so-called five main senses is extremely limited. With the naked eye we can only detect a fraction of the available total on the electro-magnetic spectrum and yet, if we can't see it with the naked eye, then we don't believe it to be present until our limited science proves it to be there.

A family of graceful swans, two gorgeous white adults fol-lowed by four adorable, fluffy grey signets, glided gently by just a few metres away, leaving only faint, almost imperceptible, yet ever-expanding ripples upon the placid waters.

There is so much that we cannot see and yet we create the-ories based on what we do see, plus what, with our constrained cognizance, we imagine might be there or what we actually want to discover there, often setting up our research and experiments to determine what we want to be revealed, usually dismissing a full spectrum of anything that cannot be seen and yet can be felt by others with more perception to the unseen energies of our world. In doing so, we do not allow room for everything that is there, that is not seen. We often base our theories upon our own limited view of the Universe, disregarding much that cannot or should not, in truth be overlooked. Everything that is, is inter-active and everything matters, everything influences the whole that everything is part of. That we can't actually see the con-nection doesn't mean the connection is not there. We know not what is unseen because we have reduced ourselves to over reli-ance on the main five senses. All our senses are limited in this way due to the reduction and limitation of our own attitude to-wards the human body we occupy and our constant flight away from the fullness of the being we truly are.

Redeveloping and reclaiming our sixth sense, clairsentience, which is the ability to feel and read unseen energies at play, chang-es all of this, allowing the truth to be felt within the body, ex-posing the delusion that has betrayed our other five senses. At the moment we no longer feel the outplays of the energies that we are simply marionettes for, we no longer choose the energy we serve, we simply allow ourselves to be controlled by the con-cealed and deceptive energy of spiritual creation.

Nearby, the stillness was shattered by the screeching and squabbling of dozens of seagulls as they aggressively fought for the scraps of bread being thrown to the multitude of ducks nearby. A group of adults with several small children had gathered to feed the seabirds, causing them great agitation. Where there had been stillness before the human intervention, now reigned chaos and discord amongst the creatures affected by mankind.

Returning to her ponderings about energies and control, what next came to her attention was religion in general. The religions we know today are based upon interpretations of certain ancient written texts that are believed to have come from known prophets or world teachers. These religions do not seem to be felt and lived in truth from the body, they are taught parrot-fashion, through induction, indoctrination and fear, to enrapture the growing worshippers, locking them further into the confederate of dark forces. This is a corruption of what religion is meant to be. One cannot feel the true energies beyond the five senses through the process of indoctrination, senses and abilities to read the energies at play are quashed by the one energy that thrives upon our reduction, thus further deepening our deception of the truth.

Is religion a way of returning to one's soul, the soul we all seem to have separated from? Is this return accessed through energetic awareness and conscious presence such that we begin to re-develop the clairsentience that enables us to feel and read all the energies and forces at play, around, in and through us all the time. Could this be the true meaning of religion (re-uniting with one's true self or returning to one's soulful being)? Is anything else simply a faux copy or a bastardization of the one true religion that all other religions have been created from? Is this fact of the true meaning of religion then incrementally undermined to become yet another depreciator of the One-Truth that we all come from and shall return to?

Are we not totally ignorant of the most important and powerful sense that we have, due to the fact that from birth we are actually indoctrinated into a way of life that is a complete reduction of what and who we are? Then forced and coerced into believing this narrative, we are fed how life is supposed to be, dependent upon which country, culture, religion and family we are born into. Parents that have previously been indoctrinated by their parents, and so on back through generation after generation of the past, did the same with their children in the belief that they are doing the right thing.

Just because most of humanity does it this way, it has become the normal way of living, but it does not mean that it is the true way. If we look at the absolutely horrendous state our world is in, it is quite the opposite, it can only be seen as the proof of the ever-deepening incremental forgery of life as we now see and know it to be.

She then thought of an example close to home, drinking alcohol and how normalized that has become all around the world. It is possible to see the sheer ridiculousness of this indoctrination. Personally, she pondered, I don't drink, I have though tasted different alcoholic beverages through the years, but they have never agreed with me. My body has rejected it, realizing that to me it is a poison. The problem is that drinking alcohol has become completely homogenized in society, so much so that, when I or others choose not to drink, the 'normal' drinking people around think that there is something wrong with me or anyone else not partaking, that we are strange, are ex-alcoholics, or such boring people, too religious or even a member of some kind of weird or harmful sect that takes too much care of themselves.

In other words, if we do not fit in with this normalized way of living, we became social outcasts, anomalies to be first of all judged and ridiculed, then on some level tolerated by what is in effect the 'grand cult of normal alcohol drinkers'. We are often avoided due to our severe abnormalities of not wanting to destroy our own bodies, not wanting to reduce our awareness or diminish our capacity for cognition and memory. Basically, the way society looks at drinking is completely inside-out. It tries to inculcate every member to take part in activities

that are severely harmful to those who succumb to participation. This inside-out thinking goes way beyond the use of alcohol to diminish who we truly are; it is a method that is repeated within every aspect of the society we have built on this planet.

She was suddenly aware of movement beside her and as she turned to the right her eyes met with a young golden retriever, standing quietly gazing at her. As she reached out her hand, it joyfully skipped away towards a young couple walking hand in hand along the pathway. She smiled knowingly at the beautiful moment of interaction.

Society is fabricated upon these harmful constructs that are championed as being forward thinking, progressive, transformative and innovative and yet the results are plain to see. We have a media that does its utmost to conceal, manipulate, deceive or simply overlook reporting on some of the worst degradation ever seen. Did slavery come to an end in the 19th century or are there more people 'trafficked' and enslaved now than ever before? Children and young women in particular are kidnapped and forced into sex-slavery, prostitution and to be forcefully engaged as participants in the somehow socially-acceptable pornography industry. Many people of affluence, politicians, celebrities and businessmen are involved in this debasement but are continually protected by this corrupt system, by an elitist ring of entitled men in all walks of society. Poverty is rife and yet the richest people on the planet increase their fortunes at a formidable rate and are allowed to avoid paying taxes. War, illness, disease and the corruption of health systems in general are driven by huge corporations in order to increase profits.

Parenting is almost non-existent; parents are often more interested in their own careers than in actually raising a child to be anything other than a slave to the current system within which they themselves are enslaved. Most of the entire population of Norway are fed the illusion that, at any cost it would be idyllic to own a large spacious home with a panoramic view over the fjord, the lake or the mountains, that each adult should have a modern reliable and somewhat expensive car, they should aim to own a winter cabin in the mountains and for the summer have a motor boat or a yacht moored in the harbour, that they should be up-to-date in having the latest off-road or on-road bicycles, skiing and snowboarding equipment. Entertaining guests should be done with the finest foods and most renowned wines and spirits. In other words, do everything possible to show how successful and refined they are.

Both parents often work full-time to enable this so-called successful lifestyle, but what then happens to the children? After the first twelve months of their lives, although it often occurs before, children are delivered to the kindergarten. Here it may take several months for them to settle in as they often cry relentlessly to be with their parents as every day they are quickly dumped off, enabling the parents to scurry off to get to work on time. They have known only the warmth and safety of their own homes and suddenly their parents leave them behind with a group of strange people and lots of other small, distraught and confused children, deposited in the same way. All the crying and distress is composite proof of how devastating it must feel for them.

She could now hear the joyful shrieks and laughter from the sandy beach nearby, she turned to observe a group of young children splashing and frolicking in the sea. A group of adults sat in deckchairs on the beach close by, deep in conversation, and a couple of toddlers sat in the sand with buckets, spades and several other plastic implements. It was after-all a beautifully sunny summer Saturday and with this gorgeous weather the local beaches would always quickly fill up.

She continued ruminating, thinking further about children and her own working life as a schoolteacher. School does not seem designed to evolve children but rather to reduce and individualize them, set them in comparison and competition with each other. Every few years the sitting Government decides to introduce some kind of school reform to improve the standard of education and without fail it has the opposite effect. Each year it seems that schools have less money available to employ the relevant staff and the school hours for the children and youth are reduced to the absolute minimum. Sickness of overworked and stressed-out teachers also takes its toll and unqualified reserve teachers are brought in to cover the gaps. Norway has a reputation of having the noisiest schools in the world, with some of the poorest levels of discipline and the levels of education are constantly dropping. More and more children and youth are being taught via computerized methods, based upon limited and disingenuous sets of information, ultimately designed to create profit for their creators/purveyors, all to the detriment and reduction of the students.

Lessons are mainly by rote learning where pupils are graded on how well they remember the disseminated information they have had to read through or practise and regurgitate. It's not that Norway has a particularly bad schooling system; it is more or less as equally unscrupulous and deficient, as most other westernized countries around the world.

What if, when children come to school they could be truly met by their teacher, that the first lesson is that of connecting with the teachers and the other pupils. Maybe the next lesson would be learning more about energy! The fact is that everything in the Universe is energy, and this leads to the fact that everything must be because of one energy or the other. What if children were to learn first what the different types of energy are and how they can choose for themselves and know the consequences of the type of energy in which they live their lives? They would swiftly be more able to access the wisdom behind these teachings that are infinitely more valuable than learning to recite poetry, remembering their times tables or working out the value of 'x' in an algebraic equation. Yes, these practical abilities need to be developed but the system is failing tragically and all that we do is to keep applying hopeless 'band aids' to the gaping sore that can have no possible effect whatsoever other than to add to the already malign, discordant situation.

Should we not teach and learn the greatest lessons of life first rather than apply this forlorn system upon our beautiful children? They could learn the differences between cooperation and competition, that evolution and true development comes from the former rather than the latter. Or that true loving observation diminishes the incidence of jealousy, encouraging children to truly learn how to lovingly respect each other, free from any petty form of judgement. It could all be so much simpler if we were able to step away from the dark energies that are in control here. The system in control is so steeped in spiritual creation that it seeks only to further entrench our children into the miasma of the ever-deepening rot and decay of what is supposed to be an education system.

The shrill scream of a young child suddenly pierced the serene atmosphere. Elisabeth turned to observe the hectic activity, as a distraught young girl ran up through the shallows to a concerned lady within the group of adults on the beach. She had seen it many times before, children playing gleefully in the sea only to fall foul of a stinging jellyfish lurking out of sight. The lady, possibly the girl's mother, fished out a bottle of still water and a tube of ointment from her bag. Almost every Norwegian parent had these tools at hand within their beach bags. The beautiful warm summer weather in Norway often brings with it a plentitude of Lion's Mane jellyfish to the coastal waters.

The commotion quickly died down but there remained a residue, an air of anxiousness within the group as the children moved out of the water onto the beach for safety. Two of the men within the group used a net to fish out the offending jellyfish and move it to a more innocuous location.

Roar awoke to the distant sound of the door closing as Elisabeth left the apartment. Groggily, he slowly reclaimed his sense of awareness of the surroundings and the dull headache pulsing at his temples. He remembered his dinner with Anders and the four beers he had consumed, realizing immediately the significance of his body's messaging, that there was no longer any room in his life for alcohol, at all. He gently maneuvered his body carefully out of the bed and walked straight to the shower. He stood under the powerful torrent of the showerhead for the next ten minutes gently changing the temperatures from hot to warm to not exactly cold but a lesser level of warm, and then back again through the scale until he felt the dullness let go and began to feel more alive again.

After he had completed his morning ablutions he dressed in shorts and a light short-sleeved top, then he too went out for a morning walk. He had walked this route with Elisabeth repeatedly during the last six months and by the time he had reached the beach he could see Elisabeth in the distance sitting on the sea wall. He made his way slowly along the beach towards her, appreciating the stillness and the true beauty she emanated from within.

She turned as she heard the sound of his approaching footsteps, smiled and turned back to look across the shimmering azure fjord. He came and without a word gently sat beside her on the sea wall and he too gazed out across the blue waters. They sat in silence for several minutes until Roar broke the reverie and began to recount the events of the previous evening in full. He left out no detail and completed the story with his realizations and conclusion this morning, that he could never drink alcohol again. He could feel how damaging it was just to drink four small bottles of beer and that if he were to do this on any regular basis the amount of devastation he would be causing his body would be horrific.

Elisabeth had listened in silence, allowing him to express in full and by simply observing his movements and the way he spoke she could read the sincerity; she could feel and read the energy he exuded. She smiled, opened up her arms and gave him a long uninhibited hug without any form of hesitancy or judgement. She stood up, held his hand and gently pulled him up. 'Let's walk,' she said.

They made their way along the coastal path, through the park and down into the small harbour at the centre of the town that was now slowly starting to come to life. The little café on the quayside had opened and people stood in line for their morning pick-me-up coffee. They continued through the town and up the hill to the south. They would, when they reached the hotel at Skiphelle beach, loop around through the forest towards the town hall, up through the woods, past the old cannons and back down to their apartment. As they walked, they began to talk again.

'You know it's not just alcohol that damages our health, it is everything we do, our every movement, every word, gesture, thought and intention is either healing or it is harming, there are no in-betweens, no neutral ground,' Elisabeth exclaimed.

Roar quipped instantly, 'Do you want me to give up cigars, skiing and take up Pilates and meditation then?' with a slight hint of irony and irritation.

Elisabeth read it immediately and calmly replied: 'I don't want you to do anything Roar. It's all up to you to make your own choices but both you and I now know, well in fact we have always known, what our true movements are, what actions are hurtful, which foods are nourishing, even the type of music we listen to can bring with it an energy that can be either nurturing or toxic. We just know it and our bodies will always let us know if we are being abusive to ourselves or not. The body always, in one way or another offers signs that we can then either choose to read or not.'

Roar replied: 'It is now obvious to me that drinking alcohol, as fun as it may be, is not something that my body can deal with anymore. But even though I know this, there still is an enormous attraction to it, to the buzz that it always gives me. Why is it so difficult if my body knows this, why does it want more?'

Elisabeth answered: 'Is it your body that wants the alcohol, or is it something else? Your body can't speak to you in words, it can only give you signals, such as the reaction you had last night, to what is for you, a very small amount of beer. The signals you get are often health warnings, like getting heartburn from drinking coffee or eating certain types of greasy food. A big indicator for me was the way I react to dairy products, my sinuses become blocked and my breathing gets hampered by the sheer amount of mucus my body then produces. It can really be as obvious as that but there can be more subtle signals that we can learn to read, like small aches or pains out of the blue, dullness or sleepiness after eating certain types of food, or the way the body can become racy after coffee or a piece of cake. It becomes a process to be aware of the signals, to read them and to make the necessary adjustments. As I have worked with these bodily signals, I have gradually lost much of my dullness, I am less lethargic and have become a lot lighter in my outlook on life and the way I communicate with other people is much more joyful.'

Roar grimaced as he spoke, 'so you are saying that the best form of medicine is how we live our lives, life is either good or bad medicine.'

After they had walked through the small central harbour that housed a selection of pleasure boats of all shapes and sizes, from small, motorized dinghy's up to forty-foot luxury yachts, they continued on past the community aquarium and into an area of narrow streets with quaint, brightly painted, small wooden houses. Many of these old buildings were precariously perched on the rocks overlooking the fjord, they were adorned with various nautical bric-a-brac and festooned with numerous flower boxes containing a lustrous juxtaposition of glorious blooms of all colours, shades and sizes. This little town, that could be so cold, foreboding and insulated during the long winter certainly blossomed during the short summer months.

Elisabeth continued: 'It is difficult to change when you have lived in such an ingrained and destructive pattern for most of your life and who knows, maybe for many lifetimes before that. My experience of this when I discovered what dairy products were doing to me was that my body was telling me something was wrong and yet there was something within me, stuck within my head and often repeated to me via the deceptive black box stuck on the living-room wall, saying that chocolate was okay, that yogurt in the morning was good for me, that my lunchtime cheese sandwiches were healthy. It got to the point where I had difficulty breathing at night, as soon as I lay down my airways would become clogged. As I was so congested, I had to breathe through my mouth and always woke up feeling more tired than when I went to bed the night before. I was addicted to nasal spray to get some semblance of a proper way of breathing and I felt exhausted and anxious for much of the time.

'Fortunately, a few years ago, through my old Pilates group, I met a lady called Janne who lived in Oslo, she had had similar problems and advised me to try giving up dairy products. Although I did love my cheese and my yogurt, I decided to try it. Things gradually improved and after about four months I could breathe freely at night. I could breathe, breathe properly and for the first time I could remember, I didn't feel constantly tired. I stopped using nasal spray and it helped me to begin to see life in a different way and of course, it helped me to listen to what was going on in my body, what it was actually communicating to me.

Roar looked at Elisabeth, thinking about the way she lived her life, the amount of green vegetables and salads she consumed. He would never feel satiated if he ate the same way as her.

'My body told me I had to change my lifestyle, choose a different way of looking at the world. I found that my body – our body – tell us everything if we are attentive to it. It presents us with the truth about everything we do, in one way or another and we can't get away from that. We can either listen and take heed or we can override the signals and continue to blast the body with our unhealthy habits and harmful choices. Each body tells everybody just where they are at, most of us don't choose to listen, ultimately ending up with one or other, or several forms of lifestyle illness, disease or with some kind of serious incident, just as you have experienced.'

They started to ascend the steep hill up from the end of the main street, heading south out of town, the very hill Roar had walked on his fateful escapade after the New Year's Eve party. In fact. they were now about to retrace his steps all the way down to the hotel by the beach on which he had collapsed. Each time Roar walked this route it would bring back the memories of the evening that seemed to be so long ago. He brought his attention back to what Elisabeth was sharing.

'It wasn't just giving up dairy products, almost anyone can probably do that with the pure force of willpower, if the threat to their health is severe enough. I learned that if I stopped myself when the cravings first began and at that moment, I could look at what it was that I was feeling that would try to convince me to eat or drink something that I knew was harmful to my body. I discovered that it was a combination of me starting to feel something that had hurt me in the past and to then, through comforting food, dull myself down to avoid feeling that hurt, through the enjoyment of these pleasurable creamy tastes spreading from my mouth throughout my body, thus dulling my senses. The hurts would then be covered over once more, and I wouldn't need to feel it.

'By no longer indulging in these cravings I could experience some of the hurts of my past, feeling the lack of self-worth that had been etched into me from the first moments I could remember. My parents, unknowingly, for they thought they were doing the best they could for me, even though they made the choices to not be aware of what the best was, gradually instilled within me the image of a fragile little girl. In a way, they convinced me, although in truth I was asking to be convinced, that I should grow up to become a good housewife and mother to the children that I most certainly would have at some time in the future. It was assumed that I would become this pretty dainty bauble for the pleasure of my future husband, to love and obey his every whim. It wasn't just my parents either, this continued from extended family, friends of my parents and then on to school and within all the after-school activities. The fact is that it is not just me, it is almost every girl on the planet that gets sucked into this system to churn out young women that struggle with feelings of self-worth, their own self-image, and self-respect. Men on the other hand, are taught and learn how to exploit and abuse these weaknesses, often reinforcing the hurts that women carry, adding to the cause, driving them to hide the hurts deeper and deeper within.'

They had reached the plateau, the top of the climb up from Droebak, an area that afforded stunning views not only across the fjord but southwards towards the open sea. Roar stopped at the exact point where he had stood face-to-face with the great elk. He looked from side-to-side for any signs of wildlife before he proceeded onwards.

'So it was that I entered upon what became an unequivocal and now unrelenting series of revelations that changed the direction of my way of living completely,' continued Elisabeth. 'Each time I had this experience, rather than avoiding feeling behind the deep wounds I carried, another layer of defence would be scraped away, revealing a little more of my true self that had been hidden within. This has been going on for years now and as you can see and have experienced from living with me this has allowed me greater detachment from all the dramas in life. I realized that all these emotional dramas are but illusions designed to enthrall us and to keep us captive within this current abusive system.

'As you can imagine there is more to it than simply giving up habits and addictions as well as all other forms of distractions and pastimes that in truth keep us from being consciously present within our lives. There is something within us, a wayward part of our being that doesn't want us to become aware of what the real truth is, a part that is in fact aware of the real truth but doesn't want us to live within it.'

'As you speak Elisabeth, I can feel part of me wanting to tell you to be quiet, I just don't want to hear it and yet there is another part that simply knows I need to listen and accept what you are saying to me. It is like my insides churning around, like a constant unrest.' Roar interjected.

They turned off the road just before the entrance to the hotel opposite the large beach carpark. The winding pathway was steep and narrow, taking them uphill through the forest mostly consisting of birch, spruce and pine trees with a smattering of oak and hazel. Beneath the mature trees of the forest green were swathes of blueberry bushes with tiny dark deliciously sweet, ripening berries ready for the taking. The meandering pathway that wove its crooked course between the tall members of the woodland was just wide enough for them to walk in single file. As they climbed what seemed to be ever upwards their conversation stopped as they concentrated upon following the serpentine trail. They came upon patches of open ground without any green coverage, there the pine needles had amassed and after weeks without rain had been dried almost to a powder, ready tinder awaiting the heated spark.

Onwards and upwards, they continued, the climb broken only once to cross a small road through the forested area. At the pinnacle of the climb Elisabeth remarked, 'I always loved this part of our walk up the steep path through the forest, it really does get the heart pumping, doesn't it?' Roar nodded whilst taking a few deep breaths.

They continued in silence for a short while until they once again came out of the forest into a residential area and made their way down towards the town hall and past the school at which Elisabeth worked.

Elisabeth then continued. **'Our body is made up of divine universal particles and consequently we are inextricably connected to and moved by the Universe. Thus, we are undoubtably part of the whole of the All that is. This I like to describe as the all-pervading energy that governs All that exists, but some may call it God or refer to it in the name of some other deity. Somewhere within the All that is, through the choice of free will, a wayward force has incrementally unleashed what we now call human life, which became what we now perceive to be our reality. This is now the only ill-conception anywhere within the beauty of the All, anywhere within the Universe. Individually, within each of us this wayward part can be known as the spirit. This spirit in its playground, along with its deviant compatriots (all of us), seeks to expedite dark forces within this temporal reality, the constructed illusion in which they experiment with their free will to create. No matter how far they stray from the Universal oneness, they are still contained within it, within the All. They cannot escape the truth as they must one day relinquish their farcical foray and return to the All, from whence they separated.**

Roar found all this talk of spirits, God and ill-conceptions difficult to swallow and yet there was something strangely fascinating that compelled him to listen even more intently.

She continued, 'For it is so that we have all been part of the illusion, and so many are determinedly anchored to it, desperately remaining disconnected from what is our true essence, choosing instead to be lost within the falsity. We willingly allow ourselves to be charmed, beguiled or baffled by this spiritual energy. It has become our reality which is so far removed from the truth that we will refute, attack and abuse anyone that reflects true veracity, or in other words, hold anyone in contempt that lives from the heavenly or soulful energy. The truthful are vilified, tarred and tarnished, denigrated and scandalized until they are smirched and smeared with the very labels and perverse accusations that are diametrically opposite of their true representation.'

They walked from the road and up past the football stadium, once again in an ascending trajectory, they followed a track up past a tiny kindergarten along another winding track. At the top of the rise, they walked under a stone-built archway covered in shrubbery and wild grasses.

Elisabeth stopped speaking as they came through to the other side to be confronted with a battery of huge old cannons that were originally installed during the 19th century as fortifications to defend against any invasion. Later on, at the start of the 20th century, they served as a line of defence when Norway declared its independence from Sweden in 1905, after five hundred years of living under both Swedish and Danish rule.

They scrambled up above the cannons and sat on the lone bench which was probably one of the most spectacular viewpoints in the whole town, overlooking the fjord, several islands and the countryside beyond.

Roar was now deep in thought, trying to digest all that Elisabeth had said. Yes, he had witnessed the changes in the way she had been living, but during that period of time he had pulled away from her. At that time, he wanted anything other than to align to her straight, clean way of living – it was no fun, she had become even more serious than he had thought her to be. No skiing, no partying just neat, tidy, healthy living and always looking deeper into herself and expressing her feelings, simply had not appealed to him. Well, it did appeal to part of him but obviously not to the controlling delinquent part that had ruled his life until January 1st this year and still wanted to maintain that control no matter the cost to his physical body which was, in truth, even to him quite alarming.

They sat for a while in the glorious warm sunshine, closed their eyes and allowed the heat to permeate their bodies. When the summer sun shone from dawn to dusk Norway was such a sublime place to live. They remained in the stillness of this moment for the next few minutes. They opened their eyes, turned to look at each-other, and smiled.

Roar spoke slowly: 'I can understand what you are saying about the wayward spirit within us, as I have felt this so many times, in many different ways. I could be hard at work concentrating on a project, putting my full focus on it, when out of the blue an idea pings into my head proposing something that is almost irresistible, such as walking down to the local restaurant for lunch for a steak and a bottle of deep red Malbec wine. This idea might then lead me to trying to chat up the waitresses and a lunch break that suddenly turns into a three-hour drinking session, important work becoming insignificant in the moment, the work being delayed or having to be done by someone else. Once alcohol was in my body it was like a whole group of spirits and some of their demon friends, had taken over my body for one big party and any outcome then became possible.'

Elisabeth simply asked: 'Do you ever ask yourself why, why you chose to allow this to happen, why when you know that you are in a relationship with me, that you not only disregard your own body and your whole being but you also disregard me and others such as your work colleagues and the women you chase and may or may not have sex with?

'It's not simply allowing the wayward spirit to have its merry dance, having a bit of fun, it's also willingly choosing harm, both to yourself and in fact everyone else around you. Could it also be something deeper than this, something that you avoid looking at, preferring to choose all different forms of distraction and indeed, self-destruction rather than face what is there, to face the grander truth, taking full responsibility for everything that you are?'

Roar replied: 'Yes, there is more and yes, I do allow myself often to be controlled by what I would call sudden impulses but it feels like the impulses come from the stream of thoughts that continually return to be spun around in my head until it gets to the point that I have to act. The thoughts telling me I am thirsty or hungry, the thoughts and images of women and different sexual encounters. Thoughts that lead to thoughts that lead to more thoughts in a never-ending spin inside my head. The desires and the impulses come from these ever-returning thoughts. I have realized though, that these thoughts seem to be somehow programmed in me to keep me away from facing or knowing the truth.'

Even though Elisabeth had heard about and accepted all of Roar's previous infidelity, every time he talked about it, mentioning the word sex in conjunction with other women, there was sharp pain in her stomach. Showing her that there was still more to uncover, that she was not clear of the pain this had caused her. This was a reaction to what she herself had been willing to overlook in order to keep the peace, something that could no longer be allowed in her body.

He continued: 'As long as there are thoughts, keeping me entertained, letting me feel the excitement and the fun of the way I have been living, then I don't feel what might lie beneath. My thoughts are like my own private world of self-indulgence, no-one else is eligible for admission, no one can examine my desires, infatuations and fantasies. No one is privy to what goes on in here, I don't confide or reveal my secret world to anyone, and I have always tried to live out or experience everything I could. It has always been about what I can get out of life and there has never been contemplation about why I want to get all these things. I have always thought that I was living and experiencing a sort of ultimate way of life. Successful in business, fit, healthy and good looking, gift of the gab, confidently charming with the ladies, I figured that I was living every man's dream but at the same time there has always been something missing, something more to be done or achieved. No matter how successful I became, I wanted more, more money, more admirers, more recognition, more of everything I considered life was about.

'Then, boom, I end up in the hospital at death's door and re-alize that everything I have done, achieved and experienced is worth almost nothing and I suddenly feel a huge gaping hole in my life, a nothingness, worthlessness, and I am now realizing it is time to ask the question ... why? Why do I never stop to ask the question why? Why am I here, what is it all about, what is it all for? Why is there no room in my head for respite, peace and quiet, why is my head full of self-serving, self-oriented schemes and indulgencies, frustration and pointlessness?'

Elisabeth replied: 'After all you have been through recently, all that you experienced, almost dying, it may sometimes feel dark and meaningless, but it can also be seen as a great opportunity to turn your life around and find your true purpose in this life. It seems to me that you have been given some great revelations regarding your previous way of living, you are receiving some incredible flashes of truth that could be guiding or offering you the options to start to move in a different direction.

'Each time we are given true revelations it is an offer available for us to embody into our way of living life. These revelations can assist in breaking that almost constant stream of distractive thoughts that churn around within our heads. Revelations of-fer us moments of settlement and stillness, moments to feel our true being, it is up to us to take these moments and expand with them. Our moments of tranquility can quickly be overrun by the force of dark thoughts but there may be an uncomplicated way to reclaim our true harmonious space.

'It can be from within the practice of simple meditation, learning how to bring yourself to stillness and to develop a more consistent conscious presence. It's about learning how to be with yourself in your every movement, to a point where you only think about what you are actually doing, you only do what you currently think, staying aware and present in everything you do. There is then no place within your being to house an incessant stream of dark repetitive non-sensical thoughts that can often take over our whole being. It's not something that normally happens all at once, like an overnight change, though it can be that, it does take time and a certain amount of commitment. Once the true benefit of the settlement it brings is experienced regularly, it becomes a natural choice to undertake a more devoted practice that helps instill an innate obedience and dedication to living a life more attuned to the Light of the Universe.'

She paused momentarily, looking directly into Roar's eyes, seeing the distinct sparkle of Light that she had never noticed before. Roar gazed back into her eyes as they held each other for what seemed like an eternity but was actually less than thirty seconds. Once again, they smiled to each other as Elisabeth spoke once more.

'You might now be thinking that at this moment in time it may seem impossible but if you look at it simply, you have already been practising a way of life that you were obedient and dedicated to, and you did this tremendously well. It is just that it was done within the harmful dark energy, which as you well know almost resulted in your untimely demise, in this life at least. What if you simply changed your allegiance from one energy to the other, you already know how to be dedicated and obedient, what if you do it in the energy of being present within your life, living attuned to the Universal Light. You have already felt and intimately know the truth. Is it possible for you to return to it and to live within it?

'As you reclaim what is your own inner space, the stream of useless, repetitive thoughts will gradually diminish and a greater clarity can be discovered as the inner fog that not just you, but all of us walk in, steadily dissipates. This also helps to provide the opportunities to heal the inner hurts we all carry with us throughout life, the hurts we try to protect ourselves from through all our ingrained behaviours, the hurts we don't want to feel and yet they are the keys to release us from this form of self-imprisonment we have chosen. Behind the ceaseless chatter of the mind are the protections and ill-behaviours built up over years, and even lifetimes to avoid feeling the hurts that continually fester within the body.

'The hurts that we do not attend to are like everything else, they are comprised of energy, and un-dealt-with, ill-energies stored within the body may eventually seek release from the body and that may come in the form of physical or even mental illness or disease. We could at this point ask ourselves, do illnesses and diseases just happen or is there a root cause for everything? Does everything that occurs, happen because of one energy or the other? Stress and anxiety are great examples of this, and they almost always relate to the continual circulation of ill-mental energy spinning around in the mind. These may often be precursors for many of the, more or less, serious physical ailments such as cancers, kidney and cardio-vascular disease, or just stiffness, aching joints and migraine headaches.'

Roar nodded and said: 'I understand everything you're saying Elisabeth, I can feel the care and the truth in your words and I'm just wondering about, or even starting to get an idea of some of the issues that I may have buried and avoided looking at, essentially for my whole life. That I have behaved in a way that has been harmful to myself, continually ignoring the pain and avoiding the answers that were inside me all the time. Just by stopping the thoughts for a short moment allowing myself to truly feel my own body, a wave of sadness seems to flood up from within me.

'It seems like a sadness of being alone, separate from everyone, in particularly a lack of real contact with not only my father but my mother too and any other true mental or physical connection with anyone. I think this is part of the reason why I seek exciting experiences, emotional, physical and passionate highs for exhilaration. I have always sought the next level of euphoria and yet after each peak there is a trough, a sense of emptiness which leads onto seeking another new high point to lift myself up again. I just can't feel real connection with anyone now, except with you. In the past, I have done my utmost to sabotage our relationship and to keep you at arm's length in case you asked me to be more than I felt I could be. Just now, this makes me feel like I need to be doing something – so I don't have to think any more about it, not to feel what is here and yet I know that herein lies the opportunity for true happiness, that is a constant joyful way of living.'

Elisabeth interjected: 'Yes Roar, just as I, and most women I know, have issues with their own self-worth, most men seem to have issues regarding being rejected, ignored or neglected at a very young age. I think this can often lead men to develop unhealthy patterns of deportment such as insecurities, possessiveness, unreasonable jealousy and a myriad of other irresponsible habits and behaviours. As you can imagine, it is different in each individual case but almost everyone is brought up in a way that may cause them to have these kinds of issues throughout life. Until that is, they step back and realize there could be another way, they return to some level of awareness and discover a true purpose in living human-life. We all intrinsically know what lies beneath the layers of protection, the habits and behaviours we have developed to not see what is there but so few of us are willing to actually stop for a moment and go there, because what may be revealed can be painful to re-experience and express whatever feelings may be attached. But, once expressed and released from the body it can open up to a way of living that becomes free from the sadness and pain and therefore the ingrained ill-habits can be much simpler to let go.

'Men can be rejected in many different ways that may not, at first glance, even seem like rejection. Take your own rejection as an example; your mother was there all the time but didn't give you much attention other than feeding, clothing and tidying up after you. You were simply given toys and other gadgets to distract you from a true connection, to keep you occupied and pacified. Your father was never there, he was completely committed to his banking career so everything else in his life was secondary to his bank. He never spent any time with you or developed any real bond or connection with you. How did this make you feel?'

Once again, she looked directly into Roar's eyes, waiting for a response to the question. Roar turned away as he became a little teary. He felt saddened, but had no words, he signaled Elisabeth to continue.

'Two parents and neither of them were prepared to connect and spend time with you, to provide an upbringing that might possibly leave you free of all the hidden issues, in particularly the outplays of your deep-seated rejection that you now have. In a situation like this it is so easy for a child or even an adult to feel victimized, to not want to take any responsibility for their own situation and to go into blame. We often say it was all the parents' fault, they didn't look after me, they neglected me or they abused me, often resulting in the willing adoption of the role as a victim. This is such a dangerous path to go down even though it may feel justifiable to blame others, in the end, no true good will come from it. On the contrary, it can lead to the formation of harmful patterns of behaviour and a way of living life with a total lack of self-responsibility. Whenever anything goes wrong in life it is always someone else's fault, it is never our own fault.

'We often think about situations in life in an isolated manner. That is, we don't stop to see the whole and instead we look to the individual part, just the tiny piece that has gone wrong. We ignore the fact that everything is interconnected and may not be solely related to events taking place within our present life. There is also a very important point to be aware of when sorting through the feelings and emotions connected to the issue of rejection, and that is that it could be related to your past-life momentum into this present life. Could it be, that because of your issues with separation and rejection that this was one of the reasons you actually chose to be born into your little only-child family with Harald and Solveig? That this would ensure that you could continue in the same patterns and the same momentum that you may have done so for many previous lifetimes. This may or may not be relevant as you dig deeper into the root causes of what is there inside you to be revealed.

'Something else that is prevalent in the cause of rejection in young boys, and the men they become, are the images of expectancy of what real men should be, that all aspects of society continually saturate both parents and children with. We have all seen, firsthand, how we classify children, girls and boys. Immediately from birth we try to separate them with the use of colours and the appropriate apparel, dolls, cuddly toys and what is much worse, the way we start to speak to them. As they grow, we instill them with what we think they should become, we speak to girls and picture or project upon them the roles we think they should fill, such as, good wives and loving mothers. We speak more harshly and play more roughly with the boys; we want to toughen them up so they can be big and strong and become real men. When in truth both boys and girls are beautiful, fragile, tender beings that need the same guidance, attention and intimacy as each other. They do not need to be formed by the corrupted ideals and beliefs of this out-of-control society, modelled and forced to become anything but the innate beautiful being they truly are.

'Focusing on boys though, they are often brought up to be tough and physically robust, to be strong and not express feelings and emotions, to not be a sissy or too soft. Using phrases such as, "big boys don't cry" or "you're not really hurt", "just get up and get on with it". So, we take these tender young baby boys and start to mould them into what we and society at large consider grown men should be. We actually demand that these gorgeous little beings separate from their innate beauty and tenderness and take on the facades that are considered correct in the eyes of the current ruling dark narrative and the sold-out generations of the past that have gone through the exact same process of separation from who they truly are.

'Consider any of your own friends that have had a son and how they have indoctrinated them into their own view of what being a man is and all the different components, opinions and deceptions that are included within that. The first thing I noticed were the clothes that they put on the boys, not only were they predominantly blue but also had designer labels and often the colours and names of their favourite football teams, sometimes with the names of favourite players too. Even the child's bedding would be something like racing cars, spaceships, some other macho theme reserved for boys, or once again the colours and emblems of that favourite football team.

'They begin with rough and tumble play, taking them to skiing lessons almost before they can stand up, then its karate, jujitsu or Tae Kwando, its football, handball and stooping out from the highest diving platform into the sea. It is forever pushing them beyond their comfort zone, creating fearless, individual and what society deems to be masculine young men that often become centred upon their own achievements, their own self-advancement, what they can get from this temporal divisive world. It is possible that they become totally engrossed in their own success and in out-competing their peers and everyone else. They may become completely detached from their own true self and only interested in what they personally can get out of life, that is externally, in the form of achievements and material possessions. They can become single-mindedly interested in the attainment of recognition for whatever their preferred endeavours might be, in reality, completely sold-out to the dark forces of spiritual creation. This can lead to entering into relationships, looking for fulfillment not even realizing they are looking to avoid or diminish their own separation from themselves. Relationships are then often doomed to become a misguided set of agreements and caveats to exist together as well as possible without exposing one another's underlying, soulless separation, issues and hurts.'

Roar smiled in respet at what was almost a diatribe directed at the way society is set up to cause this great individuality and separation. It touched him deeply, as he recognized his own lifestyle within her words. It was a brutally honest rebuttal of the lifestyle he and the majority of those he knew, had for years signed up for. An incisive exposé of the falsity of the current system of living that humanity had waywardly indulged in.

She spoke further: 'When a woman comes along asking a man for true intimacy, they, both the men and the women, simply have no idea of what is being asked for, what intimacy truly is. Many see intimacy as any form of physical touch and/or any variation of sexual intercourse in every possible context or setting. Their idea of this way of being intimate is most likely conceived as that is all they have ever known; all they have ever seen.

'Sadly, this is getting steadily worse due to the proliferation of, and addictions to, pornography. It is often the first introduction to sex-education for many, thus the societal norm for intimacy is becoming more and more like hard-core sex. Everything that is presented to them regarding intimacy has at least sexual undertones and at the other end of the scale means nothing more than physical and often violent sex. Pornography has become so abundant and ingrained into men's everyday living, and worse, the obscene level to which porn now goes and is watched on a regular basis by hundreds of millions all around the planet, completely corrupts and programs them to steadily harsher levels of what they now believe is intimacy, but in truth is pure abuse.

'It seems to me that they want to re-enact what gets them off on the computer or television screen, to have the brutal or the cold, hard tenderless sex that they watch at every opportunity. In doing so, this in many cases alienates them completely from any form of intimacy with any partner, no matter the gender or orientation. Living life based on ideals gathered from perverse, vulgar and brutal pornographic films and images does nothing other than cut themselves off from their own self-connection. Being so separated from who they are, it may become impossible for them to be intimate in any true sense of the word. This often involves a significant element of secrecy; thus, they cannot be transparent or freely express anything, in any way, from their true essence.'

Roar replied: 'So why is it that there can be such a wide view of what intimacy actually is? It's all very confusing, as you have said many men have a highly sexual view of what intimacy is.

I have always looked upon it as being something that is private and sexy, it could be hours of touching, caressing, lovemaking, getting down and dirty with each other, an exploration of everything and in every angle and position. If it's not all this, all that I thought it was, then what is it?'

Elisabeth said: 'Could it be Roar, that intimacy is not a physical act, not any form of doing? That it is in fact a state of being – and from that state there is a movement in true connection with both oneself and the All that is. Thus, an opening up of space with stillness and observation, simply allowing the Light of truth to come through without putting any corrupt or pre-determined pictures and images of what our own personal opinion of intimacy is upon what is inherently there. Presenting openness and transparency without any expectations to whoever you are offering intimacy to. Therefore, none of the things either you or I previously thought were intimate are anything to do with intimacy. They are actually distractions and distortions away from it. The word intimacy itself has been corrupted to mean anything and everything rather than what it truly is.

'It can be that intimacy does not even need to come from the spoken word although conversation from alignment with the true Light of the All, untainted by the dark forces of illusion, would be from a place of intimacy. Intimacy is evolving and expanding away from the dark consciousnesses, away from the selfish ideals we run with, from that which controls the human system. Anything that is from or for the human self has nothing to do with true intimacy. Intimacy can simply be a beholding of another or others, within the Light of the Universe.

'Maybe not knowing what intimacy truly is means that we are, in one way or another, rejecting our true selves, rejecting anyone and everyone that we associate with. Could it be that from being and feeling rejected we have somehow lost sight of what true intimacy is? Therefore, we don't really know how to interact with others in a true way, which causes us to do the opposite, which is to form secretive, inter-dependent and conditional liaisons

or arrangements instead of open, unconditional, transparent, loving relationships.'

The sun was now beating down upon them as the temperature started to soar. They looked towards each other, stood to embrace and made their way the short distance down the hill towards their apartment.

Chapter 8

RE-ACQUAINTANCE WITH THE DEVIL

It was a bright Saturday morning in early September, London bathed in the warm autumn sunshine of 1902. Grace Lightfoot had now been the live-in housekeeper for Richard Billings for over two and a half years. They had developed a beautiful loving relationship as dear friends and fellow students of themselves and of living a truly purposeful life, reflecting a different way of being to everyone they knew and everyone they encountered upon their way. No subject between them was taboo, everything could be discussed, even the more sensitive subjects not often conversed upon between women and men. They were completely relaxed, and open with each other and both could see and feel the enormous benefits of this way of communicating leading to a harmonious and joyfully open, expressive and expansive relationship. Richard was both friend, companion, substitute father and teacher all rolled up into one generous and caring elderly man.

Although Grace still had moments with dark thoughts and painful recollections of the time spent at the House of Darcaster in Kensington, these tended to pass rapidly as she quickly learned to accept what had been before and to move on from it. She accepted that there was actually learning in everything she had experienced. She now knew that there could be absolutely nothing gained from remaining in the role of a victim of abuse. Holding on to the pain, humiliation and hurts served only to prolong the agony and suffering, and that letting go of the anguish avoided and dissipated the festering of these malignant energies that had no place within her body, in fact they have no place in any person's body.

It wasn't a question of forgiving George Darcaster as she had come to accept that the evil energy that came through him was much more damaging for him than it was for her. It was the vile forces coming through him and not the sad and lost man that had perpetrated the ill deeds upon her. Yes, Mr. Darcaster should be punished for his crime but the system of justice in this country would never allow that to happen. In the end, only he himself had aligned to the dark evil of spiritual creation, seemingly feeding him the thoughts that formed the choices he made to live his life in this way. Knowing, yet apparently unknowing that ultimately by living under the control of these dark energies he would eventually have to pay the price in lives to come. Karma is the great leveler, no one walks free from the accumulated ills of lives lived in waywardness. Everyone must one day return to the Light of the Soul.

Richard had left the house quite early in the morning to open up the bookstall for the hordes of Saturday travelers that would be passing through London Euston Station. It never ceased to amaze him how many people swarmed around the streets and that it was now calculated that London had reached a level of population of over five million people which was around twenty percent of the total population of the whole United Kingdom. He loved to people watch, to observe humanity both in all their glory or in their degradation, to behold and feel the love he held for all of them. He felt every single one as they flocked and thronged in, out and through the station entrance focused on their own particular tasks or destinations.

He could sense the energy and the forces that drove them on their individual journeys through this life. It was incredible to see with such clarity and to register the dark power that controlled most of their movements. From the rich businessmen with their single-minded focus on wealth and prosperity heading to the first-class carriages, to the poor working-class passengers crammed like sardines into the dingy third-class compartments. There was such a startling difference between the wealthy and the poor and yet there was a remarkable similarity within the manner commanding their movements. All but a few were acceded to the fact of class differences. It was ingrained within their bodies, it was the accepted norm, they either loved or hated the actuality of it, depending on the separate levels of ascendency within the hierarchy of social rank.

There was a consciousness of supremacy that seemed to govern the activities of the masses, rich, poor and those in-between, all marched to the same entrenched tune of the haves and the have nots. Privilege and arrogance extolled by and oozed from the upper echelons of society whilst misfortune, deference and despondency hung like a pall of sooty fog over the commoners, the lesser inhabitants of this grand but at the same time, in many ways, grotesquely depraved and grimy city. Deeper than this controlling supremacy consciousness he could feel that there were other energies, forces and consciousnesses at play here, some quite obvious, whilst others were much more subtle, all there to control humanity, to hold them sleeping within this ill illusion, that was both the pleasure and success, or the suffering and toil of human life.

George Darcaster had been spending much more time at his house in Kensington as the expansion of his business interests in London had gained great momentum during the past two years. Ideally it would be most effective if he were to move the family home to London but knew his wife would have none of it. She was safely ensconced at their stately home, Alexandria Hall, in the hills to the east of Manchester and had absolutely no intention whatsoever of moving to London.

George liked to keep abreast, in great detail, of everything that happened in all areas of his many divergent businesses, so much so that he would rarely delegate to others anything that he held to be of importance and in doing so found it increasingly difficult to cope with the sheer volume of work he now had to undertake. He was working at least twelve hours almost every day, he rarely had the time for anything other than work. He found himself drinking more alcohol just to enable him to stop thinking about work and to get some sleep. This inflamed his heartburn and general bodily discomfort to the point where he now felt, more often than not, exhausted and knew that he was gambling with his own health. In reality he knew that he had to make some important choices. He had to trust some of his managers, to give them more responsibility to lessen his own load, but even within these thoughts he could feel his own reluctance, he wanted to be in control, he wanted all the recognition and all of the power that came with it.

Mrs. Davinia Roebottom, the housekeeper and replacement for Grace Lightfoot had been carefully selected by Alexandria Darcaster. Davinia had been a long-time acquaintance of a good friend and came highly recommended. Davinia was a forty-two-year-old childless widow, having lost her husband in the early stages of the first Transvaal War in 1881. Mrs. Roebottom was a stout and robust, mature and highly dependable, no-nonsense lady originally from Sheffield, although she had worked in several homes all across the country and came with impeccable references.

She had started work at the House of Darcaster on March 1st, 1900 and had quickly settled into her routine of keeping the house. She cleaned and catered for George whenever he was in London, generally ran the household and more importantly she kept a wary eye over his comings and goings as she was also there to be an observer of any potential wrongdoings. She had understood that Mr. Darcaster had a roving eye when it came to the ladies but so far, the only notable item of concern she had noticed, was the amount of food and alcohol the man consumed. She had never seen such a voracious appetite and thought that this could not be a very healthy fellow.

This morning Mr. Darcaster would be travelling to Manchester and had requested a full breakfast to fuel him for this long day of travel. She had laundered, pressed and packed his clothes and other necessities into his considerable trunk. She had also ordered a Hansom cab to arrive at 10.30am. He would now be staying in the north of England, working mainly between Manchester and Liverpool for the next three weeks. He had spent the best part of the last three months in London and Davinia was looking forward to a well-earned break from serving Mr. Darcaster.

In the little house in Barnsbury, Grace went joyfully about her chores on this bright and sunny morning and looked forward to taking a walk into the city to do a little shopping and to drop by at the bookstall at Euston Station on her way.

She put on her newest ivory coloured skirt and blouse with a pale blue sash around her slim waist accompanied with a lace hat to match, a small blue lace handbag completed the outfit. Grace was often out and about in the summer months so her face and hands had a warm olive hue that added to her overall healthy appearance. She looked quite stunning as she swished out of the front door into the warm sunshine.

The cab pulled up outside the Darcaster residence at precisely 10.30am, was promptly met at the front door by the ever-efficient Mrs. Roebottom who asked him to kindly take the trunk and Mr. Darcaster would be out directly.

Two minutes later, George climbed into the cab and away they sped towards Euston Station to shortly be met by chaos in the traffic bound streets. One of those new-fangled motor omnibuses had been involved in an accident with a smaller horse-drawn vehicle and both were now blocking the road. The wily cabby with many years of experience driving through London's streets, after a quick consultation with George, turned the cab around and set off in a different direction. This would take a little longer but he assured George that they would still be in good time for his 11.30 departure time.

All this extra concern did not reduce George's already high blood pressure and he could feel the anxiousness rising. He didn't want to miss this train as the next possible departure would be more than three hours later and may cause him the inconvenience of an extra hotel stay in Manchester instead of being able to reach home in the early evening. As the cabby weaved in and out of the smaller back streets in order to find a route around the stagnant traffic, George grew more and more impatient and could feel the heat rising in his cheeks. He took out a cigar, lit it up and proceeded to puff manically upon it in a vain attempt to calm himself and to lower his blood pressure level.

The cab emerged from a side street onto the main thoroughfare and the end destination was suddenly in sight. George sighed with relief but could still feel the blood pumping in his veins and had that familiar light throbbing at his temples. He sat back in the seat and drew in the smoke from his cigar appreciatively, trying to calm himself further. The cab pulled up at the station entrance and the cabby hopped down, placed George's trunk by the door, accepted payment and was gone in a flash leaving George to find his way to the platform.

Grace and Richard stood together deep in conversation behind the counter of the bookstall as George Darcaster dragged his trunk inside the station looking for a luggage porter. Out of the crowds emerged a young man pulling along the large luggage trolley behind him and immediately asked George if he needed assistance and to which platform he might be leaving from.

George snapped at him immediately: 'Of course I need some bloody help, take this trunk to Platform 2 and wait for me there.'

The porter, used to aggressive and abusive travelers bowed his head, biting back his own anger. 'Yes sir, right away,' he courteously replied.

For many years he had dealt with these high and mighty toffs being so arrogant and impolite. He had learned to outwardly maintain his calm although seething with irritation inside. He loaded up the trunk instantly and made off at speed towards Platform 2. The crowds parted in front of him and seemed to instantly swallow him again and he disappeared as quickly as he had arrived.

George walked over to purchase the morning newspaper. He arrived at the bookstall and addressed Richard, asking him abruptly for *The Morning Post*. Richard broke off his conversation with Grace, turned and recognized George Darcaster. With a look of surprise, he turned back towards Grace as she too turned to look George Darcaster, full in the face.

Grace's expression did not change, the Light continued to shine from her eyes as she took in the apparition before her. George Darcaster on the other hand was dumbfounded, his jaw dropped in shock as the blood seemed to rush to his temples and the throbbing instantly increased. He felt a stabbing pain in his chest and the whole station seemed to spin around as he lost consciousness and tumbled to the ground in front of the bookstall.

Richard and Grace, almost dumbfounded, stood still for a few moments before they sprang into action. Richard checked George's breathing, which was shallow but steady and his pulse which was quite faint but seemed to be beating regularly. Under Richard's direction they placed him in a comfortable position on his side with his head resting on a small pile of newspapers. Richard placed his coat over George to keep him warm, he then asked Grace to stay with George as he went to the Station Manager's office to call for an ambulance.

Twenty-five minutes later an ambulance arrived at the station entrance and the medical team came to treat George. They swiftly decided to take him to the hospital and asked if anyone knew him and if they could accompany him to Charing Cross Hospital. Grace, taken aback at first, quickly resumed her calm and agreed to accompany the ambulance. Richard looked straight at Grace as if to say, 'you can handle this' and told Grace as she was leaving to ask for his nephew again, Dr. Samuel Billings. The ambulance wasted no more time as the horses were whipped up to speed, they galloped through the streets making good time, it took a little more than fifteen minutes before they were headed into the hospital and enquiring to the whereabouts of Dr. Samuel Billings.

Ten minutes later George had been wheeled into a treatment room and was now being examined by Samuel Billings. He had heard the description of the events at Euston from Grace and further been informed of his current condition by the ambulance team.

George regained consciousness, and after a short examination it was quite simple for Dr. Billings to confirm that he had almost definitely suffered some kind of heart problem. He had seen many patients suffer in this way, with varying outcomes and many did not survive. He knew that this was a very serious condition requiring at least a six week stay at the hospital with careful treatment and diet administered by the hospital staff. This seemed to be a disease they knew very little about, although it frequently appeared to afflict gentlemen of import and stature, who led stressful lives, along with a rich and plentiful diet.

He informed George of the severity of his predicament, that they had treated him with morphine to relieve any pain and that he would need to stay in hospital for the next four to six weeks being treated in this way to give himself a chance to recover. The doctor told him that it was a very serious condition and if he was not careful about the way he lived he may have a relapse that could possibly be fatal. George nodded his understanding but couldn't really feel the seriousness of the situation, instead he felt quite elated, calm and serene. George discovered that morphine was a blissful sensation not unlike the third glass of port, although greatly more relaxing, almost completely carefree.

George then remembered the bookstall and the face of Grace Lightfoot. He asked: 'The young lady at the station, what has become of her?'

Sam replied, 'Ah yes, Grace, she and the bookseller acted quickly to get you brought here to the hospital and she accompanied you in the ambulance; she is waiting in my office.'

Samuel itched to say more, to tell George that it was he that had saved Grace's life after she had been so brutally raped, abused and forced into an illegal abortion by him, but he knew how unprofessional that would be and may in fact cause the patient harm, so he clenched his teeth together, stayed tight-lipped and kept his thoughts to himself. From his experience with similar patients, he knew that George was in a very precarious position and that any shock or stress during the first few weeks of recovery could cause another seizure that may be fatal.

George was becoming drowsy and after a long pause he asked, slurring his words; 'Could you ask her to come in to see me? I wish to speak to her.'

Samuel thought for a few seconds but knew the answer as George closed his eyes and fell asleep. Once more he checked George's breathing and listened to his heart before leaving the room and returning to speak to Grace.

'It is difficult to know how serious his condition is, but it is most certainly his heart, and he will need to be very careful in the weeks to come and even that may not be enough. So many times, we have had patients with similar conditions that seem to be making a recovery and sadly have a re-occurrence of the same issue and we are helpless to save them,' Samuel said after he and Grace entered his office. 'He is sleeping at the moment, but he has asked if you would come in to speak with him.'

Grace replied calmly: 'I can come back later this afternoon to see him although he may not enjoy the words I have to say. In the past I have hated this man so much but all that has gone now, although I still hate everything he stands for, the way he and others in high public office or standing look down upon the rest, abuse anyone they choose to at their whim. He and his ilk are lost to a consciousness that makes them believe they are supreme, that they are born to rule and control others.'

Samuel asked: 'How does it feel to meet him again under these somewhat strange circumstances, the man that almost caused your death two years ago?'

'I have a calm feeling of detachment, but don't get me wrong, I do hate his actions, they were absolutely despicable but then again, I know now that he is but a puppet of the evil forces that control him. He is more damaged now than I am, he has always been so in this lifetime. He did abuse and defile me and at the time you and I first met I was broken and close to death, but this process has made me much stronger and much more aware of what goes on here in this wicked world. I could have succumbed to the atrocities I have experienced but, with the guidance of your lovely uncle I have regained much of my true inner strength and have evolved greatly as a human being as a result of this,' Grace replied.

'When I was treating him, I felt a rush of anger and hate for him and struggled internally to avoid speaking the words that wanted to explode from me. Instead, I said nothing, regained my composure and treated him as any other patient I might see. I can't choose who to treat or not to treat based upon what I know about their personal lives. In my eyes everyone has got to be the same, I have sworn an oath upon this,' said Samuel.

'Thank you for all that you do, Sam, you are a wonderful man,' she said as she made her way to the door. 'I trust the hospital will contact his family to let them know what is going on.'

Richard stood looking quizzically at Grace as she arrived back at the bookstall waiting to hear the outcome of the earlier events.

'Please, do not keep me in suspense, how is George Darcaster and how is my wonderful nephew at Charing Cross,' he smiled.

'Your nephew, as you well know, is a lovely man and is currently caring for the dastardly George Darcaster as he would any other. Mr. George Darcaster on the other hand may not be so lovely but for the moment he is still alive and will be in hospital for several weeks to come, that is if he manages to become well again. Just before he fell asleep, he asked Sam if he could speak to me, and I will return later to hear what it is he has to say for himself. His collapse is most likely due to a problem with his heart and Samuel said he must be very careful about how he lives his life from now onwards,' she replied.

Richard asked: 'How does it feel when you see before you how George Darcaster's ill-ways have resulted in his downfall – and that his collapse should happen the first time he sees you in the full glory of what you have now become? Many people would just write this off as a coincidence but you and I both know that coincidences do not exist and that everything that happens, does happen for a reason. It can also be a great opportunity for George himself to see and feel the untruth of his misguided choices, to take a look at the dark energy he has been aligned to and to realize for himself that he has not been living in a true way.

'A brush with our own mortality can often be the key, or the defining moment that invites us to go deeper into our living way to assess its validity, or lack thereof. It is of course a definite warning, a moment of possible learning, an opportunity and not necessarily a categorical turning point. We, as human beings often do not heed the messages that come through our bodies. It seems that, in this current life, many simply cannot or will not change no matter how deleterious the outcome. Many do recover, as may George Darcaster, but that does not mean he or any other will live their lives any differently in the future.

'During his recovery he will have the space and the opportunity for contemplation, potentially a stop moment that could be exactly what he needs to re-assess the way he lives his life and his abusive ways. When I say abusive ways, I don't just mean the way he has treated you and no doubt other women but also the people he interacts with in general. It is so, that such a man, to become so abusive towards others is always, in some ways abusive to himself first, whether it be physically, mentally, or both. He can either see his situation as a moment of bad luck, an ill-occurrence that was not his fault and thus avoid taking responsibility for all his own actions that have brought him to this point, or he may look upon the way he has lived his life thus far and realize that he has been abusive and irresponsible and he may then wish to change his ways.'

At that moment a tall, well-dressed man with black hair and olive skin, seeing Richard and Grace deep in conversation, picked up a newspaper from the stand and handed over a sixpence, laying it quietly upon the counter, turned and headed out through the main entrance into the late summer sunshine.

Richard continued: 'Something to also consider is the fact that he may have long ingrained patterns of behaviour due to experiences in one or more past lives. He may have been a woman abused by men and now the darkly controlled spirit within him that has not an ounce of care for the human body it possesses, chooses to be, not only the abuser of its own body but the abuser of women. The spirit-driven man that is aligned to the forces of creation has only lusts and desires that it craves to fulfill with no true regard for the collateral damage it may cause. In fact, it craves collateral damage and emotional reactions of all kinds as its very lifeblood. We must always remember that we are all the same in essence and with everyone we meet to try to see, appreciate and love that inner-quality first but at the same time recognize the source of the energy that drives the actions coming through each person, be it from the soulful Light or from spiritual creation.'

He paused for a few moments, as though deep in thought, before going on: 'Whatever happens, it is not a problem for you if you do not choose it to be so. When you visit him, all you need to do is recognize what kind of energy is coming towards you, simply continue to emanate the inner beauty of what you truly are, stay with your essence in whatever dealings you have with him, or with anyone else in any other situation for that matter. The energies that are at play here will surely try to infiltrate into your body to generate thoughts and reactions to what has been in the past, know then that you are only here to be in the present. As long as you stay within the current moment, the evil energies that come at you through George Darcaster, that can come through everyone or anyone else, can hardly affect you. Even if you do feel a reaction, such as anger, fury or irritation, and you do feel dark tendrils of spiritual creation begin to seethe within you, there is still no need to judge yourself, that will only allow its dark forces further access into your body. Simply accept that it is there and return to your essence and to presence. Accepting the fact that no one, neither you nor I, or anyone else is perfect, it may then be easier to avoid that dark energy expanding within, thus curtailing any greater reaction of anger, irritation, rage or even sympathy.'

Grace said: 'I understand all that you are saying but I still have some doubts about this spirit character that is causing so much chaos inside everyone. How do we distinguish between the human being, the spirit and the soul? How can we be all three at the same time?'

Richard replied: 'It generally is a question of awareness of everything we do, of our own movements, thoughts and intentions. When we assess or try to comprehend something, anything really, that befalls us in life, we more likely than not do this purely from what is often referred to as the instinctive, human perspective, that is, from using our five main senses. This is generally all we now know when we live in our reduced state of being unaware that we are much more than simply human. This is just as our spirit, or more correctly stated, the grand collaboration of all separated spirits that make up the forces of spiritual creation, have designed it to be. In doing so we are often completely oblivious to the energies that are actually at play here. We are deliberately fed the thoughts that we "think" by the dark forces that tell us that we are only human beings or that we can live only this one life and go straight to heaven or hell when we pass over, or some other illusive narrative in a similar or not so similar misleading vein.

'Whatever the dark energy feeds us will be an attempt to reduce us to be less than we truly are, continually controlled by our wayward spirit puppet-master. To avoid the reduction that we are a part of, we need to revive our most powerful sense, that of clairsentience, the ability to feel, be aware of, sense and read the subtle and not-so-subtle energies at play in and around us.

'It is a question of unfolding and expanding the whole of what we are, our metaphysical being, rather than residing in the constriction of what we have become, which is the de-limited spiritually controlled thought-driven physical human body and its self-entitled machinations. As you so rightly ask, how can we be all three at the same time? We can be all three and yet we cannot.

'When incarnate we are obviously always in a physical human body, which is a vessel of expression for either the Light or the opposite, it cannot be both at the same time. An important point is that we are creations of separation, of and by the dark

225

spiritual collaboration and yet we are created from the divine particles of the Universe, for no other particles exist, every particle comes from and is equally part of divinity. Although we are created by the dark forces, they had no recourse other than to create from the grandness of all that already is, the Universe. They provided the created human beings with only a meagre subset of their own intelligence in order to have complete control over the sphere of existence that includes humanity. This control has been mostly successful for many millennia and has brought humanity to where it is at present, in complete and utter disarray, self-destructive, with shocking levels of inequality, arrogance, abuse and irresponsibility. For the dark forces, being human is an experiment, the human body a plaything, to experience and distract from the yearning and pain felt from separation from their soul and the One Soul.'

As she stood listening to Richard's words Grace could feel a discomfort within, a tension, as though something inside her was being exposed. She became agitated and, in the unease, she glanced away, looking around at the people in their never-ending chaotic cacophony of movement and sound. By shifting her position and refocusing upon Richard, she regained her calm and the inner turbulence passed as quickly as it came.

Ever-observant Richard gave Grace the space she needed to compose herself and to come back to a place of stillness before he continued. 'As the spirit-controlled human, with the provided limited intelligence, we exist in the created illusion of the constructed system of living we now endure here on Earth. There is also a constant pull from the Light of the One Soul which exists in and through every divine particle of everything that is, including every atom of the created human body. When this constant, yet subtle pull back to the oneness with the All becomes strong enough it can connect to a level of soulful wisdom and intelligence that is far deeper than that of the disconnected wayward spirit, allowing the human being via its divine particles to embark upon a return to Truth. A return from whence we came, gently pulling the reluctant spirit along with it. At first this return

226

may be of an intermittent nature as we strive to understand the full potential of what we are and where we come from and to comprehend the machinations of our own disconnected spirit. Initially there can be a great deal of equivocation and turmoil as the dark forces seek to sabotage the human consciousness and bring it back under spiritual control. They, the dark forces, will in fact never let go, not until this miscreant force itself has been dissipated, that is when all spirits re-align to the One Soul they all originally separated from.

'Stepping out and away from the way of life that is the illusion and the commitment to an existence in service to the evil spiritual forces, steps us into alignment and into true service for the power of the Light, to universal wisdom, for all of humanity and to all that is. In service our responsibility to be and reflect all that we are extends to everyone on this planet no matter their energetic alignment.'

Grace nodded serenely without a word, as Richard continued.

'Our constituent parts, Spirit, Soul and human consciousness, though there are never all three in action at the same time, they are never not all there, present in every moment, at least until the wayward spirit returns to be at-one with the soul. The universal particles that make up the human body contain the wisdom and intelligence from whence they came and as such they seek to play their part in the continued expansion of the All. It is therefore inevitable that All will return to its truth of origin and that the futility of the nefarious spiritual collaboration is doomed to crumble no matter how much they delay. This is an inevitable, unequivocal fact. Although futile, the interruptions caused by the sinister forces, that will create and do anything at any cost to avoid returning, can mean that humanity must strive on for several hundreds, possibly thousands of years before the inescapable return actually takes place.

'We can naturally feel when we are connected to the true source of energy, from the Light of the Soul, the whole body becomes at one with it and there is an innate knowing and an all-pervading stillness in every particle. There is a harmonious presence both of mind and body that cannot be disturbed by the dis-ease and ill goings-on around us. From this natural loving state, it is possible to feel and discern the deceitful energy of spiritual creation and choose to no longer align to it.'

They fell into silence and there was no more to be said at that moment. Grace felt to continue on with her errands, holding the resonance of the teachings imparted by Richard's words as a guide to re-imprint how she moved and would thereby go about her daily endeavours.

Later that same afternoon, Grace returned to the hospital to once again meet her incapacitated abuser, the man who had callously and unrepentantly raped and beat her on a multitude of occasions, the man that had balefully ignored her pleas to stop, had only become more infuriated and violent when she had resisted his advances. Showing no regret, he had sent her to the back-street abortionist that had almost caused her death. Since that time Grace had recovered well and through her association with Richard Billings she had personally evolved as a human being in so many ways. Even though she could feel the same old Grace was still there, she felt her inner-state-of-being and her current levels of awareness had given her a whole new outlook on what life was truly about.

Although the years of torment at the hands of George Darcaster were mostly accepted and she could see them as a point of learning and expansion, occasionally she could still feel the defilement of the dark seething energy trying to creep back into her body and her mind, calling her into reactions of anger, disgust and sadness just at the very thought of him. Now she was about to face him, converse with him for the first time since she had escaped his evil clutches. Or, she thought, the clutches of the dark evil force that he allows to come through his body to attack her and many others. She considered that by attacking her he had attacked everyone, as we are all interconnected. What we do to one person we do to everyone. Although we think we are separate and act as individuals, we cannot but affect the All. With our actions, all our movements and intentions, we either embellish or we detract from the whole that we all belong to.

As she was about to open the door into his hospital room she stopped, making sure that she was focusing upon her own body and its movements, only thinking exactly what she was doing, clearing herself to allow through the Light of the universe that she knew she was a part of. Staying present, not reacting, having no judgment, she knocked lightly, pushed open the door and entered the room.

George was sitting in bed, propped up on a multitude of pillows. He smiled meekly as she advanced towards the bed. Grace genuinely returned a smile back as he pointed to a chair near, but not too close to the side of the bed. She nodded and sat down, focusing on seeing his essence first, that equal tender and gorgeous essence that she knew they and all others were from. Calmly she looked into his eyes and asked him what he had to say to her.

'George Darcaster, I have come along at your bequest – as you can imagine I was a little reluctant to do so, what is it you have on your mind?'

'I have been feeling ill for some time now,' he said. 'It began even before you left the house and the saddest part of it is that I knew all along that it was the way that I was living that was making me ill. It was so obvious, as I ate and drank obsessively and hurried from one meeting to another, one town to another, my body continually showed me in many ways that this was not a healthy way, but I just couldn't stop. Even my own doctor had told me many times that I needed to slow down at work and to be more careful with the quantity I consume and quality of ingestion, but I just didn't listen, it was the only way that I have ever known. I always do what I want, and no-one stands in my way, I decided long ago that no-one will stop me from achieving my goals.'

Grace interjected calmly, quietly yet firmly: 'Why are you telling me this story, in what way does it concern what you have done to me?'

George's face reddened as he reacted to her words and struggled within himself, to keep his calm. The first thought in his head was, how dare she, the sheer impudence of this upstart of a woman, who does this servant girl think she is? He bit back the words that were forthcoming, calmed himself as the redness slowly dissipated whilst Grace watched, fascinated by this show as she could easily read from his expression and energy he emitted, exactly the thoughts he was thinking. She also realized that the introductory story he was telling her was in fact a prelude, his way of attempting to justify what had happened. Whether he had any sense of remorse remained to be seen. She sat back and spoke, 'Please continue with what you have to say and I will try not to interrupt you too often.'

George took a few, long, deep breaths as he again fought to regain his composure, as everything she said seemed to rile him, it was all way above her station. She had certainly changed during the last couple of years. Eventually he began to speak, trying to take a different tack. He spoke slowly.

'As you know the life that I have lived so far has been one of privilege and I have in fact been of the opinion that I am deserving of this, deserving of everything I have worked so hard for, but today I could have died and now feel how tenuous my grip on life actually is. I have been so dedicated to work for what feels like my whole life and now I'm asking myself, what has it all been for? I have used and abused many people, all for the sake of getting what I want and not really knowing why I want it, other than everything was there to be taken. I'm asking myself, what is the driving force behind the way I choose to live my life, risking everything to have more wealth even though I now have more than any man could possibly need. What is the point, when I die I can't take it with me, it's all going to someone else, it seems so pointless?'

George, loose tongued under the influence of the considerable doses of morphine, didn't seem to realize that he was still completely consumed with his own self, talking only about how it was for him, speaking now to the young lady he had so blatantly abused, violently, sexually and mentally. He could not see or feel that he wasn't even sorry for what he had done to her as he was only consumed with his own self-pity, that he was now the victim, therefore Grace and in fact everyone else should have sympathy with and pity upon him. Grace recognised this energy coming from George, she saw how conniving it was and was determined not to allow it to violate her body and being.

Gently, yet firmly she asked him, 'Do you mind if I say something Mr. Darcaster?'

This simple question seemed to stop the flow of self-pity, of the sleezy, deceitful energy that oozed through him. He looked straight into her eyes for a few seconds, feeling the strength of her being and simply nodded for her to speak.

Not wanting or even needing any form of apology or even attention of any kind she addressed him, powerfully holding herself in presence, keeping her steady gaze upon him. 'Since my near-to-death experience at the hands of your back-street abortionist two-and-a-half years ago, I was given the opportunity to look at life from a different angle. It took quite some time for me to let go of the extreme hate that I had for you and what you represent. Over time I have become clearer about who I am and why I am here, why all we human beings are here and what our purpose in life is, and I know that my purpose, everyone's purpose comes from relinquishing all that is of the self. I, like you and almost every other person in the country, in the world, have spent lives focused upon ourselves, our survival, our security, our needs and wants, our wealth or lack of it, completely ignoring the bigger picture and a true purpose in life.

'You have much wealth, your wife and family, all the servants in your grand houses and all the workers within your factories, warehouses and other businesses and yet you set your own needs and desires above all of these, it is you, yourself only that comes first, that is your main priority. You may say that you care and provide for your family but is that not simply a secondary effect of your own self-motivated ambitions to become successful, rich, powerful and influential?'

Again, George reddened, and yet did not speak as he felt the words of truth penetrating his body. He did not feel any anger or bitterness coming from Grace and thus, with accompaniment of his steady supply of morphine he was able to stay calm and not fly into a rage as he normally would if he had any notion of anyone trying to criticise him. Unmoved, she calmly continued to speak. 'Within everyone there are certain degrees of un-dealt with hurts and harms that distract us from a truer purpose in life, that capture and keep us bound together with the self within. I have found a more fulfilling way of living by working through my own internal wounds that have absolutely contributed to defining my 'self' image and I do have many inner scars, some of which you were very much involved in. Then taking a serious look at how damaging it can be, not only to my own being but also all those I encounter, I observed the possibility of re-focussing my living way onto the well-being of everyone and everything, to look upon all as my equal brothers and sisters.

'I know we have been taught that we are all different, that some are to be rich and some poor, some are to be upper class, some middle, some lower and those that live in abject poverty, begging on the streets. There are some born in England whilst some in France or India or any one of the multitude of countries around the globe, some speak French, some English and some may speak Chinese, but all of these facts are simply superficial individualities whereas inside we are all the same, we all bleed the same blood and have the same organs, we are all from the same source and will one day return to that heavenly source. All that we are given of the separative teachings, religions and schoolings are nothing but destructive to the oneness we all originate from, they seem designed to separate us from each other. Relinquishing our individuality, our self-interest, selfishness and our separative goals in life for a living way of equality and working for the good and evolution of all men and women, may that not be a worthy cause?'

Grace sat back in the chair and waited for George to respond, or react, having no expectations that he would understand or that he may be willing to change his ways. George sat quite still for what seemed an age but was in fact a little less than two minutes, as neither of them spoke. At some level, he felt the truth in her words but at the same time all of this went against his lifetime of home-grown ideals and beliefs, everything he was, everything he knew and everything he had ever done.

Eventually he spoke. 'Miss Lightfoot, those were powerful words, and it seems that you have indeed stepped out of your shell and uncovered your hidden wisdom since last we spoke. What you say is all very interesting, but do you think that the world will take any notice of a young woman with what may safely be called radical views that go against everything the establishment stands for? If it were not for men like me with ambition and drive, where would our creativity and evolution be, would we not still be in the primitive ages with nothing but spears, bows and arrows and other archaic implements? There would be no modern civilisation, no Great British Empire and very little wealth and prosperity.'

Grace understood exactly what George was talking about and knew that in some ways, within the materialistic view of the world he was not far off the mark but in truth as everything was a question of which force one is aligned to, that is the force of spiritual creation or of soulful Light, he was firmly entrenched within the dark energies and therefore what he had said could not be of truth. She wondered to herself, if he would be receptive to an explanation of the two forces at play here and of course she was aware that he had not actually asked her for this. She knew that unsolicited preaching of her recently attained and lived wisdom to anyone that was not ready to receive it was like a red rag to a bull and would only provoke an opposite reaction. She realized that it was he, George Darcaster, that had initiated the conversation and that in fact she would have preferred to never see him again. As she pondered this, she realized that it was exactly this confrontation, or discussion opportunity that was required, as within her reluctance to see him again lay the seeds of something inside her, yet to be fully dealt with.

It was not a question of forgiveness or forgiving him, for in what he had done lay the road to judgement and who was she to judge any other person for what they had done. For her, she knew that all he had done to her had happened and would never happen again, this she needed to accept in full. This was purely an opportunity for her to learn, evolve and detach from all that was connected and caused by the forces of spiritual creation. She could feel the truth as she contemplated the thoughts that had come to her, that what she had experienced through George Darcaster and the path her life had taken after the night of the abortion may never have happened had she not suffered at his hands. As for George Darcaster himself, there may not be justice and physical punishment in this life for what he had done, as the judicial system is rigged by the evil spiritual forces to serve its minions. But the true repayment of Karma would at some point be forthcoming and he may be given the opportunity to learn and experience his own reprehensible behaviour in return.

After what felt like an eternity in her own thoughts, but in reality, was just a few seconds, she replied, 'Mr. Darcaster, let me put something quite simple to you; could it be that the establishment as it stands today is not created in the interests of all equally and due to this fact, it is a biased and unfair system that ought to be changed? Also, this system is run by the privileged few, first and foremost for the gain of those that are already privileged, to the detriment of the lower classes and in particular the poor and deprived at the bottom of the pile. The system and those that run it actually take advantage of those that have nothing, abusing them to further increase their own material profits.

'What I am about to say may seem to you to be a little preposterous but please do listen closely to all of it. Everything that is, is controlled by forces much greater than anything we may have imagined. Yes, Governments and businesses seem to have control over the masses and in a way, they do, but there are unseen forces much greater than these that ensure that they themselves are mere puppets of these dark powers. Every rich and powerful man, woman or even child, that believes that they are superior to those less privileged, that thinks they are better than the workers or beggars on the streets, are given these thoughts from a source outside themselves. Those that cannot see that each person is of the same value, are simply lost to the dark consciousnesses that feeds them every thought they have. That provides them with the financial success and acumen they think they have been deserving of. They are all lost within the consciousness of supremacy and obediently do the work of the dark force of spiritual creation. Upon this abundant Earth there are more than enough resources for every man to live comfortably and yet there are the greedy few that want more, much more even though this self-indulgent avarice is detrimental to so many others, they do not care if others suffer and die of starvation, as long as their wealth continues to increase.'

Through his morphine induced fog, George registered her words and squirmed a little in his discomfort and irritation as he perceived them as a direct attack upon his own self-important person.

'There are in fact only two possible forces to align to. One is of a dark creation; the other is of Light and true fortitude. Fortunately, I found the Light of heaven in my darkest moment, when so close to death. It was a great struggle and I needed the help of truly good people to pull me through. I could easily have become consumed by hate, blighted by the forces of spiritual creation, looked upon myself as a victim and become lost in self-pity, save for the people around me. I am honoured to have these people in my life, there are so many others that are not so fortunate. It is through my affinity to the Light that I am able to be with you today, face to face and be clear of the burning hate towards you that threatened to devastate me and destroy the rest of my life. When I am present within the Light, the dark forces of spiritual creation that rule our little planet cannot touch me. Only when I let my guard down and lose my own connection to God and the Light, may they enter.

'If it were not for men like you George Darcaster, persecuting and desecrating women at your whim, by your arrogant entitlement, where would the world be? Because you have an aptitude for making money and taking advantage of economic opportunities does that bring any real progress to the evolution of mankind? Does it not bring greater separation and inequality, as you increase your wealth on the back of exploitation of the poorest workers and do you not supply the British war machine with both ammunition and weaponry that cause the deaths of countless thousands across the globe, all in the name of progress? Did you ever stop for just one moment to contemplate upon what the true evolution of mankind is and what that would look like? Would that have anything to do with the construction of greater and taller buildings or larger and faster ships, speedier railways or automobiles, and for that matter, any other industrial advancement? Did you ever consider that there may be a greater purpose to industrial betterment, that it could be for all the people and not simply for the profit of the already wealthy few?'

Grace felt an edge of excitement and irritation coming into her body; she stopped and took several slow, deliberate breaths, felt the movement of the air in and out of her body and gradually brought herself back to the centre of herself. There was so much to say but she realized that George was no longer capable of really listening to her, he was becoming sleepy and obviously needed to rest. She realized that she had given him much to ponder upon if he actually could come down from his shadowy, lofty perch and deign to do so. She looked straight into his eyes that were dulled by the medication and the events of the day and saw how frightened and vulnerable he actually was, the hard and austere outer layer could not hide that. She realized that he understood everything she had to say but would probably dismiss it all and choose to continue living the same lifestyle until at some point it would take his life. Not from pity, but from a sense of service, she asked him if he would like her to return the following day. He drowsily nodded as she said goodbye and turned away.

The following afternoon, Grace arrived at Charing Cross Hospital and was shown into the office of Richard's nephew, Doctor Samuel Billings and asked to sit and wait for the doctor who would be available in a few minutes. Sam arrived a little later and they greeted each other warmly as was their way ever since their first encounter over two years earlier. After a few minutes catching up on their well-being, Sam came to the point of why she had been led to his office.

'Mrs. Darcaster has arrived and is in the room with Mr. Darcaster at this very moment,' he said. 'So, I thought it best that you be forewarned of any such confrontation. I do not know how much she has been informed about the situation, but she does know that it was you that brought her husband to the hospital. She is though, quite eager to meet you and has asked to be informed upon your arrival. It is understandable if you do not want to see her but, if you do, I will make this office available to you as I will be attending to my patients for the rest of the afternoon.'

Grace pondered for a short while and smiled. 'I would love to see Mrs. Darcaster, even though these circumstances are not very fortunate. She has always been very generous and propitious with both myself and my parents who have worked in her household for many years. I also think that she knows her own husband and what he is capable of. The truth of this situation will probably not come as so much of a shock to her. I have no reason to protect Mr. Darcaster from the truth of the deeds that he has done and I think she would expect nothing less than that. Mr. Darcaster has feathered his own bed and now has no other choice than to lie in it, at least at this present time.'

Sam nodded in agreement. 'If you wait in here, I will let Mrs. Darcaster know that you have arrived. She will probably be along quite sharpish.' He stood and promptly left the room.

Less than ten minutes later there was a gentle knock on the office door, Mrs. Darcaster stood waiting for a reply as Grace opened the door and asked her to come in. They had not seen each other for more than three years since the last time Mrs. Darcaster had accompanied Mr. Darcaster on a business trip to London. They stood opposite one another, looking directly into each other's eyes. Mrs. Darcaster could see the fire in Grace's eyes, she understood that this was no longer a naive young woman but a strong, independent and beautiful lady that had grown tremendously during recent years.

They sat opposite one another, either side of Sam's desk and after exchanging some pleasantries Mrs. Darcaster asked pointedly, 'What happened to you? Why did you suddenly leave the house in Kensington, what did George do to you?'

Grace replied: 'What did he tell you had happened?'

Mrs. Darcaster shrugged. 'He said that you had not been keeping up with your work and had become distracted by a man that took up most of your thoughts. When he had questioned you about it, you had become guarded and upset. The next time he had come to London you had left the house without any warning, simply taken your belongings and moved away. He had subsequently assumed that you had taken off with this new man in your life.'

Grace smiled at the ridiculousness of the false narrative George Darcaster had uttered to his wife and replied, 'Do you actually believe any of that?'

'No, not at all. Your mother did tell me that you were fit and well and had found new employment that you were very happy with. You understand that I have been married to George for many years now and I know how selfish, uncompromising, callous and brutal he can be with some people. He sees himself first and what profits only him, above all else. If it were not so difficult for women to divorce men, I would have done so many years ago,' she spoke softly. 'Now tell me everything that happened, every detail, leave nothing out.'

Grace took a deep breath and began from the beginning. She recounted that the first time he had assaulted her was just about six months after she had moved to London to become the housekeeper. She told Mrs. Darcaster how, at first George had been very charming, witty and generous but soon he became too familiar, touching her inappropriately and commenting on her looks and her figure. She had been embarrassed and knew not how to ask him to refrain from this behaviour. One evening at dinner after he had consumed a copious amount of his favourite alcoholic beverages … 'as I cleared away the crockery, he was decidedly tipsy and became more covetous and grabbing, touching my breasts and buttocks. When I asked him to stop, he flew into a rage and started shouting that he owned me and that I should never speak to him in that way or deny him anything he wanted to have.

'I excused myself quickly, left the dining room with the dishes and began to wash-up, hoping nothing more would happen. After completing all my tasks, I made my way up to my room on the top floor and got myself ready to sleep. I felt a little shaky and it took quite a while for me to fall asleep but eventually I dropped off. I was woken by Mr. Darcaster, he was naked, he had pulled off my bedding and was ripping at my night-clothes; he was like a wild animal. I screamed for him to stop and he slapped me across the face, I struggled and he hit me again and again until it came to the point when there was no struggle left. I thought he would kill me. He pushed me face down on the bed, I could hardly breathe, and this is how my maidenhood was violently taken from me. He was so aggressive, demonic and monstrous and I truly feared for my life. It seemed he would stop at nothing until he killed me. I sobbed myself to sleep that night as I tried to think of an escape route, truly knowing that there was no way out of this predicament I had allowed myself to be trapped within, other than living on the streets which we all know is a fate worse than death.

'From then on, I lived in fear, never knowing when he would attack me again, always hoping that you would be travelling with him. Every time he came to London alone, he would abuse me, every time I would struggle and beg him not to, every time he would beat me, ignoring my pleas, seeming to enjoy hurting me. I was trapped, here alone in London, I knew no-one except for an old bookseller at the station and a few shopkeepers where I regularly bought the supplies for the house. I could not go to the police for who would they believe, the lowly servant or the rich important businessman? Mr. Darcaster also threatened me into silence, saying he would throw out my parents from their position in your household. He promised to put them on the streets and ensure they would never gain employment anywhere else. I put myself into this untenable situation without enough forethought and it almost cost me everything and could also be devastating for my parents.'

Grace continued the long painful tale to Mrs. Darcaster, absolutely everything about every incident, every beating, every time he abused her, holding back nothing. She thought to herself as she spoke, how easy it was to express herself about all these events, all the pain and suffering she had endured, how healing it was to speak about it. She realized that through it all Mr. George Darcaster had not been in control of himself, it was the force, the dark force of the savage spirit that he had allowed to come through him. He had actually given himself away to this consciousness of entitlement, greed and supremacy and that had taken control of his life. It produced the evil within him that had almost taken her life, without an ounce of care. Yes, he had chosen to align to that energy and in doing so was responsible for all the evil atrocities that he had enacted upon her. She also realized that she could not hate him, he was just the conduit that evil spiritual creation had controlled. She could, though, hate the dark evil spiritual forces that held full jurisdiction over him.

She told Mrs. Darcaster the story of her confrontation with Mr. Darcaster the night he had sent her to the abortionist. All the bleeding in the days that had followed and how close to death she'd come; how she had collapsed in the hallway and been found by Richard Billings, the bookseller, the gentle-man that was so much more than a man who simply sold books. She went on to tell her about Doctor Samuel Billings, another of the men that had saved her. They now sat in this doctor's office and the same man was doing his upmost to save the life of Mr. Darcaster. She told her about Richard Billings and how he had offered her employment and along with the cabby had helped her collect her belongings and move to her new abode.

She also told her that even though these experiences had almost destroyed her, they had led her to a much greater self-evolution, a personal expansion that she could never have dreamed of, which had led her to be able to gain a much clearer view of the world. As crazy as it may seem, she had to go through all the pain to come out on the other side with a new way of being, a new way of living life, a completely different outlook on everything.

Mrs. Darcaster sat silently through it all, feeling the whole range of emotions cascading through her body, everything from intense rage and anger with her husband George and his abuse of Grace all the way to sadness and empathy for all the pain Grace had been through. She also thought of her own situation and her life with George and the fact that she had known what he was capable of and had let Grace become his housekeeper alone in London. She felt responsible for everything this young lady had experienced and yet, she gazed upon this amazing being in front of her that had become so much more than she ever was before. She radiated love and beauty, it emanated from her whole body and sparkled from her eyes.

Eventually she spoke. 'I am both shocked and stunned by everything you have said, all that he has done to you. Most of all though, I am amazed at what you have become, you are no longer that young girl, that young woman, you have become so much more, a glorious and powerful woman. I would love to hear more about you and how you have developed so wonderfully in such a short time.

'As far as George is concerned, if he survives this medical condition, he will have to recompense for everything he has done. He can no longer continue to victimize and maltreat everyone he feels to. I doubt that he can change his ways so I will finally try to be rid of him, divorce him, if possible, but at least, no longer have any dealings with him. Similarly, I want to prevent him ever having access to any of our children ever again; he rarely sees them anyway so I doubt that will cause him any distress.

Mrs. Darcaster stood up, moved around the desk and extended both hands to Grace: Grace took them and Mrs. Darcaster pulled her to her feet. They came together, embraced and held each other for several minutes, completely open, with no resistance. They moved slightly apart and looked into one-another's eyes for a few seconds, as if to seal an agreement that they would work in cooperation and absolute openness on their future journeys.

Mrs. Darcaster asserted: 'Now let's go and take a look at that devilish brute, I'm sure he would appreciate us coming to see him together.' She smiled broadly, took Grace's hand and led her out of the office.

Chapter 9

LESSONS IN LOVE

By the early autumn of 2002 Roar had sold the luxury mountain cabin and had invested the proceeds into a beautiful house overlooking the fjord close to the town centre of Droebak. It was moving day, a day of completion, September 18th. All his belongings had been transported to the new house and this was his last morning living with Elisabeth. It had taken more than two years to come to this point where both were clear of attachment to each other and ready to move on with their lives in separate homes. They had agreed to not simply walk away from the relationship they had together, but to spend the time needed to uncover everything that had not been true within it. Thus, when they came to this point where they both new that their relationship had run its course, it was complete and the only true move forward from here was to continue life as friends.

They could honestly say to each other that they loved the other more now than they ever had done before, that now they were so much closer to knowing what love truly was, whereas when they first came together, it was something completely different. Knowing love when one does not truly know oneself can be something of an impossibility, as love is not really love unless it is the living way, a constant state of being, a loving, judgement-free state of observation rather than the falsity of all the emotional variations of love touted and championed by society, the film industry, TV, entertainment, books, magazines and the mainstream media.

There had been many discussions during the previous two and a half years, many moments of honesty and openness for both of them. There had been many layers of falsity and illusion to peel away from the protective layers they had been swaddled in. They had both felt the pain and the hurts they had built their separate and collective realities upon; they had identified and reduced the incremental mendacity that were their lifelong patterns of behaviour and released themselves somewhat from their individual self-inflicted imprisonment within this delusion.

There had been the love they thought they had for each other, the love Elisabeth thought she felt for Roar and the love Roar felt he had for Elisabeth. They had given each other the space and time to feel what lay behind the ideals they held as love, images of love that evoked particular emotions and reactions within them. This had revealed that not only their individual relationship with one another, but their societal relationships in general were, at best, loveless concoctions of conditional arrangements. This all based upon an ever-varying set of falsified ideals and beliefs that were being fed to them and everyone else, absolutely all the time and from every possible angle. Society, as a whole, was and is on a completely wayward path and almost every individual was upon their own self-created variation of this fractiousness, depending of course, on their own versions of self-image, self-interest and self-serving hopes and aspirations.

Although having an ideal of what love can be is often a very complex, multi-faceted and illusive conundrum, Roar had gradually realized that his headstrong behaviour was a misguided search for intimacy, true intimacy. The outplays of his defiant pursuit were the often alcohol-induced, never-ending pursuits of any woman he found to be attractive in the hope of that perfect match in every way. He chased that vague picture of his ideal woman that he carried around in his head, although he had never really quantified the exact measurements of what the perfect match would be and thus wouldn't recognize her if he had ever found her, which he wouldn't because no such 'ideal' woman actually ever exists.

Even in his sobriety, he still had no clear idea of what he wanted from a relationship. In truth he knew not what the words love, intimacy or relationship really meant. In this dilemma, he was not alone, as most of humanity seem to be seduced by the constructed ideals that are fed to us by all forms of media, by parenting and being parented, the education system that is deliberately set-up to lessen who we are and all other spiritually-tainted walks of society. They concluded together that they and mankind in general are all being deliberately distracted and misled to avoid waking up to the truth and the enormous multidimensional potential of what we truly are.

He had discovered that there was so much about society that he had simply taken for granted as being the way it is without ever questioning or realizing that there could be another way. Books, TV series, film, magazines, radio and every other media portrayed the many aspects of love we have been indoctrinated to believe are the truth and yet there is not an iota of authenticity about any of it. He had been so sucked in and convinced by the colossal amount of deceitful effort that lay beneath the murky waters of the presented images of what love should be that it was difficult to accept that there could actually be something else that was truly love, that it could simply be a harmonious observational state and way of being.

He now felt like a child bereft of his toys, floundering in the dark with no idea of what to do or how to take responsibility for his own choices. He wanted to cry for his mummy but knew there was no help to gain from that quarter, it was all up to him now.

It all started very early in life for him, his journey away from love and into the tainted images of what love is for a society devoid of true awareness. He could see it more clearly now. How, in general, newborn babies are most often deeply cherished and unconditionally loved by their parents for the first few months of their lives but how quicky it changes, how swiftly that love becomes more tentative and provisory. Most newborn children are love and emanate only love which is most often reciprocated by the parents without any form of expectation or demand being put upon the love. By the time a child reaches the age of six to twelve months certain behaviours are already deemed to be appropriate or inappropriate, a child is trained in the expected ways of a certain culture, religion, society or household and only rewarded with love for the anticipated and accepted responses and behaviours rather than to be guided and beheld in that state of unconditional love no matter what. This immediately indoctrinates the child with conditions in regard to love, instilling the child with appropriate behaviours for which they will be rewarded with a form of attention, that is anything but love.

From his own vivid memories of childhood, he could remember being cherished, subsequently pampered and trained in a subservient, even self-sacrificing way by his mother and to this day she still looked upon him as her child, attempting to mother him at any opportunity. She gave away her own power to him, which helped enable and encourage him to manipulate, disregard and disrespect both her and then ultimately other girls and women that entered his life. That is not to say that there was not already something within him that wanted to take advantage of his mother's subservience, that there was a pattern of old, possibly from previously lived lives that sought out and gleefully accepted the offered donation of acquiescence. But had he had the reflection of a woman truly connected to her divine sacredness, to the All that is, from birth onwards, then what may he have then become?

He mused further: Had he been a subservient woman, or even a slave? Had he ever acquiesced to men such as himself. He shuddered at the thought of being abused by himself, still not quite comfortable as the alpha male he was, with the thought of another man, even himself, invading his body, even though it would have been in another lifetime as a woman. He smiled wryly to himself.

On the other hand, his father had always been distant, yet both strict and demanding in certain areas of his life, wanting him to be academically intelligent and develop a successful business career as he himself had done. He oversaw Roar's childhood from a distance, without too much interference but still keeping tabs on his academic performance that he never thought was good enough. He expected Roar to be an A+ student, insisting he had the potential to be the best in the class and was therefore continually disappointed with his average B- performance. From very young, his father's interest was about what he could become and how much he could earn, rather than taking him to the park, the swimming pool or up in the mountains to ski as most of the other children did with their parents. Instead of an open, loving relationship together they developed a cold, cheerless and intermittent arrangement, only seeking each other out when absolutely necessary, which was not often and became more infrequent as the years passed by. Like most children in relation to their parents, who adapt to the situation, often glorifying them until perhaps, they experience or observe the relationships their friends have with their own parents. It can come as a shock to children when they witness other seemingly more loving relationships in other families, that they then observe and gain a greater perspective on their own family dynamics.

This happened for Roar; he saw his friend's families spending time together, he was sometimes invited along and felt the togetherness, the caring of and for others, on the other hand, he also witnessed the squabbling, disagreements and emotional outbursts that occasionally came with it. It was so much more fascinating and refreshing, unlike the cold, quiet home he belonged to. He loved the noise, the passion and the activity that were so stimulating and yet different within each of his friends' homes. In the end, he would much rather spend time anywhere else, just somewhere that would take him away from his own home.

He grinned to himself as he recalled the times when he had crept home silently in the night with a girl in tow. How they had stifled their giggles in an attempt to remain undiscovered. He wondered if his parents ever knew what was going on.

His mother strongly discouraged him from bringing his friends home, often saying that his father would prefer the peace and quiet when he got home from work. Although they had a beautiful house, Roar became ashamed of his own home, actually avoiding bringing his friends there, unless it was absolutely necessary. Until, that is, he became so obsessed by the opposite sex, then he became bolder and more guileful.

He realized that the relationships his friends and their families had were far from perfect but compared to his own family they were preferable. He felt it would have been much better to be in a large family full of squabbles and dramas rather than the quiet, cold and distant, only-child existence he had experienced. Although he now knew that his own situation was a great opportunity for him to learn and grow from the lessons that were actually on offer. He also realized that the relationships between his friends and their parents were just as false as his own with his parents; they had just adopted other ways of not living the full truth of what they were.

Many of Roar's relationships thus became based upon his ability to charm and manipulate people into doing what he wanted without any real sense of remorse when he let others down or emotionally upset them. His aims in life were based upon his desires rather than any real plans and this proved to be generally successful for him on the temporal level. Behind his positive, cheery façade he was cold and cynical in his business dealings, many would say borderline corrupt or even worse. Underneath the manipulating, charming, seemingly happy exterior lay a sad, hurt and rejected little boy that had turned to alcohol and other excesses for self-medication in order to avoid his feelings of rejection and low self-esteem.

It had been quite a journey for Roar to re-live the cold and distant experiences from his childhood, feel the separation from his own family and in particular the distancing from his own inner being that had allowed him to behave in such a selfish and yes, corrupt and atrocious manner. He quickly realized that it served neither himself nor anybody else to berate and be self-critical; it was much more beneficial to no longer live that way and to now reflect a different, more caring attitude to life and everyone around him. Blaming his parents for his own behaviours was no longer an option. No matter what his parents had done or not done, it did not matter, everything that he did, everything that happened to him in life was his own responsibility.

What hurt most was the feeling of separation from his own true self, it was the greatest hurt he carried inside himself. This he found was nothing to do with his parents or his childhood, it was in fact that he had chosen to distance himself from his own inner-being and the one soul we are all part of. He knew that his true purpose in life was to live from the inner Light that flowed through him and that he could live from that Light at any moment as he could equally from the dark evil forces of spiritual creation that had controlled him for so long. It was a seemingly eternal choice of these two sources of energy, did he live from disconnection of spiritual creation or did he choose to live from connection to the Light of the One Soul? Living from the Light of the Soul enabled him to relinquish his self-oriented behaviours whilst spiritual creation kept him trapped in his old self-abusive patterns. It seemed to be a simple choice, live by and for the self or live purposefully in service for all, himself equally included.

After realizing the truth of his disconnection from his purpose in life, it may have seemed to be a simple decision to live in a more soul-full way but, this often proves much easier said than done. Roar now felt he had lived previous lives more connected to the true Light of the Soul mainly because of the reoccurring and vivid life-like dreams of Grace Lightfoot in the Victorian era in London not so many years ago. He not only felt Grace in his dreams but also that she was with him in a way as he moved about his life in Norway. Recently he had felt the imprints of other past lives he had lived that in truth had been under the control of dark spirit-driven forces. In his current life as in many other lifetimes he had been on a wayward course, accruing unwanted patterns and momentum that continually held him and attracted him further, more deeply into spiritual creation, that constantly attempted to weaken his new resolve. Conversely, his previous lifetimes spent in truth and particularly his life as the young lady in London, stood him in good stead in his own internal battle between the Light and the dark, his own evolution back to the soulful Light.

Whatever we feel about Reincarnation and the fact of Karma, whether we deny it, ignore it, dull our senses so as not to feel the truth of it, does not matter. It is here and we will at some point have to take responsibility for the reckless and irresponsible way we live our lives. If not in this life, we will simply keep on coming back, life after life, until we can no longer deny it, so why not accept it and get on with it now? Do we have fun living in this current way, partying hard, hurting ourselves and self-sabotaging in the delay of our return or do we rejoice with joy and truth, in the glory of true presence all the way back to the One Soul?

Roar had realized that there are always points of Light within this sea of disparity we call the human race, that stand immovable as lighthouses in the dark stormy nights, unwavering as they shine through the raging tempest of emotional human life. Whilst lost in spiritual creation his redeeming steadfast Light had undoubtably come through Elisabeth, she had provided the spark that had slowly re-ignited his internal flame, allowing him to step away from the brink of the infernal lightless abyss.

It can often come as a surprise, or even quite a shock, for many once-wayward beings embarking on a return to the soulful Light to discover how deeply embedded we all are in the illusion of 'self', the 'I', the 'my' and the 'me'. How everything we do, even though we may look upon some of it as being good or charitable, is in fact done by and for the 'self' within, to make my-self feel better, to let others know that I am a good person and to be recognized as such or even to give the impression that I am not a cruel businessman and that I do care about others.

How often do we see global players using faux charity to change their ill-begotten public image? The I, that through the corrupt mainstream-media, changes the image of the me from the notorious, avaricious, ruthless and super-privileged entrepreneur to the kind, generous and caring philanthropist seemingly doing good across the globe. When enough effort and wealth is invested in

the right places the spurious transformation can convince enough of the public that some miracles do happen.

It is often difficult to uncover all the reasons behind our selfish, self-orientated, self-serving or even self-sacrificing ways and attitudes that lead us away from the true Light of soul-full living. We, each one of us, members of the confederate of recalcitrant spirits, have made it deliberately difficult for ourselves, we continually feed the counterfeit dark forces that hold us within the evil of the spiritual creation that pervades this world we must live in.

It was difficult for Roar to fathom just how complicated the setup had been created to be, although he slowly learned to recognize the ways and the means of the wayward spirit inside himself. Even more perplexing was the extent of the control of his spirit that seemed to be beyond his grasp, outside of himself, as a puppeteer pulling his strings, feeding him the thoughts and impulses way beyond his control. This was his own self, that was not truly a self, with so many different aspects, so many different games it played at the expense of the pervaded and controlled human being that he was much of the time. He felt a little like Pinocchio before he lost his strings to become the real boy.

The greatest flaw in the creation of a human vessel is in the building blocks of the construction. Each particle, every atom within the human body comes from the Universe, there are no other particles available, thus the human being is fashioned from the divine particles of God and therefore will always be pulled back to their true calling to be at-one with the All. Within every human being there will always be the irresistible pull back to its divine purpose, likewise there will always be a compelling call for the spirit to return to the soul it once separated from. The unnamed cricket (Jiminy in Pinocchio's case) on our shoulder, live or in etheric form, will always be there to call us back to truth.

In the meantime, the spirit uses every trick in the book to avoid feeling the hurt of its own separation and to delay its inevitable return to soul and the one soul we are all part of, stubbornly continuing all its illusive antics here on Earth.

Roar could feel the wisdom he was given whenever he was attuned to soul-full living, present within himself, allowing him to
live more in line with the natural cycles of life here on Earth and
of the Universe. He could feel it in his own breath even though
he didn't need to focus upon it. The in-breath of his presence infused him with the stillness of the Universe and the purpose of his
very being, his out-breath brought his stillness and purpose into
motion, in harmony with Heaven, to what could be described as
the path of return, in service for humanity. Him-self being the
same as every other self, equal brothers and sisters caught in the
chaos of the unrelenting dark spiritual forces, but all with equal
opportunity to step away and into the Light of soulful presence.

He realized that whenever he was not in tune with or connected to the Light of his soul, the forces of spiritual creation were at
play and he was often oblivious to the fact. There are only two
options, connection to Light or connection to the dark forces,
there is no neutrality. Any time he was distracted, if he reacted
or was emotionally contracted, a myriad of thoughts would run
around inside his head using every angle and evoking every emotion to hold him away from the truth that could only be found
within his own conscious presence.

When connected, he instinctively knew that obedience and
devotion to the greater vibration of the power of Light, to the
movement of our own solar system and the cosmic constellations
of the Universe, brought a greater access to the true intelligence
of the Ageless Wisdom held within its unceasing communication
of All that is. This did not mean submission or subservience in
any way but a surrender to a joyful harmonious connection to,
expansion beyond that which lies within and way beyond this
current realm of life. The more he was obedient to the routines,
rhythms and cycles of his current existence, the more clarity he
attained in regard to his own purpose in life. What needed to be
done seemed to fall naturally into place. Of course, there were
some hiccups along the way, there were doubts, desires and addictions he still needed to attend to, that would stealthily creep
into his thoughts and his movements. His obedience was by no

means perfect and would probably never be so, but all-in-all his life had changed so much that he hardly recognized the man he was, compared to the man he had become at this point in time.

His life had now drastically transformed, he felt like a completely different person. The real Roar had slowly risen from the ashes of that calamitous New Year's Eve party that now seemed so long ago. Instead of being dedicated to his past abusive, self-destructive way of life, he was mostly dedicated to a life of wellness and responsibility, a life of caring and equality. A life of love, truth, joy, harmony and stillness, the five real qualities of soulful living that came naturally when in the Light of presence.

Returning to the way of the Truth of the Soul may seem like an arduous path to take when we are caught up in the drama, the drudgery, the suffering or alternatively wallowing in the abundance and seeming success of material life, or any other of the Machiavellian variations of living human life we have been fed through our allegiance to the dark forces of creation that eternally seek to keep us cemented within our backward and restrictive self-serving attitudes. The illusion of life that has been created here on Earth is the antithesis of soulful living and intentionally so. Living from connection to the Soul brings a simplicity that cuts through the miasma of the infinite number of complicated offerings available from the darker side. Spiritual creation is the ultimate in deception and our own spirit is the practised and accomplished, consummate liar, so in truth we are the spirit, the spirit is us and we are the deceiver of ourselves, in particular, when we choose to believe that we are no more than human beings. This is so hard for many to believe and inconceivable to accept particularly if we are seen to be doing good. Do we ever ask ourselves, "Are we simply doing good for others or are we doing good to be recognized and praised for doing good, in the end, to feed the self and its ego?" If it is not simple, if it involves layers of complication then it is not from the true soulful way, it must then be from the devious realms of spiritual creation.

Even now, knowing everything that he knew, it was so easy to fall into the traps and trimmings, the comfort and the convenience, all of the rewards constantly offered by the dark forces. No matter how well he had stayed with himself during the day there always seemed to be something more, a sudden surprise, an old friend expecting him to go for drinks, one distraction or another. It could be as simple as a sudden thought entering his head, telling him to pick up the TV remote control, switch on the TV, thus automatically switching off his connection to the Light, then suddenly two hours had passed by completely engrossed in television programmes and advertisements with a totally mind-numbing effect, before realizing what had happened and choosing to regain his connection, coming back to presence.

It was almost comical how easily controlled he was at times, it was as if an outside force or an unseen entity, maybe the Invisible Man, could press his buttons and turn his switches on or off. Thus, in a blink of an eye, he would do something he moments before had just decided he would never do again.

It could be stopping by the supermarket on the way home from work to buy the ingredients for dinner, walking around the aisles determined to pick up only healthy food and drink. Some fish and green vegetables in the shopping basket, a thought gets into his head to buy himself a large pack of potato crisps, a diet coke and a block of his old favourite milk chocolate, overriding his previous determination not to buy anything unhealthy. He walks out of the supermarket, already munching on the potato crisps. He feels that after being so focused and present all day at work that he now deserves a little pleasure in the form of the salty and sweet tastes he just purchased, knowing and yet not considering the effect this will have on the rest of his body, not considering the chain reaction now taking place.

After arriving home, he is preparing his dinner whilst continuing to eat the crisps and drink the diet coke that he knows will upset his stomach.

After dinner he clears up, not wanting to 'check-out' watching TV, he picks up his laptop computer, replies to a few emails whilst eating the chocolate and soon, unconsciously, but not so, he finds himself lost in the world of the internet, reading posts about how beautiful it is to drink wine watching the setting sun on a beach in Mykonos or to ride a motorcycle along Route 66 in the USA. Suddenly the whole evening has passed him by, reading empty articles on his computer, leaving him feeling tired, frustrated and disconnected from his own body.

How much of life just passes us by in this way, how many hours do we spend not even present within our own body? Are we living life or are we being moved by something else that does not want us to be aware of it? Could it be that we are in a grand puppet theatre, living life in some kind of Punch and Judy show, with someone or something else's hand stuck up our behinds, making all our moves for us?

Thankfully these episodes and urges happen less and less, sometimes he even puts the rewards in his shopping basket, takes them to the check-out, and suddenly deciding he won't have them after all, leaving them at the check-out.

Roar eventually noticed that absolutely everything is a set-up to take him out, distract him away from what he now knew was his natural and harmonious inner vibration. It was not only himself but the whole of mankind, every person on the planet is targeted in order to keep them enthralled and firmly residing within this swamp of deceit. Those realizing their true origins are subject to even more attention from the devious forces of spiritual creation in order to draw them back into the mass deception. The whole system of society, every little nuance, was designed to knock, not just him off balance but everyone else too. Designed to become the illusory reality we all fall for, we are sucked in and thoroughly indoctrinated to the point that we believe everything we are fed by every aspect of the implemented system of living and seemingly controlled and overseen by those above, the men of power. Although it may apparently be that these powerful men that are running this fraudulent shit-show, often hidden behind many layers of deceit, they are in-truth the manipulated marionettes under the impulse to think that they run the system but are unwittingly controlled by the supremacist consciousness they are obedient to and yet seem so oblivious of.

They are, in fact, so sold-out they knowingly serve their unseen Masters of self-appropriation, avarice, arrogance, ascendency, ruthlessness, callousness and brutality all rolled up within this consciousness of supremacy, letting naught stand in their way of inflicting depravation, deceit, duress and devastation upon humanity. They as we, live our lives firmly ensconced in this grand illusion of being only human, thinking that we only live this one life and thus must live it 'in full', partying carelessly, unstoppable and indestructible, that is until lifestyle disease catches up with us.

When we do get sick, we often malign our situation as misfortune, do what is needed to recuperate if we can, even give up our addictions and ill-habits. If and when recovered, we can return to the style of living we had prior to becoming ill, strangely and frequently resulting in relapse or some other unfortunate disorder. And yet we still believe that our intelligence is the upmost, greater than any other occupant of this planet.

Living within the constructed confines of spiritual creation is often complicated, there are also innumerable variations and levels of what we think are the lifestyles we are choosing for ourselves. The question is, are we being fed the impulses that make our choices for us? Perhaps it can be compared to psychosis, that the whole of human life may in fact be psychosis on a grand scale. It seems that living as a human has a whole range of what we call normal and acceptable behaviours dependent upon our nationality, culture or religion and many other social and tribal factors such as which sports team we support, our preferred alcoholic drink or even our sexual preferences, basically, everything that humans do.

Good is often a greater evil and can be more deceitful than bad!

For example, it is touted throughout society, that alcoholic beverages such as wine and beer, with very little credible proof, are in some way good for us. It is said that a couple of glasses of wine in the evening to help us relax and unwind is also good for blood circulation, the cardio-vascular system and Diabetes 2, amongst many others. Many espouse a cool beer in the afternoon sun as a deserved reward after a hard day's work. Across huge swathes of the western world, it is considered normal to consume large quantities of alcoholic beverages, to have alcohol at every celebration, even a child's baptism or at the funeral of loved ones. No matter if they have inadvertently died from the effect of the very poison their death is celebrated and/ or commiserated with.

Often ignored within research papers proving the benefits of alcoholic beverages are the facts that alcohol is a known toxin, immune system depressant and carcinogenic which has been proven to cause many life-threatening illnesses and diseases such as cardiomyopathy, congestive heart failure, strokes, cirrhosis of the liver, kidney damage and so much more, in addition to reducing the body's resistance to viral and bacterial attacks.

Roar had been there himself with his fondness or, in complete truth, his addiction to alcohol. He knew, from personal experience, only too well how dangerous it could be. He, like so many other Norwegians, took any and every opportunity to take part in what are the socially accepted and expected drinking sessions, or in other words, acted on any excuse to get smashed.

Since having no choice other than to stop drinking if he was to reclaim a healthier lifestyle and subsequently to live a more vital, vibrant life, he had realized just how much many devoted drinkers frown upon those who do not drink or have managed to stop drinking. Non-drinkers are often ridiculed, judged and rejected by their former social circles, they may be deemed to be boring or plain weird, not interested in having fun, too serious and party poopers. Some of his old friends, after trying to persuade him to join in the drinking simply gave up and no longer cared to call. Whenever he called them, they were usually too busy or had other appointments and priorities. He had puzzled over all that he had observed the last two years, how many of his so-called friends were no longer around. It was as if their whole relationship had been alcohol dependent. If the main catalyst for the arrangement was no longer there, then the contract had been broken and therefore should be terminated. It seems that some drinkers did not care to be observed by non-drinkers even if they had been friends for thirty years.

He came to the conclusion that it had nothing to do with him no longer drinking alcohol, but everything to do with the reflection they saw of themselves as he stood steadfast in his new way of living. They looked upon themselves in full knowledge of the extent they were hurting, not only themselves, but all those around them. They could see and feel the full extent of the internal, external and collateral damage being caused; they experienced the irresponsibility of their actions and knew it was because they did not want to feel the truth. They did not want to feel the extent and the depth of their internal hurts and anyone walking a path of true responsibility was a grim reminder of their ill-predicament, their ill-lifestyle choices. He had broken the conditions of their unwritten contracts to always be one of the fellow collaborators within the confederated dark spiritual collaboration. His previous agreement with them was to always remain oblivious to the Light of the Soul and the magnetic pull back to the Universe and the One Soul the vast majority are separated from.

He contemplated that if he started with the premise or even the knowing within his own body, that he and everyone else are more than simply human, that we are all deeply soulful beings, it offers a great living foundation for life in general. This he could feel within his own body if he allowed his awareness to be open to it. Through simplicity it is then revealed and realized that the attributes of the soul are purely love, truth, harmony, stillness and joy, whatever we take on that is not of these attributes cannot be, in reality, what we are. All our patterns of behaviour, all of our ingrained and indoctrinated ideals and beliefs, our selfish ways, all of our habits and addictions, all of our judgements, comparisons, competitiveness and complications, everything that human life has become are fabricated and divisive layers of illusion, a form of psychosis entwined around us, masking the true essence of what we are, each layer building another

illusory chapter upon another as we fall deeper into the narrative of evil spiritual creation, lost in the incremental falsity we believe to be our reality. For we no longer know what truth is in this world, our perceived reality, every truth we know is an individual, false truth, the only true Truth can be when we all have the same Truth, for how could it be otherwise?

Taking the concept of a One-Truth a little further, he realized that each individual truth no matter how close or how far away from the soulful Light they may be are all in reality variations on the same dark deceit. Though they may seem to be, none are closer than any other, to the true One Truth of our Soul, the One Soul, and living from within the presence of this soulful Light. Many of the truths we live and die by are designed to be close copies of the Universal Truth of the Light and yet that is what they are, merely copies that can never truly represent the All, only deceptive manipulative versions that may be similar to it. For those that think they live the truth are fed the thoughts that make them believe that their truth is the One Truth and that all others are untrue, the wrong belief: Is this not how righteousness arises? It brings in the corruption of right and wrong, which leads to comparison and judgement, accelerating to dispute and conflict that leads to war and devastation and a multitude of other temporal ills that abound in this world.

He deliberated for a while upon the notion of right and wrong and how odious and contrived they actually are. It is all connected to the initial choice or positioning to either one of the two sources of energy, the Light of the Soul or dark evil of spiritual creation, simplicity or complication. Living from a deep connection to the Light there is only simplicity, there is no comparison, competition or judgement, there is no right or wrong, there is an acceptance of all that is wherever it may be, only the One Truth and connection to the All that the Universe is. Here, in the Light, there is only love, truth, harmony, stillness and joy, here there is no judgement, there is no abuse of any kind. There is a universal knowing, a loving observation of the All without reaction, thus no judgement and therefore no wrong, no right. Even when faltering, there is an acceptance rather than a judgement, for in Truth there can be no perfection whilst we live within our human bodies.

Choosing to live from the connection to spiritual creation immediately allows in complication, ideals and beliefs, the judgement of others, emotional desires and reactions, the need for recognition and of course the deception of the untrue truth in the form of what is right and what is wrong, what is good and what is bad. In fact, all the facets of spiritual creation are a complex intertwined set of deceitful constructions designed only for the entrapment, delay and distraction of the unsuspecting human fabrication. Because of our complicated way of life where everyone has their own sets of ideals and beliefs, and because we judge each other all the time, knowingly or not, we all have our own individual slant on what is right and what is wrong on everything that is said and done, whether expressed verbally, outwardly or held within. If seven to eight billion people have their own take on right and wrong about everything that is going on, this drives complication and complexity with billions upon billions of judgements with no one truly in unison to what is right or what is wrong, what then is the truth? The overarching structure of society can only ever be a fuzzy line laid down by those with the most power to decide what all the inhabitants must adhere to, what is erroneous or what is proper. A middle way, a mix of different truths to pacify or satisfy as many as possible is still nowhere near the true truth.

When illicitly appropriated power is exerted upon human beings, there will be dissent, there will be opposition and there will be abuse in many ways. It is ill-gotten power, because at this time on Earth there is absolutely no leadership that is not corrupt, political power is purchased by those of gross-wealth, in order to not only keep that wealth for themselves but to multiply it at the expense of all others and in particular those that have the least. It is these spiritual creation-driven devotees that purchase the rights to decide what is right and what is wrong at local, national and global levels. They live aligned to the dark force of the supremacy consciousness that enthralls everyone, whether obediently aligned to it or in reaction to its outplays. They are not the evil that is at play here but merely puppets of it, they have chosen to align to it though they are not the real perpetrators of it. It is the consciousness itself that is the resident and persistent evil, a force that can only survive for as long as we continue to partake of any of its malevolent offerings.

This evil force is fed and maintained by our every reaction and all the willing contributions we donate to it. Without our donations it cannot exist, it is of our own doing and only we can undo it. Only living from the soulful Light can banish spiritual creation. We, ourselves, are the creators of all that is this dark poison, moving into and from the Light re-imprints our own dark footsteps that have assaulted the Earth for millennia.

Observing spiritual creation and its evil shenanigans, all may seem bleak, but the magnificence that awaits us all upon stepping away from it and into the Light is beyond stupendous. The majesty and power of what we are returning to dwarfs anything and everything on offer from within the depths of the gloomy unawareness to which we currently attend.

At our point of birth, though we are mostly free from the machinations of this evil dark spiritual plan that encompasses the whole planet, could it be that at this moment we are closer to the Truth than at any other point in our lives? Excluding the precious few soulfully transcended parents that have returned to the Light, we humans are born to parents that have been indoctrinated into the systems of spiritual creation as all others have been for lifetimes past, woefully lost in this psychosis of humanity. They believe they live the truth, unwittingly dragging their own offspring down to wallow in the seething swamp of dark deceit along with themselves. They believe in the subterfuge and yet at their innermost being they all know and can feel the true Truth through the dark fog they have chosen to become lost within.

Each day that passes, children are dragged deeper into the heinous treachery, taught how to be emotional, how to react, how to adopt beliefs, how to individualize and separate from their fellow human beings. They are taught a combination of all the things that harm them, that they are better than others, they are the best, the most beautiful, the precious, the most intelligent, the idiot, the ugly child, the worthless, the useless, and the unwanted. From the open and loving children that are born, we create all the mixed-up individualistic adults with all their separative views and beliefs. Daily, more and more layers are then added to this ever-deepening dark psychosis we call human life. It is not surprising that we have a world population with an ever-increasing rate of serious psychological illnesses, insanity, suicide and psychoses, which seem to be running amok all across the planet.

As Roar contemplated all this, he found it difficult to digest the magnitude of the evil at play. There seemed to be nothing that was not tainted by the poisonous tendrils of these heinous dark forces. He also realized that every child and every adult, deep inside, knows the truth even though the dark spiritual forces try to convince them otherwise.

We are from the Truth, from the Light of the One Soul and therefore this is what we are in essence and what we know first before all else is fed to us.

He could feel that there was a certain momentum within his current life that he sensed was from past experiences, past incarnations and that every human had their own impetus from lives lived both in the depths of spiritual creation and from within the soulful Light. Even though the forces of spiritual creation are very powerful here on Earth, they are but a tiny speck, insignificantly miniscule when compared to the colossal might within the universal Light. Spiritual creation is but a tiny blemish, a spot of smut within the magnificent Light that we are all from. Human life and the currently controlling spirit world are the only transgression, the only malignant misalignment in the splendour of the All that is.

Everyone, he thought, large or small, young or old is constantly being offered the opportunity to return, to leave behind spiritual creation and choose the Light. The opportunity to wake up from the dark slumber, to step out of the swamp, to peel away the layers of temporal psychosis and return to the heavenly Light we are all from. The wayward and fractious spirits within each of us know that they must one day return to the Light. They stubbornly fight, frantically trying to avoid this inevitable conclusion, clinging on vehemently to individuality and identification. Their only recourse to this avoidance of truth is their subsequent fashioning of an existence of emotional suffering and or excitement and the delay of what cannot be stopped, their inescapable return to Soul. The soulful Light on Earth grows ever more powerful pulling everyone and everything back to love, causing the confederate of spirits in resistance and reaction to, in any way they can, create and cause ever more drastic and dramatic measures to obstruct and hamper what is, in the end, the unavoidable return to oneness with the All.

Roar mulled over some of the ways in which the trappings of temporal life enticed, seduced and intrigued him, and most of the rest the of humanity, into the temptation and the rewards of living within and in support of the vile concoction that is spiritual creation. There was so much more than he imagined. It went way beyond the buzz of the first few beers or the chill, carefree feeling from smoking marijuana. His body was becoming more sensitive to both food and drink, music and sounds in general, and even to the way he and others around him moved.

Sometimes he would stop for petrol and pick up a spicy hotdog, a large pack of salted potato crisps, a pack of three freshly baked sweet raison buns or some other treat on his way home from work. This often happened if he had had a long day at work where he had been particularly responsive, not been in emotional reaction, remained mostly connected to himself and had hardly been distracted by anything outside of himself during that time. Then suddenly whilst driving home, rather than simply appreciating his day and accepting this way of being as the norm, he had allowed himself to enter into thoughts of pride or self-congratulation, allowing tiredness and dark spiritual energy to creep in thus sparking a desire or an entitlement for some kind of salty or sweet reward. The sugar or salt content would lift him up for a little while but then the amount of stodge he consumed would leave him feeling bloated and uncomfortable. This could often lead to a poor night's sleep and the creation of a chain reaction, then becoming more distracted and less productive at work the day after.

At times it was so easy to let himself get distracted, particularly after a good day at work. He might come home late, have something light to eat, sit himself in front of his computer and almost unconsciously open up Netflix, watch three or four episodes of some exciting Marvel action series and again not be able to get a good night's sleep because of the energetic disturbance he had allowed into his body. It came to him that all these things he rewarded himself with – the TV, Netflix, fast food, sugary drinks even listening to his favourite rock music – were more punitive, rather than beneficial to his personal evolution.

It was a long process to let go and to renounce all these things that he thought were perks and goodies. Now he realized the 'rewards' were in fact, not only detrimental to his body but also took him out of awareness and conscious presence. Previously, he was sure he deserved these rewards for doing a good day's work or for signing up a new client on a big new contract, but now realized that they were simply dark spiritual sleight of hand.

He had listened to music all his life without giving it a second thought, with no idea that it could be harming him. He knew now that everything that is not nurturing and healing, must be harming and that there is no neutral ground. Music, as with everything else in life and the Universe, is energy. The energetic source of any music needed to be discerned. Logically, whatever energy the musicians were allowing through themselves would be reiterated and amplified through the music they produced. The more he listened to that music the more he would absorb the energy of it into his own body. He had given this much cogitation and reflection as he felt deeply attached to his music collection; there were so many memories of concerts and parties and so many emotions connected to his favourite songs. He loved to sing along in the car as he drove to and from work and in-between appointments and meetings. At the gym he would use particular tunes to bring through more energy and aggression to help him move more weight.

Hearing certain songs would bring up a whole range of emotions, sadness, elation, sympathy and bliss, anger, remorse, shame and happiness, a real roller-caster ride. This, he realized, was the proof in the pudding, the energy of the music was toxic, took him out of his presence and washed him away into a world of past and current emotional experiences. Many of his favourite artists had either passed away or were no longer able to perform due to the lifestyles they had lived. Some had died through ailments primarily caused by alcohol addiction and others from drug-over-doses. The music they had produced would have been fueled by drink and drug dependency through their alignment to the dark spiritual forces. This is the energy he had willingly allowed to infest his body and contribute to his own wayward lifestyle.

It was now much easier for him to feel it, although the attraction to it was still strong. Whenever he did listen to it, he could feel how quickly he was assimilated into it, its vibration took over his body, moved him and reproduced its own words and pernicious energy through him. He would sing the words he knew so well with all the emotions he could feel, all the wailing sadness, the angry impudence, the sexual lust and the abusive misogyny. It was all there flowing through the music and flowing into and through him and whoever else that listened. It came to the point when he decided it was impossible for him to listen to this music because he could often feel the hooks within him and the tendrils drawing him towards it. He was disgusted by it and had started to hate the controlling and mesmeric dark energy that lay behind it.

Roar had realized that he was in a grand process of return that involved renouncing absolutely everything that was not of and from the soul, refuting all that was on offer from the evils of spiritual creation, thus returning to the Light from which we all come. Renouncing all that he had been and done led to re-imprinting his way of living. The greatest problem was that many of these darker ways were so deeply ingrained within him that they felt inexplicably difficult for him to let go of, even though he could plainly see how damaging they were.

He had to laugh at himself as he contemplated all these things he once loved; he lived for these activities, hobbies and pastimes, they were more precious to him than anything else. And yet he could feel the surge of pure joy as he was able to let go of most of his attachment to them.

It had been revealed to him, he could see it, that human life was structured in a way to complicate and confuse to such an extent that it prevented the majority from seeing and experiencing the Light of the Soul, that they are all undoubtably originally from. Individuation and separation are the result of our currently accepted way of living and unfortunately, they are conveniently what most would now call our normal way of being. This subterfuge includes nationalities, religions and cultures that are constructed to give a false version of brotherhood, togetherness and at-one-ment. We can be fervently nationalistic and yet within our nation we are often divided into a class structure. We can be at odds with people from other religions, cultures, or even fans of opposing football teams or some other kind of sport. We may support our own nation, but why should that create a difference between us and other countries?

We only see others as our equals when it is convenient rather than that being a permanent footing. His life had always been about him, as an individual, outcompeting or manipulating others to get what he wanted and yet when the Norwegian football team played an international match, he would become fervently patriotic and he would join together with most other Norwegians as if they were all one, no differences and the best of friends. They would then, as a group, turn their disdain towards the offending national team from whichever country they were battling against, generating a febrile hate towards an unknown group of people from a country in which on some occasions they might spend their summer vacations, then loving the

266

country and the people within it. Admittedly these episodes had almost always been under the influence of alcohol and when the event was over and the fog had cleared, he would return to his individualism and indeed a certain level of contempt for other sections of the Norwegian society.

Further to this, he could feel how this form of convenient and short-lived congeniality had temporally served him well in both his personal and business relationships, how he could instantly turn on the charm or incite sympathy at the drop of a hat, to achieve his own personal aspirations, often to the disservice of others. He realized that it was not just often, it would always be to the detriment of others. Although it may have seemed to be to his advantage, in truth it would also be more harmful to himself, ingraining these hurtful patterns deeper and deeper into his own body, digging himself further into the murky hole of spiritual creation.

He had always seen himself as quick-witted and fun-loving with a sharp sarcastic tongue. He considered himself smarter than most others around him. He didn't need to try hard, the humour and arrogance seemed natural to him, people liked him as long as his acid remarks were saved for others. He had now realized how awful he had actually been, everything he did was calculated and contrived in order to serve his own personal wants and needs, that is until his levels of sobriety dipped below and beyond the pale. Then it was as if he had been commandeered by some crazed entity that drove him towards his own self destruction. Trying not to be self-critical in any way, he reasoned that what he had thought was his social and intellectual intelligence was not intelligence at all; they were rather extreme levels of abuse, self-abuse, irresponsibility and stupidity. He could though feel his own self-judgement within these thoughts and that this was also harmful. Yes, he had been all these things and more but now that he was climbing out of the murky swamp, he could see that he had to accept everything that had gone before and to let it go and not carry this baggage along with him any further into this life. By living from the point of newly attained realization and settlement with it, he could move forward, leaving most of his excessive past behind.

This dark form of intelligence he was in the process of eradicating from his life, the same intelligence that infests most of humanity in one way or another, had nothing to do with true intelligence and real wisdom. The dark intelligence that he had been controlled by was not true intelligence, it was a seething conniving construct designed to infect all it came across, the more it polluted humanity the more it was amplified by those living from it. It circulated around and around the planet through all means of communication, constantly contaminating every walk of human life. The so-called knowledge provided by this ill-intelligence continually embedded the waywardness of the dark forces into what we call human life, in fact it forms earth-life into what the great majority now believe is their normal way to be.

Roar had now concluded that life is simple and straightforward when we are connected to the power of the Light, although he deliberated, why do we do our utmost to complicate everything in so many ways? He thought back to the way he had been living prior to his life-changing event on New Year's Day 2000 and how complicated his life had been. He remembered all the complex lies and deceitful strategies, both within his relationship to Elisabeth and all other aspects of his life. How difficult it was to remember the full intricate web of lies he had spun and how in the end Elisabeth had known what he was doing as had many others. It was strange how he had been both deceitful and yet at the same time uncaring about being exposed for his deceit. He would beguile and concoct the most ridiculous scenarios not really concerned for collateral damage and potential fallout. He wanted what he wanted, there and then and he would go the necessary steps to achieve that, regardless of who he might hurt in the process. Whatever way he lived in one area of his life, that was what he brought to all other areas, no matter how well disguised he may have thought it to be.

There was still something in him though that wanted to be seen as a good person, he compared himself to other men and other business leaders. He imagined that he was at least as good as, if not even better than most others in similar positions. Whatever happened he did not want his reputation to be a bad one, he did not want to be thought of in an unfavourable way. He had seemed to be afraid of being judged even though, he had to admit, for him judgement was an on-going and daily activity that he found extremely difficult to stop. At least now he felt that he was much more aware of when he judged people, he kept it to himself, didn't spread the judgement any further and gradually started to stop those judgmental thoughts entering his mind.

He became aware that every time he met someone, the natural instinct for him was to give them a quick once-over, to analyze who they were, how they looked, what kind of person they were. It was in fact an instant judgement. This natural instinct, he thought, was just the same as everyone else. We all do it. He now knew that this was no natural instinct, anything but; in fact it was more like the opposite of natural. Nothing we do as human beings is our natural way until we actually re-connect with our true inner essence. There we will find all that is our real way of being.

At our innermost we find our true way, we find an innate stillness, harmony and joy. Living from this stillness we emanate love; we observe and offer judgement-free space for all to express just as they feel the impulse. From this space, and this loving and affriming observation, there is no emotion, no comparison, no competition, no judgement and no reaction.

What is it we human beings most often do when offered such space? Do we attempt to fill it with our own self-inflicted issues, adopted and inherited idiosyncrasies and ingrained behaviours? When we are firmly ensconced within the world, controlled by the dark forces we concoct and construct a life full of illusionary attributes, excuses and behaviours to avoid living the full and true being that we are. Spiritual creation often plays on the need for security, to have confidence and the adopting of outgoing personalities, but at the same time it infects people with self-worth issues, often causing them to withdraw, giving them a lack of confidence and insecurity. When we live from the Light of the Soul, we see through the illusion cast before us, from the offered space we see and feel ourselves in full. From this place there can be no insecurity because we no longer have an attachment to being a 'self' and no addiction or desire for the materialistic trappings offered from the devious illusions created by the evil dark forces. Confidence, or lack of it, is replaced by a conscious presence and a connection to the ageless wisdom of the Universe that knows all and responds to what is needed.

In the presence of and with God, there can be no withdrawal, or contraction away from the fullness of our true being. The Universe is within our every particle, where everything is known, hence, connection to our true selves reveals the wisdom of the All.

Chapter 10

LIFE GOES ON

George Darcaster died from massive heart failure at Charing Cross Hospital four days later. Although he was still at the hospital, nothing could be done to save his life due to the irreparable damage already done to his own body through his successively wretched lifestyle choices. Alexandria felt relieved that she would no longer have to suffer through her awful marriage with George and yet, at the same time, she was angry and frustrated that he had managed to die just when she was in position to make life hell for him.

The Darcaster's two teenage children were unmoved by it all. They were neither greatly saddened nor were they ecstatic. It was a total non-event, the passing of an almost never-present, arrogant authoritarian father they rarely spent any time with at all. They had a close, loving and intimate relationship with their ever-present mother who had steadfastly refused to have them sent away to boarding schools. Alexandria had chosen to both self-teach and to bring in well-respected tutors for the subjects in which she had little experience. For a mother to spend so much time with her children was almost unheard of amongst many of her peers, often considered frivolous and pampering. Although when George was home, there was a completely different regime, the children could be seen from time to time and only heard, as long as that was from a great distance. Even at mealtimes the children would not be allowed to eat at the same table as Alexandria and George.

It was a sad fact that when their father was home, they would see less of their mother, although the lovely servant staff more than made up for this absence. They would often eat their meals in the kitchen with some of the servants. In particular, Arthur

Lightfoot, the butler, and his wife, Evelyn the housekeeper, who would make light of life and take great care of them. They would laugh and joke, having such a jolly time together, which was a stark contrast to the stern, serious airs of their father especially.

When Grace heard the news of George Darcaster's demise her immediate thoughts were of how he deserved this, and it was indeed a repayment of Karma. She realized where the source and flow of these thoughts were coming from, stopped immediately and for a short while, breathed gently through her nose concentrating on her own movements until her presence returned. She recognized that the thoughts were in reaction to her own pain, the hurts he had so fiendishly inflicted upon her, rather than a response from the place of stillness and understanding in which she often lived her days. In spite of all the harm George had caused her, she was able to relinquish all the emotional reactions that tried to enter her thoughts and any sense of judgement about him deserving to be punished or to die for all the suffering he had inflicted upon herself and others.

She knew that through this sudden death he had received a clearing and a healing from his soul that would serve him in his following lives to come, it may give him the opportunity to choose a different way of living in whatever body he arrived in for his next incarnation. Whether he chose to accept and embody what was being offered to him, or not, remained to be seen.

She pondered for a while upon the process of death, dying and rebirth. She wondered if death was not actually dying but a transition, or a rebirth, to another plane of life, possibly the spiritual fourth dimension. Would this then be a prelude to coming back to human life through what we call birth, but maybe in the fourth dimension it is like a death or some kind of penance or simply Karma and another opportunity to get it right, the possibility to embark upon and return to a more soulful way?

How long would all this go on for? She knew through her previous discussions with Richard and was confirmed by what she could feel in her own body, that we would each individually continue on this cycle of birth, Earth-life, death and so on until all were ready to leave, which could be several hundreds or even thousands of years. When enough of us human beings, whether incarnate or not, have reached a level of expansion such that we have walked far enough upon the path of return to the One Soul, we may then be ready to leave this plane of life permanently. When as a one humanity we have sufficiently relinquished the chains of the individual 'self', thus, ultimately recognizing and guiding each wayward spirit inside every living being back to at-one-ment with their Soul.

How many lives have we already lived she asked herself? How many lives have we wasted in the glorification of this temporal, materialistic and immoral human life mostly filled with selfishness, hate, suffering, malice and injustice or at best living in a state of semi-permanent-to-permanent emotional reaction?

What are we if we are in fact more than human, if we are recalcitrant spirits that have separated from our true origin, constantly delaying our never-ending call back to soul? Could we be fragmented, highly intelligent, multi-dimensional beings on a wayward detour upon this tiny planet Earth? What are we doing cavorting around inside human bodies on this tiny little microcosmic speck we call our World? She could feel that she was much more than just a human and that at the same time she knew there were many forces at play here to make her think that she was less.

Through her time spent living with Richard, Grace discovered that there have been many teachers in the past that have presented living sutras that unfold the Ageless Wisdom throughout the millennia. This unending lineage of teachers and presenters have often been labelled as Prophets, Saints or even Gods, although they are in human form as are we all. It happens that we often take their teachings, whether it be from Hermes Trismegistus, Zarathustra, Patanjali, Pythagoras, Siddhartha Gautama, Yeshua, Mohammed or one of the many other, known or now lesser-known presenters. We then proceed to completely re-write, or at best re-interpret or disdainfully bastardize these teachings until they become no more than tools of control, forming manipulative and prejudicial doctrines devised for a small few to exercise control over the masses of our fellow human beings.

During their lifetimes, these presenters of Ancient Wisdom were without exception persecuted, slandered, defamed, physically attacked and in some cases murdered by those that profess to be the true source of enlightenment and authority. Could it be that this alone can be understood as evidence of what is the true Truth? That anything that is not inclusive of everyone cannot be for the evolution of All, that if it discriminates against any other in any way it therefore cannot be from Truth?

If a dogma or tenet is designed in a way that exerts control over its followers or discriminates against non-followers in any way, if it involves conversion, coercion, indoctrination or persuasion at all, has it not then departed from the All that is truly Truth? Has it then been moved away from the Light of the Soul, if it was ever originally from there, then deeper into the world of spiritual creation? If religious movements or organizations are formed on the basis of these teachings, do they hold true to what has been delivered? Could any corruption of this, past or present, such as any historical acts of violence, genocide, warmongering or any other form of abuse in the name of God or any other deity, in fact, anything that is not from 'love and in service for all beings', be defined as obvious, tell-tale signs that the particular doctrine in question holds no soulful Light, that it resides in spiritual creation. Once it is ensconced within, can it ever return to be a truthful way?

The majority of us, humanity, with very few exceptions, would rather not live our lives based upon the Ageless Wisdom teachings, instead we turn them around, interpreting them to suit the way we choose to live. Thusly, we avoid the responsibility the tenet calls for and substitute this with greed, comfort, ecstasy, bliss and all sorts of pleasurable or indeed painful experiences in order to not feel the truth of what has been delivered to us. We avoid living what we are and where we come from. Could it be that the real purveyors of Truth are most often attacked, defamed and persecuted? Are they not often prosecuted under false witness by a corrupted judiciary and if they have too much momentum, even eliminated?

As the greater majority of humanity do not seem to want to awaken from their convenient slumber (preferring to wallow in unawareness), they still seek to avoid living from the soulful Truth, preferring the deceit of spiritual creation and will commit any or all crimes, even write laws to solidify the untruth as statutory. Many of the true presenters of the ancient wisdom have had the teachings that they have delivered ruthlessly corrupted, partially or completely expunged from the documented history we now know, but their work will always be felt, it is continually and eternally imprinted in soulful Light upon the Earth and cannot be so easily erased. This History, we are now force-fed from birth, is the product of many revisions, in order to erase and corrupt all works of veracity from the past teachers of candor.

Grace could feel who and what she was, she felt that she was much more than a human being living in her human body for this one life. She felt her own expansion and evolution from what she had been, with more certainty each passing day, in fact it was more like a return to her true self, her true way of being. She felt the particles of this, her flesh and blood human body tingle with a lifeforce which she knew instinctively came from her acceptance of the Light, the energy of her own soul, and of the One Soul of which we are all a part. At the same time, she could feel her resistant spirit within twisting and turning, trying to hold on to its separateness, the individuality it thrives upon would stop at nothing to avoid relinquishing, to prevent returning home to Soul from whence it came.

She felt further into the existence of the spirit, that it is both within her body and without. It is a wily character that houses an intelligence far beyond that of the human being alone, yet far reduced from that of the Soul which it is part of and will always be inextricably interconnected to. The mind of the human being is controlled by its maker, the spirit, and yet the human body is built from universal particles, the divine atoms of God. When aligned to the Light, the particles of the human body may become soul infused, thus accessing the intelligence and wisdom of the Universe, for which the irresponsible spirit is no match. The spirit is dependent upon temptation and trickery, using weapons such as security and comfort ever enticing the human aspect away from soulfulness. The spirit wants to keep us in what it has defined as the human mind, within the physical brain, but this again is simply one of the deceptions it depends upon. It tells the human that it is intelligent and that it is an independent thinker from the place of this defined mind, whilst itself wielding intelligence far greater than it allows the limited human being access to.

When aligned to the power of soulful Light we simply feel and know that the mind of the human being is within every particle of the body. If you think that you, alone, have independent original thoughts then could it be that you have been led into that thought process by the miscreant dark forces? We do have thoughts and ideas, but they are always spawned from the consciousness or energetic source one is subject to, either from spiritual creation or from the Light of our Soul.

She thought again of George Darcaster as an example of subjecting himself to the dark spiritual forces. He was seen as a sharp, decisive, intelligent industrialist, an innovator through the eyes of most people in the upper echelons of society. He would often be praised in the newspapers for his business acumen but never openly criticized for his failings. None of his peers would question his ethics or the treatment of his employees, the state of his health or the way he abused both himself and the people around him. He had proved himself to be without scruples, beyond a shadow of a doubt to be an instrument of a dark arrogant, narcissistic and supremacist force.

His employees would be paid as little he could possibly get away with and he would attack the unions at every opportunity. He had greatly profited from the sale of armaments and ammunition used for the destruction and slaughter of many thousands of people in both India and South Africa. And, of course, he had raped, beaten and abused her on many occasions, ultimately almost causing her death. God only knows who else he had abused in this way, of how many others he may have taken advantage, what he may have done to them and what had become of them. He took what he pleased from whomever he deigned, whenever he felt the impulse to indulge himself, regardless of the legality or the pain and suffering he caused others.

Grace came to a point of realization. She wondered, are we not all caught out by the deviousness of the dark forces, in the way that we become so attached to our own thoughts, particularly when we think we have ideas that make us feel good, bad, better or worse than others, more or even less intelligent, or any other thought that takes us away from the fact that we are all the same and all are equal? In truth we may have different expressions of our equality, but this is not necessarily a deviation away from the oneness and equivalence with all others. It is in falsity that we are fed the thoughts to think we are worth less or more than others.

It may be said though that when we are controlled by contrivances of spiritual creation, we develop what we could call a spiritual pride which is basically an ownership or a claiming as ours of the ideas we are fed. We believe what we think about are our own original, endemic thoughts. This could not be further away from reality. An energy always ignites and controls our thought patterns. The only way we can affect our own thoughts is in the choice of aligning to one of the two energies that are on offer. We choose either the energy of soulful Light, which is the responsive, loving, judgement-free energy, or we choose the energy of the dark creation, which is the emotional, self-oriented energy proliferated by the grand confederate of wayward spirits.

From her place of inner quietude, Grace pondered further; that if we believe our own intelligence is superior to that of others because we are able to decipher complicated equations or write a complex thesis on the workings of the solar system or in fact for any other reason, then have we not truly succumbed to the forces of dark spiritual creation? Likewise, if we choose to believe that we are stupid, that we are lesser than others, that we have no real worth, if we put others upon pedestals in worship or exaltation, that we must keep to our designated class in life, all this is equally the work of the dark forces and our alignment to that which is of the evil spiritual creation. Thinking that we should worship another or judging that we are worthy of worship are two sides of the same coin, maybe both are simply variations of being lost in the divisive fog of dark creation.

Contemplating academic intelligence, people of power, clergy, civil servants, businessmen and everyone else of that ilk, she considered: maybe if our purpose or goals in life are not for the true betterment of the whole of humanity, not in seeking the return to the soulful way for all, could we then say that we are choosing something lesser, something that is tainted and certainly not from the Light of the One Soul? Is it not black or white, with no grey areas in-between and no contamination of either? Is it from the complication of spiritual creation or from the simplicity of the soulful Light, from the wayward spirit or absolute truth? Spiritual creation attempts to create separation at every opportunity, which is every moment, of every day. Is it possible that we may be so far separated from the truth of who and what we are, that we can no longer see the difference between what is from true Light and that from dark licentiousness, that we have become oblivious to the existence of the two opposing energies?

In the end, could it be that the claiming of the ownership of our thoughts blinds us to the fact that we do not think independent thoughts, we are only ever given the impulse to think from our chosen energetic source, either the consciousness of soulful Light or the murky depths of spiritual creation. Grace felt the spaciousness of her own thoughts. She knew instantly that they came from a place far beyond her own human body. She had no need to own these thoughts, instead feeling a gratitude for them flowing through her consciousness and knew beyond any doubt, that they came from her alignment to Soul.

Until we attain a state of Oneness, that is to be at one with everyone and everything, the cycle of life, death and rebirth undoubtably must and will continue.

In the aftermath of the passing of George Harald Darcaster, his wife Alexandria inherited the majority shareholding in Darcaster Industries. With the help of her father, who was a well-known lawyer, she was able to maximize the sale of all Darcaster Industries' assets within twelve months of the date of her inheritance. The house in Kensington was quickly sold and that dark chapter permanently closed, and all-in-all Alexandria was now an exceedingly rich woman with enough wealth, if applied astutely, for many years and several generations to come.

Alexandria though, was not one to rest upon her laurels and her excessive riches would not go to waste. She decided immediately that some of this inheritance should be put into righting the wrongs of, not just the legacy of her husband but some of the ills of the country in general, repaying the lesser fortunate, the oppressed and victims of some of the malice inflicted upon them at the hands of those of the supremacist classes. Through many discussions, that would often include Grace Lightfoot and occasionally Richard Billings, they devised plans to help both children and young women out of the worst destitution and into more significant ways of life. Yes, it was true that there were many men too that suffered under the present system, the corrupt way of the world and some men would be helped but that was not the main focus for Alexandria and Grace.

The Alexandria Movement as it would be duly known, focused first of all upon the plight of homeless children and secondly upon the scourge of prostitution within the larger cities in England. The movement purchased land and property to build and develop both suitable, comfortable and practical accommodation as well as education and re-education centres for their forthcoming clientele. Their teams would ultimately be selected from people within the environments upon which they focused. They recruited adults that had survived living on the streets and had escaped the world of back-street prostitution that knew how life was for those on the bottom rungs of society. Other employees came from diverse societal classes that were vigilant and aware of the corruption and inequality, that had a genuine wish to help change the hypocrisy and injustices of the current distorted and disunited system.

They put together teams in London, Birmingham and Manchester, consisting mostly of experienced, robust, steadfast and considerate ladies with several magnanimous, reliable and tender men that could more easily approach and reassure the streetwise urchins and the cautious, mistrustful women of the night. Their potential clientele did not believe or trust in charitable organizations and were wary of anyone offering something for nothing. Many had experienced or viewed the cruel machinations of the supposedly 'good' workhouses designed to help the poor but were, in truth, simply traps to exploit and work them until they dropped, fell ill and ultimately died. Many found that it was safer to live on the streets or within the packed slums than to enter in through the doors of a workhouse. It was not a question of good or bad but of the lesser of the two evils that ran this immoral and discriminatory way of life.

As the organization grew, the teams made up mostly from the streets, evolved and expanded in many ways. It became a true calling for many, living life in service to both themselves yet equally to their clients.

Little did they know when they initiated the Alexandria Movement project that it would become more than their full-time occupation, it would be a lifestyle. Alexandria and Grace, though there was a large age gap, became life-long friends and close colleagues.

As they grew ever closer, more transparent and intimate with each other through their constant and committed devotion to the project and to humanity, they opened themselves up, steadily more accepting of themselves, one another and all those whose lives they blessed. There were no secrets, no hidden emotions, no concealed comparison or jealousy, everything was laid bare. Grace noticed how similar the effect of her own openness and honesty on Alexandria was exactly the same effect that Richard had had on Grace herself. They both realized that this could be the way for all relationships to bring true joy into being and a true marker for how not only women but also men, could interact together.

Richard Billings, even with his advancing age, became involved in the project. After all, he had jovially stated: 'I am accustomed to roaming the streets at night looking to take care of lesser fortunate young ladies.'

He continued with his part-time work at the bookstall and would be out on the streets with his team several evenings every week. This he would continue to do until, at eighty-nine years of age, his body became too frail to continue the work on the streets although he remained avidly involved in a more back room clerical engagement.

Active within the organization until his penultimate day, Richard Billings, aged ninety-three, passed away in December 1911 bequeathing all his worldly goods to his adopted daughter, Grace Lightfoot.

Whilst eating dinner on Saturday evening he had remarked to Grace that he was feeling exhausted and yet complete and that his time in this life was almost over. He was full of joy as he bade goodnight and goodbye to Grace as she retired for the evening, knowing that he would not wake for another morning. Grace also knew that this would be their last meal together, tears streamed down her cheeks as they hugged each other for the last time.

'Goodbye Richard, I love you so deeply and will cherish all that you have given me, all that you have opened my eyes to, everything that you are and will be. You are truly an angel, sent from Heaven.'

Richard died quietly in his sleep. His body was still warm when Grace went in to see him early the next morning, it was now but an empty shell. Richard had left this plane of life, moving on to the next. She sent word to Dr. Sam Billings to come as quickly as possible, he arrived within the hour. It was still dark outside, only 6.45am on a Sunday morning in mid-December. He knew why he had been asked to come; he had seen the frailty and the decline in Richard's physical health over the last few years but had still marveled at his astuteness, his profound wisdom and sharp mental acuity even up until the previous week when the three of them had eaten dinner together.

After checking his uncle's body, Sam wrote out the death certificate. At 'cause of death' he stopped and felt for the truth, even though he knew he would write 'natural causes'. He felt that there was much more to say than that. He looked up at Grace, as she looked back quizzically.

'I was just wondering about his cause of death; it is normal and expected to enter "natural causes" or some other reason such as 'consumption' or "tuberculosis". I just feel that there is no room to express the truth of Richard's death or indeed how he lived his life. I wish I could write that Richard Billings died of living a full, joyful and expansive life; he brought harmony and truth to everything he did. His body could no longer contain the magnificence within and his essence had moved on to greater realms of life.'

Grace, once again with tears of joy in her eyes, replied: 'That is so beautiful Sam, and so very true. He was a divine being and has left behind this frail body to further evolve. Maybe we will know him in his next incarnation although you might agree, neither of us have any unresolved issues with him, so that may not be necessary.'

'Richard told me last night, after dinner, that he was ready to leave and I knew it was true. We said goodbye to each other and I thanked him for all that he was and everything he has done for me. I know, beyond any doubt that he left this life joyfully and does not expect anyone to mourn for him. He has already paid for a cremation service and would like his ashes to be spread in Hyde Park. He desires no burial and no gravestone to mark his passing. This life has ended, he will definitely not be looking back upon it and would not wish for anyone that knows him to dwell in the past either.'

Two weeks later there was a short service at the crematorium. Richard had outlived most of his own generation but there were still many who knew him and they came to pay their last respects. There would be no wake or celebration, nothing was required. After receiving his ashes, Grace, Alexandria and Sam took a cab to Hyde Park to spend an hour wandering through Richard's favourite pathways, finally emptying his ashes around the foot of an old horse chestnut tree where he often sat to ponder upon life's mysteries, injustices and its unfolding magnificence.

Returning home from Hyde Park, Alexandria dropped Grace and Sam off at the house in Barnsbury. Saying goodbye to them Alexandria cheekily declared that Sam ought to ask Grace to be his wife, causing both of them to blush profusely. As the cab drove away, they watched and waved, turned to each other and without a word, stepped into each-other's arms and held one-another for the first time. Eventually they released each other from this beautiful embrace that neither of them wanted to let go of, turned and hand-in-hand walked inside the house.

From that moment, they knew that they were constellated to be together, just as Alexandria had also known it before she had spoken those profound words. She was simply performing her duty as an instrument of Heaven to make their next step a simple one. She could feel the love between them and yet read the hesitancy and insecurity in the air. She loved both of them deeply, no longer able to watch their slow dance around the class differences between them and the expected societal propriety, realizing that it was simply for them to get on with what was needed, to say yes to what was on offer for both of them. To step out of the constraints of a tainted system. Needless to say, from that moment onwards they never looked back.

Alexandria, at short notice, became a wedding organizer. She had all the contacts and all the resources she would need. As her first official act, she had decided that she would open up Alexandria Hall for what she referred to as the Wedding of the Century. She spared no expense and would not hear of any payment from either Sam or Grace. This was, as she often expressed, pay-back time. Alexandria, with the help of her very able housekeeper,

Grace's mother Evelyn, took care of every detail for the wedding. They had also arranged for a two-month long honeymoon, travelling around the country to visit all the relatives of the two families that were unable to attend the wedding ceremony and several of those that did.

Grace Lightfoot married Dr. Samuel Billings on May 12th, 1912, at Alexandria Hall. The ceremony and celebrations thereafter were simple yet elegant in the spectacular surroundings of this great stately home. Grace had never dreamed that she would wear such a dress and celebrate in this lavish and, yet for her, a most familiar environment.

From the first unfortunate yet blessed moment that she had met Sam after regaining consciousness, he had held a place in her heart. Along with Richard, his uncle, the men of the Billings family had been her true champions in so many ways, opening up a new path in life culminating for now, in this astonishing wedding. However, she did not give them all the credit for the self-evolution she had brought to pass. Once awoken to the power of the Light, she embraced it with her whole being and would continue to do so.

They would never have their own biological children due to the internal damage caused to Grace by the illicit back-street surgery all those years before. They did however bring Light to the lives of thousands of homeless, desperate children and outcast young women, the veritable untouchables of this cruel society, to whom they dedicated their lives.

Chapter 11

ᴀND SO IT GOES

Roar awoke from a deep sleep. His dream had been so vivid, in a similar way to his first experiences of Grace Lightfoot. He had once again felt Grace, been with her, a part of her, this time, as she drew her final breaths. He felt the contraction away from the Light that had been on offer, the disconnection, disappointment and judgement that had tainted her dying process.

Grace passed over in June 1953, at the age of eighty-one, twenty-five years after her husband Dr. Samuel Billings. She had worked tirelessly throughout most of her adult life for the benefit of those less fortunate than herself. She had felt the effects of two world wars and the tragedy of the great depression in between. Her own steadfastness and dedication had been shaken by the level of atrocities committed by mankind upon their fellow human beings. It was inconceivable that after the Great War of 1914 – 1918, humanity would once again enter into such wholesale slaughter where tens of millions of people would suffer and die due to the evil manipulations and machinations of dictators, so-called politicians and conniving industrialists under the ultimate control of the dark supremacist consciousness. Evil spiritual creation would stop at nothing to prolong its perverted and tyrannical reign on Earth and sadly Grace was unable to avoid reacting to its malevolent subterfuge.

By the time mid-20th century arrived the population of the United Kingdom was mostly gripped by fear and the desperate search for personal security amid wholesale destitution and poverty among the lower classes. Once again, the minions were being punished, beguiled by the duplicitous chicanery of those controlled by the nefarious power of the dark forces.

Roar understood that Grace, in her final two years of life, had fallen for the deception of the dark forces, had allowed disappointment and disgust and thus judgement of others to debilitate her obedience to the power of the Light. Mostly alone, she had been entrapped by the construct of loneliness, had withdrawn from life, stepped away from truth to hide in her books and await the end of her own mortality in her current life.

He realized that the events of his present life, along with all the momentum, observations and learnings from Grace and other past incarnations were here to aid his own settlement and acceptance of Universal Light and to expand beyond the levels of connection and awareness he had previously lived. He knew that everything mattered, and that there would always be, at least in this lifetime, dark forces that would attempt to knock him off track: To, in some way, cause him to react and contribute to their endless quest to create an incessant and disturbing circulation of conflict, jealousy, judgement or any other emotional energy that helps maintain this malicious dark agitation.

He could also see that spiritual creation is boundless in its disregard for human life, that the human body is of no consequence to 'It', whatsoever. Earth is a mere emotional playground that may seem real and is, in the sense that we are in human bodies and mostly believe that we are only human. It is this belief, amongst many others, that we are only human beings, that keeps us captured within the game that has been designed, created, presented and manipulated by the unseen malevolent dark forces. What a masterpiece of shadowy deception it is!

Later the same day, Roar and Elisabeth were in the park by the sea, sitting on either end of the park bench, openly chatting as they always did, whilst watching the children playing on the nearby climbing frame. They each had a large bag positioned between them on the park bench, full of the necessities required for an afternoon with the children in the park.

Although their physical relationship had ended prior to that fateful New Year's Eve all those years ago, they had grown ever closer and more non-physically intimate as the years had passed. Every two weeks or so, they would arrange to meet, often, weather obliging, they would bring their children down to the park to play. During the winter they would still meet, and it could be to do a few hours of gentle cross-country skiing in the locally prepared tracks or at one of the outdoor ice-skating rinks close by. They would always pack a healthy nourishing picnic no matter which activity they chose to do.

They both had sons, who at the moment were twelve and eleven years old, with their respective partners. The boys were down by the sea, out of their line of sight, doing some of their usual activities, foraging along the beach, trying to catch crabs and other small aquatic creatures in the shallow pools, particularly along the rocks at the end of the beach. Elias, Roar's son, was seven months older than Tobias but they constantly played together, living close by in the centre of town, attending the same kindergarten and even sharing the same class at school. They had become close friends and spent lots of their free time together, played together, often ate together and did school homework together. They were completely at one in their harmonious play and never antagonistic towards each other in all the hours they would spend together taking part in other activities.

Elisabeth asked: 'How have you been recently, Roar?

He hesitated for a few moments before he replied: 'I could just say that I'm feeling fine and leave it at that but both you and I know that that is just avoiding giving a proper answer to the question. That replying in this way is just like saying everything is not okay and don't ask me about it because I don't really want to talk about it and you don't actually want to know. It's so funny that in most cases the question is asked expecting the 'I'm fine' answer and hoping to avoid a deep and full response too. It's like an unspoken agreement, I'm fine, you're fine, now let's move on to speak about something more banal like what we watched on TV last night or catch up on the latest gossip that is circulating around the town, anything that keeps us stuck in the absurdity of what we are fed to be normal human life.

'So, to answer your question truthfully, in general I'm feeling great, as the days, weeks and years go by, everything becomes clearer and it is easier to discern truth within the falsity that is all around us, even if I haven't always particularly wanted to see it or do anything about it. It has become so obvious to me now, that certain things that I have been extremely attached to do nothing more than distract me from being my true and full self, delaying my return to a more soulful way of living. I know it's there, right in front of me, even so I still allow certain activities and I must say, evil constructs, to impede and obstruct my way. It feels disgusting because I know that I am not only delaying myself. It's more than that. Collaborating with the dark forces in this way means that I am harming not only myself, but adversely affecting everyone else. I am willingly contributing to the malaise encompassing the whole of humanity and I don't want to be a part of it any longer.

'It's more than a question of just giving up something that I know I shouldn't be doing, though these are things that are so ingrained in my way of life that it feels natural and, in a way, automatic, a must do, no matter what. It has always been like this and almost everyone I know lives this way and yet I can now feel it so clearly when I am in it, that it is a ridiculous global construct that keeps all of us enthralled within it. For me it seems, more than anything else, it is sport, in particular football and it seems that almost everybody I know has an addiction to it, watches hours of it, talks about it. For men, in particular and for an ever-increasing number of women, it is a serious, life-and-death business and a time-consuming addiction. It may sound a little crazy referring to sport and football as evil constructs but they are quite simply malicious fabrications. I'll try to explain this more clearly: I figure that anything that takes us away from our inner stillness, that causes emotional reactions, inner disturbance, excitement, elation and disappointment, that is not contributing to the wakening and true evolution of mankind, is distracting, detracting, abusive, harming, is of malevolent design.

'In Norway we have a long tradition when it comes to supporting football league teams from other countries and in particular the Premier League teams from England. We often refer to England and the United Kingdom as the "Ball Island". We all grew up with a live football league match from there, televised every Saturday afternoon ever since 1969 on our then only TV channel NRK. For many of us it became the highlight of the week, everybody chose their favourite team, the whole family sat around the TV cheering their teams on. We all talked about the game on Monday mornings at school. It was part of our way of life that became a tradition that is even stronger, more embedded in society now as we get to see football every day of the week. You could say it was a tradition that became an obsession and an addiction'

Elisabeth listened closely to Roar's words. She had experienced his football addiction; how much he drank when the 'match' was on and how his moods could swing from one extreme to another. He would be elated in one moment only to be angry and almost depressed a few minutes later, and often there and back again several times in the space of a two-hour football match.

He continued: 'You know how interested in all different sports I have always been and, in particular my somewhat fervent support for my favourite football team, Manchester United. I never missed a match, wherever I may have been I would somehow find a TV so I could watch the game or at worst I would listen to a radio commentary. They have been so successful during the recent decades, which has only helped enhance my interest even more, always expecting them to win and really getting emotional if they didn't. I get frustrated and angry, even get into arguments with some of my friends that support Liverpool Football Club. We make fun of each other and the teams when they lose, baiting and insulting one another, the members of the team, their managers and supporters in general. It sometimes feels more like war than sport.

'There is nothing that would stop me from watching them, it was always the highest priority, even interfering with deadlines at work and any relationship I was in. Watching the match and having a few drinks with the boys was prioritized way ahead of any woman that was in my life. I can't even remember when or why I became a Manchester United fan; it seems to have always been this way. If something ever got in the way of me watching the match, I would feel so much agitation and unrest through my whole body, more so than actually watching it, although watching the match was something of a roller-coaster ride, with lots of emotional highs and lows. I remember, not too long ago, they were playing an important Champions League match whilst we had family around to dinner. I couldn't concentrate properly on the conversation at the table, I had to excuse myself so many times to go to the toilet, when in reality I was just sneaking off to look in on the game and check the scores. I was totally pre-occupied with it and it left me completely disconnected from everyone else at dinner.

'When I did go to see them playing live, which, as you well know I did quite often, it didn't matter how high the price tag, flights, hotels, match-tickets, I would pay almost anything to be there and then brag about how much money I had spent doing so. During the match I would get so excited and emotional about it, singing, screaming, shouting at the players or the referee and jumping around gleefully whenever they scored a goal. My behaviour simply makes no sense at all when I look at it from a different angle, when I step back and observe what is actually going on, it becomes quite shocking, even disgusting.'

Elisabeth smiled lovingly as Roar described what had been his own normalized behaviour and attitude towards something that he now realized was so ridiculous, pointless, meaningless and in truth self-harming. It was more like a prison in which he had willingly incarcerated himself for so many years. He had at last rediscovered the key, or more candidly, he had decided to take the key out of his own pocket to unlock the prison doors.

Roar went on: 'Now I have come to the point where I don't feel that it is a sport anymore, if it ever was. We have an elite group of self-centred, rich, overpaid young men *(this is not a judgement on them, they have simply made a choice to sell out to the same conscious-ness that I have been a willing devotee of, just in a different way)*, run-ning around a field chasing a big leather ball with thousands upon thousands of brainwashed deluded fanatics, like myself, baying for blood on the sidelines. Then there are hundreds of millions more bellowing and screeching at the televised version, trans-fixed to that black box on the wall or in some way positioned as the altar of worship centrally in the living room, in groups, in pubs and bars, or in individual homes around the whole world.

'It's also a fact that the fans are now the meal ticket for a glob-al football industry that demands loyalty and squeezes as much money as possible out of everyone that becomes hooked into the consciousness of it, whether it be from ticket sales, TV-channel payments, football accessories, fan clubs, credit cards or any oth-er schemes they can devise to maximize their profits at the ex-pense of the loyal captivated supporters.

'Looking beyond the material, temporal aspects of the game, I can see how sinister the consciousness that drives football actu-ally is. I can feel how it has hooked me in, when this happened as I was still a young boy and how it has built up and intensified throughout my life. Eventually it became an integral part of liv-ing the deceitful lie that is the life I have lived. For a great many, in particular men, it gets to be even worse than I experienced it, which I must admit was pretty severe. It becomes all-consum-ing, the primary priority, it comes before everything else. It is a matter of life or death, some will and have, actually, fought and died for their chosen club or country team.

'The dark forces behind football are so powerful that they de-mand we indoctrinate our own children into it as swiftly as pos-sible. It provides all the necessary props, such as bedding for the baby's cot, football kits for all ages, of course, starting from zero upwards, shoes, slippers, football boots even for new-born ba-bies, jackets, hats, kitchen utensils, doormats, you name it and it can be found with the team logo emblazoned upon it. You can even get a car respray in your team's colours. Sit the kids down in front of the TV to watch the match or take them along as soon as they are remotely aware of what is going on, get them brainwashed into supporting our team as quickly as possible to avoid the chance that they may choose to support another that maybe your deadliest rivals.'

They looked at each other, as both could feel the power within his words. Elisabeth could feel the depth of the renunciation Roar had gone through to bring forth these realizations. Roar felt the grip of the dark football consciousness relinquishing further as he continued.

'It has been a long and arduous task to shake myself free from the evil consciousness that is professional football and I still am not completely clear of it yet. It is everywhere I look, in the newspapers every day, on TV during each news broadcast and there are televised matches every weekday evening as well as for most timeslots throughout the weekends. There are endless re-runs of matches from all around the world and it is now possible to see some form of football twenty-four hours a day, seven days per week. Every time I switch on my computer something will pop up to remind me or give me a link to something concerning football.

'I realized that it is not the football in itself that is the problem here, but my attachment to being distracted from being consciously and continually present within my own life, thus preventing me from being my full and true self. Once I realized how evil this consciousness is, it became an easier process to disconnect from it, although some of its malicious tendrils still infiltrate my body and being, constantly searching for a chink in my armour, a crack to prize its way back in to present itself within my own thoughts. Much of the time I do not entertain it, don't follow it or read anything about it on any form of media. Then suddenly, what seems like a bolt out of the blue, a thought enters my head telling me to check the football results which leads to online media and suddenly I'm watching the highlights of the previous match. Instead of being angry, disappointed or hard on myself, I simply accept that I have been away from myself, observe the controlling energy behind it and return to presence.

'Slowly I have become less attached to the team and their results although I can still feel the level of attachment to them winning and their toughest opponents losing. I do now realize just how ridiculous the whole of this story I am narrating to you is, as I am doing it. It's not only absurd but nauseating too, as it's not really about supporting a football team, that is just one superficial surface layer. What is more sinister are the layers lying beneath that, the energies of the grand illusion that affects, controls, perverts and destroys the whole of society, the whole of humanity. Through supporting a football team, I am not only an advocate of the dark forces but indeed a champion of all that is evil in this world.

'Without my supportive donations and the subscriptions of the masses, spiritual creation cannot exist. If we no longer contribute evil will have its termination, it can and will be eradicated from this plane of life. Even as I am saying these words, I feel a form of release from the control of this dark consciousness that has had a grip on me for what seems like the whole of my life and for eons prior to that.'

Elisabeth replied: 'I can feel that, of all sports in this world the football consciousness seems to be the most enthralling, it is powerful and quite overwhelming. It has infiltrated the whole planet and every echelon within society, even women are now becoming enthralled by it, confirmed by the growth and professionalizing of the women's game. When I look at it from the outside, it could be compared to any of the mainstream religions or even an extreme religious cult of some kind, in the way that it captures the young within its devout families, indoctrinating them into its intolerant judgmental regime. It is driven and perpetuated by forced conditioning on so many levels, maybe worse than religion in that it is even more focused upon hating the rivals, crushing them at any cost. There is a complete lack of integrity, there is cheating, play-acting and deceiving the officials, all of which is accepted as gamesmanship as if it's totally fine if you can get away with it, as long as victory can be gained. Parents and family, social media, mainstream press, TV channels, peers, fashion industry and absolutely every possible channel are used to recruit into the cult of football.

'The people are to idolize the so-called heroes in the arena of the mighty football gladiators. Supporters are encouraged and inspired to become fanatical, to fight and die for their team, the rivalry often depicted in the terminology of war, a matter of life and death with the poor brave participants suffering injury and heartbreak, joy and elation on the grand battlefield that is the football pitch. Is it not pure evil to take innocent children and deliver them into the arms of this vicious and evil cult that takes hold and never wants to release them again? Because we are captured by this consciousness, we willingly sacrifice our own children upon its altar, as we do ourselves. Instead of stepping back to feel what is actually going on here, feel the energy behind it and renounce the evil that lies there, we devote our lives to it.

'It's not just football though, it is every sport you can think of. Some people become addicted to all sports, it doesn't matter what they watch, as long as there is sport to be seen. I was never really interested in it, even though almost every weekend in every winter season, my parents would watch the cross-country skiing, downhill skiing, ski jumping and Nordic biathlon events on TV, without fail. Whenever the Winter Olympics or the Skiing World Championships were played out, they made it into a family event, dinner around the TV whilst we cheered on our favourite Norwegian skiers. I could feel then how easy it was to get sucked into the atmosphere, the patriotism and the excitement of the occasion. Skiing for your country, most importantly, defeating the old enemy – Sweden – next door. Little old Norway performing better than everyone else, we are the best country in the world, we are above all others, they are inferior to us.'

'Yes, you are spot on with that Elisabeth,' Roar exclaimed, 'that's exactly how it has been for me. Sport has been so important in my life, not only watching it at every opportunity but taking part in it too, particularly winter sports. Downhill skiing at high speeds has always been so exhilarating for me and even now during the winter we still go up to the mountains occasionally. I have slowed down though, much more controlled, I don't take any wild chances the way I used to do. The thrills of the speed and not knowing what is around the bend or below the next drop were part of what I lived for but I have realized that this recklessness and carelessness is also a way to disconnect from my inner being. To have short-lived thrills, temporary highs that always need another adrenalin rush and another beyond that. Of course, yet more ways of detaching from my true self and avoiding seeing the utter mess of the way I lived my life.'

Elisabeth pondered, 'I don't know where or how sport came to be, it just feels like it has always been there, in every culture, at least in every one of the so-called civilized cultures. What I'm beginning to wonder is whether sport is civilized or is it the opposite of that? Are our cultures and societies civilized at all? When we look at the amount of war, poverty, greed, abuse, murder, rape, deceit, defamation, propaganda, lies and everything else you would imagine could not be present in a civilized culture, then how civilized are we? Sport is closely associated with competition, comparison and jealousy or envy, as is education, employment and even family life in many ways. You could say that absolutely none of this is a remotely civilized way of human interaction. How has humanity come to this point and what would it be like if we could step away from all of it? I wonder if by calling ourselves a civilized culture we are actually signifying the opposite, wanting to claim something we are not, something that we are obviously so far away from.'

Roar added: 'Role models, that's what our top sportsmen and women are being presented and projected as on every form of media we have. They often have so much money that they don't really know what to do with it. In certain situations, they seem often to make quite poor choices. It can be drink and drugs related, sexual assault, physical violence, driving offences or other more serious crimes, thereafter claiming innocence and using expensive lawyers in an attempt to escape from the irresponsibility of their actions, at least in the short term. It seems that it is often related to self-gratification, satisfying needs that they have, without respect or consideration for the harm it could be doing to others. Many of our children grow up idolizing these athletes and modelling themselves upon their sporting prowess along with their ill-actions and behaviours, committed to their own competitions and becoming the best at their chosen activities.'

Elisabeth replied: 'Success in competition it seems may be somewhat proportionally linked to self and self-centredness. The more successful an athlete is the more they seem to be self-consumed and in disregard of others. Well, this is not just concerning athletes and sport, I imagine it is the same in any area of societal life. The way children are taught to be, act and play, encouraged to be the best, the quickest, the smartest, the kindest, the nicest, it is all designed to instill, cement and solidify the self-importance by out-competing their peers whatever the chosen activity. It works the same way in the school system, children are rewarded for performing above their classmates rather than being taught and guided in the arts of communication, cooperation, collaboration, equality and respect. Competition is such a loaded instrument that breeds disrespect, comparison, judgement, divisiveness and jealousy, all the negative attributes and qualities needed to unfortunately further feed the corrupt ways of our inequal and degenerative society.

'You could ask though, why do we accept this within society if it is so harmful? Although, is it so prevalent because that is what the masses are demanding and thus, what is provided? There can be no supply without the demand. Every which way we turn we are faced with competition with its deleterious consequences and yet we indulge in it, we bay for more, we never seem to have enough of it. Thus, we can perhaps surmise that humanity is indeed not yet ready to awaken from the dark slumber, not yet prepared to step away from the dark forces and return to the Light from whence we all came.

'It is quite simple, we either live from the Light or from the dark. Our current world is almost totally dominated by the dark forces of spiritual creation that bring us all forms of debasement, deceit, competition and the like. Most people are completely lost within it. They choose to live, believing in the age-old illusion that is offered to us all as 'the way that life is', simultaneously avoiding the inner knowing we all have, but choose not to access. In truth they are living "the way life is not".

'Spiritual creation has become normalized, hiding in the safety and security of being part of the deceived masses even though the dis-ease within us all signifies the truth hidden within. The joy, harmony and love afforded from stepping away from spiritual creation into the Light of the Soul is obvious for all to see. All see and feel it and yet take precious few steps towards it in these current times. It is and has been so, that those living from the Light are seen as a threat to the continuity of the embedded dark ways and thus they are derided, attacked, slandered, threatened and often persecuted in order to perpetuate the dark rule here on Earth.

'As soon as there is a movement from true Light with any amount of momentum, the dark vultures will circle and their demons will awaken to blacken, disavow, and attempt to destroy all that is of truth. For there are those among us that are sold-out slaves of the dark forces, such that they wield great power upon this human plane of life, whether it be in a position of judicial power, a political mouthpiece or a person of great material wealth. They will carry out any conceivable ill-doing in order to perpetuate the reign of the malevolent spiritual creation which is upon us.

'You can safely say, that if you step forward and live from the Light, others will automatically accuse you of being 'too clean', of hiding your dark secrets, for they will refuse to relinquish any of their fellow lost and licentious brothers and sisters. There will be those who will clutch onto any who are pulled back towards the soulful Light, retain them by their sides within their tethered purgatorial existence, firmly imprisoned in spiritual creation. They will feel the enormity and the truth of your chosen way and yet will seek to denounce and deride the reflection that you bring, casting doubt and suspicion at every opportunity, using all the dark tools on offer. "He cannot be so happy all the time, there must be something wrong with him, he must have some dark secrets somewhere", or "she doesn't drink or smoke, has no bad habits, eats healthily, goes to bed by 9pm every evening, she must be in some kind of weird or harmful cult". Using all the standard, pathetic circulatory gossip, speculation and rumour spreading without a grain of truth at their foundation, with the plan of simply repeating the lies enough times in order that they will stick, they will become the chosen dishonest-truth of those who want to remain ensconced within the dark.'

★★★

They paused for a while and gazed out across the deep blue waters of the Oslo fjord. Roar turned again to look at Elisabeth and said: 'You look more vital, radiant and beautiful now than you have ever done before. I can't believe that in just three months you will be fifty years old, you look so youthful, clear and fresh.'

Elisabeth replied: 'Thank you Roar, I do feel amazing and as you know the way we look and feel is a reflection of the way we live our lives and now more than ever before I am completely focused on being responsible for my every movement, looking after myself. Truly caring about my whole being is just a natural way of life for me now. I don't just live this way for me though, it is for everyone I know, for Tobias and Elias, for you and your wife Amalie and of course for my husband Sebastian, all the pupils, not just in my class but in the whole school, all of their parents and anyone that knows me and even those I pass by on the streets. I look at it like this, our every breath matters. Every word, thought, movement and intention, everything I do affects everyone around me, anywhere and anytime. There are only two options regarding our every action, we either heal or we harm and my purpose here is to heal, it is what my current incarnation is about, it is my job here and now in this lifetime on earth. As such I will take responsibility to do my upmost to reflect a true way of being. Show who and what I am, to be completely honest and transparent with everyone.'

Roar interjected: 'You could also say that it is everybody's responsibility to live responsibly if we are going to change the destructive course mankind is heading on.'

Elisabeth continued: 'You and I, Roar, have come a long way from the lives we once led; we were caught in an entanglement of arrangements, lies and illusions that we believed were real. We have changed much of our ways of living and the results are plain to see. They do not go unnoticed and because we live in a world built for and by what is a corruption within the Universal Light, reactions are, and will be forthcoming. Dark forces will challenge the truth we represent. All life here on Earth is but a tiny blemish within the magnificence of the All and consequently, must one day return to that grandness from whence it came.

'It may seem that at this present moment in time humanity is becoming more wanton, reckless, careless and irresponsible. The levels of corruption, deceit, abuse, and evil seem to have reached a new atrocious high and there seems to be little hope that things may change enough to avoid our own self-destruction. On the other hand, individuals here and there and small pockets of people across the world seem to be waking up from the dark slumber in which they have been caught up. It may seem but a tiny few compared to the size and power of the corrupt systems that control the world, but it is all about the collaboration and building up of a true momentum of change from within each person that can eventually reach a tipping point where responsibility, equanimity, transparency and absolute honesty become the leading lights.

'Only this fundamental transmogrification, a metamorphosis back to our original being can end the malaise, the endless suffering of the wanton spirits controlling mankind's currently devastating path. We have everything we need at our fingertips, passing through us all of the time, just as we also have all that we, the confederate of misguided spirits have together created

299

and irresponsibly chosen before us that has become our current, yet illegitimate truth.

'We all know that what we live here on Earth is not it, nowhere near it. In fact, it is most often the exact opposite or at best a deceptive bastardization of who and what we are truly meant to be, and why we are here. There are many questions to be answered. We have all the questions and we know all the answers and yet we choose to live in our own purposeless-built illusion of distraction, reduction and suffering, avoiding the magnificence of what we truly are.

'At some point in the not-too-distant future, though probably not within this lifetime nor many to come, we all will reclaim our magnificence. There will be no more evil spiritual creation on this planet, the Light of the Soul will permeate All and everyone will return to the One Truth.'

THE END

EPILOGUE

As a further pondering upon some of the content within this book, it may be helpful to highlight the unfathomable extent of an almost absolute corruption, which we could describe as a seething dark consciousness which permeates all things within our temporal lives, ensnaring almost every person on the planet, young or old, no matter what colour, culture, religious belief or persuasion, thus, in fact, controlling the entire world we live in. What is this improbity, other than an all-encompassing consciousness that holds us all enthralled until, that is, until the moment arrives when we realize that we are more than what it tells us we are? We are much greater than it is, yes, still within it, yet stepping free of its sordid tentacles, enabling us to live a more cognizant, multidimensional existence.

The greatest mal-achievement of this force of mass degeneracy is that it, or some other overpowering consciousness closely akin to it, has fed us, that is the whole of humanity, all of the thoughts we think. Our idea of ourselves is that we are untainted, that we are free, or other self-deceptions such as we are not the sinners, that we are good people, that we fight for democracy, justice and freedom for all, that we are in 'the right', but are we? Do we not often have thoughts such as, 'yes, it is corrupt over there, but here it's not so bad', or, 'there is a certain level of immorality, but that is something that always happens, we just have to live with it'. And hence, we accept the iniquitous way life has developed and in doing so, we actually support and assist its colossal deviation and deprivation. To be free of this putrefaction, do we not need to have zero tolerance of it, know that no amount of deviance is acceptable. If we accept any sordidness, are we not then tainted by it?

This all may seem ominous, ghastly and totally out of control, and it is true that we of mankind are in an utter mess, but there is Light (pardon the intended pun) on the horizon. There are some amongst us that have stepped out of the glutinous swamp of separation and individuality into the fiery light of the Soul, that again walk with divine footsteps upon this earth. There are many more awakening from the dulling, deceiving grasp of the dark spiritual creation that held us all obliviously ensconced within its concocted illusion, many now realizing the truth with eyes that could not see but are now discerning veracity from the colossal ill-prevarication. It is an occasion of monumental upheaval as all things must change. It begins now.

Could it be that we are simply choosing the comfortable option, the easy way out, rather than examining, admitting and renouncing what our own levels of wretchedness are? Do we ever ask ourselves what it is within us that is so agreeable to this disparity and consequently the astronomical levels of incongruity throughout all walks of society? If we work for a living, pay our taxes and give a measured portion of our money to charity, pray to our respective deities, we consider ourselves free of the debasement within society. We cannot help but be aware of the debasement, but we are experts at pretending we don't know.

Strange or not, as this may seem, the word I find most synonymous with corruption is 'self'. Could it be said that where there is focus on 'the self', there is defilement and divisiveness?

Could we describe the relationship between 'self-centredness' and gross ill-behaviour as exponentially proportional? The greater the self-interest, self-serving, self-advancement, avarice, competitiveness, self-ambition and all the other attributes often touted as factors for success in our nefarious world, the more prevalent, atrocious, monstrous and despicable our actions become.

Sadly, in the world in which we now live, ill behaviour controls everything. Tainted human beings controlled by an unscrupulous dark supremacist consciousness, the very apex of the fraudulent pyramid of human success is reserved for those most willing to submit their bodies to the control on offer, those most willing to do its bidding, purchase, exploit, eliminate, kill, destroy, manipulate, and abuse, anyone and everyone if need be, in order to attain and remain at what they observe to be their deserved place at the pinnacle of this wayward illusion we call human life.

There is a brazen arrogance that only the shameless wayward spirits would be audacious enough to, through their human marionettes, wantonly flaunt their ill-conceived plans and from a position of supremacy dismiss any dissension as 'conspiracy theory'. We have seen and heard it so many times, anyone questioning the current lopsided system or proposing another way, are branded for life by the instruments of propaganda (mainstream media, social media and perversive fact-checking organizations). The truth is there, it is hidden in plain sight. The debase labelling and public pillorying of those revealing the truth cannot stop its emergence indefinitely. As the Light of the Soul intensifies, the dark spiritual deceit becomes more obvious and exposed, more desperate and will begin to crumble.

Through a little research, reading the freely available propaganda and the lines in-between, it is not conspiracy, but rather 'in your face' that a global takeover has been executed, covertly planned in meticulous detail, to such an extent that those governed by this dark supremacy consciousness now own and control most politicians, huge swathes of the mainstream press, big tech and social media platforms, the lawmakers, the judges, police force, military and any other officials deemed necessary to preserve their immunity from responsibility for their actions and from prosecution for their reprehensible ill-deeds. Let us not be deceived by those portrayed as the saviours of humanity or marketed philanthropists, for they have the resources to create any identity they wish to have, whilst conniving surreptitiously in the background to maintain the status quo and indeed capture an even greater slice of the pie.

Unfortunately, this does not free all others from the accountability for their own levels of adopted falsehood, for they are indeed much the same as the so-called 'big-players'. It could be that some are on their own ladder to the false illusion of what success is, the picture of material advance painted by the dark evil forces that maintain the delusive images of what is normal and accepted, or indeed others that are simply caught by the reaction of envy and jealousy to it. It could be said that it is black or white, do we in any way allow and/or accept infraction or do we not? We allow the violation within ourselves, simultaneously accepting the levels of abuse taking place above and around us. We may observe the high-level, grand deception, we may even verbally denounce it, but without looking at and dealing with our own iniquity, we are still contributing to the seething abomination.

To delve a little further into this conundrum, maybe it is time to take a closer look at what indeed 'the self' is.

A CLOSER LOOK AT 'THE SELF'

There are many differing theories, writings and conjecture around what exactly comprises the human being, whether they be of psychological, scientific, philosophical or religious origin. Here in this Epilogue and indeed within the book itself, there are references and discussion in regard to the composition of the human being. Science has been unable to discern, psychology has many theories, and religions are in disagreement as to the biological anthropology and spiritual origins of the human being. Because of these schisms in thought it seems that it cannot be unanimously agreed upon in any way and thus it may be postulated that maybe none of it is true, or maybe there are differing amounts of truth within each position. Possibly indicating that, here again, the dark malfeasance has played its part to contaminate, confuse and to separate human beings from each other. What if we are all one and the same? What if 'self', individuality and this concocted separation only serve to keep us distanced from one another and thus distanced from what are our true selves?

Was there a Big Bang that initiated this Universe? Did God simply create everything within six days, resting on the seventh? Or was there some other event or process that produced all that we see and feel around us? Science often produces theories in one century or decade that are, at some point, later disproven. Science has an interesting way of claiming the definite knowledge, proposing it has all the relevant information only to realize at a certain point further down the line that, it had overlooked particular factors, or had been totally unaware of other aspects or considerations and thus the then most recent theory was indeed incorrect.

Science can also choose to demonstrate certain theories designed only upon a limited set of criteria simply to prove what is wished or desired to be proven. Evolution of man, it is now generally accepted without any real proof, came from the apes based upon sporadic finds of sculls and other bones dating up to seventy thousand years ago, ignoring the fact of advanced technologies far superior to our current capabilities that date previous civilizations, possibly, hundreds of thousands of years prior to our stone age and neanderthal finds. This is far beyond the currently presented theory and stubbornly held onto timelines. Inexplicable finds have been unearthed but, as yet they are not accepted and do not fit within the narrative of mainstream science. And thus, so do our education systems still stubbornly teach our school children that we have evolved from the apes or some other equally incredible fairytale. It seems that we have to cling onto the current stories and illusions until we find something else that completely negates them. Why does it take eons to let go of the concocted stories of the past?

Let it be said though, that science has created some amazing technological advancements but sadly this is often driven purely for monetary profit or military advantage, weaponization first, general public and the poor must stand at the back of the queue, cap in hand in the hope of reaping any rewards from these advancements. Seldom, or never, are discoveries created and developed for the true good of all the people. Why is this not at the forefront of human development? Is evolution based sole-ly on technological advancement and what is good for the elite few? It seems to be okay to test new technological and medical progress in the name of financial profit, upon the unsuspecting public, with any ill-effects conveniently and rapidly swept under the carpet by the totally corrupt companies, politicians and me-dia. And, of course, the totally checked-out population that are willingly deceived and baying for comfort, for security and to be healed or saved by what is being offered and produced.

It seems that we need a new theory or indeed, how about the real truth if it is in some way possible to discern it through the miasma of lies and corruption? It seems that, as long as we are stuck in this world of 'self', egotism, separation and individual-ism, it is impossible to live in a truthful way.

Returning to the 'self' conundrum, is it possible for us to re-connect to the essence of who we truly are and in doing so will all be revealed? What if we remove or more correctly stated, rein-in the indulgent, wayward self, not to become self-less but to replace the self-orientation and selfishness, with soul-fullness?

Contrary to the old rhyme, little boys are not made of snips and snails and puppy-dog tails, neither are girls made of sug-ar and spice and all things nice. This may be an obvious state-ment but let's start with it anyway. We are all made up of exact-ly the same divine Universal particles and driven, controlled or impulsed by a life-force from either one source of energy or the other. One energetic source is of Universal Oneness, Harmony, Stillness, Truth and Love whilst the other is everything that the first is not, the antithesis of it. The primary and original energy, literally the first in existence, is the soulful, Universal Light. The secondary and plagiarized energy is the dark spiritual creation, a force, that is at work solely on this planet Earth.

The next statement/question will certainly be contested and even ridiculed by some but possibly accepted and pondered upon by others, which is, just the way it is right now:

Is it possible that we are all on the cycle of birth, human life, death and rebirth to then do it all over again and again until we learn that we are all equal in our divine origins? Furthermore, is it possible that between death and rebirth, we spend time on the spiritual plane of life, or we could call it the fourth dimensional plane of life, a dimension that is right here on Earth, right beside us and yet we are unable to see it? This is therefore postulating that we do have a spiritual element to the human being and that this part of the being is actually immortal. What if we expanded that thought, could it also be said that it is not the human body that has the spiritual element to it but quite the opposite, the spirit has a self-created denser human part that it controls and uses for its own entertainment, distraction and exploration? So it is, that the human body and personality, after each life, perishes and only the spirit moves on to the next plane of life and from there to its next human incarnation. This cycle of Reincarnation will continue until all spirits let go of their wayward adventures and return to soul and the One Soul they have all separated from.

Moreover, could it be that, initially the spirit was part of the soul, which resides on the soul plane or within a fifth dimension that is here, adjacent, above and beyond the third and fourth dimensions on Earth? The spirit aspect separated from soul to experience the world of creation within the fourth dimension, and much later, after observing physical life, it decided to enter into the third or physical human dimension, to experience it for itself. The first movement of the spirit away from soul was the moment that the 'self' and the corruption of Soulful Light were created, bringing about an imbalance within both the spirit itself and the Universe. After eons of existence in the fourth dimension, a certain confederation of spirits created human beings on Earth to experience the physicality of their own creation by partially incarnating within the created human being.

The human being though, is created from the divine particles of the Universe through which there is a natural magnetic pull back to equanimity and at-one-ment with the Soul and the Universe. Therefore, when in human form there is an eternal unrest within this human part of the spirit due to the agitation and unsettlement of the separation from the whole and the resistance to the magnetic pull of its inevitable return to equilibrium.

It is not the point here to go into detail about our true origins but let it be said that, here on Earth, as human beings, we are living only a fraction of what we truly are. The consideration suggests that everything can be felt by everyone if we choose to align to the energetic source that is Universal rather than the source that comes from the confederate of wayward separated spirits that reside only here on Earth within the third and fourth dimensions as previously described.

We are led to believe that our conscious mind is solely within our heads and yet it is plain to see that each particle, each atom contains a level of intelligence that we, as a human race, are still unable to fathom with the so-called high intelligence supposedly placed between our two ears. Could it also be said that within each of our divine particles resides the access to all the wisdom that the Universe is?

We human controlled spirits 'think' that by blindly crashing, destroying and deconstructing streams of particles (aka Hadron Collider) we can uncover knowledge that will evolve humanity or more likely develop new weapons of mass destruction and/or massive streams of income. What if by re-connecting with the Light of our soul we could access wisdom way beyond these puny human attempts to break and destroy everything we come across?

We, under the control of the wayward spirit, have an arrogance, a self-belief, that we are the most intelligent species, that our kind are capable of creating what is needed to comfortably enjoy life. And yet, we do not have the intelligence to live in a way that does not lead to a deadly range of lifestyle illnesses and diseases. Through our poor or **unintelligent, unwise** lifestyle choices we knowingly create, promote and prolong ill-health instead of intelligently choosing to simply prevent it, we also willingly take recreational drugs, eat junk food, drink from small to copious amounts of alcohol and/or sugary beverages, we physically thrash our bodies and avoid being consciously present within them. We still call ourselves intelligent but is this truly intelligence? It seems to be nothing more than irresponsibility, stupidity and in fact we could even call it a slow form of suicide.

We could consider that the human consciousness combined with the Light of the Soul and the pull within the Universal particles, that make up the human body, are constantly at work, drawing the spirit back to its inexorable return from whence it came. The self is the spirit-controlled part within, that resists this return, that wants to continue living its capricious life of pain and suffering, experiences and emotions, ideals and beliefs, the crazy roller-coaster ride that human life can be.

Could it be that the whole current purpose of human life now is to evolve away from the farce we have willingly been drawn into, renouncing the created illusion of what human life has become? Can we then let go of all attachments to it, to return to the soul we have separated from?

'Self', or the spirit controlled human consciousness along with its ethereal puppeteer are the stumbling blocks, the well-practised subversives that cling on to keep extending this miserably reduced existence here on Earth. Life after life, rebirth after rebirth, pain and suffering, bliss, the constructed yet elusive search for happiness, emotional experiences, comfort and security, all things nice and good, all things evil, exciting and stimulating, everything possible to avoid truth and delay the inevitable return, back to where it all started.

What is it that we are so determined to resist? Could it be that the spirit is afraid to no longer be the individual demonstrative self, that returning from eons in separation from the soul means that it must give up its singularity and in doing so embrace the All that it and every other being is part of? The self would no longer be 'the self' but part of the divine magnificence of the oneness of all souls, hence part of the One Soul.

Imagine the control, deception, distraction and diversion exercised by the fourth dimensional spirit in order to enforce the limitations of intelligence, wisdom and realizations upon its human being simply to continue its vain attempt to delay its own return to soul.

In addition to the exposition about creation and the wayward spirit, herein follows a short example of how words relative to, not only this book but all that is, can be debased by humanity, within our lie-infested world, driven by ever-increasing levels of incremental deceit and forgery.

Truth, true and truthful are often used words that we could say have been tampered with beyond any shadow of doubt. So much so that we now have the position in society whereby the truth is defined individually, every being on the planet has their own version of what truth is for them. In an attempt to create some sense and order within this malaise, or perhaps to further confuse the issue the powers that be are constantly creating new versions of overarching truths that are subsequently implemented in order to control and govern the masses. Conceivably, what is happening is that each individual 'self', is moving and behaving in ways based upon their own personal set of ideals and beliefs, which in turn are based upon protecting their undealt with hurts and the exercising of the momentums they carry throughout life and lives past. Thus, moving around within their own 'truth' in conflict with, yet reluctantly accepting or not, the authorities, various religions, centres of culture and indeed every other group, gender and being on the planet. The inner conflict this causes is suppressed and a new truth paradigm is introduced, the corruption of the word truth to allow everyone to have their own truth but to be submissive to grander truths imposed upon them from above. *The greatest problem being that none of it can possibly be truth.*

The major ensuing situation is that those with greatest power, wealth and influence, the apex of human predators, the elite purveyors and expediters of what the truth is allowed to be, have almost complete control and therefore it is their individual and exclusive truths that trump any other individual or group truth. Within this grand complication, the desired bias and corruption are achieved, and no-one is allowed or even able to see or feel what the true truth actually is.

Is it then an impossibility to experience the true Truth as long as we are run by this wayward 'self'?

There are those, currently only a few, that have to some extent been able to re-align the self, or in other words, bring 'the self' back to or towards its soulful infusion or reunion. Returning to soul is an inevitability for every human being and every separated spirit, no matter how long and hard they fight to resist it. This may not be a simple task, as each being, each self, has lived many lives and created its own separate set of lived imprints throughout its sojourn here on Earth and previously. These imprints, the being will need to clear and re-imprint on its way back to soul, which may for all be similar in ways but ultimately will be different from all others. To reiterate, every individual will have what could be similar and yet different unique ways to return to the oneness of the All that is. In other words, it will be to walk the path in reverse of the track that brought them to their current state of individual separation.

The true Truth, or in other words, Energetic Truth (in regard to the choice of aligned to energetic life force, either the healing Light of the One Soul or the harmful force of spiritual creation) is known and felt by all. As such, the Truth will be rejected by those still intensely embedded in the constructed illusion that is human life, or contrarily, accepted by those ready to return to their soulful origins. Whenever it comes to pass that we are witness to a true presenter of Energetic Truth, and it has happened many times during past millennia, how will this person, these persons be received?

The evil purveyors, gatekeepers and disciples of separation and individualization, of segregation and dissemblance will assail and bombard, will defile and denigrate, will stop at nothing to destroy and discredit all who deign to utter energetically truthful words. They will believe within themselves that they are the truth, that they are the authority, that anything that is not acceptable to them can and must be eradicated.

If one teacher of Truth falls, others will always come in their place. It will never cease, for the simple fact is that we are all originally from the Light of Truth and one day all shall return to that place of divinity.

Although this may be incredibly difficult for many to accept; anything that is not from the Light of the Soul, from universal at-one-ment, must then be from the dark coalition of creation, the deceitful confederate of separated spirits. If we do not consciously make the choice of one or the other, Soul or spirit, Light or dark, then the choice is made for us, in choosing not to choose our own alignment we thus choose not to align to the soulful energy, and so choose, unconsciously as it may seem but in fact consciously, to align to the spirit, the energy of the created dark fraudulence. The possibility of energetic alignment is always there to choose, every moment of every day, if we think we have not chosen we have only deceived ourselves into believing this fact.

Energetic Truth = soulful connection, living in at-one-ment with all, within the All.

The current meanings of the words Responsibility and Integrity are two more examples that have been deftly vulgarized to become vested upon the debasement of what our societies have become.

It goes like this:

Responsibility means accepting, in full, the culpability for yourself, your own actions and anything you do or are involved in. It may be expected that you align to what is conventional and, accepted as normal for the majority within your particular society. If, for example, segregation and discrimination are prevalent factors within a certain country or society, it will be the expected norm, the responsibility of the general public to maintain this arranged and accepted level of abuse. Equally, if the education system teaches untruths, encourages competition, comparison, thus jealousy, separation and individuality, the children will be trained to carry this harming behaviour as a programmed responsibility into the world.

What use is this poisonous form of responsibility? Smoking cigarettes was previously the accepted norm, touted as healthy and relaxing in many societies until enough people demanded the truth be uncovered. Even now, when everyone knows how harmful smoking is, billions still partake. Is that responsible?

Integrity means the adherence to your own personal moral code, or the code defined by the authorities above you, in any and all circumstances. Possessing integrity can be described as being true and honouring to oneself and all others, never demeaning anyone. If your moral code is based upon the waywardness and degradation of a decadent political system, where then lies your integrality?

On the other hand, if we preface responsibility and integrity with the word 'energetic' we can take it to a whole new level, we are thus given wholly true and complete meaning to these words.

Energetic responsibility is the responsibility of energetic choice or alignment, aligning to and living from the Light of the Soul or the opposite, not aligning to the Light, thus living from the dark energetic creation of the confederate of wayward spirits. Thus, being energetically responsible is living soulfully (without perfection), every movement and intention is from a place of love, no harm can be caused, only healing. This would be the premier and most important choice every human being is faced with. Delaying the choice is not possible, but every moment gives a new opportunity to re-make the choice and re-align to one or the other.

Energetic integrity comes from the alignment to the Soulful Light. It is to no longer adhere to the corrupted moral personal or societal codes that fraudulently run our communities, our countries, or the world and do not work for everyone equally. It is to live in true service to the whole of humanity, seeing the energetic truth and honouring all from that loving, living way.

AN AFTERWORD FROM THE AUTHOR

This book, *Unfolding Grace,* is a work of fiction with fabricated characters and events. There are though, some references to historical incidents and situations that may differ slightly from the actual recorded episodes. Although, it could be said that all recorded history is, in fact, mostly opinion, propaganda and conjecture put forward on behalf of those in ascendency and authority, that further retain or allow others to be in the position to document it (the historical forgery). These historical references are in no way an attempt to depict true or false chronicled happenings, they are nothing other than a background for this heartfelt story.

It, the story within this book, is however based upon commonly felt wisdom, known human behaviours and ordeals that have transpired in the past, present and, as they undoubtably will continue to do so, in the future.

It may be said that the world we live in is geared up around dishonesty masquerading as truth. Low levels of dishonesty are often the levels most criminalized whilst high levels of dishonesty are likely portrayed as honourable or desirable and therefore protected, proclaimed as being the truth.

Unscrupulous systems have been put in place by the deceitful beings controlled by a dark and arrogant supremacist consciousness to avoid or replace anything that is truthful, supplanting it with outright treachery and duplicity. Truth, as described previously, is so distorted that we may ask ourselves, 'Can it be categorically stated that there is no real honesty anywhere to be seen in those that have the pivotal roles in our societies?' It does not stop with the people in powerful prestigious roles of office. It is all of us. We have succumbed, en masse, to the beguilement and corruption that we have called for and, so, is copiously on offer to us.

Whenever anyone stands forth and presents Truth they will be duly attacked, labelled, besmirched, vilified, defamed, threatened and tainted with any and every poisonous brush that the vicious annals and channels of our current corrupt society possess, for they cannot stand to feel the reflection of what lies at the heart of every man, woman and child, what lies at the inner-most-essence of every human being. There is but one Truth. How can each individual have their own truth? The fact of individual truths exposes the corruption of the word 'truth'. Truth can only lie beyond the 'self'. Therefore, until we relinquish 'the self' with all that makes up each individual set of ideals and beliefs, we will remain lost within the corruption of our current maniacal, self-destructive and treacherous lifestyles and governing systems.

Within this book there are discussions, musings, thoughts and observations that may refer to different religions, cultures and other ways of living and being that suggest that our life here on Earth may not be all that it seems. It is not written as an afront to anyone's personal belief system but it does question the fact of beliefs in general, whether they are individual, for a smaller group or a global quasi-community. (The word 'quasi' is used to prefix community because of the current levels of abuse, selfishness, jealousy and disregard communities generally hold within.) It also asks if these beliefs are ever exactly the same for two individual beings or purely constructed by and for the 'self' and therefore as all else connected to self, they are simply another adulteration of the truth.

What if, as many may agree, we are much more than simply humanoid beings living one life here on Earth and then it's either over into heaven or hell, or some other convenient variation, or a more nihilistic approach, that we live only once and at death there is nothing more? What if all the mainstream religions have originally been created from truthful words and teachings, but thereafter been conveniently desecrated by dark forces to separate and control huge swathes of humanity? Within *Unfolding Grace* are discussions suggesting it is possible to return to the original

'Energetic Truth' that has been presented on many occasions, in many different ways throughout time.

There is now no doubt that we have overwhelming proof that throughout millennia nothing has ever truly worked, no system, no form of governance nor any form of institutionalized religion has brought about a harmonious and joyful existence for any substantial part of humanity. Killing, terrorism, war, persecution, rape, abuse, slavery or the more modern term human trafficking, child sex-trafficking, suicide, prostitution, poverty, greed, the list is endless and yet we persevere with the same systems knowing they are totally unfit for purpose.

We live in ways that debilitate us. In general, we live longer yet physically sicker lives in addition to the ever-increasing numbers suffering from various forms of mental illnesses such as the dreaded Alzheimer's. Could there be another way of living that would allow us to live lives that are more healthy, more transparent and more purposively aware, that might lead us to living fuller, consciously present and harmonious lives? Perhaps it is simply the type of energy and the subsequent consciousnesses that we continually align to that may need to change, consequently systems of living that do work could naturally be implemented.

And yet at this present moment we have institutions and organizations with so much power, it is they that decree they have the jurisdiction and the knowledge, their claim is that science has the only real proof of what is true or false, anything else is insignificant. As all other elements of this complicated and degradingly infected society, science dances to the tune of those that pay for their convenient and advantageous resolutions, that their truth shall be proven no matter what the cost may be in currency, environmental damage or in the loss of human lives and dignity.

We are continually attempting to fix the problems and quandaries of the world using the same energy, the same mindset, with the same consciousnesses and same systems that created the problems in the first place; this is so obviously a non-starter, yet we seem to believe that 'it is the only option we have'. If we are ever to change the ill-ways of mankind, may not the obvious answer lie in changing the energy and the consciousnesses from which we have so destructively lived and operated from?

Is the evidence of the failure of the current lopsided setup not plain to see? How much more proof do we actually need to have before we choose to reverse our absurd march into oblivion? In proving what is true and what is false we are often hypocritical. We look at the world in general, what the human race has done and it is obvious that we are living in a detrimental way, but science says we are evolving, asking us to look at technological advancement, look at how long we are living but don't look at what we have done to the planet, don't consider that we are sicker than ever, don't look at the inequality, don't look at what the state of the world may be for our children, grandchildren and generations to come. How can we call ourselves an intelligent species when we constantly cause so much harm to ourselves, each other and the environment we live in?

Do we not ever learn, is it not a fact that some countries depend and thrive on a war-based economy? Without war their commercial systems will start to fail, if not fall apart completely. What have we, humanity, come to?

We have come to a point in time where anything that cannot be seen and witnessed with the five main human senses or quantified in a way laid down and certified by the controlling scientific authorities, cannot have any true worth or meaning to society. Anyone quoting personal experiences, anecdotal evidence as proof of a healthy lifestyle or that they have felt that they have lived previous lives or are given messages from Heaven or some other cosmic plane of life, are often derided and negatively labelled in one way or another if they have not been scientifically proven. Science seems to base itself on selective theories that are proven in regard to the preferred, limited criteria available or conveniently chosen. This is then held and promoted as truth until the next scientific genius produces another theory that expands upon or even disproves the one held previously to be undeniable certainty. Flat Earth anyone?

Are we even capable of fathoming the depths of the Universes? Do the answers lie within our own bodies or do we search outside of ourselves? Do we actually know how our bodies truly work or are these just theories put together based upon our limited knowledge? Do the answers to our existence lie within the access to our own consciousness through deepening into constant conscious presence? Or can we think ourselves to the answers using brain power? That would be the same brain power that designs nuclear and chemical weapons of mass destruction, exercises greed, inequality, selfishness, and levels of recklessness beyond comprehension. We could say the proof is in the pudding and looking at the state of our present world, the pudding is sour and rotten to the core, proving we human beings, in general, are undoubtably moving in a totally misguided direction.

If we live in a world, or for that matter, Universe, where everything is energy in one form or another, down to the most minute particle, to our every word, desire, thought or intention, as well as, every movement and action, surely, we need to first look at the type of energy in which we live our lives, the energy that is the impulse for our thoughts, our ideals, beliefs and behaviours. If we look at the current energy in which we choose to live our lives, could we not describe it as divisive, self-serving, disregarding, recognition-seeking (including self-sacrificing, being good or nice, justification and being right or wrong), unconscious, irresponsible, reactive, emotional, judgmental, antagonistic, competitive and everything else that has led us to the complete decadence and inequity of everything that living on this Earth currently is?

What if we could live our lives in the energy that is the opposite of all of the above, an energy that would inspire us to live a life of awareness, dedicated to being in service to each other, everyone and everything else, where 'the self' is no longer the construct of ingrained ideals and beliefs with its only goals being looking after number one, entertaining itself and exercising its own dreams, desires and selfish whims?

What if it could be that we primarily live our lives energetically, based upon Energetic Responsibility and Energetic

Integrity, thus removing all that is corrupt and untrue, allowing life to flow and be of Energetic Truth, the only truth that actually exists, for how can it be that each individual has his or her own version of a conveniently tailored, egocentric truth to fit themselves as and when suitable?

Let us stretch this question of Truth or the one energetic truth to religion and the obvious fact that all the mainstream religions are different and thus there is a maximum of one religion that can be energetically true. Further, we could then ask, are any of these religions complicit in any way, past or present? Have they promoted persecution, retribution, separation, discrimination, prejudice, enmity or any other connivance? Do they protect or cover-up ill-doing of its clergy or any of its members in any way, protecting them from prosecution or disclosure of the harm they have done to even one human being? If the answer is yes then, is there any way that a religion can be true if it entertains, conceals or supports such ill-ways? Not only that but as long as the dogma and doctrines taught and preached by those that are in positions of responsibility within these religions do not promote the teachings of energetic awareness, the fact of the One Energetic Choice, that we only have Free Will to choose if we align to Soul or spirit, what then is it that they are actually conveying?

Once we have chosen our energetic alignment, either to Soul or spirit, all else flows from this, living lives of loving soulful obedience in harmony with the All that is, or the opposite, a continuation of the erratic, emotional, disconnected and oblivious living that has brought us to this crucial point that can be described as a human catastrophe.

To learn texts from holy books in the way of a parrot, no matter how truthful the writings appear to be, does not bring through the lived energetic integrity of what was originally spoken and written. They cannot be lived in full as long as 'the self' reigns strong, as long as it is 'an untamed, wayward self' that interprets the teachings based upon its own individual, self-serving truth, as long as it is a self that willingly accepts the interpretations of others without question, can it be Energetically True?

319

What does religion really mean and how has it been corrupted? Have we not corrupted even the word 'religion', as we have, without fail, corrupted most other words within every language, in every culture and country across the planet? Religion may simply be the return to unity, a oneness that we have left behind, a return to the 'harmony within' that the controlling, recalcitrant etheric bully fights so hard to avoid, a realignment from eternal unrest to the soulful splendour of the essence of what we are.

Why have we built such flamboyant and expensive 'houses of God', and would a God actually have any desire whatsoever to be worshipped? How could there be a religion that is based on judgement or praises, worships a deity that is imagined sitting upon high and deciding who has been good or bad, who has been faithful and just, who has worshipped in the houses of God and who has stayed away?

God, or the Universe, is within All that is. We are from God and of God. We are his children and thus we are the same as him. In truth, we are all gods currently living as un-gods and as a complete reduction of what we truly are.

ADDENDUM

Nothing that is written, simply comes 'out of the blue', from nowhere. Is it then possible that whatever is forthcoming is not from us but vibrating through us? It's not our idea or our inspiration, it is given to us from whichever energetic source we live our lives from.

As previously mentioned, we – humanity – are the outplay of the desires of the etheric spirit, created to experience physicality as human beings with limited awareness, constricted by our incognizant dependence upon our five rudimentary earthly senses. Although, through the universal particles that make up our physical bodies we are able to access multidimensional intelligence beyond that of our ephemeral creators thus giving us the possibility to access both the life-force of our puppet-masters and the life-force of the One Soul, the Light of the Universe. Of the only two available energetic sources of life-giving force, we can live from, as planned and designed well before our primary inception as human beings, we here on Earth are unanimously subjected to the inexorable persistence of the force of deceptive spiritual creation. As human incarnations controlled by our predominant recalcitrant etheric beings, existing on a high of our own power of creation, we steadfastly refute the always-present call back to our origin, the true source of Universal Light. Despite this constant ephemeral spiritual bombardment there is within our divine particles an ever-present, inexorable magnetic pull back to our true Universal origins. The ultimate energetic responsibility of each individual is to which source of life-force they will align to and correspondingly which call will be answered.

There is and have been many movements and many teachers of what is known as the 'Ageless Wisdom'. Most mainstream religions are originally conceived from these teachings. True presenters are often attacked (and imprisoned or killed) by figures of power, controlled by the dark spiritual forces. The teachings, no matter how well documented, are always re-interpreted, contaminated and often completely bastardized.

When a new presenter appears in this modern-day society, how will he be received?

Within this book there are references to certain teachers and presenters of what are often called 'the teachings of the Ageless Wisdom' and as such this whole novel has come about as a result of my own limited, yet timeless study of the Ageless Wisdom teachings which are, in this current era, being earthed, that is, brought through and presented, by the Australian Healer, Author and Philosopher, Serge Benhayon.

As soon as a presenter of such presence, power and Light gains a foothold, a certain measure of audience or a substantial following with true movement and diction, as their design dictates, there commences the expungement of the ill-ways and spurious imprints of the dark force of creation. The dark, evil monsters and ghouls will undoubtably gather around. Demons and perpetrators of heinous malignancy in the form of 'detractors', will stealthily crawl out of the woodwork to stop at nothing in their quest to destroy what is of the soulful Light, what is of love. Then beyond the demons, the enslaved minions, the unprincipled evil vultures, writers of falsity (so-called members of the press, newshounds, sensationalist journalists) and evil donors of concocted mendacity will assemble to attempt to tear at the flesh of those they are committed to assail. The evilly constructed system of disenfranchised living we powerlessly adhere to, including authorities such as the courts of law, gleefully take part in the abrogation and demonizing of both the presenter and his words of truth.

Serge Benhayon, as many of those before him, has in recent years relentlessly endured such vicious assailment, an unceasing vitriolic assault, not only upon his own person but upon those of numerous family members and friends. Unmoved, he stands steadfast whilst deception, fabrication and forgery abound.

All arms, branches and cohorts, the lost soldiers of the despicable seething spiritual creation, will coalesce in a frenzied, delirious attempt to pollute, dilute, pervert 'what is' into 'what is not', desperate to destroy any compelling presenter and their words of Truth.

IN DEEPEST GRATITUDE

For more than twenty years the impulse to write a book has repeatedly been felt, it has come and gone without productive return. Finally in the year 2021, I have listened, aligned and responded to this divine offering from heaven and the enclosed pages are its consummation.

This book is testimony to the limitlessness of the magnificent, golden offerings in the form of the Ageless Wisdom teachings presented primarily by Serge Benhayon under the banner of Universal Medicine. Without the teachings brought through by Serge, I fear that I may still have been wandering aimlessly in the realms of spiritual creation, searching blindly for answers to the false existential questions within fraudulent consciousnesses that had left me unable to see the riches not only before my own eyes but constantly passing through me. And to paraphrase a line from an old song, 'I was indeed, a beggar unable to understand that for the whole time, I was sitting on a beach of gold'. I was unable to access the riches that I and everyone else have in our possession, whilst the key to unlock this golden treasure of Ageless Wisdom we sit upon is always firmly within our grasp.

Could it be that there is only true worth in the wisdom that is beyond that of our current human existence, that nothing that is on offer within the human material realm has any real substance or permanence? Each life we live is a mere steppingstone upon our way of return to the higher realms from whence we came. Each life can be lived either in delay of that return or in the purpose of the acceleration towards our (all of us) inevitable onward departure.

I was looking for answers within the delimited, permitted scope of my own self-restricted mind of my chosen reality, 'thinking' that I was on the right track, that I was evolving as a human being when in truth I was allowing myself to be manipulated by the ever-present, ever-active *self-serving, wayward and controlling character (the etheric spirit) that operates both within and outside of myself.*

As Serge often presents, we have only one real choice to make, to move in the energy of 'fire' (Light) or 'prana' (spiritual creation), that is the source of energy we align to, everything else is fed to us following on from that initial energetic alignment. All our thoughts, words, actions and intentions are energy. We do not think our own thoughts, we are moved by the energy we adhere to. We are led to believe that we are individual, that there is a me, a self – when the complete opposite is true.

Although this book is primarily a work of fiction it would not have been possible without the teachings presented by Serge and other members of his family, notably Simone Benhayon and Natalie Benhayon, that all together have enabled the unfoldment and expansion of my own living way. These teachings and my own evolvement are, of course, reflected within the pages of the book.

In closing this short addendum, a heartfelt thanks to all that are upon the Way of the Livingness, that are students of the Ageless Wisdom teachings that equally, in their own way, contribute to the movement of All upon the path of return.

For any of our fellow awakening brothers and sisters, please pay a visit to: https://www.unimedliving.com

A thousand thanks (tusen takk) for journeying this far.

ACKNOWLEDGEMENT

To those who have inspired, assisted, guided, and loved, we are all part of the same Whole, the Oneness of everything, the love for all is immeasurable.

Special thanks to Gayle Cue for the introduction to and joyful journey through the editing process. It's simply amazing to experience so much gentle judgement-free guidance.

And to Neil Gamble for being the guinea pig, the first reader and for your constructive, unwavering feedback, guidance and support.

To my dear wife Rebecca for all the love and support, second proof-reading and all the magnificence you bring to our life together. We are love, we are one.

To all at Novum, thank you for the whole process from inception (i.e. acceptance of the manuscript) to delivery of the physical book.

Born in 1959, Wigan, north-west England, Christopher Murphy also lived in south-east England and London before moving to Norway, residing there for twenty-five years. These locations provide the settings for this, his first novel, Unfolding Grace.

His life is now devoted to living life in true integrity for All equally. Christopher spent many years walking the 'wayward path' that feeds us the illusion of our current individualized way of life. In the realization that we are all far greater than our current self-restricted appearance, he is now committed to uncovering deeper truths of all realms of life. This clarity enables him to live this life and lifetimes hence in true service to humankind. He is a student of himself and 'Ageless Wisdom' teachings and is dedicated to each member of the equally magnificent multidimensional family we are all a part of.

Christopher is married, has three adult children and lives in Richmond, Surrey.

The publisher

*He who stops
getting better
stops being good.*

This is the motto of novum publishing, and our focus
is on finding new manuscripts, publishing them and
offering long-term support to the authors.
Our publishing house was founded in 1997, and since
then it has become THE expert for new authors and
has won numerous awards.

**Our editorial team will peruse each manuscript
within a few weeks free of charge and without
obligation.**

You will find more information about
novum publishing and our books on the internet:

w w w . n o v u m - p u b l i s h i n g . c o . u k

Printed in Great Britain
by Amazon

18435714R00192